MW00337426

BOOKS BY MARIA FAGYAS

Court of Honor
Dance of the Assassins
The Devil's Lieutenant
The Widowmaker
The Fifth Woman

COURT
OF
HONOR

Maria Fagyas

Simon and Schuster   New York

COPYRIGHT © 1978 BY M. BUSHE-FEKETE
ALL RIGHTS RESERVED
INCLUDING THE RIGHT OF REPRODUCTION
IN WHOLE OR IN PART IN ANY FORM
PUBLISHED BY SIMON AND SCHUSTER
A DIVISION OF GULF & WESTERN CORPORATION
SIMON & SCHUSTER BUILDING
ROCKEFELLER CENTER
1230 AVENUE OF THE AMERICAS
NEW YORK, NEW YORK 10020

DESIGNED BY DIANNE PINKOWITZ
MANUFACTURED IN THE UNITED STATES OF AMERICA
1 2 3 4 5 6 7 8 9 10

LIBRARY OF CONGRESS CATALOGING IN PUBLICATION DATA

FAGYAS, M
   COURT OF HONOR.

   I. TITLE.
PZ4.F156CO   [PS3556.A34]   813'.5'4   77–27114
ISBN   0-671-22498-0

PART ONE

1

The dress was delivered late, barely allowing her time to slip it on. It was of pale blue chiffon, its floor-length skirt appliquéd with Bruxelles lace medallions at knee height and along the bottom. The short sleeves were flounced into two tiers above her elbows, and the neckline dipped low to leave her shoulders bare. She fretted impatiently while Lotte struggled with the intricate hooks that closed the back, then she sent the maid to tell Hans Günther that she would join him shortly. First she had to find the court gloves she had bought on her last shopping trip to Berlin. They weren't in the box she thought she had put them in. On the verge of panic, she rummaged feverishly through the drawers of the dresser, then saw the gloves lying on the console table, where Lotte must have thrown them when she laid out the shoes, stockings and the lingerie her mistress was to wear that night.

After a quick look in the mirror, Alexa grabbed her wrap and went to the salon. She found her husband as she had left him half an hour earlier, standing, watch in hand, in the middle of the room, a frown of annoyance clouding his handsome face.

"At last," he snapped when he heard the door open. Then

he turned to her and his petulance changed to open-mouthed wonder. "God, you're beautiful!"

She had expected a reprimand for being late, and his impetuous praise perplexed her, although by now she should have been used to his mercurial moods. She froze on the threshold, still waiting to be scolded.

"Stay where you are. I want to look at you." His extended hand halted her as she was about to approach him.

The nervous pounding of her heart, caused by her mad rush when dressing for the imperial soiree, was slowing down. His approving gaze felt like sunshine on her face; it was warming her all over, despite the chilly May breeze blowing in through the open windows. She moved close to him and offered her lips for a kiss, but he ignored the overture and reached out to tuck up a wisp of hair that had come loose at the nape of her neck.

"Now that's better," he said. "I really should congratulate myself for what I've achieved with you in three years." He flashed a self-satisfied smile at her. It was the same smile she had seen on many an owner's face leading his race horse into the winner's circle. She turned away to hide the fact that once again he had succeeded in hurting her with a remark he had meant as a compliment.

"I wonder why you married me when I was so hopelessly gauche and dowdy."

"Because I was Pygmalion and could see the future Galatea in you. A modern-day Pygmalion."

The blood rushed to her face. "Except that Pygmalion turned a lump of ivory into a live woman, while you have turned a live woman into something cold and dead."

The angry bitterness of her tone wiped the self-satisfied smile off his face. He put his arms around her, careful to avoid crushing the corsage pinned to her gown, and pulled her into a conciliatory embrace. "Don't be silly. What I meant was that you look better now than you did at nineteen. What's wrong with that?"

Still not placated, she freed herself. "Shouldn't we be leaving?"

"Not yet. I ordered the carriage for seven-thirty."

"You told me seven-fifteen," she flared. "Why? If I had known that, I wouldn't have rushed. I was so worried I'd be late."

"You would've been late if I hadn't tricked you."

"Oh, Hans, that was unfair." Annoyed, she dropped into a chair. "Now there is nothing to do but wait."

"You always complain that we never spend time together alone, just the two of us. Now we are."

Yes, she had complained, not once but many times, and with reason too. He seemed more of a stranger now than during the first weeks of their marriage. The more anxiously she expressed her need for him, the less willingly he responded to it. He did not exactly neglect her; he merely paid more careful attention to her trivial problems—clothes, social contacts, vacation plans—than to her emotional ones. He treated her more like an ornament of than a partner of his life.

"I have news for you." He interrupted the silence that had grown oppressive around them. "There is a chance you might run into one of your Hungarian relatives tonight."

She frowned, puzzled. "Hungarian relatives? At the New Palace?" Her sole Hungarian relatives were her grandparents, an old couple living in dignified poverty on a small farm in western Hungary.

"Your brother-in-law, or rather ex-brother-in-law. He has been appointed adjutant to the Monarchy's military attaché; he has been in Berlin about a week now. I'd heard about it last night, meant to tell you, then it somehow slipped my mind."

"Nicky Karady in Berlin?" For a second her voice broke and she choked as if a hand had clamped down on her throat. She was close to tears. There she was, dressed in pale blue chiffon, flowers in her hair, ready for an evening of music and excitement, as if Beata, her twin sister, had not burned to death in a fire on an August night in 1904. Now she lay in the bronze coffin her widower had provided for her in far-away Hungary. Alexa felt as if the scar tissue of her half-healed wound were being ripped off by a cruel hand. She *did* want to meet Nicholas Karady again, but in private, not amid the pomp and glitter of a court affair.

"I cannot understand the Austrians." Hans Günther's voice broke through the cloud of grief that had enveloped her. "To appoint a Jew to their Berlin Embassy! As clerk perhaps, but not to the military attaché's staff, a post which calls for social contact with our officers' corps."

It took a few seconds for Alexa to react. When she did, it was with outrage. "What do you mean, a Jew? Karady is no Jew!"

"All right, a half-Jew. Isn't his mother Jewish?"

"And what if she is? He made a wonderful husband to Beata, that's all that matters to me." She should have added, *A better one than you have been to me.* "They were gloriously happy."

"For ten, or was it eleven months? How can you tell whether that glorious happiness would have outlasted their second year, or their fourth or twenty-fifth? Anyway, you only knew your sister's side of the story."

"You just don't believe there can be such a thing as a perfect marriage, do you?"

"No. No relationship can be perfect. That is what's wrong with you women. You expect happiness to be a permanent condition."

Whenever his moments of discontent occurred, she was the target. If only she could revolt, but he still had absolute power over her. To be so helplessly in love with one's husband could have been heaven, if only the husband weren't Hans Günther von Godenhausen. Nevertheless she protested. "Beata *was* happy. I know she was."

"So she said in her letters, but there is nothing as tolerant as a white sheet of paper."

"Can I help it that there was no other contact between us?" Alexa said. "I wanted to visit her, but you would not let me. You didn't even let me go to her funeral!"

She closed her eyes and relived with painful clarity the moment when the news of her twin's death had reached her. Hans Günther had left some time earlier for Borstedter Feld, where cavalry exercises were in progress. She had been about to take a nap and was half asleep when Lotte entered with the telegram, handed it to her and, instead of leaving, lingered on. She had obviously peeked at the message and was waiting with morbid curiosity for her mistress's reaction, Alexa thought.

Her eyes glided over the words. She understood each one, and yet they failed to make sense to her. She felt Lotte's stare fixed on her face. "Give the mailman a tip," she said. When Lotte made no move to leave, she raised her voice. "What are you waiting for? Get out!"

Muttering under her breath, the girl shuffled out. Left alone, Alexa reread the wire, including those mysterious abbreviations that have meaning only for postal clerks. Beata had died in an accident, her funeral would take place two days hence, was the gist of the message signed by Nicholas Karady. . . .

"Beata is dead," she had said out loud. She felt no grief, only a numbness of the kind produced by an injection of a painkilling drug.

As she lay on the sofa, the disturbing moments of her childhood, when she had wished her twin dead, flashed through her mind. Not really dead, just gone, abducted by some mythical strangers who refused to let her return home but kept her forever as their very own.

Suddenly grief attacked with the fierceness of a whiplash. She rose and started feverishly to prepare for her journey to Hungary. She had to leave the same evening if she wanted to be in Sarkany in time for Beata's funeral. She ordered suitcases brought down from the attic, and by the time Hans

Günther returned from duty she was packed. His first reaction was sympathy befitting the occasion; he gently kissed away Alexa's tears, then he called in Lotte and ordered her to unpack her lady's luggage. No pleadings, sobs or tantrums could make him change his mind: Alexa was not going to Hungary, and that was final. His duties tied him to Potsdam. He could not accompany her or find a suitable traveling companion for her in time. . . .

His voice brought Alexa back to the present. "We were newlyweds; I didn't want to part with you, not even for a week. Was that so bad?" He chucked her playfully under the chin. She found the sudden warmth of his smile as disconcerting as she had his petty malice a few moments earlier. She often wished he were ugly and unattractive, not tall and lithe, his face unlined except for a few laugh wrinkles at the corners of his eyes. She was grateful for the small mole on his left cheek which kept him from being outrageously handsome.

Some men were loved because they were robust and virile, born conquerors; but with him it had been his elusiveness that fascinated her. He presented the challenge of a prize to contend for, yet winning him had never been synonymous with owning him. She believed that he was faithful to her, yet his love was like a rainbow—bright, many-hued, seemingly within reach, but in truth ephemeral and intangible.

He was one of the most popular officers in the Gardes du Corps and, lately, a favorite of Emperor Wilhelm II. Always proper and friendly in public, he could also be maddeningly distant at home, causing her to feel wretchedly abandoned. Then he would unexpectedly utter a tender word, take her into his arms, and suddenly she would feel sheltered and immensely happy.

Thadeus, his orderly, entered to report that the carriage had arrived. "Please," Hans Günther told Alexa on their way out, "for a change, be attentive to the old ladies of the court. Especially to Countess Keller. The empress is devoted to her, and so is His Majesty. For some odd reason, she can tell him things that he would never take from anyone else."

"I'll be charming," Alexa promised. Funny, she thought after they had started out for the dinner given by Wilhelm II, in honor of Franz Ferdinand, heir to the Austro-Hungarian Monarchy's throne, Beata wasn't like me. She was never bored with balls and receptions. In one of her last letters she wrote me how thrilled she'd been to be presented at the Hofburg. Being addressed by the old emperor was an unforgettable experience for her. I wish I had her joie de vivre. I wish she were in my shoes tonight.

In 1905, on the anniversary of Beata's death, Alexa had finally obtained Hans Günther's consent to visit her twin's grave in Sarkany. By then, she had learned the gruesome details of the tragedy. While Beata's husband had been in Vienna on official business, a candle, carelessly knocked off a table, set the rug smoldering in her bedroom in the Sarkany castle. She had suffocated before the staff noticed the fire that subsequently gutted the entire left wing of the building.

Situated west of the Danube, Sarkany was a hardly discernible speck on the map of the Monarchy. After crossing from Austria into Hungary, the railroad traversed gently rolling country, lovely to look at, but less than ideal for farming. The Count Karadys owned three thousand acres of it and a castle. Alexa's grandparents, the Rethys, owned two hundred acres and a modest manor house.

The Rethys' only son, the twins' father, had become involved in a shady affair involving a forged promissory note and committed suicide. A year later his Prussian-born widow followed him to the Sarkany cemetery, leaving her daughters, Alexa and Beata, to their grandparents' care. At twelve, Alexa fell ill with tuberculosis, and the impoverished Rethys had to choose between praying for a miracle or giving her up to her mother's rich sister, Rose von Sedlitz, who could pay for a

15

cure in an expensive Swiss sanatorium. After weeks of agonizing they handed Alexa over to the aunt.

Revisiting Sarkany after an absence of nine years proved to be a frustrating experience to Alexa. She had planned it as a journey of expiation, a pilgrimage to prove her love for Beata, a love still strong enough to reach her twin across the gulf that separated the dead from the living. She had hoped somehow to express how painfully she had missed her sister during their long separation, how many times she had whispered Beata's name, hoping for some telepathic communication over a distance of a thousand kilometers. For the first twelve years of their lives they had not once been apart, then suddenly they were separated, never to see each other again.

At twelve, when she had left for a foreign land with an aunt she had not known before the journey, Alexa carried along a disturbing secret resentment against her grandparents. She thought they let her go because they considered her a burden and a nuisance. She knew that she had been sickly and restless as a baby, her cries keeping the house awake night after night. As a toddler she had to be closely watched to prevent her from engaging in mischief or having an accident. In school she was bright but disobedient, a troublemaker. Beata, on the other hand, was from the first day of her life a joy to her grandparents. The word "beata" meant happy, and she was a happy child, content with herself and the world. Nothing disturbed her calm. Even during rare fights with Alexa or the farmhands' children, her anger lasted only brief moments, leaving no bitter residue of resentment behind.

In the sanatorium recovering from tuberculosis, as well as in her aunt's home in Berlin and later in Potsdam as Hans Günther's wife, Alexa continued to remember the Rethys' farm with deep longing, a place where life had been simple and secure. She was certain that once she set foot on her grandparents' land again she would be rid of all her doubts and grievances and feel loved and wanted as never before.

16

It was not to be. She felt as though she were in a theater watching a stranger impersonate her on the stage, the reunion with her grandparents being part of the performance. They seemed so different from the way she had remembered them, like actors wearing makeup to appear aged.

In her quest to establish contact with Beata, Alexa asked to see all the pictures taken since their separation. There were only two rather blurred daguerreotypes dating back to Beata's adolescent years and a few good likenesses showing her as a young wife. Instead of helping, they merely confused and disconcerted Alexa. The person in the photographs looked like Alexa, only the clothes were different. Even the face framed by the bridal veil was hers. No matter how hard she tried to visualize Beata the woman, to Alexa she remained a frail little girl waving tearfully after the train that was taking her sister away to Switzerland.

That journey from Sarkany to Davos remained one of the most painful memories of Alexa's life. Aunt Rose had descended upon her grandparents' house with the fury of a tornado and despite her frantic protests swept her up and carried her away. The Rethys stood by impassively, assuring Alexa that the separation was for her own good and that she would be brought back when she was cured, a promise she refused to believe.

Alexa spent the first three months in Davos in a kind of traumatic shock. She lost weight, and the benign jocularity of Dr. Berend, chief physician of the Germania Children's Sanatorium, grew more and more forced when he read her fever chart. Her cure was brought about by Felicitas von Hartwegh, her new roommate. The daughter of a Prussian foreign service officer, Felicitas had many an interesting story to tell Alexa about her travels. She seemed sophisticated to Alexa, but she was still a little girl and mischievous enough to be good company. The word "felicitas" meant happiness, while Beata's name meant happy, and the odd coincidence caused

17

Alexa to conclude that her roommate had been selected by a higher power to fill—if only temporarily—the void left in her life by Beata's absence.

Before Felicitas's arrival, Alexa's world consisted of Sarkany and vicinity. St. Josef's Church in the town of Komárom was the tallest building she knew and the Karadys the most prominent personages, a mere notch below Greek deity. Her roommate's reminiscences caused this once fascinating world to appear suddenly poor and shabby to Alexa.

On the train her aunt, Rose von Sedlitz, had hinted that later she might take Alexa to live with her in Berlin. At that time this had terrified Alexa, but later she wondered if Berlin wasn't worth a visit. She thought of the women of Sarkany, wives of gentleman farmers, some fairly affluent, others barely keeping the wolf from their doors, all wasting their youth on unruly children, on straying husbands, on coping with lazy and thieving servants. Always insecure, they lived in a deadly fear of epidemics, hog cholera, foot-and-mouth disease, of hailstorms, droughts, floods and unwanted pregnancies. She wondered if as a general's niece in Imperial Berlin she would not have a more interesting time readjusting to the world of the healthy than as the granddaughter of an impoverished old landowner in Sarkany.

Adalbert von Sedlitz, Rose's husband, had behind him a brilliant military career, and he was now assigned to the General Staff, which gave him entree into court circles. By marrying him, Rose had made an even more splendid match than her rich family had hoped for when they provided her with a dowry large enough to capture a distinguished though penniless member of Prussian military nobility.

Despite her earlier protests, influenced by Felicitas, Alexa wrote to her aunt that she would agree to go to Berlin, provided it was only a visit. Her consent was an empty gesture, however, because Rose von Sedlitz, now her legal guardian, never intended to send her back to her grandparents.

When told of her aunt's decision to keep her in Berlin for

good, Alexa reacted with a tantrum; but no arguments or tears could move Rose. The many thousands of francs she had paid Dr. Berend were an investment that entitled her to a profit: the presence of a child in her childless home.

The battle lasted two days and ended in Alexa's surrender. For Rose it was a Pyrrhic victory, and in the ensuing years Alexa's resentment of Rose fluctuated between violent hatred and mild dislike. They both learned to live with it as people do with chronic sinus conditions—something unpleasant but not painful enough to keep one from functioning.

Rose von Sedlitz, née Lutz, had had a postcard prettiness at sixteen; but at forty-one her face looked like a peach left to desiccate on its branch, with lines of petulance running from the corners of her mouth. Her body, seemingly put together of mismatched parts, appeared heavier than it really was. She had a fast, aggressive walk that prompted the household help to call her, behind her back, the charging bull.

The Sedlitzes' apartment took up the entire third floor of a house on Kronen Strasse in the center of Berlin. Four of its spacious high-ceilinged rooms faced the street; the others, including the kitchen and bathroom, overlooked the courtyard. The two cubicles where the servants slept had windows the size of portholes which opened onto an air shaft.

After her arrival Alexa was assigned a sofa and half of a wardrobe in the sewing room facing the yard. She was told to rest until suppertime, when she would be introduced to the general, who had sequestered himself in his study and left word that he was not to be disturbed. The memorable meeting took place half an hour later when he emerged from his seclusion to have the light meal that was always served him at six-thirty sharp.

With his short compact body that resembled a tilting-toy mannikin, his ruddy complexion and thinning copper-colored hair, General Adalbert von Sedlitz was far from the heroic figure described by his wife.

"So this is our little Magyar!" was the general's jovial

greeting, accompanied by a friendly pat to Alexa's cheek. He was, as Alexa realized later, in one of his exceptionally benign moods, making small talk throughout the meal, even a few puns to the worshipful delight of his wife and Fräulein Elsa, her awestruck companion-secretary-seamstress.

At first Alexa was amused by the household's attitude toward the general, but she soon found it degrading and revolting. From Rose down to Minna, the scullery maid, they treated him as though he were a victorious occupation force with authority over life and death and they were the defeated army.

Katie, the old cook, was the only exception, permitting herself an occasional joke at his expense. Probably because of her droll sense of humor she managed to get away with what for the others would have been lese majesty. What amazed Alexa most was the fact that during the five years she had spent under the general's roof she never once heard him raise his voice. On the contrary, it was with his inscrutable and impenetrable silences that he struck holy terror into his flock. The silences could last for days, even for weeks, with no one aware of what had provoked them.

It was a week after her arrival that Alexa first experienced what she later called "Siberia on Kronen Strasse." For days the quiet and chill of a tomb descended upon the apartment whenever the general was home. Its occupants must have been blessed with unusually sharp hearing, for the faint click of his key turning in the entrance door lock was sufficient to scare them into Carthusian silence. Katie alone refused to be hushed. She sang, whistled, quarreled with Minna, slammed doors, rattled dishes and pounded schnitzels with enough force to kill a calf.

Alexa wondered whether the general preserved his silence away from the house as well. Later, when she became better acquainted with Berlin's social life, she realized that his sullen moods were strictly for domestic use. Neither intimidated nor angered by them, she took them in stride, especially since the day he revealed that his pique was not directed against her. Catching her alone in the narrow passage between his study and the bathroom, he suddenly pounced upon her and fondled her sprouting breasts with his hard, stubby fingers until they hurt. No matter how carefully she tried to avoid him, he managed to grab her time and again, always during his melancholy periods and always in stony silence, as though their not being on speaking terms somehow made his caresses accidental and impersonal.

At first shocked, she later reacted to his attacks with a mixture of contempt and amusement. She decided not to denounce him to her aunt. She knew Rose would not believe her and that she, Alexa, would lose the power these secret encounters gave her over the general. His lust revealed to her what a forceful weapon her body could be, a knowledge she might find useful in the future.

After the farm in Hungary and the Swiss sanatorium, Berlin with its wide avenues, palaces, museums and cathedrals amazed and fascinated Alexa. That it also had dirt, poverty and block after block of dilapidated, ill-smelling tenements she realized only much later. The men and women who attended her aunt's at-home days were of the clique that exercised a decisive influence upon the present and even the future of Imperial Germany, perhaps of the entire civilized world.

From their conversations she gathered the vague notion that in the new and impressive Reichstagsgebäude on Königs Platz an assortment of unruly civilians, among them a group of brawlers called Socialists, were trying to undermine the security of the state. Thanks to the wisdom and moral rectitude of the Kaiser and of his loyal army, the efforts of the rabble were destined to fail.

There was no limit to the admiration Rose and her lady friends lavished on the emperor. Elsewhere, all over the globe, only one sun rose in the sky, but Prussia was blessed with two—the celestial body and an even more luminous one,

Kaiser Wilhelm II. His handpainted portrait hung above the big sofa in the Sedlitzes' salon, and his autographed photo decorated the general's desk in the study. His and the imperial family's daily activities were the main topic of conversation at Rose's parties, also during the private hours she spent in the company of Fräulein Elsa.

At times her aunt's hot flushes of Prussian patriotism touched off a rebellious fury in Alexa. Asserting pride in her Hungarian heritage, she would engage in angry quarrels with her aunt, which ended in name-calling, tears, being slapped and banished to the sewing room. Her aunt, terrified by the general, could turn into a veritable despot, taking her revenge for his petty cruelties by inflicting the same treatment on servants, tradesmen, laundresses, artisans and poor relations.

After three months at the Sedlitz home Alexa decided to return to Sarkany. When her aunt refused to let her leave, she started out on her own. At the Anhalter Station she bought a ten-pfennig ticket to the platform. Having previously studied the timetable, she had no trouble finding the Dresden–Vienna train, which was due to depart within a few minutes. Afraid that her expensive-looking clothes would draw attention to her in the crowded third- and fourth-class coaches, she settled in a three-seat compartment at the end of the first-class car. A sticker on its door read RESERVED, and she hoped that whoever it was reserved for would not appear. She pulled down the blinds on the window and locked the door.

The wheels were already turning when the conductor opened it with his passkey for a General Staff colonel. At Grosslichtenfelde the train made an unscheduled stop and Alexa was taken off and held prisoner at the stationmaster's office.

Although unsuccessful, the escapade nevertheless had its benefits. It caused Rose to realize that despite the small fortune she had spent on restoring Alexa's health she could expect no gratitude in return. When the captive Alexa was returned home, instead of a frightened and repentant girl, Rose was confronted with a wild creature spitting insults at her.

"I hate you! I won't stay with you! You had me dragged back now, but let me warn you I'll be off at the first opportunity."

For a long moment Rose remained speechless. No one had ever talked to her with such disdain. She was so surprised that she broke down in tears. "Is this the thanks for all I've done for you?"

"I wish you had done nothing for me."

"You would've died just like your mother."

"I wish I'd died just like my mother." Then the ultimate insult. "I'd be better off dead than living in this damned house!"

Rose was still at a loss for a properly stern reply. The girl appeared to be ready to leap at her jugular vein. In truth, Alexa was awestruck by the ferocity of her own outburst, her almost uncontrollable hatred. She froze, expecting retribution, then saw the tears in Rose's eyes and understood that she had won. It was a moment never to be forgotten, the great switch in their relationship. Rose had lost the whip hand and she had gained it. Like the general's secret caresses, Rose's impotent tears unshackled her niece for the rest of her stay in the Sedlitz home.

She had discovered strange cracks in what had seemed like an impenetrable armor of meanness in her aunt. It seemed that Rose loved and wanted her, perhaps because blood was thicker than water, perhaps because the presence of a child in the house filled, if only partially, the emptiness of being the unloved wife of an unlovable man.

Alexa was enrolled in a very expensive girls' day school, and with dancing, piano and French lessons was given an education befitting a von Sedlitz. The general's intermittent pawings continued, becoming bolder as her boyish body acquired soft curves. Once he tried to reach under her skirt and she slapped his face. Rose was much too blind to suspect her husband's lust for his niece, and her reaction to Alexa's new prettiness was a mixture of family pride and an aging woman's envy. Alexa no longer found her whims infuriating. She knew they were the growls of a defanged and declawed lioness.

Alexa met Hans Günther von Godenhausen in the spring of 1900, a few days before her sixteenth birthday. He was the general's nephew, the son of his sister and a Junker baron who had been killed in the Franco-Prussian War in 1871.

Alexa had concluded long before the meeting that the bond between the general and the young captain was a great deal stronger than the usual uncle-nephew relationship. Since the seventeenth century, almost all male Sedlitzes had served and several had died as officers in the Prussian army. Two hundred years of long and bloody wars gradually thinned out the once numerous branches of the family; and by 1900, Adalbert, Rose's husband, was the last von Sedlitz, and Hans Günther the only male child produced by a Sedlitz woman. With his perfect physique, nimble brain and devotion to duty, he was the son denied the general by a cruel fate, the only human being he deeply and blindly cared for. Alexa had often heard her uncle turning lyrical when fantasizing about the brilliant career his nephew was destined for. She had no doubt that the general was willing to go to any length to further that career. Her aunt slavishly shared her husband's dreams for his nephew.

Hans Günther's photographs as a cadet and later as a second lieutenant were kept in a velvet-bound family album in the Sedlitzes' salon. Even as a boy he was strikingly handsome. Tall for his age, wide-shouldered, slim-hipped, his skin showing no traces of acne, the common curse of adolescence, he looked like a young Böcklin god come to life.

From Munich, Godenhausen was transferred to the First Army Corps in Königsberg, 589 kilometers from Berlin, then, in 1900, to the elite Gardes du Corps, that Kaiser's own regiment, stationed in Potsdam. His first social call in Berlin was made on the Sedlitzes.

In life he was even more handsome than his pictures. What set him apart from other attractive men was the way in which he ignored the impression his good looks made on people. At thirty-one he still acted like a man without a care on his mind.

He became a steady fixture at the Sedlitzes' home, calling on them every time he was in Berlin. Alexa had become a beauty and *she* knew it. Young and not-so-young men lost their heads over her, while Hans Günther treated her with only big-brotherly affection. He was still single and, as far as she knew, had no woman in his life. Through the local grapevine she heard that before his transfer from Munich to Königsberg he had been involved in a scandal. Gossip making the rounds in the Berlin garrison hinted at a drunken orgy at the residence of a French diplomat who was later recalled to Paris. The nature of the scandal remained a mystery to Alexa.

Alexa had fallen in love with him at first sight. Frustrated and humiliated by his easy camaraderie, she flirted with every attractive young man who showed interest in her. She was much too young for these meaningless flings, and they infuriated her aunt. As usual, the general kept out of their fights, only his attacks of melancholia became more frequent and longer lasting. Alexa fell into the habit of venting her frustrations on him, pummeling him with her balled fists every time he tried to fondle her. He endured the punishment in silence and always came back for more.

Among all the young men who crossed Alexa's path, there was only one who could have taken Hans Günther's place in her heart—that is, had he lived.

Lieutenant Schenker's death was called an accident. Yet could a bicycle ride taken on an almost vertical slope into the swirling torrents of the sea below be called anything but suicide?

Alexa remembered that he had left in a somewhat apprehensive mood for Wilhelmshaven to board the yacht *Hohen-*

zollern and join the Kaiser's annual summer cruise along the coast of Norway. The prospect of spending weeks as adjutant to a general, in the immediate proximity of the All Highest, failed to delight him. On shipboard, in all male company, the Kaiser was known to be a boorish host. During calisthenics on the windswept deck he would sneak up on his stooped guests and with well-aimed kicks send them sprawling. He demonstrated his approval of younger men by pinching their cheeks or buttocks. He had fingers like pliers and their touch left red marks on the men's skins.

According to the first reports, the lieutenant had lost his balance on the slippery rain-soaked deck and fallen overboard. Stories of a drunken brawl leaked out later. The Kaiser had kept to his stateroom for days after the "accident," and when he reappeared his face was bruised and his lip cut.

Alexa wondered what ignominy had driven a man of Schenker's quiet, dreamy disposition to lifting his hand against his emperor, an offense for which, according to his honor code, the sole fitting penance could be suicide. She shed bitter tears for Schenker. Besides being a tender and devoted friend, he had had one virtue that had set him apart from all her beaux: he was a patient and eager listener, an ideal companion for a lonely girl who had failed to make female friends her own age among the priggish, inhibited daughters of the Prussian upper class.

Later, when her grief subsided to the passive acceptance of her loss, she had to admit to herself that she had never really been in love with Schenker. What she had felt for him was a deep affection that was untinged by any hint of sexuality. He would have made a good, dependable husband and given her a life of peace and security. But was that all she wanted from the future?

Too much was happening in Berlin for people to dwell on a small individual tragedy like Lieutenant Schenker's mysterious drowning. These were the golden years of the Kaiser's

26

reign, when he still could refer to God as Germany's great ally and to himself—only in private, of course—as the Almighty's favorite son. If not exactly Jesus Christ, he was at least his younger brother. Not even the news that his uncle Edward VII's very successful visit to Paris had resulted in a definite rapprochement between France and England could shake his self-confidence. He was building a navy that would soon equal England's, and should it come to war his army would overrun France in a week.

In 1903 the Sedlitzes spent their summer vacation on the island of Norderney in the North Sea. It was here that they received Beata's letter announcing her forthcoming marriage to Nicholas Karady.

"It's incredible! Unbelievable!" Alexa cried. "She's become engaged to Count Nicky. As children, we both had a crush on him. Beata always said she would marry him, but I made fun of her. Yet it's true! It has become true! Isn't that marvelous?"

Suddenly she was seized by a homing urge as forceful as the drive that causes pigeons to return to their cotes and lost dogs to their masters' hearths over distances of many hundred kilometers. Above all there was her longing to see Beata again.

"The wedding is on the fifteenth!" she exclaimed. "I'll have to be there at least a week earlier. There isn't much time, is there? Will you come too, or do you want me to go alone?" she asked her aunt.

It was a simple question, yet it seemed to disconcert Rose. "Well . . ." she began, then paused. "I'm afraid neither of us should go."

"What do you mean neither of us?" Alexa raised her voice. "I don't care what *you* do, but *I* shall go, and that is final!"

Oddly enough, her aunt remained calm. There was even a touch of loving kindness in her eyes. "It seems things always happen at the wrong moment. That's life. I was going to tell you but wanted to wait until it became definite." She lowered her voice to a confidential whisper. "Hans Günther wants to spend his leave with us. I suspect he is getting serious, my dear."

Uncomprehending, Alexa frowned. "Serious about what?" Her aunt emitted a girlish giggle. It was hardly becoming. "About you. Who else?"

Alexa had not seen or heard from Hans Günther since the end of May. Speculations about Lieutenant Schenker's mysterious death had weighed so heavily on her mind that they overshadowed her secret infatuation with Hans Günther. Now her aunt's news rekindled the fire that for a while she had considered extinguished.

According to an old saying, a person is not irrevocably dead as long as he is remembered by someone he loved. At Schuchardt's Hotel in Norderney, Lieutenant Schenker was now dying for a second time.

"Hans Günther never showed any interest in me." She had sensed a touch of uneasiness in her aunt's tone, and she wondered if her hint at Godenhausen's serious intentions wasn't a lie to keep her from attending Beata's wedding. "I never thought he cared. There are ways for a man to let a girl know."

The glow of benevolence faded from Rose's face. She looked peeved. "What did you expect him to do? He's a gentleman who wouldn't indicate his feelings to a girl until he was absolutely sure of himself."

"Hans Günther hasn't seen me for months. Why is he suddenly sure?"

Rose gave her a withering look, then turned for the door. "All right, my dear. I'll send him a telegram and tell him not to come. And you go and attend your sister's wedding to that Jew."

She was halfway through the room when Alexa stopped her. "No, don't wire. Let him come." Her voice sharpened. "And Karady is no Jew. He is a very fine man, rich and handsome, and Beata is a lucky girl to get him. She is madly in love." Alexa sighed. "Good God, what am I to tell Beata? That I won't go to her wedding because Hans Günther has suddenly become serious."

Rose watched her from the corner of her eye. "Think it over. You can still change your mind. He won't be leaving to join us until early tomorrow morning, so there's still time to wire him."

Alexa spent the rest of the day composing a letter to Beata in which she tried to explain why she could not go to Sarkany. While scribbling draft after draft, she marveled at the strange whim of destiny that arranged for them, twins living apart and separated by frontiers and hundreds of miles, to find their future husbands during the same month of the same year. The words "future husband" caused her to reflect. What if Rose had been lying?

With a shrug, Alexa crumpled up the paper. She was going to wait with the letter until she learned the truth about Hans Günther's intentions.

The sky was overcast and a rough northeasterly blowing when Hans Günther arrived late on the following afternoon. The crossing from Norddeich, a thirty-minute trip on calm seas, took more than an hour.

During the first few days of his stay the weather was bad. There was nothing else to do but to sit in the lobby, read, play cards or use the fleeting minutes when the rain stopped for a brisk walk along the beach. At long last, on the fourth day, the sun reappeared and Hans Günther invited her to go for a walk with him. She was relieved when Rose decided not to chaperone her as she had on her strolls with other young men.

They passed Conversationshaus with its restaurants, theater, game and reading rooms, then the newly built modern section which contained the bazaar and the expensive little boutiques selling French and English imports. Skirting the village green, they took the path that led to the lighthouse. They were halfway to it when Hans Günther reached out for her and took hold of her arm.

"Come, let's climb to the top of the dunes and sit down. I love to look at the sea. Especially when I'm not in it," he added with a chuckle.

They laughed, which broke the strange tension that had made her tongue-tied during the walk. When clumps of sand gave way under her feet, he placed a supporting arm around her waist. Suddenly he stopped and lifted her up until her toes barely touched the ground. Holding her in a tight embrace, he kissed her on the lips. She felt an elation, an intoxication which spread through her body. Later, whenever she recalled the moment, she knew it was the zenith of her entire life. Nothing that happened to her before or after could match it.

He released her and they continued in silence up a dune where they found a grassy spot at the top and sat down. He took her hands and kissed them. "Will you marry me?" he asked.

Later she wished she had been more restrained, had kept the words from gushing out as though a dam had sprung a leak inside her.

"Will I? Don't you know how much I love you? Ever since I first met you! Even before. I sneaked a picture of you from Aunt Rose's album and hid it in my desk drawer. Before going to sleep, I used to take it out and—"

A strange expression on Hans Günther's face cut her short. He had pulled back and was watching her as if he were an audience and she an actress performing her big scene. For a second their eyes met, then, realizing her embarrassment, he smiled guiltily and embraced her.

"You're adorable." He kissed her lips, then her eyes. "I love you. How could a man not love you. God, you're so beautiful. And so very young." He paused for a second, his smile fading. "I love you, but there is something you must remember. I'm not nineteen like you."

"Almost twenty."

"Not twenty either. I wish I were. Perhaps I would be a different person if I had met you at twenty. But when I was twenty, you were five, so there you are. A man is exposed to all sorts of temptations. He might succumb to them or defeat them. I've been through a lot, survived a lot. Now I want to start afresh. With you. I'm not the easiest man to live with. Marriage will be a new experience for both of us, although with a difference. You grew up with the thought that one day you'd be married, and you're prepared. I'm not. For a long time marriage seemed inconceivable to me. I'll have a more difficult period of adjustment than you will. You must take that into the bargain when you marry me."

Though the words had failed to, the tone succeeded in warning her of an obstacle, a threat, that she would have to overcome to make her marriage work. Suddenly she felt depressed.

"Are you sure you want to marry me?" she asked.

Gently and lovingly he cradled her face in the palms of his hands. "I am sure. I just don't want you to walk into this . . . this thing blindfolded. Marriage is . . . well . . . how shall I explain it? Today we have gorgeous weather. For almost a week we had windstorms. Tomorrow it might rain again. Nevertheless one mustn't lose heart. No matter how long it rains, the sun is bound to come out at the end. All one needs is patience."

They celebrated their engagement with a dinner given by the general at the restaurant of the Strandhalle. Hans Günther remained two more weeks. They bathed in the sea—three dips and out—took long walks and kissed and embraced whenever they were allowed sufficient privacy by their elders. They behaved as a well-bred and proper engaged couple in love were supposed to.

In a long letter, Alexa notified Beata of her engagement and sent her regrets for not being able to attend her wedding. Beata's answer, in which she too noted the strange caprice of fate that helped them both find husbands within the span of one month, wished Alexa happiness and expressed hopes for a meeting in the near future.

The Karadys were honeymooners in Italy when Alexa Rethy and Baron Hans Günther von Godenhausen, captain of the Gardes du Corps, were united in holy matrimony at the garrison church in Potsdam.

Alexa had been looking forward to her wedding night with a mixture of impatience and alarm. She did not know what to expect. The only detailed information she had ever obtained on sex was from a classmate at the Obere Töchterschule who claimed to be an expert on the matter. An ugly sallow-visaged girl with clammy hands and bat ears, she seemed to derive a special thrill out of shocking her listeners with facts found in her coroner father's books on forensic medicine.

Despite her strong aversion to the girl, Alexa repeatedly joined the group of her classmates attending the impromptu seminar. What they heard about the sex act was more confusing than enlightening. In bed, men were supposed to go to all sorts of extremes. On the wedding night they turned into beasts, ripped off the bride's clothing, tore her apart and caused injuries that never really healed. Most women hated "it," and if they didn't they became whores.

The day before the wedding Alexa had been tempted to ask her aunt about the physical aspects of marriage, but she decided not to. The picture of Rose copulating with the general seemed embarrassingly grotesque to her. Perhaps they never did, so it was useless to go to Rose for information.

Alexa need not have feared the wedding night. Hans Günther was in no hurry to possess her. On the train he waited in the corridor of the wagon-lit compartment for her to undress, then took off his clothes in the dark and went to sleep in the upper berth. Their marriage was consummated after a leisurely dinner and a second bottle of Veuve Cliquot ordered from room service at the Badischer Hof in Baden-Baden.

Drunk with champagne and with his caresses, she was much too confused to know what was happening to her. He had switched off the light and lay down beside her in complete silence. He began stroking her, then guided her hand to his penis, a limp chunk of flesh which, to her surprise, slowly grew hard and erect. She had seen paintings and statues of naked men with their organs hanging like oversize prunes that were backed up by what seemed like small tobacco pouches. Now suddenly his organ had a life of its own. It felt silky-skinned, smooth and throbbing. She wanted to say something, ask, but he placed his hand over her mouth.

"Be quiet," he whispered. "For God's sake, don't talk. Everything will be all right, just don't talk."

He stuffed a pillow under her back, then parted her legs. This is it, she thought and froze. She felt him fumble nervously, his whole body shaking.

"Help me," he exploded, strangely brusque and peevish, "or I'll just give up and go to sleep."

Confused and hurt, she obediently relaxed. She felt a sharp pain and disregarding his order to keep quiet, cried out. The pain persisted for some time; later she could not remember how long. He left her abruptly and rolled off her with a groan. Something hot and thick was flowing out of her, and the horror stories of her ex-classmate flashed through her mind.

"I am bleeding," she whimpered.

He threw her a towel that he had placed at the foot of the bed and turned on the light. She wiped herself. A thick white liquid colored by a thin streak of blood showed on the towel.

"You'd better get down and use the chamber pot," he told her.

She stared at him bewildered. Never in her life had she urinated in the presence of a man. Not even when she was ill and the man was her doctor.

33

"I will not!" she blurted out.

"Then go to the W.C. It's down the hall. I don't want you to get pregnant the first night."

She remained awake until the light of dawn filtered in through the slits where the panels of the heavy drapes met. Shouldn't there be more to a wedding night than some awkward fumbling followed by a sudden and penetrating saber thrust? From the moment they had entered the bedroom, Hans Günther seemed to be performing a premeditated and mechanical ritual that had no relevance to anything that had happened previously between them.

Before the wedding she had hoped that the strange remoteness that at times separated them like a six-foot wall would crumble in the privacy of their shared bedroom, but now she suspected it never would. Not completely.

By the second week of their honeymoon they had reached an almost comfortable plateau of mutual adjustment. No longer expecting fireworks, she became satisfied with his gentle though impersonal modus operandi in bed. Twice he even succeeded in causing her to reach a climax. She continued loving and desiring him, but slowly, like a mother growing used to her infant's retardation, realized that he lacked the fundamental capacity to enjoy sex fully. His wit and gaiety brightened her days, but at nights he became like royalty, full of good will yet strictly adhering to the rules of court etiquette: she was not to address him without first obtaining permission.

On the whole they had a pleasant time except for minor incidents which revealed to her that he was prone to sudden, inexplicable fits of anger.

One evening she put on a dress fashioned by Fräulein Elsa after a sketch in the *Modejournal*. He had preceded her downstairs, and when she followed him and stepped from the elevator he glared at her, pale with rage.

"Where in the devil did you pick up this ludicrous outfit? At the flea market?"

She blushed. "It came with my trousseau. It's a Vivienne

34

model, copied by Fräulein Elsa. Vivienne is the most expensive couturière in Berlin. On her shield it says, 'By appointment to Her Majesty Empress Auguste Viktoria.' "

"I am not surprised," Hans Günther muttered. Evidently his allegiance was restricted to the person of the All Highest but not to his spouse. "From now on I'll tell you what to wear. And don't ever let Fräulein Elsa sew as much as a fig leaf for you."

He ordered several outfits for her from a dressmaker on Sophien Strasse. They were expensive and Alexa wondered how he could afford them. She knew his family had no money, and his captain's pay was barely enough for the standard of living befitting his station. It was only much later that she heard of a trust fund a mysterious Godenhausen uncle had settled on Hans Günther. As a boy Hans Günther had lived with this uncle for a year and traveled with him to Turkey and Egypt. On the rare occasions the Sedlitzes mentioned the uncle it was with reluctance and disapproval.

The newlyweds stayed in Baden-Baden until the first week of October. The weather remained mild and sunny and so did Hans Günther's mood. He lost his temper only once more, this time over an ostrich-feather-trimmed hat Alexa chose to wear with one of the new suits he had ordered for her.

"Must you always dress like an organ grinder's monkey? Won't you ever learn?" He dropped the hat into the waste basket.

She stifled a sob. "Is that reason enough to hurt and humiliate me?"

"Yes, it is. And I am going to hurt and humiliate you again and again until you learn." He stepped to her, his blue eyes under the long silky lashes fixed on her face. "You are beautiful. Nature's masterpiece. As perfect in your own way as the Venus of the Capitol. Can you imagine Venus wearing a hat like that?"

Her face was tear-streaked, nevertheless she could not help laughing. "You're crazy. I am no Venus. Too skinny for that.

35

I always hoped my breasts would grow, but no. Perhaps when I get pregnant, or after my first child."

"I don't want you to change. Child or no child. Now wash your face and let's go. I need the exercise. Thank God we're leaving soon. I'm beginning to feel like an animal in a zoo, or a dancing bear kept on a chain attached to a ring in his nose. The difference between me and the bear is that my ring is on my finger." Seeing her eyes brim over with tears, he pulled her into his arms. "Don't. Don't be so sensitive. I love you, it's only that I'm not used to being idle. That's something women never understand. My life has been duties, discipline, regulations. Then suddenly no duties. No marches, only strolls. All right for old men, perhaps not even for them. Remember Bismarck, how he went to pieces after his resignation. And he was seventy-five, not thirty-four."

She washed her face and they left for their usual afternoon walk. Two days later they boarded the train for home.

In addition to her trousseau, her aunt also paid for the furnishing of the apartment they rented in Potsdam. The choice of style was left to Hans Günther, who, as everyone agreed, had impeccable taste. An ardent champion of the art nouveau, he insisted on having everything made to order in Paris. For a long time Alexa felt she was living in an interior decorator's display window. She almost felt homesick for the clumsy mock-Gothic buffets, the no-style armchairs and the wide comfortable beds of the Sedlitzes' apartment.

Their first at-home afternoon was attended by such dignitaries as General Kuno von Moltke, commandant of Berlin, Councillor Lecomte of the French Embassy and two aides-decamp to the emperor. The party was a great success and everyone agreed that the Godenhausens were the most attractive young couple of the Potsdam military set. . . .

36

2

And indeed, they still were considered to be, these three years later, Alexa thought as she sat in the carriage next to her silent husband.

There was little traffic on Linden Strasse, but upon reaching Brandenburger Tor the carriage was slowed down to a snail's pace by the line of vehicles gravitating toward the New Palace. It was a twenty-minute crawl from the park gate to the entrance. When the Godenhausens alighted, Hauptweg was still dotted with the twinkling of carriage lamps, the air filled with the snort of reined-in horses and the squeak of wheels coming to a sudden halt.

Although Franz Ferdinand and his morganatic wife, née Countess Sophie Chotek, were received en famille by their imperial hosts, close to four hundred guests, among them the entire diplomatic staff of the Monarchy's Berlin Embassy, were invited to the dinner honoring them. Had Sophie been royalty, the occasion would have called for a state banquet, but she presented a delicate problem, and entertaining her required special arrangements. It was decided that she and her husband would be welcomed with warm hospitality but no pomp. In Vienna the implacable Prince Montenuovo, Emperor Franz Josef's Lord Chamberlain, had always seated Sophie at the low end of the dinner table. This caused endless friction between him and the archduke, which still failed to bring the wife one chair closer to her husband. At the New Palace, Marshal of the Court August zu Eulenburg suggested that the guests be served informally at individual tables, the archducal couple sharing one with Wilhelm and his Auguste Viktoria, who was called Dona by her family.

The Godenhausens, as all guests, were instructed to proceed to the Grottensaal, a high-ceilinged room with sea-shell-covered walls and moldings inlaid with semiprecious stones. At eight o'clock sharp the descent of the imperial party from their private apartments was announced. In the Grottensaal lines formed as if on command, ladies to the right, gentlemen to the left, flanking the aisle through which Their Majesties, His Highness and the ex-countess would cross to the Jasper Gallery, where the dinner would be served. It was at this moment that Alexa caught sight of Count Nicholas Karady, her twin's widower.

Although she had not seen him since her childhood days in Sarkany, she recognized him immediately. He had been a cavalry lieutenant then, now he was a captain on the General Staff. Despite the few gray streaks in his charcoal-black hair, he looked younger than his thirty-five years. From his paternal ancestors he had inherited a tall muscular body, an aristocrat's commanding presence and a handsome angular face with piercing dark eyes. On the whole his was a fine face, not easily missed in a crowd, and once noticed not easily forgotten.

As a member of the Austro-Hungarian ambassador's entourage, he was placed at the head of the line. His expression betrayed only mild interest in the hubbub about him, certainly not the first festive gathering he had attended. Invitations to Mount Olympus are a great honor to ordinary mortals, but after a while their novelty wears off, especially if the gods make the same speeches over and over and offer the same menu. Or was it not ennui that made his face seem to be the only somber one among faces flushed with anticipation, but the two-year-old pain not completely gone? Alexa wondered.

As his eyes passed over the room they halted on her face. Alexa saw him turn deathly pale. For a moment he seemed to be holding his breath. He took a step forward, as if wanting to rush to her, then his body slackened and he moved back into the line. He stared at her with an expression of disbelief, then quickly averted his gaze, as if unable to bear the sight of her. He had never seen her as an adult; it was the resemblance between her and Beata that had revealed her identity to him. His discomposure was so obvious that she wondered whether the people around him had noticed it. From mutual acquaintances, and also through the grapevine stretching between Vienna's and Berlin's military circles, she had learned that he had been inconsolable after Beata's death. He was still vulnerable, or the presence of Beata's twin wouldn't have upset him with such intensity, Alexa concluded. Her heart went out to him. He was a complete stranger to her, yet she felt that their common grief was a closer tie between them than even a blood relationship.

The entrance of Marshal of the Court Count August zu Eulenburg had hushed all conversation in the room. There were the three obligatory taps with the marshal's ivory wand on the floor, then the count moved down the aisle, closely followed by the All Highest, as Wilhelm preferred to be called, with the ex-countess on his arm, and by Franz Ferdinand escorting the empress.

Alexa had seen Kaiser Wilhelm before, yet watching him enter, she was once again surprised by the man's evident self-consciousness, like an actor greeting his admirers at the stage door. Even his nods to acquaintances had the quality of a performance.

He was shorter than his portraits led one to believe, slender, but compact and well-preserved for his forty-seven years. A hint of a tan acquired at maneuvers colored his sallow complexion. His waxed mustache, a tonsorial triumph over the forces of gravity, was still as martially upturned as ever.

An intemperate egotist, he was known to use every public appearance for histrionics, always wearing the proper costume to fit the role. On this night, dressed in the gala uniform of the Austrian uhlan regiment bearing his name, Wilhelm chose to act the benevolent uncle entertaining a nephew forgiven for a youthful misstep.

The misstep in person, the woman on his arm, seemed to take the great honor of being dined by the emperor of Germany in her stride. She was full blown and well put together, radiating health and contentment. The smile she bestowed on the men and women lined up along her path was friendly and without the slightest touch of pride or sarcasm, although she knew that some, especially of the Austrian contingent, had done their utmost to malign and humiliate her before and after her marriage. Archduke Franz Ferdinand, tall and slightly stooped, his gala uniform inelegantly tight over his middle-aged belly, was in one of his unusually benign moods; his wife was being welcomed at a ruling monarch's court with all the honors due hereditary royalty.

Passing the Monarchy's Embassy contingent, displeasure clouded his eyes, then he nodded curtly to the bowing ambassador and turned his attention back to the empress. The ambassador was a Hungarian count, and Alexa had heard that there was no love lost between his countrymen and Franz Ferdinand, who had never been completely at ease in his role as heir apparent to the oldest throne of Europe, a role in which he had been unexpectedly cast after the mysterious suicide of his cousin, the Archduke Rudolf, at Mayerling.

Empress Auguste Viktoria, a woman of forty-eight and the mother of seven children, had the florid complexion, the curves, the solid flesh, the soft manageable hair and clear untroubled eyes of a typical German housewife. She wore a dress of purple damask, the fabric of which would have made perfect upholstery material for a sofa. It had a low-cut bodice which left her shoulders bare. Her bosom, amply plump under a flawless skin, reminded Alexa of the velvet cushions jewelers displayed their wares on. Her necklace of diamonds, rubies and several strings of pearls lay carefully arranged on it as though being offered for sale. The Order of the Golden Fleece was pinned to her dress above the right breast.

After the imperial party had settled down in the gallery, the foursome cozily sharing a table, the marshal of the court signaled for service to begin. Alexa saw Nicholas seated between a dame d'honneur to the empress and the wife of a Bavarian diplomat, two rather attractive women. Throughout the meal he seemed to be paying only polite attention to them, rarely contributing more than a short remark to the conversation.

Alexa and her husband were dining with the very distinguished group that was referred to somewhat disparagingly as the Liebenberg Round Table, named after Prince Philipp zu Eulenburg und Hertefeld's country estate in Liebenberg. Eulenburg—a man of great charm, a poet, playwright and composer, but most importantly Emperor Wilhelm II's best friend—sat between Alexa and the Countess von Hohenau, the only other woman in the party of eight.

Ever since Wilhelm's ascension to the throne, no imperial decision had been made without Eulenburg. For close to nineteen years it had been the prince and not the Kaiser's chancellors and ministers who had shaped Germany's foreign policy. His unique position had made him an easy prey to attacks from the extreme right, the extreme left and frequently from the center as well. He and his friends were called a secret camarilla, and veiled hints were circulating about certain unsavory practices within their group. They even reached Alexa's ear, but when she asked Hans Günther for an explanation regarding their nature he told her they were the kind of poisonous gossip no successful man could escape in politics.

The military commandant of Berlin, General Count Kuno von Moltke, with his dreamy eyes and the long-fingered hands of a musician, was seated on Alexa's right. He was one of Eulenburg's closest friends and supposedly owed his brilliant military career to the prince's support. Despite the best efforts of his tailor, there was the hint of soft curves under his tight-fitting uniform, and his face had the cherubic prettiness of a small boy turned fifty.

The Frenchman on Alexa's left, Councillor Lecomte of his country's Berlin Embassy, was an honorary member of the Liebenberg Round Table. Slight and pale-complexioned, wearing a thin dark mustache that looked as though it had been dabbed on by some disrespectful graffiti artist, Lecomte had, supposedly because of his weakness for blond Nordic cavalry officers, a great admiration for Prussia and her military. He had been credited with repeatedly soothing his government's indignation when it was aroused by the Kaiser's outbursts against France.

Count Wilhelm von Hohenau, aide-de-camp to the emperor, and Colonel Count Johannes von Lynar of the Gardes completed the party.

Alexa knew that her husband's acceptance as an equal by the Round Table, men fifteen to twenty years older and a hundred times more powerful and richer than he, puzzled many people. Not her though. Without being especially witty or anxious to please, Hans Günther exuded the kind of mysterious attraction that made matinee idols out of moderately talented actors. At first meeting the impact of his good looks was softened by a hint of vulnerability that drew men as well as women to him. He responded to their flattery with the proper measure of cordiality, never discarding the invisible armor that no friendship could completely penetrate.

Throughout the meal the center of attention remained the imperial hosts and their guests of honor. The Kaiser ate little, mainly because he hardly stopped talking. His voice, once youthfully strident, was now dulled, not by age but by the operation he had undergone for the removal of a polyp in

42

1903. It became lost in the din of general conversation; only his loud laughter broke through with growing frequency, flashes of lightning in an overcast sky. He seemed to be having the time of his life, which astounded Alexa. Only a few days earlier there had been rumors floating in Berlin about the nervous breakdown the Kaiser had suffered when it became evident that the Algeciras conference had ended in a shattering diplomatic defeat for Germany.

Chancellor Bülow and his elegant Italian wife were seated at a table to the right of the Kaiser's party. His presence was a surprise to everyone. Only six weeks earlier he had suffered a fainting spell—some called it a light stroke—while addressing the Reichstag. He was driven home in an ambulance and later advised by his doctors to take an extended vacation. His presence at the dinner tonight marked his first public appearance since his illness.

Another Moltke, Helmuth, the new chief of staff, nephew of the legendary hero of the Franco-Prussian War, dined with the Bülows. He was the most impressive man present, and would have been in any gathering. The very paragon of a cavalry officer, he appeared to be mounted on horseback even when on foot. In London it was said that the Kaiser had made him chief of staff hoping that his martial looks would strike terror into Edward VII's heart.

The dinner was followed by the ritual of the Sprech Cour. The imperial and archducal couples strolled through a series of rooms addressing guests, exchanging pleasantries, making small talk. The Godenhausens were instructed by an aide-de-camp to remain conspicuous, for the emperor had expressed his wish to address them.

With about a dozen men and women, mostly strangers, they were herded into one of the small salons. Everyone stood around in awkward silence, eyes avoiding eyes, bodies keeping their distance from other bodies. A man stepped on a lady's train, a woman dropped a fan, there was some clearing of

43

throats and discreet coughings with hands covering mouths. A few secret yawns. Suddenly with the force of a trumpeting elephant, or so it seemed in the cathedral stillness, an elderly man in tails and white tie blew his nose. In the crossfire of shocked gazes, he shamefacedly stuffed his handkerchief into his pants pocket. It made a slight bulge with one hemstitched corner still hanging out.

At long last, preceded by two footmen who took up positions at the double-winged doors, the Kaiser, accompanied by the archduke and an aide-de-camp, walked in.

After addressing three others, the Kaiser halted in front of the Godenhausens. The sovereign's portraits, framed and hanging on walls, or reproduced on ashtrays, mugs, plaques, pitchers, postage stamps, silver and gold coins, always showed him to be virile and handsome. Now at close range he looked like an old ferret sniffing out the shortest way to the henhouse.

Before presenting the Godenhausens to the archduke, the Kaiser threw a few facetious quips at Hans Günther. Judging by the escorting aide-de-camp's expression, they were an unscheduled interruption of the Sprech Cour. It seemed to Alexa that it was the gaze of Hans Günther's blue eyes, reverently fixed on the imperial face, that was keeping the apparently mesmerized Wilhelm from proceeding with the ritual. She herself, frozen in deep curtsy, rated no more recognition than a friendly nod.

Franz Ferdinand acknowledged her curtsy and her husband's stiff bow with a smile that spread over the lower part of his face but failed to reach his eyes. When the Kaiser mentioned that Alexa was Hungarian, even his half-smile faded.

The All Highest's exit from the room brought the people back to life. His words were repeated and analyzed with an awe worthy of prophetic revelations.

"This has been the third time His Majesty has singled me out for an address," Hans Günther told Alexa as they were headed for the Tanzsaal from where the strains of a Strauss waltz played by the house orchestra were emanating. "Uncle

Adalbert mentioned the other day that my appointment to aide-de-camp seemed within the bounds of possibility."

She gave him a surprised look. "You never told me."

"Sorry. I know, I should've, but it is too good to be true, and I am superstitious."

Later she was surrounded by her court of enamored subalterns from Hans Günther's regiment, sitting out a dance, when she felt her cheeks burning. As if following a telepathic command, she shifted 'her gaze and saw Nicholas Karady standing alone at the far end of the Marmorsaal. With sudden decision she rose, excused herself to the young men and, dodging dancers, made her way through the crowd. Realizing that she was headed in his direction, he rushed to meet her halfway.

"I am mad at you," she said without waiting for him to speak. "You've been in Berlin for some time without letting us know. We had to learn it through the grapevine. I am your sister-in-law, remember? Or is that a thing of the past?"

He stared at her, speechless, then blurted out, "God, you're so much like her!"

From close up she became aware of the telltale signs the years had marked his face with.

"So much like her," he repeated in a whisper.

"I think that's good." Embarrassed, she corrected herself. "I mean, good for me. I look into the mirror and think, That is Beata. She is alive, in me. We'll grow old together and die together." She blushed nervously. "Sorry. That's sheer nonsense." She wished he would reply, but he kept silent. "Aren't you amazed that I recognized you? After such a long time. But, of course, you haven't changed much." That was not true, yet he failed to protest. "Besides, I knew I'd see you tonight. My husband told me. Come, let's look for him. I want you to meet him."

"I already have. Prince Eulenburg introduced us."

"Do you know Eulenburg?"

"Very well. He's been a friend of my family from the time

45

he was German ambassador to the Monarchy. One of the most fascinating men I've ever met. I have nothing but admiration for him."

He spoke with a vehemence, as if he were expecting a protest from her. "Everybody adores him," Alexa reassured him. She added, "Almost everybody." Footmen were passing with champagne-filled glasses. She took one and gave him one. "Come, let's find a place where we can talk," she said, suddenly switching to Hungarian. "There is so much I want to ask you." She led him through a series of rooms to the small salon where she had been presented to the archduke.

"You seem to know your way around here," Karady said.

"Not really. But I've been in this room before." They settled in a corner. Except for three bemedaled civilians conversing in animated Dutch, they were alone.

"Isn't this nice and cozy?" she asked. "Seems it has been reserved for us. At least one can sit down here. Anywhere else one must stand. Standing and waiting, that's what life is at this court. I often wonder how the older dames d'honneur manage. They're like horses, fall asleep standing. I swear I've seen old Countess Keller do it. But that's not what I wanted to talk to you about. How are my grandparents? When did you see them last? I feel so terrible for not having written them since Christmas. I'm sure they're hurt." Her sentences came in jetlike spurts. She lifted her glass to her lips, then put it down without taking a sip.

"I saw them in January. They seemed well and—"

She cut in. "Did you tell them you were going to be in Berlin?"

"No, because I myself didn't know it at the time."

"Are you pleased to be stationed in Berlin?"

"It's a change."

She threw an inquisitive look at him. "You don't look happy." She immediately regretted having said it. She didn't want him to think she was probing.

46

He shrugged. "Should I?"

"I'm sorry. I mustn't pry. It's only that throughout the dinner I kept watching you and—"

"I thought you didn't even notice me."

"I certainly did. You were seated between two attractive women and looked clearly bored. Or sad. I wondered which."

"Neither. Just observing the scene. Getting my bearings."

"If you want to be au courant come to me. Except that Hans Günther thinks I am prejudiced." She lowered her voice. "He is so terribly Prussian. Deep down, I mean. He denies it, but the truth is that patriotism is his religion and the Kaiser his idol. If the Kaiser ordered him to, he'd walk barefoot over blazing coals like those crazy fakirs in India and feel no pain. The Kaiser can do no wrong. It's the Socialists and the Reichstag who are the root of all evil. If it were up to him he'd line them up against a long wall and shoot them dead."

"I didn't know you were interested in politics. German women seldom are."

"German women! The kind you meet. I can well imagine the topics they discuss with you."

"You still don't consider yourself German?"

"Heavens, no. People around here call me the little Magyar, which, make no mistake, isn't meant to be flattering. At best they consider me a mongrel." She gazed at him, her eyes exploring his face. "You too are a mongrel. I mean, to them. And let me warn you. This isn't Vienna. People can be very cruel around here."

"I imagine they can. But don't worry about me. I've been around and have faced prejudice before. Being twice the mongrel you are, I am prepared for a few snubs. I can take them and repay them in kind."

She didn't ask him what he meant by "twice the mongrel." He had taken it for granted that she understood him, which she did. She clearly remembered his mother, Countess Melanie, a descendant of a certain Nathan Geiger, a Jewish grain dealer from Poland who had built a village feed store into a brokerage firm that controlled the entire feed market of the Monarchy. His eldest son, Josef, in reward for services rendered to the empire's commerce, was raised to the rank of baron and his surname prefixed with Gebhardt, after the village of his birth. From then on he called himself Gebhardt, yet the Geiger name remained as permanently stuck to his family as barnacles to ship's hull. He and his wife became converted to Catholicism, his three daughters married gentiles. Melanie, the youngest of the brood, made the most impressive catch: Count Ferdinand Karady.

Everyone in Sarkany knew that at the time of his marriage Count Ferdinand was in serious danger of losing his heavily mortgaged land. Melanie's dowry wiped out the mortgage and restored the dilapidated castle. It also paid for a three-story mansion, thenceforth known as the Karady palace, in Vienna's Herrengasse. Alexa remembered the excitement created by Melanie's visits to Sarkany. For short periods she had enjoyed playing chatelaine, then she would rush back to Vienna to spend her energy and time on her futile campaign to replace Princess Paula Metternich as the first lady of the capital. And on squabbles with her husband, an incorrigible Casanova. She had bought him, title and all, with the Geiger millions, and for thirty-eight years she had fought a losing battle to keep him bought.

"Sorry," Alexa said. "I shouldn't have brought up the whole thing. It was most tactless of me."

He gave her a long warm look. "I am glad you did. Now I know you are *you*. You look like her, sound like her, yet . . ." He paused. "She was reserved, almost shy. You are not."

She laughed. "No, certainly not. Not shy. I wish I were. It would be safer. Nevertheless, I don't understand why I took such . . . such liberties with you. Probably because we were talking in Hungarian. I could never have talked this freely to

48

you in German. Besides, we're related, aren't we?" He nodded and she went on. "I'd hate to see you hurt."

Before he could answer there was a voice calling from the doorway. "Oh, here you are! I've been looking all over the place for you." Hans Günther was crossing to them. "So you have managed to meet!" He turned to Alexa. "Don't you think it's time we left? Unless you want to help the staff lock up the palace." His tone was clipped and chilling.

Alexa was surprised and embarrassed. Never before had he been rude to her in front of others. She wondered whether Nicholas had noticed it and, if so, what impression it had made on him.

She pretended to be unconcerned. "What's your hurry?"

"I'll be on duty at six in the morning, which means that I'll have to get up at four-thirty, while you can sleep until eleven. Where is your wrap?" Again the sharp tone. Now she was convinced that Karady's presence had prompted it.

"In the cloakroom." She offered her hand to Nicholas. "It's been so good seeing you again. You must come and visit us. Could you make it next Friday? The last Friday of each month is our at-home day. Any time from four in the afternoon. Promise you'll come."

He held her hand for a long moment before lifting it to his lips. He had most likely sensed Hans Günther's impatience and did it deliberately. "I promise. I certainly will."

Taking leave, Godenhausen was once again the very image of cordiality. "Don't restrict yourself to Fridays. Any time you're in Potsdam," he said in his friendliest Prussian. To Nicholas's ears his r's sounded like pebbles rolling down a rocky hillside. "And please let me know if I can be of service to you. Introducing you to people, taking you around, showing you the sights. We have no telephone at the house, but you can always reach me at the Gardes du Corps regimental command post." He gave Nicholas one more warm handshake. "I hope you'll like it here, Karady. Of course, Berlin isn't as

49

sophisticated as your Vienna. We're a young empire, so don't be too critical of us."

Two months earlier, in the middle of March 1906, Nicholas Karady had been notified that his request for transfer from Vienna had been granted. From April 1, he would be detailed on duty as adjutant to the Monarchy's military attaché at the Berlin Embassy.

The assignment surprised Nicholas. It wasn't exactly the post he had hoped for.

"May I ask a question off the record, sir?" he addressed General Hartmann, his superior at the deployment section of the Austro-Hungarian General Staff.

Hartmann nodded. "Go ahead."

"Why Berlin, sir? Why me, with my background? General Conrad knows that I am half Jewish."

"By now you must have learned how to handle that problem. If it *is* a problem. I personally don't think it is."

"Probably not in Austria, sir. In Berlin it used to be an impenetrable wall. A Baron Bleichröder had to leave the army because his colonel barred him from the officers' mess, and Goldschmied-Rothschild was considered acceptable for the diplomatic corps but not for a lieutenant's commission in the army reserves."

"You're talking of the past. Times have changed since. The Kaiser himself has changed. Today Albert Ballin, a Jew, is supposed to be one of his intimates."

"Because he is the head of the Hamburg-America Line. The Kaiser can talk ships with him. Now that he is building a fleet to rival England's, anything that moves on water has priority with him. He probably senses a kindred soul in Ballin. But I have no ships, not even a canoe. I'm still waiting for your answer, sir. Why me? Or aren't you supposed to tell?"

The general contemplated for a moment. "I think General Conrad wanted a man who was not in sympathy with the

Prussian military and had good social connections with Italian, British and French diplomats. If the Prussians keep their distance, don't give it a thought. We're not interested in Germany's military secrets, because we can read them in the London *Times*. The *Times* gets its information straight from the horse's— I mean, the Kaiser's mouth."

"I'm afraid General Conrad overestimates the importance of my social connections."

"You have one that could be very useful to us. You're still in contact with Prince Philipp zu Eulenburg und Hertefeld, aren't you?"

"I am, but the prince is no longer in active service."

"He is still the Kaiser's best friend."

So this was why he had been chosen by the chief of staff, Nicholas thought.

"I don't promise you much fun in Berlin," the general said. "During the late nineties I was there for a week and hated every minute of it. However, I hear the city has changed. Become a real metropolis. Anyway, you won't be there forever. Two, three years at the most."

Not exactly delighted with the turn of events, Nicholas nevertheless had no regrets about leaving Vienna. Having to part with Mitzi Hahn, soubrette of the Theater an der Wien, the lastest in the succession of women he had slept with since Beata's death, was more deliverance than hardship. He had tired of Mitzi, but she held on to him with an ever-growing passion that made a break impossible.

He had long passed the stage when taking a woman to his bed would leave him with a sour aftertaste of self-loathing. By now he was leading a monotonous but otherwise not unpleasant life. The first in line of his mistresses had been a family friend ten years older than he. It was about a month after Beata's death that she brought him a basketful of red roses and words of sympathy whispered during tender embraces. The softness of her mature body stirred up a sudden, irresistible hunger in him, and wasting no time on gallantries, he made love to her right there on his drawing-room sofa, a fragile piece rather inadequate for such vigorous physical exercises. After his moment of lust, once again in control of himself, he showed her to the door with the brusqueness of a man getting rid of a troublesome peddler. He refused to see her again and practiced complete abstinence for a long time afterward.

It was a period of intense suffering for him. His grief was as physical a reality as the pressure of shackles around a convict's ankles. During none of his waking moments was he free of pain; Beata's death remained a dark backdrop against which his daily life was being enacted. Suffering had its high and low tides, and at its peak it manifested itself in crying fits rather unbecoming to an officer. Unable to control himself, he endured them in secluded places such as men's rooms in restaurants or foliage-hidden park benches. In his pre-Beata years, he had regarded hours spent in solitude as welcome pauses, but now he found them insupportable. Nevertheless he preferred solitude to having his mother and her friends around. Her efforts to lift him out of his "morbid state of mind" by introducing him to marriageable girls or complaisant women annoyed him no end. His father, to whom he had never been close in the past, showed a surprising degree of understanding. He would take him to dinner or the races or obtain invitations for him to hunts on friends' estates in Hungary.

His second fall from grace occurred on one of these occasions. This time it was the daughter of his host, a young woman separated from her husband. The affair, a pleasant relationship satisfactory to both parties, lasted several months and ended with the woman's reconciliation with her husband.

What amazed and disturbed Nicholas was that having a mistress failed to relieve his grief. On the contrary, a touch of self-condemnation caused his sorrow to become even more oppressive. In the beginning of his widowerhood he accepted the return of his hunger for food to be a perfectly natural development, but now, no matter how he tried to reason with himself, his hunger for sex demeaned him in his own eyes.

After a year and several affairs, both his neurotic self-hatred and the intensity of his grief began slowly to lessen. The cold emptiness that followed was no comfort either. His inability to feel even the mere semblance of an affection for any of his women distressed him. A believer in Christian morality, although not in a Christian God, he disapproved of the cynical and promiscuous man he' had become. With half of his life still before him, his future seemed like an immense desert with no roads leading into or out of it; the ever-receding line of the horizon was its sole boundary. Religion or ambition could have built that missing road, but he had no propensity for either. He worked well and intelligently at his chosen profession, because he preferred work to boredom, but derived no satisfaction from it. Having been born to money and social position, the idea of acquiring more of the same failed to excite him. Power could have served as a goal—for many of his kind it did—but he had no longing for power either.

Ten years before, Nicholas had spent a few days in Berlin and had left with no desire for a second visit. As the carriage rolled down Wilhelm Strasse, he was surprised by the cold splendor of the avenue, the old, the new and the restored palaces with their fresh coats of paint, wrought-iron gates and virgin-clean windowpanes. There was an unmistakable grandeur to the scene, and it brought Emperor Wilhelm's official portrait to his mind: an aging Lohengrin, steel-helmeted, high-booted, bemedaled and wrapped in a tentlike white cape. Ruler of a young empire, the Kaiser was as flamboyant as Franz Josef in his plain military tunic was dull. The Hapsburgs' sprawling gray-walled Hofburg in Vienna was dull too. The streets leading to it had the anemic pallor of old photographs. Dull but dependable. A native son could return to them after an absence of years and find them unchanged. Even return to them blind and still feel his way around, thanks to the old cracks in the pavement and the chipped curbstones left unfilled and unsmoothed.

Traffic in Berlin was spirited and dense compared to Vienna. The profusion of carriages, their glossy bodies adding touches of color to the scene, was surprising. It was a city with three million inhabitants and still growing, and getting bigger and richer. Vienna was the past, Berlin the future.

When Nicholas reached his hotel, the Kaiserhof, the concierge, a small man with the dignity of a freshly crowned Napoleon, personally escorted him to his suite. Furnished in the German version of Louis XVI, with heavy plush drapes and crystal chandeliers, the salon overlooked Wilhelms Platz, a wide square with the bronze statues of Frederick the Great's generals.

The noble warriors, attired in tight tunics under wide-skirted coats adorned with buttons and embroidered loops, their sleeves cuffed to the wrists, their leggings reaching from instep to thigh, made a heroic impression, especially General von Schwerin, immortalized, leading his troops into attack with standard in hand. Nicholas wondered how they had endured the long marches and the rides under the hot summer sun or in drenching rain in all that finery, always ready to go into battle at the sound of the bugle. His father had fought in Austria's war against Prussia in 1866 and received a flesh wound at Königgrätz. It wasn't the danger of being killed that he recalled most vividly, but the lice, the bedbugs, the socks rotting on his feet, the smell of his own body after days without changing his clothes. The splendor of the eighteenth-century uniforms was supposed to instill in all Prussians a large dose of amor patriae.

It was late in the afternoon, and, like bees out of a hive, swarms of officers were pouring out from the Ministry of War and streaming down Wilhelm Strasse. Basically they were not much different from the Austrians around the Hofburg; it

54

was merely the civilians' meekness in yielding them the right of way on the sidewalk that Nicholas found odd. Again, it might have been his imagination, prejudices brought from Vienna, that caused him to mistake the civilians' politeness for subservience.

The orderly assigned to him was to report for duty the following day, so instead of calling for a hotel valet he unpacked himself.

From his eighth year to his fifteenth he had had a tutor who, under the pen name Lysias, was a regular contributor to a Viennese periodical with Socialist leanings. Dr. Schauffele was determined to mold Nicholas into a self-sufficient, unspoiled human being. When traveling, he insisted that they stop at modest hotels, even pensions. At the Karady palace in Vienna or the castle in Sarkany, he saw to it that the staff refrained from kowtowing to Nicholas. It was no simple task to have a boy living amid the most wasteful luxuries of the nineteenth century accept near-Spartan standards, but because of his pupil's level-headedness and his own devotion to ideals, Dr. Schauffele succeeded splendidly.

Sincerely fond of his tutor, Nicholas was distressed and puzzled when the man was suddenly dismissed by Count Ferdinand and, what's more, barred from any contact with his ex-charge. The count had learned that Dr. Schauffele's name had appeared on the list the police kept of persons suspected of homosexual activities. Nicholas was told about this only years later. The cruel injustice inflicted upon Dr. Schauffele outraged him. Whatever the man's sexual preferences were, they remained his secret. Not once did he reveal any other sentiment for Nicholas than a teacher's tender concern for a lonely boy entrusted to his care.

Hanging up his uniform in the wardrobe, Nicholas recalled his youthful travels when he had unpacked not only his own but the aging Schauffele's luggage as well. The good doctor had since been laid to rest in Vienna's Central Cemetery, but a whiff of bitter smoke emanating from a locomotive, the sight of a hotel concierge handing over a room key or a station porter loading suitcases into a cab unfailingly conjured up memories of happy journeys taken all over Europe by a fat man and a skinny boy, both equally eager to explore and to learn.

After the Godenhausens had left for the cloakroom, judging by the hubbub coming from the entrance hall, the imperial hosts and the archducal couple were retiring, prompting a general exodus of guests from the New Palace. Nicholas found himself alone in the salon. The Dutchmen were gone, had probably left while he was still too deeply absorbed in talking to Alexa to notice their exit. Ever since his arrival in Berlin he had planned to call on the Godenhausens, but some inexplicable reluctance had kept him from it. Now Alexa's uncanny resemblance to Beata left him dazed. He needed time to collect himself.

Ready at last to pick up his greatcoat and shako, he passed through the Apollo Saal and found himself falling in step with Prince Eulenburg, who was also headed for the cloakroom. The two men had not seen each other since the prince's resignation as Germany's ambassador to the court of Franz Josef. Despite the difference in their ages, Eulenburg had always shown a warm interest in Nicholas. There had been occasional letters from him, volumes of his poems and sheet music of his latest songs. Now it appalled Nicholas to find the prince looking tired and older than his fifty-nine years. His face seemed like a faded daguerreotype; only his eyes and voice remained young. The eyes were smiling even when the lips were not, and the voice imbued the harsh Prussian consonants with dreamy softness. As always, there was an air of sophistication about him, the kind that unfailingly commands attention.

"My dear Nicky, how splendid to see you again! I was away

56

at Liebenberg and heard only yesterday that you were in Berlin. How are you, my dear boy? Happy, unhappy, merely contented? The rumors I've heard about you don't seem comforting. I understand you still live by yourself, with no intention of making a change."

"If you mean, Prince, that I have no marriage plans, that's true."

"I know, it is too early. Only two years. Nevertheless, life without a family isn't worth a farthing. Perhaps I am saying this because I am blessed with my dear Augusta and six lovely children, gifts from heaven. I don't know if I'd ever survive without their affection and loyalty."

He spoke with deep emotion and Nicholas detected an underlying bitterness behind his tone.

"I don't imagine survival has ever been a problem for you."

"People think that the emperor's friendship is a great blessing. It is, except for the jealousy it creates. For twenty years people have been after my hide and still are."

Shortly after his arrival in Berlin, Nicholas had heard rumors of a secret investigation of the prince's private life supposedly conducted by the Berlin police. Suspected of homosexual leanings, mainly because of his association with known pederasts, the prince had become the target of an insidious campaign. Nicholas first heard the gossip from one of the councillors of his own embassy, a man who was aware of his friendship with the prince. He responded with an indignant outburst few captains of the Austro-Hungarian army could permit themselves when dealing with a high-ranking foreign service officer. Because of his wealth, background and indisputable virility, Nicholas could and did.

Despite his determination to expel all biased notions from his mind, Karady now looked for signs of effeminacy in Eulenburg's manners and appearance. He found gentility, a touch of world-weary lethargy, but no limpness of gesture, no nasal whine to his soft baritone. In the twentieth century,

57

he was a nineteenth-century man, addicted to colorful speech and poetic similes. Coming from others, they might have sounded stilted; but coming from him, they had charm.

"What people?" Nicholas asked, pretending to be unaware of the rumors.

"At the moment, two of the most ruthless men in Germany. Does the name Harden mean anything to you?"

"Yes. I know of his publication, the *Zukunft*." He didn't want to add that he also knew of the periodical's past mudslingings at the prince.

"It is nasty, vile, scurrilous, but widely read. And quoted and feared. Ex-Councillor Holstein of the Foreign Office used to be one of its targets. Harden had accused Holstein of being a member of my secret camarilla that exercised power without responsibility. This was his attitude until two days ago, when all of a sudden he proclaimed his reconciliation with Holstein. My first reaction was confoundment. My second, alarm."

"Why should their reconciliation affect you? I remember it was shortly after my arrival in Berlin when I read the news of Friedrich von Holstein's resignation from his post. People at my embassy told me he'd been forced to quit because of the Algeciras Conference debacle. I understood that many heads were rolling. Holstein's was one of them."

"Ever since his resignation he's been looking for the guilty party. Chancellor Bülow and Foreign Secretary Richthofen were above suspicion. Both had been stricken with apoplexy a day or two before His Majesty countersigned Holstein's resignation letter. Incidentally, it was probably his tenth or twelfth such letter. Each time he had been convinced that both the Kaiser and the chancellor would beg him to reconsider. It was another instance of his crying wolf. Unfortunately for him, it had been decided that the government could function without him. He was no longer indispensable. It so happened that on the fatal day of the signing I had lunch with His Majesty. This circumstance was sufficient for Holstein to decide that I was the person responsible for his fall. Richthofen had escaped his wrath by joining his Maker—after all, Holstein doesn't feed on carrion—Bülow by taking a long time to recover. Secretly he is still terrified of Holstein. So is the entire Foreign Office. The ex-councillor is the proverbial man who knows where the body is buried, in fact many bodies."

"I can't see what harm a man no longer in power could do you?" Nicholas asked.

"Just wait and see. Holstein is implacable." The prince seemed to be a deeply disturbed man. The fact that a person of his reputation and social standing considered himself an easy prey to a vendetta puzzled and disturbed Nicholas. He wanted to change the subject. "Are you staying in Berlin for a while? If I may, I would like to call on you."

"I'm afraid I won't be able to stay. I've been away too long from Liebenberg. The season has exhausted me. Above all, I need a rest, to be in shape for the summer. I value His Majesty's friendship, but the twelve-year difference in our ages is beginning to show. His schedule is staggering. Every June there's the week of the Kieler regatta; in July a cruise along the Norwegian shoreline; in August a brief rest in Potsdam; in September the Rominten hunts; and in November there's shooting at Donaueschingen—all between his visits to my Liebenberg. This year after Rominten I shall take a vacation. Most likely in Switzerland. As long as I stay in this country I can't possibly turn down his invitations. If I say no, he becomes emotional and complains of loneliness, which is a slight exaggeration. The palace is constantly teeming with people—the military, A.D.C.'s, officers of the Gardes—"

"Incidentally, Prince," Nicholas interrupted him, "I saw you dining with the Godenhausens tonight. Did you know that my late wife was the baroness's identical twin?"

They were crossing the great hall at the end of which the cloakroom was located. The prince halted and placed his hand on Nicholas's shoulder. "Identical twins? They've always intrigued me. If your wife looked like the baroness, she was a very beautiful lady. Breathtaking." His eyes searched Nicholas's face. "If I were you I wouldn't see too much of the Godenhausens. They're supposed to be very happy together. A most attractive couple. I understand Godenhausen is destined for a brilliant future. His Majesty is very fond of him. Besides, he has influential friends. His wife is also an asset. Half of our ladies look like geese, the other half like vultures. Baroness Godenhausen reminds me of a flamingo." He paused and reflected. "You haven't asked me for advice, but I am your friend, old enough to be your father. Besides, as you've probably heard from my critics, I'm a self-styled clairvoyant. So mark my word, stay away from them."

There had been whispers about Eulenburg's possessing occult powers, the secret of his hold upon the emperor. Nicholas gave no credence to them and interpreted the warning for what it was: a bit of wisdom from someone concerned about his well-being. A few minutes later they parted, the prince promising to contact Nicholas next time he visited Berlin.

The night was clear, the stars summery bright, yet the air was prickly with the bite of a cool May wind against Nicholas's face. It was a good fifteen-minute walk along the grounds of Sans Souci to the Wildpark station, where he was to board the train for Berlin. For the first time since his arrival he felt impressed by a place. Berlin was nouveau riche, Potsdam old nobility. Beyond the high iron railing of the wide courtyard called Sandhof lay the Mopke—now enshrouded in darkness —where Frederick the Great had drilled his guardsmen. To his left the blur against the sky was the outline of a Sans Souci palace untouched by wars or the whims of succeeding rulers. The gravel crunching under his feet had been trod upon by the old king himself. The oak trees of the park had thrown their shadows over a Voltaire taking his afternoon nap and over flocks of little Hohenzollerns playing soldier before they grew old enough to exchange their wooden rifles for real cannon.

Although he had had a long day, Nicholas did not feel tired. On the contrary, he felt alert and stirred up, a condition he had not experienced in months. It was as if he had awakened from a long dreamless sleep. He enjoyed the walk, the freshness of the air, the sprightliness of his own steps. He had no special reason to be cheerful, as he'd had no reason for the lethargy that had blunted his senses a few hours before, when his world had been wrapped in an ennui as thick as November fog. Now suddenly the fog lifted and his vision extended over miles.

Sorting out the past, he recalled times when he had felt equally happy, when life had seemed worth all the effort living called for: his travels with Dr. Schauffele, his first tour of duty with the hussars, his marriage to Beata. After Schauffele's dismissal, his journeys had become pointless. After two years in a desolate Galician garrison, army life had become boring. Only Beata had remained a constant source of delight to him. During their blessed year together there was always something to look forward to: taking her to bed at night, waking with her in the morning, a child. The child never happened, because Beata burned to death.

Now his life was a calendar printed in uniform gray. The fault lay with him—in his incapacity to enjoy trivia. Several of his women called him cruel, blasé, incapable of love. He mocked them, yet secretly envied them for their childlike delight in such nothings as a new dress, a routine compliment, a mention on the society page of the newspaper. Of all, his mother amazed him most. An ever-hopeful Cinderella, she attended every party of her life expecting to meet the prince. And she did, repeatedly, a number of princes.

He knew less about his father's emotional makeup. At twenty he had supposedly attempted suicide for a girl, and years later he had come close to divorcing Melanie for a Sarkany schoolteacher.

Nicholas inherited some good and some bad traits from his parents, but an easily inflammable heart he did not. He had loved only once in his entire life, Beata. Now walking in the brisk, alien Potsdam night, he wondered whether he was going to fall in love a second time. Or was it still the same love's smoldering fire blazing up? According to old wives' tales, men consistently fell for the same type of women. He knew a colonel who had braved a nerve-racking divorce and sacrificed his entire career to marry a somewhat younger edition of his discarded wife. It would be interesting to learn, he thought, whether there was any resemblance between the Sarkany schoolteacher and the girl his father had tried to kill himself for.

Would an Alexa with black hair, Roman nose and hourglass figure have the same attraction for him as the carbon copy of Beata? He knew she would not. But was the resemblance a strong enough lure? In two years he had become adjusted to his loss. He no longer woke up in the middle of the night shaken by the realization that it wasn't Beata's head resting on the pillow beside him. He missed her, grieved for her, though not with a stabbing, heart-stopping pain, only a dull ache. It was to remain with him forever, yet never kill him. He was reconciled to his widowerhood, but not cured of his grief.

He reached the station and found a group from the Embassy waiting for the train. Nicholas welcomed their company; it took his mind off the encounter with the Godenhausens.

During the train ride to Berlin, the conversation centered on the Kaiser. Though no longer the mythical figure of his first years of reign, people still found him intriguing. He was always good for a long, heated argument. Some, and not only Germans, considered him brilliant, others a fool or a dangerous psychopath.

The second secretary of the Embassy, Hannes Schiessler, a slight blond man who was building a career upon his reputation of being a witty raconteur, was the chief talker. As the other four in the compartment were also from the Embassy, they did not need to watch their tongues.

"Did you notice how old Willy snubbed Chancellor Bülow?" Schiessler asked. "I'm afraid the honeymoon is over."

"I've heard so many contradictory opinions about Bülow," Nicholas said. "What is he like?"

"Some call him the private mousetrap. He always knows what kind of mouse goes for what kind of cheese, so he keeps an ample supply of cheeses and catches a great number of mice. His mistake is that old Willy is no mouse but a rat. One day he might find out that his cheese won't work on old Willy."

"I think the Kaiser is mad," Schiessler said. "He's building the mightiest army and largest fleet in the world solely to scare his uncle. Because that's what it all boils down to. A family quarrel. Wilhelm is still torn between hate and love for Edward. That's what makes him so pitifully vulnerable to his uncle's snubs."

After a while the train's monotonous rumble began to have a dulling effect on the conversation. Nicholas leaned against the headrest of the seat and closed his eyes. Halfway adrift toward sleep, the mention of the name Godenhausen suddenly snapped him awake. Schiessler was talking about a party attended by several Gardes du Corps officers at the palace of Prince Friedrich Heinrich.

"You've never seen such a collection of pederasts. I couldn't figure out why the hell I'd been invited."

Someone snickered. "Couldn't you?"

"Come now, that's not funny. I had the surprise of my life when I met Godenhausen's wife tonight. She is a beauty. I hadn't even known the major was married. Now I really wonder what the hell he was doing at the prince's party."

"*You* were there too."

"Once, and never again. But Godenhausen seemed to be one of the boys. It's confusing. With a wife like that, I'd be damned if I'd ever go near that crowd."

"How long ago was that?" the attaché asked.

"About three years. If I remember correctly, he was still captain."

"He's made major since. If his name had been linked with Prince Friedrich Heinrich's he wouldn't have been promoted."

"He was promoted before the scandal. It was only last year that the prince had to resign as grand master of the Order of

63

St. John. Before that there were only vague rumors. Then his resignation proved them to be true."

"It still doesn't mean that all his friends are homosexual." A councillor who had been quiet throughout the trip entered the discussion. "A few years back the prince was involved with a woman. I know this from his ex–house marshal. He's supposed to be a rather weak man, easily led astray."

The train was pulling into the Berlin station, and the discussion of Prince Friedrich Heinrich's virility ended. The insinuations regarding Alexa's husband nevertheless weighed heavily upon Nicholas's mind, adding to his inner confusion.

3

An invitation to German Foreign Secretary Heinrich von Tscharschky's reception kept Nicholas from attending the Godenhausens' at-home party on the last Friday of May. He sent two dozen roses and his apologies to Alexa. In June he had to accompany the military attaché, his superior, to the imperial regatta in Kiel. In July Alexa left for Norderney, where, as usual, she spent the summer in a rented villa with the Sedlitzes. In September Nicholas was detailed as observer to the German army maneuvers held at Merseburg, another duty he could not escape.

On the first of November he moved from the Kaiserhof into a furnished flat in a widowed countess's elegant mansion on Burg Strasse. The central location and the view across the Spree to the royal palace and the cathedral were the reasons for his renting the flat.

After moving in, he discovered a view he could easily have done without. It was at his landlady's bedroom windows in the wing facing his. Fiftyish, but remarkably well preserved, Countess von Groen was a rather disturbing sight for a man practicing temporary abstinence. At first he gave her the benefit of the doubt. His flat had been vacant for some time, and it might have slipped her mind that it no longer was. He gallantly drew his curtains closed, but when evening came and he saw the countess's bedroom ablaze with light and her performing a version of Salome's dance of the seven veils, he could no longer ignore her intentions.

On occasions when they would accidentally meet on the landing or ride up together in the little elevator with the TWO PERSONS ONLY sign, she would be the paragon of icy decorum, which amused and puzzled him. With the weather growing cold, he wondered how long she would keep waiting for some response from him. In a way he felt sorry for her. She had chosen a tenant with the reputation of a Casanova, but one who had no taste for older women, especially not his landlady.

Late in November he received a letter from Mitzi Hahn. Mitzi and a young Viennese comic had worked out a song-and-dance act and had been offered a contract to appear in the new show at the Wintergarten, the variety theater on Friedrich Strasse. On the first of December she was to report to Berlin for rehearsals.

The letter could not have reached him at a more propitious moment. He hadn't been in Berlin long enough to become involved with amateurs or to compromise on professionals. Mitzi asked him if he still remembered her, which seemed a rather absurd question. Their affair had lasted almost a year. But that was the kind of girl Mitzi was—a bit insecure, never taking a lover's affection for granted.

The anticipation with which he looked forward to her arrival surprised but also depressed him. He realized how lonely he had been, how superficial his relations were with the people at his new post. He wired her not to wait until December but to come as early as possible.

She arrived four days later, bringing with her all the gaiety, sweetness and tinsel glitter of her own Vienna, the territory that extended between the suburb Mödling, where she'd been born, and the Theater an der Wien, where she had risen from chorus girl to soubrette. He suspected that she was in love with him, although smart enough to understand that admitting it would have added an incongruous note to their relationship. Men of his kind abhorred responsibility and moral obligations, and one of the traits that had made Mitzi a successful poule de luxe was her wisdom of always knowing her place. There were rare moments though when she failed to keep her emotions under control, and such a slip occurred on the afternoon of her arrival. They were stretched out on the wide Himmelbett where they had celebrated their reunion with a magnum of Veuve Cliquot and some very satisfactory lovemaking. He felt relaxed and pleasantly vacuous.

"Penny for your thoughts," she said.

"They're not worth a penny."

"Which means they're none of my business." Suddenly she looked crestfallen. "Nicky, did you really *want* me to come?"

"Don't be ridiculous. I wired you the moment I received your letter."

"That's true. Still I wish you weren't so . . . so distant, so difficult to reach. It's as if you were deaf and I must shout for you to hear me."

He propped himself up on his elbow and cradled her face in his hands. "Stop it, Mitzi. Don't be a nag. You weren't before, which was one of your greatest attractions. We had such good times together and shall have them again, provided you don't present me with promissory notes I don't recall having signed."

"What promissory notes? I don't know what you're talking about."

"Never mind. Put on your clothes, because I have tickets to the new show at the Metropole Theater and the curtain goes up at eight. Later I'll take you to the Royal for the best supper in Berlin."

It was pleasant to have her around. Their life fell into a pattern. In the evenings when he came home from the Embassy, he would find her waiting for him. If he had plans for later that didn't include her, she would remain in the flat, eat supper and keep his bed warm. After the arrival of her co-star, she would let the little comic console her on these bleak nights. The comedian was almost as much in love with her as she was with Nicholas, which evened up things.

Their opening in the new Wintergarten show was, despite their Viennese mannerisms, a great success. Up to then Mitzi's sole claim to distinction had been the company she kept, or rather the company that was keeping her: Nicholas. Now she became more than just another of those fresh faces that for a season or two would be escorted around by the gilded youth, then disappear into the underground strata of the lower classes from where they had come. Now she was recognized by the public in cafes and restaurants and sent flowers by unknown admirers, some of whom turned out to be rich and distinguished men, though invariably married. In a few instances, merely to arouse Nicholas's jealousy, she accepted a supper invitation. Then, afraid that he would use it as a ready excuse to drop her, she would quickly send her regrets.

It had been shortly after Mitzi's arrival that Nicholas finally decided to pay a visit to the Godenhausens. The last Friday of the month came around and there was a note from them reminding him of their at-home day. He would probably have ignored it had he not felt shielded against Alexa's attraction by his affair with Mitzi. Until then, Alexa's image had been tucked away in the deepest recesses of his mind, like the photograph of a beloved child in a traveler's wallet to be pulled out and propped up on his nightstand in some cold and impersonal hotel room. Two years after Beata's death he had discovered that her body, once the source of immeasurable delight to him, was still very much alive, although inhabited by another spirit. If the rumors concerning her husband's sexual tastes were true, it was a body waiting to be taken by a complete man. A temptation and a challenge. At twenty-five, he would have responded without hesitation; at thirty-five, her married status scared him off.

After vacillating all day, at four in the afternoon he suddenly found himself at the railroad station buying a round-trip ticket to Potsdam. He felt the same guilt mixed with elation he had experienced as a boy whenever he engaged in an escapade against Dr. Schauffele's orders. This time there was no tutor to disobey, only his better judgment, yet the warning was just as loud and clear.

"I am so glad you came at last," Alexa greeted him, sounding as if she really meant it. She wore a blue velvet dress, its collar and cuffs trimmed with lace. Her hair was brushed off her face and wound into a heavy coil at the nape of her neck. She looked like a schoolgirl, young, frail and eager to please. "I was beginning to think that you were avoiding us on purpose."

She left him to welcome two new arrivals, which gave him a chance to take a look at the place she called home.

The furniture was strictly art nouveau, with no discordant ornament, lamp, vase or bric-a-brac to disturb the harmony. To the right the salon opened into a conservatory with potted palms, aspidistras and hanging baskets of fern; to the left was a formal dining room. The entire decor denoted the cold planned perfection of royal residences, unoccupied by their owners but open to guided tours on Sundays and holidays. He missed the ropes restricting the public to cotton runners laid over floors and rugs to protect them from muddy footprints.

He had heard that the Godenhausens' Fridays were known for their atmosphere of informal camaraderie. On this afternoon, however, most of the sandwiches, cakes and petits fours arranged on silver platters on the dining-room table remained untouched. Rose and General von Sedlitz were present, also an infantry colonel with his lady and a few subaltern officers. Later, a major of the Gardes arrived and immediately became engrossed in a conversation with Hans Günther in the conservatory.

It was close to eight o'clock. One of the subalterns had already left, and the infantry colonel and his lady were saying their goodbyes at the door. The colonel was finishing a long-winded anecdote when Hans Günther's orderly announced the arrival of General Kuno von Moltke, military commandant of Berlin.

His cheeks and nose reddened by the nippy winds of Potsdam, Moltke entered with the expression of a tired traveler who after a long and futile search suddenly discovers a vacancy sign on the door of an inn.

"Terribly sorry to be late," he said, his arms reaching out to enclose both Hans Günther and Alexa in one big embrace, "but I was seeing off Phili Eulenburg. He left for Territet."

Hans Günther frowned. "Switzerland?"

"Yes." He nodded.

"What made Phili leave?" Hans Günther asked. "He shouldn't have. Not now." There was more than a touch of nervousness to his tone.

Her husband's anxious concern in Prince Philipp's affairs was a new note that had puzzled Alexa for days. She had first become aware of his anger at the prince's detractors when an imaginary dialogue between two characters, "Harpist" and "Sweetie," was published in Maximilian Harden's *Zukunft*. She read the piece, yet failed to understand its intent or the uproar it later created in military circles. Although she had seen the periodical in other people's houses, the copy with the dialogue was the first issue her husband had brought home. He had left it on his desk and she picked it up and idly thumbed through it, when he suddenly pounced upon her, snatched it from her hands and tore it to pieces. Realizing that he had overreacted, he immediately apologized. However he failed to dispel her suspicion that there was more to the little parody than met the eye—her eye.

Disguised as Harpist and Sweetie, the men were Eulenburg, the poet-musician, and Kuno von Moltke, whose craving for sweets was well known. Harden had them reminiscing about their first encounter and their friendship since then. Touched upon were Harden's often repeated charges that the two were members of an evil camarilla that had ruled Germany for close to twenty years. A bitingly sarcastic piece of writing, it made fun of two honorable public figures, yet contained not one line that reflected upon Hans Günther personally, so why his furious reaction to it, Alexa wondered.

For days he remained strangely preoccupied. Although the article had been commented upon by practically everybody in Potsdam, he refused to discuss it with her. It was not brought up by the guests at her present party either. She attributed their discretion to her aunt's presence. Rose von Sedlitz, in beplumed hat and elbow-length gloves, which she kept on even when drinking tea, was the personification of all the VERBOTEN signs posted in parks, museums and public toilets in Prussia. To assume that she would read such smut as Harden's *Zukunft* would have amounted to an insult.

"Phili felt he had no choice," Kuno von Moltke said.

"Do you agree?" Hans Günther asked.

Moltke shrugged. "I don't know. It's hard to tell. There is a difference between libel and insinuation. You can fight libel, force a retraction, but how can you have an insinuation retracted? Phili wants to let the public forget. And so do I. Let sleeping dogs lie."

"I still think you and Phili ought to take action, General. Have someone talk to Maximilian Harden. Offer him money. I'm sure he can be bought. They love money. All Jews do. They can't have the position, the respect, the power open to Gentiles, so they settle for money. Send him a gift, a ring or a tiepin or a candy box full of gold coins. They love gold. Anything they can take with them when they have to run. Look at their women. Loaded down with emeralds, rubies, diamonds. It's not because they love their women more than we do ours. Hell no! It's because precious stones are fluid assets."

Alexa listened with growing concern. What has gotten into Hans Günther? she wondered. Wasn't he aware of Nicholas's mixed blood? Or was the insult deliberate, a warning to keep him from calling on them again? She dared not look at him for fear she might see his face flushed with an anger directed not only at her husband but at her too. She wished she could tell him how sorry she was.

"I am not going to send Harden a brass farthing," Moltke said with a cackle. "Harden would keep it and Witkowski would continue the attacks."

Nicholas evidently failed to understand the joke, for he asked, "Witkowski?" His casual tone put Alexa's mind at ease. Hans Günther's tactlessness had either escaped his attention, or he chose to ignore it.

"The name he was born with in his Galician ghetto," Moltke said. Suddenly, he caught sight of the display of sweets on the dining-room table. "Ah, croquembouche!" he exclaimed, and with the frenzy of a man who had spotted an exit from a burning building he started for the table. Abruptly he slowed down, realizing he was acting in character with Harden's Sweetie. Nevertheless he was unable to resist the lure of the cream puffs encased in spun caramel. After settling down at one of the small tables in the salon, he was served a cup of hot chocolate to go with the dessert.

"You have an excellent pastry cook, Baroness," he complimented Alexa.

"We have an excellent konditorei around the corner, General," Hans Günther said. "Unfortunately, when it comes to hiring servants, my wife always chooses the ones with the most heartrending bad-luck stories. So we have a cook with three illegitimate children raised in a foster home—"

Alexa felt her face redden. "Hans Günther, really—"

He ignored her. "—and a parlormaid who supports a crippled husband and a laundress who spent three years in a reform school for shoplifting."

Alexa had the choice between making a scene or pretending to be amused. She forced a smile. "She is a good laundress."

"You still have Minna?" her aunt asked with shrill disbelief.

"Of course I do. She *is* a good laundress," Alexa repeated.

"I hope you count the silver every time she leaves the .house."

"I am afraid I don't," Alexa said curtly, then turned to Moltke. "What did you think of Melba in *La Sonnambula*, General?" she asked in order to change the subject. "I'm afraid she's past her peak. Or is it only that she doesn't move me?"

"Too bad she still sings in public. She ought to let people remember her the way she was at her best. Well, that's women for you." He pronounced the word "women" with a sneer. "They refuse to accept defeat. By age, illness, by us men. I always say that we are not the stronger sex, they are." There was bitterness to his tone.

"I thought you liked women, General. Now you sound as if you hated . . ." Her voice trailed off as she noticed the expression of pique on the general's face. There was a moment of strained silence in the room, broken only by the colonel and his lady, who finally decided to make their long-delayed exit.

Nicholas returned to Berlin with the resolve to keep away from the Godenhausens. The major's unnecessary comment on Alexa's way of choosing servants kindled a slow-burning resentment against the man in him. He was also angered by his jibe at the Jews. Another such incident and he would insult or hit Godenhausen, which would lead to a scandal, probably a duel, and whatever the outcome Alexa would be the loser.

He paid the obligatory courtesy call on them next day. Without asking to be received by her mistress, he handed his card to the curtsying parlormaid and left.

For days he remained depressed. The visit, although an unpleasant experience, was like a pylon in the flatland of his existence. Mitzi noticed his low spirits and kept asking questions, which merely aggravated things.

Half the Embassy staff, including the military attaché, had left to spend the holidays at home. Nicholas had more to do

73

than usual. What little free time he had he spent Christmas shopping. Friends' children, relatives, old retainers, servants had to be remembered. His busy schedule had one advantage: it kept his mind off Alexa.

By January, when Fasching exploded with all its dogged gaiety over Berlin, the wound—rather the abrasion of that last Friday in November—had almost healed. He was invited to attend a command performance at the Royal Opera honoring the King and Queen of Württemberg and decided to take Mitzi along.

For days she had been in a state of feverish anticipation. Finding none of her evening dresses suitable for the occasion, she spent a month's pay on a Paris original. Designed for the New Woman—willowy, long-legged, a mixture of Cleopatra and Juliet, with a dash of Miss Pankhurst thrown in—the dress was blatantly wrong for her. She was no femme fatale; she was Mitzi Hahn, the girl from Mödling, no more enigmatic or mysterious than zwetschenknödel, that stodgy staple of potato dough with a plum in its center, smothered in bread crumbs and browned in melted butter, the plebeian dumpling of the Viennese cuisine.

Nicholas called for her at the Central Hotel, and as he caught sight of her descending the stairway in Parisian splendor complete with fan and shoulder-length court gloves, he could not suppress an "Oh, my God" and a chuckle.

He had always found her ambition to be considered a lady droll, and at the same time oddly touching. Acting was her chosen profession, yet her idol was not Eleonora Duse or Sarah Bernhardt but Princess Metternich, the queen of Vienna's society. He'd never before liked her more tenderly than on the night of the command performance. He practically loved her.

She noticed his astonishment and paled. Her eyes misted over. He quickly tried to restore her self-confidence. "You look lovely, my dear. Simply dazzling!"

"Not overdressed?" she asked, wretchedly insecure.

"For a command performance at the Berlin Opera? That would be impossible."

The entire court was present, and as always on such occasions, the men wore white tie or full-dress uniform with decorations. The emperor had recently recovered from a mild cold and to prevent it from recurring had ordered the house to be well heated. The result was a touch of the Sahara in the heart of an icy Berlin whitened by a sudden snow flurry earlier in the evening.

·Wagner's *Der Fliegende Holländer* was the opera chosen for the occasion. As the curtain fell after the first act and the audience rose from their seats, the flutter of fans agitated by white-gloved hands reminded Nicholas of Venice's pigeons taking to their wings at the sound of the bells of the Campanile striking noon.

He and Mitzi left their box for the gallery.

Moving through the crowd, Nicholas suddenly found himself face to face with Alexa. Smiling, she extended her gloved hand to him. He took hold of it and, turning it palm up, pressed his lips to the bare spot of skin above the last button.

"Oh, Nicky, I am so glad I ran into you! I am planning a supper dance for the twenty-ninth. Your invitation is already in the mail. Please keep yourself free, or if you're already engaged make yourself free. I want you to come. Please don't say you won't. I'd be terribly disappointed." She spoke with a breathless intensity. He was still holding her hand.

"Of course, I'll be glad to come."

He felt a nudge at his elbow and remembered that Mitzi was standing beside him. For a dazed moment he had completely forgotten her. Now he had to make amends. "I'm afraid the two of you haven't met. Permit me, Alexa, to introduce Fräulein Hahn to you. Mitzi, dear, my sister-in-law, the Baroness von Godenhausen."

The smile faded from Alexa's lips. Her head thrown back, she let her cold stare travel over the girl. Mitzi extended her hand in greeting.

75

"Thank you, Nicholas," Alexa said. "I can do without the lady's acquaintance."

She swiftly turned her back on the girl and made her way through the crowd. Speechless, Nicholas stared after her.

For a long moment Mitzi remained frozen in a pose of utter bewilderment, then she slowly dropped her hand. It fell to her side like a shot bird. She looked at Nicholas. "Why? Why?" she asked in a small plaintive voice.

The evening was spoiled and there was nothing he could do to repair the damage. Alexa's unforgivable insult angered but also puzzled him. It caused him to realize that her uncanny physical resemblance to Beata did not extend to the inner woman. Under no circumstances would Beata have humiliated a stranger as harmless as Mitzi, or anyone else for that matter. Alexa von Godenhausen was not Beata reincarnated, only her surviving twin.

The invitation to the Godenhausens' supper dance arrived on the following day. Nicholas answered it with a short note. Due to a previous engagement, he was unable to attend.

The incident at the opera had noticeably blighted Mitzi's spirits, but the ovations she received for her performances and the management's offer of a contract for the 1907-8 season helped her to regain her emotional equilibrium. The promise of work for the following year was for Mitzi the equivalent of what more staid citizens called security for life. She lived one day at a time and let the future take care of itself.

On the Wednesday following the incident at the opera, Nicholas was home alone taking care of his piled-up correspondence. His housekeeper had taken the afternoon off and his orderly, a young peasant from the Hungarian plains, was probably drowning his incurable homesickness in one of the winehouses around Alexander Platz.

The bells of the cathedral struck five, reminding Nicholas that in an hour he would have to leave to take Mitzi for a quick meal at the Café Victoria before the evening performance. When his doorbell rang, he hesitated to answer it. It was probably one of his bachelor friends from the Embassy with time on his hands in a still foreign and often inhospitable city, he thought. When the caller refused to give up, he rose reluctantly and opened the door to find Alexa, wrapped in a heavy karakul coat, a small hat perched on top of her head and a thick veil shrouding her face, waiting for him. She was holding a letter. Without a word, she offered it to him.

Nicholas stared at her. "Won't you come in?" he asked.

"I didn't expect *you* to answer the door. I only . . . only wanted to leave this. Please take it."

He was too stunned to reach for the letter. She let go of it, dropping it to the floor. Suddenly she turned and started for the stairway. Still numbed by her improbable presence, he dashed after her.

"Please, let me go!" she cried as he caught up with her. "I didn't want to . . ." Her voice trailed off and she looked as if she were going to burst into tears.

He was holding on to her arm. "You're cold. You're shivering. Come, let's go inside. We can't talk here. Come."

"There is nothing to talk about. Just read the letter."

"I will, but first . . ." Without releasing her arm, he picked up the letter, then led her through the entrance hall to the drawing room, which was heated to a cozy twenty-five degrees Centigrade by an ornate tile stove. As he peeled off her coat, he noticed that she was trembling. "Don't you feel well?" he asked.

"Read the letter," she whispered.

He tore it open. It contained one line in Hungarian: "Please forgive my inexcusable rudeness at the opera."

"To err is human, Alexa. Don't give it a thought."

"I wish I knew what made me do it. I thought you were alone, then I saw *her* standing beside you." She had spoken German; now she switched to Hungarian. "She was holding

77

on to your arm as if you belonged to her. It's been only two years since Beata . . . and there you were with this girl." Suddenly she was sobbing.

Confused, he placed his arm around her and she drew nearer to him. Her sobs stopped and her hands crept up and encircled his neck, bringing his face down to hers. Her breathing grew labored, and low moans escaped her lips in quick nervous spurts. Before his mind could grasp what was happening to her his body did, and with an intensity that caused his loins to throb. He felt a pain that was intolerably pleasurable.

Afterward he could only remember that they were fused together on the wide four-poster bed in the bedroom, and that later she nestled in his arms dozing.

He could not tell whether it had been minutes or hours when she finally opened her eyes. She sat up and stared at him as though wondering who he was. He reached out for her, but she avoided his arm and leaped from the bed. Stark naked, she picked up her batiste chemise from the floor, slipped it on, then collected the rest of her clothing scattered with his along a path that extended from drawing room to bedroom. To reach her corset she walked barefoot over his uniform tunic lying on the floor.

"I'll dress in the other room, if you don't mind. You don't have to see me off." Her tone had a rough edge. "I can find my way out."

He jumped from bed. "Alexa." He sensed a strange hostility in her. It rose like an invisible wall between them. "You can't leave. We'll have to talk."

She raised her voice. It sounded shrill and angry. "Will you please cover yourself? You're embarrassing me."

He obediently took a dressing gown from the wardrobe and slipped it on. "You're angry with me. Why? What have I done?"

She held her skirt in front of her like a shield. "Please let me get dressed. I don't like to be watched when dressing." She walked from the room and pulled the door shut.

He listened to the sound of her moving about in the drawing room, then heard her call his name. "Nicholas!"

When he entered the room, he found her fully clothed, but the back of her dress gaped wide open.

"Will you hook me up, please?"

By now he had regained his equilibrium, which for a short time had been shattered by her unwarranted hostility. He started fumbling with the hooks. "Whoever sewed these things on certainly had good eyes," he said with a chuckle.

"Hurry, I am late," she snapped impatiently.

He finished closing the dress, then grabbed her by the shoulders and spun her around, shaking her more roughly than he intended to. "What's the matter with you? Why do you act as if I raped you? Because I didn't. You know damned well I didn't."

"Let me go. I'm terribly late."

He released her. "I want to talk to you."

"Not now. Some other time."

"When?"

"Later. I promise. I can't now. I just can't. You must understand. Please—"

"I'll take you home."

She raised her voice. "No." She was putting on her hat. In her haste she stuck herself with a hat pin. "Damn," she cried and threw a reproachful look at him. "You're making me nervous." She tried to adjust her veil, then lost her patience, snatched it off and stuffed it into the pocket of her coat. She started for the door.

He barred her way. "Will I see you again?"

"Yes, if you want to. Just let me go now."

With a sigh he stepped aside and let her pass. He didn't even follow her to the hallway but remained in the drawing room listening to her receding footsteps and the loud slam of

79

the front door. Slowly, pensively he picked up his tunic and trousers from where he had dropped them an hour—or was it two hours?—before.

For the first time in his life he was mystified by a woman. He had believed he understood them, their caprices, their moods, their vanities, excusing them with the misfortune of being female. Existence in a civilized world was a complex and unending struggle for them. They had been created for purdah, and partial liberation from it was a dubious blessing. Living in a man's world, they were given the choice between the pedestal and the gutter, respect and contempt, protection and exploitation. But whatever their status—wife, mistress or workhorse—one rule applied: They were the hunted and man the hunter.

In his past relationships with women—from princesses down to cocottes—Nicholas had been the seducer. At least that was how the game was played. For the first time in his experience the parts were reversed. Whether or not Alexa arrived with the premeditated decision to make love, once she was in the flat it was she who called the tune. She let him know what she wanted and later showed no more interest in him than a customer did in a prostitute. It was he who was anxious to talk, inquire, discuss, rehash, explore, just as his women had done in the past, yet she would have none of it. He felt humiliated and wondered if it weren't better never to see her again, then the realization that the decision would be made by her struck him with painful clarity.

4

There was no cab at the stand at Kurfürsten Bridge or on Schloss Platz. Offices of the royal palaces, the Academy of Architecture and the banks in Französischer Strasse were letting out, and she had to run all the way to Wilhelm Strasse to find a carriage. By mere seconds she missed the six-thirty train to Potsdam. It was close to eight when she finally reached home. Hans Günther had already eaten. Reading the evening paper, he was still seated at the table.

"Where have you been?" he asked without looking up. "Anna had to reheat the damned stew three times and boil fresh potatoes. Now she has to boil some more for you."

"I don't want any. I'm not hungry."

He threw a glance at her over the paper. "What's the matter with you?"

She was on the verge of tears. "Nothing. I'm just . . . I have a headache. I'll go to bed now." She started for the bedroom.

He called after her in a rough tone that startled her. The unlikely thought that he had learned about her afternoon flashed through her mind.

"I asked you where you were. Won't you answer me?"

Her heartbeat accelerated. "Shopping," she said and felt her throat constricting. "I needed a few things. Fabrics and such.

I went to Wertheim's, then got hungry and had coffee at a konditorei and missed the six-thirty."

"Did you have to go all the way to Berlin to shop? Aren't there stores in Potsdam?" When she answered with a shrug, he went on. "If you really don't want supper, you'd better tell Anna. She's been waiting to clear the table. It's all right if *I* don't get any consideration from you, but the servants ought to. There is a difference between them and me, you know. *They* can give notice and leave. *I* can't. Anna is certainly no jewel, but what do you expect when the so-called lady of the house doesn't even know how to scramble eggs."

Benumbed, she stared at him. He had been nervous, even irritable lately, but never rude. She rang for Lotte, the parlor-maid, and told her to turn her bed down and to tell Anna that she needn't bother with supper.

Completely exhausted, she crawled into bed and pulled the heavy comforter up to her neck and tried to sleep. The moment she put her head on the pillow, all drowsiness left her and she grew painfully awake. She felt as though a steam hammer gone haywire were beating inside her chest; its wild incessant drumming took her breath away.

She tried to understand the irresistible force that had driven her to a man she neither loved nor desired. The harder she thought, the more confused she became. Again and again she went over the chain of events that led to their lovemaking. She found no clues. Before their chance encounter at the opera she had felt only the kind of liking for him one feels for a brother-in-law touched by a tragedy. Then at the opera when she caught sight of the ridiculously overdressed female hanging on to his arm, she became suddenly flushed with an anger that wiped out her previous compassion. For a moment it was as if she had turned into her dead twin. His taking a little whore to a command performance attended by the Kaiser and also by the King and Queen of Württemberg was a scandalous betrayal of her belief in him.

The realization that she had slept with a man other than her husband, had become a slut and an adulteress, filled her with self-disgust. There was no mitigating circumstance, no excuse like seduction or rape, because she had been the seducer and the rapist. The fact that she had experienced more pleasure in his bed than at any time during the three years and three months of her marriage made her guilt even worse.

She could not recall the exact date when she had first begun to feel uneasy about Hans Günther's conception of marital love. People considered them an exceptionally happy couple, and at times Alexa agreed with them. Hans Günther was kind, considerate and beyond any doubt faithful to her. He had only infrequent spells of moodiness when he would criticize her or commit little cruelties that hurt her. They were probably unintentional, and she tried to block them out of her memory. After all, he was all she had in the world—family, lover. She could ill afford to find him wanting in these capacities.

She often wondered what other couples' marriages were like. She and Hans Günther moved in a circle restricted to the military. While he had many friends among the men, her relationships with the wives remained pleasantly formal. There was no one she could turn to for advice and information.

What were other men like? How soon after the honeymoon did their bridegroom's ardor cool to casual camaraderie? How soon, if ever, did sex become a secondary factor in their relationships with their wives? Was Hans Günther an exception, or were all husbands like him? And were all wives as hungry for carnal love as she was?

What disturbed her most was that even on the rare occasions when Hans Günther slept with her he acted as if he were performing a duty. His attitude often drove her to assuming the role of the aggressor, which, depending on his mood, either flattered or displeased him. Even if he responded, he more often than not failed to satisfy her. He rolled off her and turned on his side, falling into a deep and untroubled

83

sleep while she kept tossing restlessly, her loins aching with unquenched desire and her heart trying to drum its way out of her chest.

Her days were no less troubled than her nights. Hans Günther expected her to be a model hausfrau, which was a role beyond her capabilities. She enjoyed good food but was willing to starve rather than cook, and orderliness was not one of her virtues. She left books, magazines, half-finished sewing, pieces of clothing, plates of fruit and boxes of candy scattered around her bedroom. Hans Günther hated disorder. Around the time he was expected home she would, in breathless haste, restore the room to its pristine neatness with the result that he would occasionally find a rotting apple in the corner of a wardrobe or a squashed bon-bon under his shirts in the chiffonier drawer.

Her handling of the servants was another reason for frictions. She had hired Anna and Lotte, cook and parlormaid, because she had been moved by their hard-luck stories. Now feeling safe in their positions, they repaid her with indolence and probably larceny, yet she lacked the will to dismiss them and start afresh with a new pair. When Hans Günther blamed her for their laziness and cunning, she bit her lips and suffered in silence.

At times she wondered if he still loved her. The most difficult to bear were the moments when he seemed completely unaware of her presence. She would address him and he would respond with the surprised look of a person who ran into an acquaintance in a most unlikely place. He flashed a smile at her or answered in monosyllables, then returned to his invisible cocoon of disconnectedness. Physically within the reach of her arms, mentally he was miles away. She never felt more lonely and abandoned than on evenings of peaceful domesticity. The more distant he became, the more desperately she longed for a word, a kiss, an embrace. He had an uncanny power over her, the kind of mystic attraction that inaccessible peaks hold for mountain climbers. She had to win him, no matter what the cost.

She heard him rising in the dining room and walking to the front door to see if it was locked. Then he turned off the lights in the hallway, a routine he performed before going to bed every night. Next he went to the bathroom to brush his teeth. There was the squeak of the faucet over the wash basin and the flush of the toilet. A moment later he entered the bedroom.

Lying stiff, her hands crossed over her chest, she pretended to be asleep.

With the precision of a mechanical doll he went, as he had done on hundreds of nights before, through the routine of hanging his tunic on the back of a chair, clamping his breeches into their hanger, placing his boots outside the bedroom door for Thadeus to polish in the morning. There was the faint odor of wool mixed with stale cigarette smoke, male perspiration and eau de cologne. Hans Günther liked to use scents, and he had a bottle of perfume secreted away in his first-aid kit.

Even though she kept her eyes closed, she knew that before slipping on his long nightshirt he paused for a brief moment in front of the silver-framed full-length mirror to cast a glance at the reflection of his perfectly proportioned naked body.

He flipped on the light on his nightstand, then crossed to her bed, bent down and touched her forehead with his lips. This was a ritual he never omitted whether she was asleep or awake. Earlier in their marriage she used to react by throwing her arms about him and pulling him into her bed. More often than not, he gently disengaged himself and moved to the safety of his own bed. After a while she became reconciled to the hollow ceremony of the kiss. It had no more erotic connotation than his tooth brushing or locking the front door.

Now she heard him drop into bed. He switched off the light and a few moments later was fast asleep. Alexa listened to the cadence of his even breathing and felt her eyes brim over. Crying made her feel better, because it was the proof of her contrition. She was Mary Magdalene washing the Savior's feet with her tears and drying them with the hairs of her head. Resolved never to see Nicholas again, she conjured up the voice of Dr. Sternwarth, pastor of the garrison church, describing the horrible tortures that awaited sinners in the hereafter. Somehow the voice failed to scare her. It was hard for her to feel truly repentant when the man she had wronged treated her with such indifference.

Nevertheless, she must never return to Burg Strasse, she thought. Whatever had happened between her and Nicholas would in due time become as unreal as if she had read it in a book or merely fantasized it. She would do her best to please Hans Günther, be a perfect officer's lady and housewife, and eliminate all the friction that tended to affect their marriage. She would become pregnant and find satisfaction in motherhood. Having made the resolution, she fell asleep.

Several times during the turbulent social season she caught sight of Nicholas at the Königliches Opernhaus or the Berlin Castle, and once at a soiree given by the Bavarian minister to the court of Wilhelm II. Each time she managed to evade him.

It was on the day that she read in the morning paper that Mitzi Hahn, having completed her engagement at the Wintergarten, had left for Vienna that her desire to see Nicholas came over her with an irresistible force.

She dressed and left the house. Halfway to the Wildpark Station she found herself buffeted by the worst blizzard of the entire winter. She could find no free cab, and the wind slapping at her face felt like the hand of an irate God. The icy snowflakes sticking to her eyelashes blurred her vision. Trying to board the horse trolley at Brandenburger Tor, she stumbled, fell to her knees and tore her stockings. Sobered by the fall, she returned home. Cuddling up to the big green tile stove of the bedroom, she felt grateful for the tumble that had saved her from a more dangerous one. She had scored a victory over herself, and even the cold that sent her to bed for the rest of the week was a small price to pay for it.

The last Friday of February suddenly destroyed her delusions. This time the apartment was filled with the sort of imbecile gaiety that characterized successful parties in Potsdam: laughter, inside jokes, glasses breaking, pastry trampled underfoot, cigarettes left burning on tabletops, smoke mingling with the odor of overheated bodies, French perfume and patchouli, blue Prussian eyes lighting up with Mediterranean fire, women's cheeks outreddening discreetly applied rouge, men becoming intoxicated with their own virility.

Conviviality was at its height when Nicholas entered. Coming in from the cold, the general merriment hit him in the face like a hot shower. He halted in the crossfire of curious stares, his eyes searching for the hostess.

Alexa was helping Rose to a piece of chocolate cake in the dining room. The sudden decrease in the intensity of the party noise caused her to take a look at the salon. Her hand holding the plate went limp, letting fork and cake slip from it. The blood rushed to her face. She quickly scraped the soft cream-filled pastry from the tablecloth where it had landed.

Rose, who had the instinct and the sharp eye of a predatory bird, threw an inquisitive glance at her. "What's the matter with you?" she asked sternly. Her eyes followed Alexa's to the salon. "Oh" was all she uttered, but her voice had the sharpness of a policeman's whistle.

Alexa ignored her question. "You'll love this cake." She served her a second piece. "Anna baked it. She's finally learned to bake, and become quite good at it . . . so . . . ." She realized the hopelessness of the evasion and left the sentence unfinished. Though not looking at Nicholas, she sensed that he was making his way to her. They must not meet in Rose's presence, she thought. She turned away from her and intercepted Nicholas in the dining-room doorway, greeting him with a much too jolly "Welcome to Potsdam! How nice to see you!"

She was pleased with herself because she had managed to hide the panic his unexpected presence created in her.

He lifted her hand to his chilled lips. Stepping close to him, she felt a trace of fresh icy air emanating from his clothes. He must have walked from the station. He seemed shorter than she had remembered him to be, probably because the other men in the room were so very tall. Most officers of the Gardes were over six feet.

She felt his eyes focusing on her face—searching, asking, waiting. He was like a hawk watching a field mouse. From the moment he had stepped into the room she was his prey. Because of the ring of people around them they exchanged only meaningless platitudes, but she knew that the question *When will I see you again?* was inevitable. And she also knew what her answer would be: *Sunday at five in the afternoon.*

The party, having absorbed the foreign body, returned to its previous lighthearted homogeneity. It was only much later when the older guests were beginning to leave that Nicholas had a chance to talk to her. She was rearranging platters on the buffet table. Helping himself to a slice of nusstorte, which he had no intention of eating, he whispered to her, his lips hardly moving, "I wanted to stay away from you, but I can't. I am going out of my mind. I must see you. If you insist, I promise not to touch you, but please let's talk. It's preposterous, but I'm afraid I am in love with you."

She noticed Rose watching them and told him in a voice loud enough for a town crier's proclamation, "Try the éclair."

"Alexa, when?"

She saw Hans Günther engrossed in conversation with a second lieutenant. He listened to the young man with more genuine interest than he had ever listened to her. The lieutenant was telling some joke, and Hans Günther responded with a burst of warm, happy, affectionate laughter. It disturbed Alexa. Why was Hans Günther charmed by the lieutenant? They were not even friends, only comrades.

"Do you think women are inferior?" she asked Nicholas.

He frowned, puzzled. "Women are what?"

It had been a non sequitur, and she felt embarrassed for having asked it. "What I mean is . . . do you feel women aren't to be taken seriously except as mothers or—" She almost said *lovers* but quickly swallowed it.

"All I can tell you, I've never taken my mother seriously," Nicholas said with a chuckle.

Hans Günther had once told her that his mother had been the only female he ever truly respected. "And other women?" she asked Nicholas.

"Some. You, for instance. More than anyone else. But let's not play games. I must see you. Tell me where and when."

From the corner of her eye she saw Rose approaching. Her heavy body cut through the crowd with the force of an ice-breaker through the frozen waters of the Arctic.

"Sunday at five," Alexa whispered.

"Where?"

"Your place."

Rose reached them. "Am I intruding?" she asked with the honeyed coyness she used when addressing good-looking men in uniform.

Alexa glared at her. "Yes, you are. Nicholas has just invited me to an orgy at his flat and I accepted."

Whenever she was shocked or angry, Rose's eyes bulged. Now they seemed to be popping out of their sockets. "You're joking, of course." She didn't seem quite sure.

"We were whispering, weren't we? So it had to be something we didn't want people to hear. Something very private."

Rose shook her head in exasperation. "Isn't she preposterous? Always this 'épater les bourgeois' attitude. Frankly, the new generation is a mystery to me. No respect for their elders, no affection, no gratitude. You offer them the best of everything—education, care, love, your lifeblood, your last penny — Oh, what's the use? Let us give you a bit of advice, my dear Count. Don't ever raise someone else's child. Not even your own sister's. You must know the saying about putting a snake in your bosom." She waited for a reaction from Alexa, and when none was forthcoming she lumbered off. Her niece's eyes followed her with the cold, unblinking stare of a reptile.

"I hate her," Alexa said in a hollow voice.

Nicholas threw a startled glance at her. The face was Beata's, but the tone was that of the same stranger who had hissed curses at him on that memorable January afternoon.

"You just think so."

"I do hate her. I always have. I'd kill her, but I'm afraid she is indestructible. If she were bitten by a viper, the viper would die, not she."

He laughed. He took her venom for sheer bravado. "I love you," he whispered. He saw Hans Günther headed for them. "Sunday," he said under his breath.

She left him without an answer and crossed to the group clustered around the piano in the salon. The second lieutenant was playing a song hit that had been sweeping the city. Voices chimed in. Hans Günther ordered Thadeus to fetch more carafes of wine and to refill the glasses. By all indications, the party would last late into the night. From the popular tune the lieutenant switched to a soldiers' marching song, so old that only three of the officers present had heard it sung in battle, while the rest merely wished they had.

More martial music followed, turning the party into a celebration of Düppel, Königgrätz and Sedan. Nicholas decided to leave. As he stepped into the street, the half-triumphant, half-lugubrious strains of "Ich hat' einen Kameraden . . ." emanated from the Godenhausens' flat. They followed him to the hack stand.

"Good God, won't they ever tire of that maudlin old thing?" he muttered to himself as he climbed into a cab for the ride to the station.

Alexa rang his doorbell at quarter past five. Nicholas had given his orderly and Frau Gerhardt, his cook-housekeeper, the day off. He had chilled bottles of his best champagne and bought enough sandwiches and petits fours to feed a squad. The weather had turned unexpectedly warm that morning, nevertheless Alexa wore her heavy karakul coat. With face flushed, her hair disheveled and a thick veil wound around her hat, she seemed as breathless as if she had just escaped from prison.

"I'm exhausted," she panted. "I got off the streetcar at Spittelmarkt and ran all the way from there. A lieutenant who was sitting at the far end of the car looked familiar— I'm not sure though. Anyway, I got off and ran. Oh, I'm so hot. I shouldn't have worn this stupid coat."

He peeled it off her and led her into the drawing room.

She halted on the threshold. "Are you alone?" she asked.

"Of course I am. I was expecting you."

They entered and she glanced around as though seeing the room for the first time. He sensed her reluctance to go beyond the limits of a social visit. Her eyes avoiding his, she stood remote and noncommittal, like a messenger waiting for the addressee to sign the receipt. Her attitude disconcerted him. He couldn't tell whether she was shy or hostile.

"Won't you sit down?" he asked.

She lowered herself onto the sofa, then, as if burned, she jumped up and moved to an armchair. The thought process that caused her to play musical chairs was much too obvious for Nicholas to miss. Somehow it endeared her to him. He stepped to her and cradled her face in his hands.

"For heaven's sake, don't be so nervous. No one's going to eat you."

He untied her veil and took it off together with the hat. "Would you care for a cup of tea or something cold?"

She patted her damp forehead with a lace handkerchief. "Something cold please. A glass of water would be fine." She watched him cross to the ice-filled silver bucket with a bottle in it. "No wine, Nicholas. Not in the afternoon. It might go to my head."

He uncorked the bottle and filled the glasses he had placed on a tray. He offered her a platter of small sandwiches. "Have a bite first. That'll keep it from going to your head. After all, you can't come to an orgy and drink tap water."

"I didn't come to get drunk." Nevertheless she picked up a glass and took a long swallow.

"Why *did* you come?"

For the first time since her arrival she looked straight into his eyes. Her lips twitched with defiance. "Don't get any false ideas. I'm not in love with you."

"I've gathered that."

"I love my husband." When he failed to react she went on with sudden fury. "I love him very much, and I'll kill myself if he ever finds out about—" She choked on the words and her eyes misted over. "I hope to God he never finds out."

He watched her with a mixture of annoyance and compassion. "Do you want to go home?"

"Yes." She nodded without making any attempt to move.

For him, the scene was beginning to take on the aspect of déjà vu. Here was a performance presented to him by more than one of his married mistresses before going to bed with him. It seemed to be a ritual that paved their way to guiltless adultery. A penitent stitch in time to keep the seams of a marriage from ripping open.

He refilled her glass. She emptied it thirstily, then held it out to him. "Some more, please."

"No more," he said.

She gave him a surprised look. "Why not?"

"Because—" He almost said, *Because I love you.* What kept him from saying it was his doubt whether or not it was really true. Did he love her or did he love the reflection of Beata in her? Was she at all lovable? Without pregnancies and child rearing and—probably—satisfactory marital sex, she was a bored, restless woman ready for mischief. Her Prussian-Protestant education prevented her from finding it fun. For a Viennese woman of her social standing, adultery was a lighthearted dip in a pool, for a Prussian it was swimming the Hellespont. If the rumors regarding Major von Godenhausen's sexual preferences were based on fact, Alexa had been kept on a starvation diet. What had brought her to his place, he told himself with a touch of bitterness, was neither romance nor affection, but the crude hunger of the flesh.

He wished he had the moral fortitude to reject her. The deal she was offering him was humiliating and unsatisfactory. In the past, women had slept with him in the belief that ultimately he would fall in love with them, which never happened. Now the tables were turned; for the first time in his life he was playing the game according to his opponent's rules.

"You had a very successful party last Friday," he said, picking a neutral subject.

"You should've stayed. We never had more fun. Lieutenant Dietrich threw up in the kitchen sink and Frau von Waldersheim did the can-can."

"That must have been a sight for sore eyes."

"It certainly was. Especially when her left breast fell out of her bodice. Perhaps it was the right one. Well, what's the difference. They're both the same: big and flabby."

They laughed. Either the wine or his amiable restraint was beginning to thaw her out of her icy mood. She had been speaking German as though using the language as an invisible wall to keep them separated. Now she continued in Hungarian.

"Oh, Nicky," she sighed. "Why must they be so . . . so different? Or why am I different? I ought to be used to them by now. Their interminable stories about horses and hunting and maneuvers. Inside jokes and gossip. Their world of barracks and parade grounds. If only the women weren't so bitchy. Proud of their names and historical titles, but basically fishwives. They watch you like hawks, count the Sundays when you miss church, catch your cook at the butcher's to ask her whether you fight with your husband, ask the friseuse whether you dye your hair. The intrigues, the barbs, the in-

93

sinuations are dropped where they can hurt most. They're more powerful than the War Ministry and the General Staff put together. If they decide that a wife is unfit to be an officer's lady, her husband will never rise beyond the rank of major."

He took her hand and kissed it. "If only every officer's lady were like you. There would never be war. No husband would be willing to leave his wife. Because men go to war mainly to get away from their wives. All other reasons are incidental."

"Funny, that's what I often think: that camaraderie between man and man is stronger than love between man and woman."

"That's not true."

"It is. And will be as long as men go off to war leaving the women behind with nothing more to do than wave handkerchiefs after departing trains."

So that was the Godenhausen doctrine, he thought, but he left it uncontested.

She reached for her glass. "May I have a sip? I am thirsty."

"Just a sip. I don't want to hear later that I made you tipsy."

"Later? Later than what?" she asked sharply.

"In five minutes . . . in an hour or tomorrow. This time I am not going to seduce you."

"Last time you didn't either, you liar! *I* seduced you."

"Suppose you did. Are you sorry?"

"I ought to be, but I am not." She rose, paced the floor, then dropped down on the sofa. "Nicky, it's terrible. I love being here. I love being with you." She reached out for him; he slid closer to her and she nestled in his arms. "I'm sure you think I sleep around, but that's not so, Nicky. I swear, never before you. Why you? Probably because you're not one of *them*. I wouldn't let any of Hans Günther's comrades so much as hold my hand. Some have indicated that they might be willing— You know what I mean. There are ways a man can let a woman know even though nothing is said out loud. But with *them*, I'd never. For one thing, I wouldn't trust them

94

to keep their mouth shut. If Hans Günther found out, he would be terribly hurt, his pride more than his heart. He'd never forgive me."

She was being frank and honest, and he wished she weren't. He felt the spark that her closeness had ignited in him become extinguished, leaving hollow darkness behind. "If I understand correctly, you consider me dependable and discreet. I'd find your opinion most flattering if I were your father-confessor. Which, however, I am not and don't intend to be." He rose and crossed to the ice bucket. "So if those are the reasons that brought you here"—he filled the glasses and handed one to her—"you might as well get high, my dear. We both might. Let's finish the bottle before it goes flat." He tasted the wine and poured it into the bucket. He emptied her glass too, then left the room and returned with a fresh bottle that he uncorked on the way. "Has it ever occurred to you that on the stage the word 'champagne' has an erotic connotation. Take French comedies or Viennese operettas. It is always champagne before getting into bed. I can't recall a single play in which the characters made love after drinking beer."

"You are mad at me. All I wanted was to make clear that I am no slut. That I haven't been sleeping around. Heaven is my witness that when I came here that afternoon I didn't come to— It just happened. And not because I felt safe with you. You could have been a knight of the Holy Grail and I wouldn't have gone to bed with you. I came because I wanted to be with you. I was afraid you might stay angry and I'd lose your friendship. I need you. Don't ask me why. Perhaps it has something to do with Beata. She loved you, which makes you special. Family! Perhaps that's what it is. You're family, so it's all right for me to come to you for comfort, assurance, whatever. For a bit of affection."

"Don't make it sound like incest," he said wryly.

She ignored the remark. "I haven't belonged to a family since I left Sarkany. Aunt Rose was good to me in her own way, yet I could never stand her. And Hans Günther. This is something I haven't told anyone. I love him, but— How shall I put it? He is my husband. I live in his home. His, not ours. It's as though I were a guest—even worse, a transient. A person looking in from the outside. My nose pressed to the glass, the way children look at Christmas toys displayed in a shop-window." She jumped to her feet. "Goodness, what time is it? I mustn't be late." She pulled out a little watch she wore stuck into her skirt's waistband. "I haven't told Lotte what to serve for supper. Lotte is the maid, but the cook's off this afternoon. I don't have to worry when she is around, but Lotte is terribly stupid. Or pretends to be to annoy me." She emitted a nervous little laugh. "Sorry. My household problems can hardly be of any interest to you."

He watched her, fascinated. She was another man's woman, here today, gone tomorrow, a comet crossing his sky with no likelihood of ever entering his orbit, nevertheless a delight to behold. She had the perfection of an ideal artist's model. Her face looked beautiful from any angle. She moved with the grace of a doe, at least so it seemed to him. She did not say anything that couldn't have been said by any other woman under similar circumstances. It was only her gestures, her half-smiles, her kaleidoscopic variety of expressions—so familiar to him from a previous life—that entranced him.

"Everything that concerns you is important to me."

"Is it really?" she asked in a small voice. Nervously she pushed the watch back into her waistband. She crossed to him and, throwing her arms about him, pressed her face against his. "Have patience with me, Nicky. I need you. I have no friend in this world. You're so good and gentle. Please accept me the way I am and try to like me a little. I promise never to hurt you, not intentionally."

To hold her slim body was a hauntingly familiar feeling. Mitzi—with her full breasts, wasp waist squeezed even more waspy by an ironclad corset, ample hips and muscular thighs firmed by the ballet lessons of her childhood—had when she was fully dressed the erotic attraction of a toy wrapped for shipping. The body he was holding now had the leanness of an adolescent boy's but enough softness to be feminine. None of his mistresses had ever fitted into his arms the way Alexa did, or Beata had for that matter.

The physical pleasure of the moment swept away all his mental reservations, although he knew they would return once he sobered up. When he kissed her, it was partly an act of passion and partly to keep her from talking. He wanted no more disillusioning frankness, only uncomplicated and soothing pleasure.

He had made arrangements with a garage owner for a car and chauffeur to drive Alexa home to Potsdam. The following day he placed an order for a Daimler coupé-limousine and began brushing up on his driving, first practiced on a 1903 automobile owned by one of his Geiger-Gebhardt uncles.

After the delivery of the Daimler he consulted a real estate firm regarding the rental of a country place within easy distance from Potsdam where he could take Alexa on their Sunday afternoons. These were the long-range plans he made for his and Alexa's combined future. In the back of his mind he still harbored the hope that there might be more in store for them than a few stolen hours.

5

After weeks of fruitless search Nicholas found and rented the ideal shelter for their rendezvous, a lakeside cottage in the village of Klein-Glienicke. Alexa was enchanted by the cottage and the country around it. On clear days they took long walks in Babelsberg Park or drove to some country inn for coffee in the afternoon. She enjoyed the excursions, despite her constant fear of a blowout that might keep her from getting home on time.

Their affair was simmering down to an almost marriage-like domesticity. No longer starved for carnal satisfaction, she played the game Nicky's way, letting him be the seducer and herself the seduced.

In her relation to Hans Günther her conscience no longer troubled her. She even felt that her having taken a lover improved their marriage. Before Nicholas she had hated the Sunday afternoons, because she had to spend them either alone or at ladies' tea parties that bored her. Hans Günther refused to miss his card games; no recriminations, sulks or tears could keep him home with her. How often had she stood staring out the window watching him, like a prisoner released from jail, walk jauntily down Linden Strasse and turn the corner of Sieges Platz to disappear from sight. Now she could not wait for him to leave. He no sooner emerged from the shadows of the porte-cochere than she too was gone.

During April, Nicholas was unexpectedly ordered to accompany the military attaché on a visit to the Italian General Staff in Rome, which meant two solitary Sundays for Alexa. She was surprised how much she missed him. Sleeping with him had still been as wondrous as ever, but she had never realized that his blindly uncritical devotion had been even more important to her than his lovemaking. For the first time in her life she was taken for a gem without defects. As a child, she had been second best to Beata; as a general's niece, out of tune with her milieu; as an officer's lady, not up to specifications. Now she was considered perfect in every way—irresistible in bed and great company in the drawing room.

On the day of Nicholas's return from Rome, she told Hans Günther that she would attend a symphony concert in Berlin. At the same time she sent a wire to Nicholas to meet her at the Klein-Glienicke boat landing. She knew she was taking chances, but it was only Wednesday and she didn't feel she could mark time until Sunday. Hans Günther did not care for classical music, so there was little likelihood that he would offer to accompany her. Anyway, he seldom showed interest in her plans unless they involved him too.

It was in unexpectedly balmy weather that Alexa boarded the boat for Glienicke that evening. Spring had come in full force to Potsdam. The day before it had still been winter, the temperature slightly above freezing, with patches of snow left under the trees of the Lustgarten. Then suddenly around midmorning a tepid breeze, feeling like a child's hand against one's cheek, wafted in from the west. Pedestrians strolled along the Havel River without overcoats, two fiacres at the hack stand at Luisen Platz let their tops down, and at eleven, as the sun came out from behind thinning clouds, the entire winter crop of new babies was wheeled to the parks. There was more laughter in the streets than the day before and fewer heated words on the trams that were now running half empty.

Alexa's wire had found Nicholas ready to go to bed to catch up on missed sleep. Rome had been hard work, with conferences every day and banquets into the early morning hours. Nevertheless, Alexa's message was like a miraculous tonic; he felt in condition to enter the marathon race or fight the nine-headed Hydra. He ordered the Daimler brought from the garage and was in Glienicke minutes before the boat docked.

They had a passionate reunion. For the first time he felt that he really possessed her, body and soul. The shortness of time allotted to them was the only thing to cloud their delight in each other. They had to crowd so much into a brief hour, so many embraces and so many confidences.

He learned from her of an event that had caused great concern in Hans Günther's social circle. On April 27 an article had been published in Maximilian Harden's *Zukunft* that, in cautiously obfuscated terms, accused the Liebenberg Round Table of being a covey of practicing deviates, violators of Paragraph 175 of the State Penal Code.

"Everyone's outraged!" Alexa told Nicholas. "Hans Günther says Harden should be stood against a wall and shot dead. As far as I am concerned, Harden couldn't have chosen a worse time. I'm afraid our at-home party on Friday won't be a success. General von Moltke has already sent his regrets and so did Count von Lynar."

The news of the article, too fresh to have reached Rome before his return, surprised and disturbed Nicholas. He gathered that Harden was pointing his poisonous pen at Prince Philipp Eulenburg. He did not want to ask Alexa for details. He wished to steer her away from the subject, but she refused to be distracted.

"Incidentally, what is a deviate and what does Paragraph 175 refer to?" she asked.

Her question embarrassed Nicholas. "Didn't your husband tell you?"

"Not exactly. He thought it concerned disorderly conduct, something like indecent exposure. He isn't familiar with the civil law book."

"Neither am I. Besides, I am a foreigner, so you'd better ask a German."

On the following morning Nicholas obtained the April 27 issue of *Zukunft*. Without naming names, the article implicated, in addition to Prince Eulenburg, three officers of the Kaiser's entourage. They were so recognizably described that no insider could miss their identity: they were General Count Kuno von Moltke, military commandant of Berlin; Count Wilhelm von Hohenau, general à la suite at court; and Count Johannes von Lynar, colonel of the Gardes du Corps.

The accusations were much more explicit than last year's veiled hints. Nicholas deduced that someone even more powerful than ex-Councillor Holstein was behind Harden's campaign against the Liebenberg Round Table. Holstein might have been Harden's partner, but certainly not his master. Both were puppets, and someone very high up was pulling their strings. The name Bülow flashed through Nicholas's mind.

No doubt Harden had chosen his weapons with great cunning. A man accused of murder or theft could in most cases prove his innocence and be exonerated, but not a man accused of homosexuality.

The four involved men must have realized this, because they maintained an aloof disregard of the attack. Harden had neither been sued nor beaten up nor killed. In the afternoons he was seen presiding over a court of admirers, or perhaps bodyguards, at the Romanisches Cafe on Kurfürstendamm.

At the Austro-Hungarian Embassy reactions were mixed. Nicholas was probably the only one to sympathize fully with Eulenburg, who, by advising the Kaiser to follow a conciliatory course in his dealings with England and France, had acted contrary to the Monarchy's interests.

That evening Nicholas attended a bachelor party at the house of Chargé d'Affaires Baron von Stoka, a corpulent Croat with a florid complexion to match the ever-present red carnation in his buttonhole. Over glasses of sherry, the conversation centered on the topic of the day, the Harden article.

"Have any of you seen Prince Eulenburg lately?" the baron asked. When his guests shook their heads, he went on. "He was in Switzerland, but I understand he's back home again. Frankly, Berlin is a constant source of amazement to me. Let's suppose a man in *our* sovereign's entourage is openly called a pederast and makes no attempt to clear his name. Do you think he could retain his position at court? Would Franz Josef go on breaking bread with him, or hunt, sail, travel or visit with him? 'Le vice Allemand,' that's what the French call homosexuality. I wouldn't be surprised if the Kaiser himself——" He stopped abruptly. "Well, what did you expect? Five years ago the Kaiser blamed the Socialists for Friedrich Krupp's suicide; he said they'd driven him to it with their false accusations. He attended the funeral, although the whole world knew that the man *was* a pederast. And Krupp wasn't even a close friend of his. Eulenburg *is,* so no wonder he sticks to him through thick and thin. Made him prince, a knight of the Black Eagle, would have him canonized if he were a Catholic." Stoka puffed nervously on his Havana cigar. "All we can do is sit back, twiddle our thumbs and watch Philipp Eulenburg and a group of pederasts blow up the Triple Alliance. Poor Austria!"

During the month of May, along with the fragrance of lilacs and jasmine blooming in the city parks, contradictory rumors of Philipp Eulenburg's fall from grace wafted through the Berlin air. For weeks the prince's name had been missing from the court bulletins. The Kaiser supposedly had sent an aide-de-camp to him demanding that he return the Order of the Black Eagle and hand in his resignation as officer in the army reserves.

The whispers were followed by an explosion: General Kuno von Moltke, commandant of Berlin, was relieved of his duties. At the same time, Count Wilhelm von Hohenau, aide-de-camp to the emperor, and Colonel Count Johannes von Lynar of the Gardes were dismissed from military service.

There was no reaction from Lynar and Hohenau. Leaving no forwarding addresses, they closed up their houses and simply disappeared from the Berlin-Potsdam social scene. Eulenburg and Moltke, on the other hand, turned for protection to the law, but were informed that the crown prosecutor refused to institute criminal proceedings against Harden.

Undaunted, they searched for other means to clear their names and requested that the Military Court of Honor bring a disciplinary action against them, thereby giving them a chance to defend themselves. When they were rebuffed, Eulenburg did not make any further attempts. Realizing that nothing he could undertake would turn public opinion in his favor, he quietly retired to Liebenberg. He had neglected to destroy or kill Harden, consequently the world judged him guilty.

Moltke refused to follow his example. Disregarding his attorney's advice, he sued Harden for libel. Count, general, ex-military commandant of the Berlin garrison, he took his complaint to a civil court, just like a common laborer or a shopkeeper.

On a Sunday in June Nicholas met Alexa at their usual place of rendezvous, a quiet side street in Potsdam, from where he drove her to Klein-Glienicke.

They had a picnic lunch in the garden: cold chicken, foie gras from Hungary, cucumber salad, petits fours and wild strawberries, all washed down with chilled Rhine wine. After lunch, a stroll along the water and some leisurely lovemaking, they fell asleep on the down quilt of the enormous four-poster that almost filled the entire bedroom of the cottage.

He slept soundly until awakened by Alexa's nervous stirring beside him. Faintly he heard the nearby village church strike

103

five. He threw a glance at her from under half-closed lids, muttered something and was about to doze off again, when he felt her shaking him violently. He sat up confused. Her nails were digging into his flesh and her voice pierced his ears.

"I am not Beata! I am Alexa! I am Alexa Godenhausen. I am me! Beata is dead! Has been for three years! It's I you've been sleeping with, not she! I! I! I!"

She jumped from bed and began collecting her clothes.

He stared at her, uncomprehending, then slowly the meaning of her screams began to dawn upon him. "Of course you're not Beata! Why . . . why, what's the matter with you? I know you're not Beata!"

"You know now, but when you're in bed with me you want to think it's she. Don't lie. Don't deny it! I've watched you many times. You close your eyes so you can pretend I am Beata."

"That's not true."

"It is true."

"For God's sake, what's gotten into you? What did I do?"

"You called me Beata. Very distinctly."

"Did I?" He rubbed his eyes to wipe away the last traces of sleep. He vaguely remembered that before dozing off he had looked at her and was delighted to notice how much she resembled Beata. She didn't always; worry, annoyance or impatience would occasionally stamp her face with an expression that was strictly her own. It was only during those rare moments when she felt relaxed and happy that he could detect the soft glow of serenity in her eyes that tricked him into believing that she and Beata were one and the same woman. "I must have been dreaming," he said.

"Then go on, dream, but without me. This isn't a séance and I am not the medium through whose body you communicate with your dead. Oh no. I am alive! A live woman and not an imitation, a reflection or a corpse!"

During the first year of his widowerhood he hardly ever

dreamed of Beata, except once, shortly after the fire. In that very vivid dream, forever fresh in his memory, he was on the south slope of the Rethys' vineyard. Tenant farmers were hoeing between the grapestalks after the horse plow had passed down the rows. He suddenly caught sight of Beata under the walnut trees that marked the border of the tract. Later he remembered that his first thought had been to keep himself from imagining that she had not died in the fire. As she came nearer and looked more and more unghostlike, he became confused. Was it the fire that had been a bad dream? Was Beata still alive, and was he her husband not her widower? He ran up the slope to meet her. Now, two years later, he could still feel the branches of the walnut tree brushing against his cheek as he took her in his arms, babbling how delighted he was to find her alive. She looked at him, puzzled, and burst out laughing.

He awakened with her laughter still ringing in his ears, her body warm and soft against his. Coming to his senses was agony, almost as unbearable as the moment when he had been told of her death. For a long time after that night, at least a year, he never dreamed of her. His mind became adjusted to his loss. She was irrevocably dead; it meant emptiness, but also a new beginning.

After his encounter with Alexa at the New Palace in Potsdam, Beata began to haunt his nights again. More and more often her identity became blurred. One moment she was Beata, the next Alexa, or rather Beata in situations that could be identified only with Alexa. She would live in Potsdam and be married to Hans Günther von Godenhausen, causing Nicholas tortures of jealousy and frustration.

He must have had one of those befuddled dreams again, although wide awake he could recall no part of it. "I know who you are. You're you. How could I take you for anyone else? There is no one as troublesome and unpredictable as you."

She was struggling with a hook on her corset and broke a nail. "Damn!"

"It's only five o'clock. Where are you going?"

"Home. And this time for good. And don't try to see me again, because I am through with you."

Her blouse buttoned up the front, so she needed no help closing it. She was already slipping on her coat when, still sleepy, Nicholas dragged himself from bed. "Be sensible, Alexa," he pleaded with her. "I'm not responsible for whatever I said in my sleep. I might have dreamed of Beata. I still do at times. I can't help it, just as you can't help dreaming of Hans Günther, which I am sure you do."

She was in the hallway struggling with the lock on the front door. He had followed her and held on to her arm.

"Let me go," she said.

"Listen to me. We've been together five months now—"

"Six," she corrected him.

"Yes, six. You've told me time and again that you didn't love me, because you loved your husband. You were always wide awake when you told me so, caring not a damn whether you were hurting me or not. To tell the truth, you did hurt me. I never thought I could be satisfied with such a one-sided affair as . . . as this one has been. Yet you meant too much to me to give it up. And you don't want to give it up either. Don't fool yourself. It's not by accident that you are here. The force that brings you here is stronger than you. Don't fight it. You may not realize it, but what you feel for me is a great deal stronger than what you feel for Hans Günther."

"That's not true," she said lamely. "Let me go. I'm late."

"I'll take you home."

"No."

"You said you were late."

"I am." She shrugged. "All right. Drive me back to Potsdam." She quickly added, "I'll let you because it'll save me time."

He dressed and they drove off. Throughout the drive she sat in cold silence.

"When will I see you again?" he asked as he pulled to the curb two blocks away from her house.

"Let me see . . ." She no longer seemed angry with him, only tired and depressed. "Perhaps next Thursday. Yes, there is a concert at the Zoologischer Garten. I mentioned to Hans Günther that I would like to attend. He doesn't care for serious music, so he might let me go alone to Berlin."

"Thursday then."

"Yes, Thursday."

"Where and when?"

"Here at three. It's an afternoon concert."

It had been one of those sudden heat waves that descend upon cities that complacently expect weather similar to the past seasons' temperature. In Glienicke, a cool breeze was still sweeping along the waterfront while on Linden Strasse people were being hit in the face by a hot wind that felt like the exhaust of a steam engine. With the drapes closed, the flat had the gloom of a damp cave. Alexa had to ring three times before a sleepy Lotte emerged from the maids' room.

She had a message for Alexa. The major had been unexpectedly ordered to take his squadron on a field trip and would be away indefinitely.

"Didn't he leave a note?"

"He was in too big a hurry for that."

Not even a note, Alexa thought. "Did he say where he could be reached in case—" The rest—*I became ill, had an accident, died*—she added silently. "When is he expected back?"

Yawning, the girl shrugged. "I forgot to ask." She yawned again. "There is still some sauerbraten from yesterday. Will it do for your supper?"

"Certainly not!" she snapped. Her anger was directed at

Hans Günther. The girl was merely a substitute target. "I want something light. Veal cutlets with parsley potatoes. And a chocolate soufflé for dessert."

"Such a fancy supper for just one person?"

"For just one person. Me!"

The sharpness of her tone killed the response that was on the tip of the girl's tongue. Her lips moved, but no sound escaped them.

Left alone, Alexa threw herself on the bed, buried her face in the pillows and wept. After three and a half years she was of no more importance to Hans Günther than the household decorative pieces that gave him comfort and aesthetic pleasure. Were he faced with the choice between her or his newly acquired Lovis Corinth still life, he would probably have kept the Corinth and discarded her.

With sudden impulse she rose and crossed to the mirror over her dressing table. The face that stared back at her was tear-streaked, red-eyed, but still beautiful. The figure was faultless too; the skin unmarred by lines or blemishes. She spoke four languages, knew and appreciated good literature, had more than a superficial understanding of the world she lived in. Why, despite all her assets, was she unable to capture the kind of love thousands of quite ordinary women could engender in their men? Her bitterness shifted from Hans Günther to Nicholas. Of the two betrayals she had recently suffered, the one inflicted by Nicholas was the most humiliating. Hans Günther's love, though pale and restrained, was all hers. Nicholas's she had to share with Beata. Share? It was all Beata's. She, Alexa, was merely the shopwindow dummy modeling a bridal gown. The once-and-always bride was Beata.

What had been Beata's secret that held a man as worldly-wise and sensuous as Nicholas tied to her even beyond the grave? Whatever it was, she was not going to fight against Beata's posthumous allure. No more Klein-Glienicke, jolly picnics on the lawn, long walks in Babelsberg Park, with a ghost turning their twosome into a crowd. If the bereaved widower needed cheering up, he could always import some willing chorus girl from Vienna to perform for a fee.

On Thursday Nicholas waited in vain for Alexa. Unable to contact her, he hoped that she would write or telephone. On two consecutive Sundays he drove out to Potsdam and parked in the side street where they had always met. On the first occasion he spent two frustrating hours behind the steering wheel being stared at by every passerby. On the second Sunday he lost patience after twenty minutes.

Later he heard that she had been to Norderney on the North Sea and had returned to Potsdam only in September. Still she remained silent. Mutual acquaintances received standing invitations to the Godenhausens' at-homes on the last Friday of each month. His name seemed to have been dropped from their guest list.

Early that fall Nicholas attended the Kaiser's maneuvers at Merseburg. As always, the imperial behavior spawned a lot of anecdotes that buoyed up the spirit of Germany's potential enemies and greatly disturbed her sole dependable ally, the Austro-Hungarian Monarchy.

Wilhelm II arrived in an unusually fractious mood, disconcerting his entourage as well as the entire General Staff. His break with Prince Eulenburg during the spring had turned him into a zealot determined to purge the Prussian military of all real or imagined moral impurities. As the weather warmed up, so did the intensity of his witch-hunt. Camaraderie, affection between two men, loyalty to friends, all became suspect in his eyes. He singled out young Prince Friedrich Heinrich for a punishment cruelly disproportionate to the offense. He deprived the prince of the services of an aide-de-camp, with the explanation that contact with him would imperil the morals of a fellow officer. He forbade unmarried princes to keep private apartments. His sons had no women, so why should their cousins sleep around, he argued. In his zeal for reform, he ordered a drive against gambling in the officers' mess halls. The campaign proved a complete failure. Many a regimental commandant was himself guilty. Besides, punishing the gamblers would have left the troops without officers.

In Merseburg, Nicholas was amazed at the money and man-hours wasted on the Kaiser's whims. Because the bathtubs at his temporary headquarters had sprung a leak in 1906, a whole pioneer battalion was now kept in readiness in the event that the imperial plumbing needed repair.

Wilhelm was in the habit of ordering troop movements without ever taking distances into consideration. To avoid antagonizing him, infantry and cavalry started the night before, rested through the best part of the following day, then completed the last stage of the march late in the afternoon, arriving at the preset hour.

Officially a cavalry squadron was assigned fifty-two horses. Because of the insensible imperial demands, a secret number of extra horses helped out whenever the going became tough. Attending military attachés of foreign powers listened with inward chuckles to Wilhelm boasting of the extraordinary endurance of his troops.

Nicholas had been looking forward to the maneuvers. He hoped they would take his mind off Alexa, but the opposite happened. Invited to a déjeuner given by the Kaiser for the foreign observers, he found himself seated next to Godenhausen, who appeared to be a member of the imperial entourage, an unusual honor for an officer under the rank of general. In his regiment he had outstripped older men with years of seniority and supposedly was in line to be aide-de-camp to the emperor.

The déjeuner was held at the regimental mess hall of the Gardes du Corps. While waiting for the emperor's entrance, the foreign guests were joined by members of the Military Cabinet, men who had been up since the crack of dawn to keep their sovereign company and now were unable to stifle an occasional yawn. Shortly after breakfast Wilhelm had retired to his tent to rest, yet his cabinet had to remain on call. As veterans of palace service, they had learned to take stress and strain in their stride, but while their spirits were willing, their bodies were not. Watching them reminded Nicholas of hack horses waiting at their stand for fares: feet tapping, heads low, eyes glazed with weariness, yet ready to move at the snap of a whip.

Finally, wearing a general's undress uniform, his withered left arm hooked into his belt, Wilhelm strode into the mess with the springy steps of a drum major. He was followed by General Hülsen-Haeseler, chief of the Military Cabinet and, since Eulenburg's fall, the Kaiser's favorite. A shameless climber for whom no trick seemed too cheap or too outrageous to worm his way into the sovereign's good graces, Hülsen-Haeseler was known to have appeared in a monkey suit, done card tricks, imitated animal sounds, crawled on his belly and dropped his pants in public—anything for imperial laughter or a kingly pat on the back.

The Kaiser halted in the middle of the room. His absurdly blue eyes searched the faces of the assembled officers with the intensity of a robbery victim searching a police lineup for the man who had stolen his wallet.

"Good day, gentlemen!" He flashed a bright smile at the guests and was promptly answered with a discreet murmur of voices. As if waiting for a photographer's camera to click, everyone remained at stiff attention.

Wilhelm approached the group. After addressing three others, he stopped in front of Nicholas and subjected the younger man's face to a thorough scrutiny. He might be searching for signs of my Semitic heritage, Nicholas thought, without being disconcerted by it. Standing at attention, he waited to be addressed.

"I hope you'll approve of our maneuvers, Captain," Wilhelm said. "After all, we're comrades in arms. Your exalted sovereign is the man I respect most in the whole world. Since the Algeciras Conference, I've realized more gratefully than ever what a staunch ally I have in his Austria."

It was another one of Wilhelm's diplomatic gaffes. To mention Algeciras in the presence of the Italian attaché, whose government, although allied to Germany, had voted against the Kaiser's policy, was in questionable taste.

It also made the rebellious Magyar rear up in Nicholas. "*And* in his Hungary, Your Majesty," he said. It gave him a devilish pleasure to remind the emperor that he had blundered twice in one sentence.

The Kaiser frowned. His ally, of course, was not Austria, but Austria-Hungary. Nicholas sensed a chill as real as a draft · from an ice house blowing his way. The half-smile had faded from the Hohenzollern face. Wilhelm disliked Jews and Hungarians, and Nicholas was both.

"Have a good time in Merseburg, Captain." The voice was even more staccato than before. He slapped Nicholas across the left arm. It was a sharp, resounding slap, rather too powerful to be the sign of imperial grace. Nicholas had the feeling that his remark would not be forgotten.

Councillor Lecomte of the French Embassy was one of the few civilians present. During the déjeuner he was seated opposite Godenhausen. When judging people, Nicholas never let their race, religion or sexual preferences influence him, yet he found Lecomte rather hard to take. A compulsive charmer, the Frenchman was out to dazzle everyone at the table. There was a touch of coquetry to his wit that Nicholas could tolerate only in women. Between witticisms, the councillor's eyes lingered repeatedly on Godenhausen's handsome face. The major seemed unaware of the attention, or he had acquired the studied nonchalance of a matinee idol used to admiration.

Throughout the meal Nicholas could not rid himself of an odd discomfort. Making small talk with Alexa's husband seemed wrong. Foremost in his mind was the thought that he was talking to the man who shared Alexa's bed. A slow-burning resentment was building up in him. Of course he was being irrational. The major *was* the husband, while he was not even the lover any more.

It had to be the major's striking good looks that antagonized him, he told himself. No doubt Hans Günther was an asset, a rare ornament to any ruler's court. Even his fellow officers paid more attention to him than his military rank warranted, although for different reasons than Lecomte and his kind. Quite obviously he was a man on the rise, and it would be helpful to be in his good graces.

"How is Baroness von Godenhausen?" Nicholas asked, trying to sound casual.

The major responded with a blank stare. His thoughts had obviously been on a different track, as if the all-male company had caused him to forget that there *was* a Baroness von Godenhausen.

"She is fine, thank you, fine. Except for the usual marital complaints. I mean boredom, too much time on her hands. Women are always surprised to find that men have a life outside the home. That they cannot be husbands twenty-four hours a day. But why am I telling you all this? You were married once, so this can't be news to you."

"It is, though." Nicholas was annoyed with himself for having dissented. Now he had to continue. "My late wife never complained of boredom. She always found the days too short." Silently he added, *They* were *short—short days, short year, short life.*

The major gave him a searching look. "I understand yours was a happy marriage."

Nicholas resented the remark. There was an undertone to it that disturbed him. He felt Godenhausen was prying. The nature of his relationship to Beata concerned only him. He and the major had shared Alexa, but Beata was his and his alone.

"Yes, very happy," he said curtly, then, indicating that the subject was exhausted, turned to the Bavarian military attaché on his right. "What is new in Munich?"

The Bavarian was engrossed in a conversation with a British colonel facing him across the table and failed to hear Nicholas.

Godenhausen refused to drop the topic. "I understand there was an unusually strong resemblance between your late wife and Alexa. Unusual even for identical twins."

"I wouldn't call it unusual."

Godenhausen ignored the evasion. "Meeting Alexa at this time must have been a shock to you."

Was it simple curiosity that prompted Godenhausen to pursue the matter or the cuckolded husband's malice? Nicholas wondered. "Not really. I had been prepared. Two years had passed between my wife's death and my meeting the baroness. Fashions change, and women change with them."

Godenhausen nodded and still continued to follow his train of thought. "Last May at the New Palace I couldn't help wondering how I would've reacted if faced with the same problem."

Now it was clear to Nicholas that the major *knew*. For a second he was tempted to grab his glass and dash its contents, the Kaiser's best vintage champagne, into the man's smiling face. He reconsidered in time. "What problem?"

"The reincarnation of a person once dear to me."

An inner voice warned Nicholas to watch for traps. If the major was aiming for a confrontation, he was not going to comply, not at the present stage of his affair with Alexa. "I don't believe in reincarnation. Anyway, my wife was unique. She could never be confused with another woman, even an identical twin."

The major obviously realized that he had shot beyond the mark and changed the subject. "We were sorry to miss you last Friday."

Nicholas wondered whether Hans Günther knew that he

had been dropped from their guest list. "Duties, you know. I should've remained in field service. On the Staff one is permanently on call!"

"I understand. Still, it is a pity we see so little of you. Alexa was very disappointed. You're the only one in Berlin she can talk Hungarian with."

Now it was the common language, Nicholas thought. As far as he could remember, he had not spoken Hungarian to Alexa in Hans Günther's presence. The major might have overheard them at the New Palace, though. "I promise I'll drop in on you next time I am in Potsdam." He had no intention of doing so. Hurt pride was keeping him away from Alexa.

"Please do. Any time. Sans façon. Your sole risk might be not to find Alexa home. Lately she's developed a passion for music. Attends every symphony concert of the Royal Orchestra. Frankly, I don't care for the classics, so she usually goes with a friend or her aunt."

If the information was intended to distress Nicholas, it fulfilled its purpose. Godenhausen *was* aware of the break between him and Alexa and was telling him of her continued concertgoing to intimate that she used it as an excuse to see a new lover.

Nicholas was deeply relieved when, after the twelve courses of the déjeuner had been consumed, the innumerable toasts delivered and answered, the Kaiser at last rose from the table. The hope that he would retire and allow his entourage to have its long overdue rest evaporated when he led the way to the adjoining smoking room for another session of conviviality. Once again everyone remained standing while Wilhelm took center stage like a Wagnerian tenor and expounded his views on the most diverse subjects, such as international politics, new discoveries in aeronautics, Goethe's love life, the value of Greek terra cotta figurines and the threat of the British fleet.

Although basking for hours in the imperial presence was too much of a good thing, Nicholas could not help admiring the man's brilliance. It seemed unlikely that he had conducted profound studies in so many areas, nevertheless his memory and the wide scope of his interests were remarkable.

At four in the afternoon the emperor at last decided to retire. Part of his entourage, among them Hülsen-Haeseler and Godenhausen, followed him to the door. On the threshold Wilhelm halted. He addressed the German officers. "So long, gentlemen. You have my permission to return to your units. Back to work! Let's make the maneuvers a great success and show our distinguished guests what important progress we have made since last year. And let them have a foretaste of what wonders we may yet achieve, given a few more years of peace, that is."

There was lame applause from the civilians, mostly foreigners. "Au revoir, gentlemen." The Kaiser waved to them.

"Au revoir, Your Majesty." The civilians bowed, the officers stiffened to attention. In a farewell gesture Wilhelm extended his hand to Godenhausen. Hans Günther bent, took hold of the hand, lifted it to his lips and breathed a kiss on it.

Nicholas expected the emperor to be startled, even vexed, but all he saw was a pleased smile behind the whiskers. The homage was repeated by Hülsen-Haeseler and other high-ranking officers. No doubt in the Prussian army it was considered as proper an expression of reverence toward one's sovereign as a stiff salute in the Austro-Hungarian Monarchy's armed forces.

As the party dispersed, Nicholas could not keep from commenting on the hand kiss. "It seems obeisance to one's sovereign is taken quite seriously around here," he remarked to Godenhausen.

If the major was disconcerted by the sarcastic undertone, he failed to show it. "What's wrong with that? Bishops get their hands kissed. Isn't His Majesty better than some holier-than-thou cassock feeding promises of a better life after death to an ignorant flock? In twenty years of his rule, Wilhelm has elevated Germany to the second most powerful empire in the world. Give him twenty more years and we'll be first."

"Let's suppose you will be. At what price?"

"Whatever the price, it will be worth it. I personally am ready to pay with my life. In exchange for what he has already given me—pride in my German heritage." He waited for Nicholas's comment. When none was forthcoming, he continued: "I don't blame you for not appreciating my views. How could you? After all, yours is a country put together out of bits and pieces like a patchwork quilt. Don't you have trouble deciding where your loyalties are? Of course, the Bible says, 'Render unto Caesar the things which are Caesar's.' Or, to be profane: 'Whose bread you eat, whose song you sing.' That ought to be simple. Unless you're a man of conscience."

Godenhausen had his eyes fixed on Nicholas's face. Without blinking, the captain returned his stare. "Am I a man of conscience? That's a tough question. Coming on one side from a long line of good devout Christians who had flogged their recalcitrant serfs, set fire to their crops, violated their daughters, then on the other side from an equally long line of shrewd Jews whose sole aim was to slip through the judicial loopholes of any country that was willing to offer them asylum, I really have trouble setting up a perfect yardstick by which to measure my conscience. Perhaps in my case conscience is the wrong definition. I ought to substitute it with instinct."

The major frowned. "I can't follow you."

"Only because we are not talking of the same thing. You mean patriotism, I mean life in general. Yours is a man's world: war games, marches, attacks, the Schlieffen Plan, the wild pursuit of the Pour le Mérite, the marshal's baton. My world is much simpler. A quiet picnic on a sunny spring day, crisp bread, freshly churned butter, slices of Schwarzwälder ham, a bottle of Rhine wine and a pretty girl to share it with me."

A shadow fell across the major's blue eyes. There was a flicker of contempt at the corner of his lips. Then the lips widened into a grin and he jovially patted Nicholas on the back. "Have fun at your picnics. I hope you won't find out that a pretty girl is sometimes harder to hold on to than a marshal's baton."

The libel suit of General Kuno von Moltke against the journalist Maximilian Harden opened at the Municipal Courthouse in Berlin's Moabit district on October 23, 1907, and lasted for six days. It was tried before a magistrate and two jurors. Because of the plaintiff's rank the case gained worldwide press attention. Every evening transcripts of the trial were delivered by special courier to the emperor's very hands.

The Austro-Hungarian Embassy had seats reserved in the courtroom for the duration of the trial. Nicholas attended most of the sessions, gaining an invaluable insight into the peculiarities of Prussian jurisprudence.

By the time the trial opened, few secrets of General Moltke's private life remained hidden from the reading public. Depending on the newspaper's partisanship, he was depicted either as a brave and brilliant soldier, a gifted musician and a man of taste and culture, or as an immoralist, a social climber, a snob, a coward, a martinet and a lecher.

Nicholas found him to be the same slightly effeminate schöngeist he had been at the Godenhausens' at-home parties, a man who felt entitled to have the respect and admiration of his fellow citizens because of his ancestry and rank. Suddenly deprived of the shelter of his pedigree, he now wore the expression of a raped spinster.

The presiding judge, an inexperienced young jurist, and his assessors, a butcher and a milk dealer, were an odd combination for a case of such importance. The plaintiff was represented by Counselor of Justice Heiner von Gordon and the defendant by Counselor of Justice Max Bernstein of Munich. Bernstein was a man blessed with a biting wit and a great power of concentration, while Gordon lacked both.

He became easily flustered, leaving the conduct of the lawsuit to his opponent.

To the judge's suggestion of an amicable settlement, Harden, a seasoned veteran of courtrooms, answered with an ear-splitting no. He added, "I, Maximilian Harden, am willing to spend the rest of my life in prison rather than retract any of my charges against Count Kuno von Moltke."

After this Moltke had no choice but to reject the idea of reconciliation.

The crowded room listened soundlessly to the judge's high-pitched voice listing the plaintiff's complaints, among them Harden's most damaging statement of calling the general a practicing homosexual. Hearing this, Harden immediately jumped to his feet. He had never called Moltke a *practicing* pervert, he shouted, merely a man of homosexual tendencies. And this he was going to prove beyond the shadow of a doubt.

The first morning was taken up by Counselor von Gordon's opening statement and a parade of character witnesses testifying in the general's behalf. Bernstein's turn came in the afternoon. The first person he called to the stand was the ex-Countess von Moltke, now remarried to the rich landowner von Elbe. Counselor von Gordon's feeble attempt to disqualify her as a manic-depressive still under psychiatric care was defeated by Bernstein's denunciation of a husband who had with his deliberate cruelty driven a loving wife dangerously close to a nervous breakdown. He also produced a medical certificate proving that since the divorce the lady had reverted to her former well-balanced self.

Despite the cool winds sweeping through the streets of Berlin, the heat in the small room had become tropical. There was a constant rustle of fans, and the air, or what was left of it, was heavy with the odor of smoke and perspiration.

Frau Natalie von Elbe was a statuesque blond woman between forty and fifty years of age. When informed by the judge that, in view of her former relationship to the plaintiff, she had the right to refuse testimony, she answered with a shrill laugh. "Thank you, Your Honor, but *I* have nothing to hide. What is more, I welcome the chance to let the world know the reasons for my divorce from the general."

The room reacted with a nervous snicker that continued for minutes. Counselor von Gordon appealed to the bench to order the courtroom cleared of the public, at least for the duration of the lady's testimony. After a brief consultation with his assessors, the judge denied the motion.

Relative quiet ruled while Counselor Bernstein began with the questioning of the witness. "Is it true," he asked, "that the plaintiff repeatedly referred to the institution of marriage as an abomination and to marital intercourse as a filthy and indecent act?"

"True."

"And is it true that General von Moltke abstained from having sexual relations with you because he had promised Prince Eulenburg to keep away from your bed?"

"Absolutely."

"And is it true that Prince Eulenburg implored you not to take his friend away from him?"

"He asked me more than once."

"And is it true that the plaintiff also told you that the family bedroom was like a padded cell in a lunatic asylum?"

The witness's eyes were brimming over and she dabbed at them with a handkerchief. "Yes, that's what he told me."

"And is it true that once in the presence of your mother he made the following statement, I quote: 'A woman is a latrine into which a man empties his filth'?"

"Yes, he did make that statement."

After each answer a low buzz rippled through the room. The judge's gavel kept hitting the desktop with dull, unconvincing thuds that had no restraining effect on either Bernstein or the spectators. The general looked like a man fighting seasickness.

"To your knowledge, madame, did your ex-husband have sexual relations with men?" asked Bernstein.

"Well," Frau von Elbe began, then paused to wait for the quiver of excitement to subside in the room, "I really can't tell. It's a subject I don't know much about. I merely found Count von Moltke's passionate love for his friends—especially Prince Eulenburg—rather disconcerting."

"What gave you the impression of 'passionate love'?"

"Some strange incidents. For instance, the prince once paid us a visit, and after he left we found Eulenburg's handkerchief on the floor. My husband picked it up and lifted it to his lips."

During the witness's testimony, the general had appeared to be shrinking to the size of a ten-year-old boy. His shoulders hunched, his chin resting on his balled fists, he had been sliding forward in his chair until he was seated on its very edge. Now a nervous tremor went through his body and his eyes widened.

"Why did he do that?" The judge continued the questioning.

"I don't know. He mumbled something like 'Phili, my Phili, my love, my dearest!"

Outraged, General Moltke jumped up. "Your Honor, I demand to be heard! That incident with the handkerchief is willfully misinterpreted. I *did* lift it to my lips, but only to amuse my wife. To tease her. It was done in fun and she knew it. But now it's been given a different shading. Frau von Elbe has been distorting the truth and—"

"How dare you call me a liar? I'm not the only one who heard him. Why, he had all sorts of pet names for his friends —'my darling boy,' 'my puppy dog,' 'my one and only.' "

The general dropped back into his chair. Except for becoming alternately flushed and deathly pale, his face registered no expression. He kept his gaze fixed upon the wall. When the judge ordered the trial adjourned until the following morning, he remained seated, letting the massive body of Counselor von

Gordon shield him from the onslaught of the curious public and the members of the press.

Next day it was Counselor von Gordon's turn to cross-examine Natalie von Elbe. Unlike Counselor Bernstein, it quite visibly pained him to touch upon the more undignified episodes of the Moltkes' marriage. He and his client were both members of the ruling class, and he felt personally degraded when talking of the pitched battles that had taken place in the house of the general and his lady.

Moltke's friends and ex-employees testified about the woman's demonic temper. They told of occasions when the general had to remain in seclusion until his face, bloodied by his wife, had healed. They willingly peppered their testimonies with direct quotes that proved the countess's familiarity with obscene and scatological expressions, supposedly used only by the lower classes.

The image emerging from the pro-Moltke testimonies was of a vicious and vulgar she-wolf, a veritable castrater of men. It failed to help the plaintiff's case, though, because from the beginning the bench clung to the preconceived idea that the woman and not the man had been the victim of the unhappy marriage. At least it seemed so to Nicholas.

During the afternoon, the general was called to the witness stand to be cross-examined by Counselor Bernstein. He readily admitted that his marriage had been a complete failure. "I had loved her with all my heart," he said, "but her conduct completely destroyed my affection for her." He paused to pull his handkerchief out and pat his moist forehead. "Nevertheless, whatever affection I had for members of my own sex never exceeded the bounds of camaraderie. So help me God."

In his inelegant Bavarian accent, Bernstein asked a question that took Moltke, as well as the courtroom, by complete surprise. "Is it true, General, that you have a standing order with the Confiserie Annabelle for a large box of bon-bons to be delivered to your house twice a week?"

Moltke stared at the man, uncomprehending. "How was that?"

Bernstein repeated the question, then added, "Remember, General, you are testifying under oath."

Moltke shrugged. "It's true. What of it?"

"Is it true that you are referred to as the sweetie by your friends?"

Turning red in the face, Moltke banged the stand with his balled fist. "How the hell would I know about that?"

"Do you admit, General, that you frequently apply rouge to your cheeks and lips in order to improve your appearance?"

If Moltke ever had, he certainly could do without it at the moment. He turned to the judge. "Your Honor, am I obliged to answer the question?"

After the judge ruled the question admissible, Moltke nodded wearily. "Yes . . . occasionally. Certainly not frequently."

Bernstein bowed from the waist. "Thank you, General. That's all for the moment."

Next Bernstein undertook the cross-examination of the plaintiff's witnesses. Despite his best efforts, he was unable to make them retract any part of their testimonies or draw an incriminating statement against the plaintiff from them. The strain of the past two days was beginning to dampen spirits. Even the spectators' rows were thinning out. After a listless hour the weary judge brought the afternoon session to an abrupt end.

Ever since her return from Norderney, Alexa had been in a restless, melancholy mood, bursting into tears over trifles. Hans Günther had terminated his vacation a week earlier than usual, leaving her in the care of the Sedlitzes. Reunited with him in Potsdam, she found him oddly distant and preoccupied. At times she felt as if he deliberately avoided being alone with her. They attended more parties than ever, yet she sensed in his hectic eagerness to surround himself with people that he was like a man who entered a dense forest hoping never to find his way out of it. She felt relieved in September when he departed for the maneuvers in Merseburg.

She almost regretted having broken with Nicholas, but hurt pride prevented her from contacting him. She recalled an afternoon in Glienicke when in an irresistible fit of curiosity she had thumbed through his wallet while he was out of the room. It contained, among documents, a picture of Beata in her wedding dress. Her first reaction was to tear it to shreds. Then the realization that in the Nicholas-Beata-Alexa triangle she, Alexa, was the victorious usurper and Beata the permanently dispossessed cooled off her anger, and she carefully slipped the photograph back into its pocket. What if now and then Nicholas had thrown a quick glance at the faded picture, wasn't it she, Alexa, whom he took to his bed? The thought had set her mind at ease. That is, until that June Sunday in Glienicke when she suddenly discovered the truth. She was nothing more to him than a handy surrogate; while he possessed her body, it was still Beata who possessed him.

On the fourth day of the Harden-Moltke trial the court, overruling Counselor von Gordon's objections, granted the defendant's request to call witnesses who would testify to alleged homosexual activities within the general's and Prince Eulenburg's circle of friends. Once again the defendant's intent to involve the prince in the proceedings became obvious.

Nicholas arrived half an hour late. When he entered the courtroom, the trial was already in progress. A tall ruddy-faced civilian—wearing a black suit that was much too tight across his wide shoulders and the hard cannonball-like bulge of his middle—was testifying.

At first Nicholas was somewhat mystified. He failed to understand the connection between the Moltke case and the private life of Count Johannes von Lynar, ex-colonel in the Gardes du Corps. Several questions and answers later, it became evident why Bernstein had called the man in black, ex-sergeant Bollhardt, former standard bearer of Lynar's regiment, to the witness stand. It was another one of the counselor's attempts to implicate Moltke and Eulenburg in acts violating Paragraph 175 of the State Penal Code.

The ex-sergeant appeared alternately cocky and ill-at-ease. To some of Bernstein's questions he responded in a beer-drenched mumble, to others with a drill-yard roar. One of his disclosures had the effect of an exploding bomb. He stated that he had been commanded, ten years before, to present himself repeatedly at the Alder Villa, the Potsdam residence of the then Major von Lynar, where he was forced to submit to unnatural sex acts, perpetrated by the count and his fellow officers.

"Was General von Moltke present on these occasions?" Bernstein asked.

Bollhardt opened his mouth, then closed it again. There was a long suspenseful silence broken only by nervous whisperings from the back rows of the room.

"It's hard to tell," he said at last, his voice sounding much too thin for his bulk. "The lights were dim. No gaslight, only candles—that was how the major liked it. A person was given all the wine and schnapps he wanted . . . Besides it wasn't easy for a person to recognize the gentlemen without their uniforms on."

A squall of laughter erupted from the spectators' benches. Bernstein looked daggers at the witness for having given such a halfhearted answer. "How about Prince Eulenburg? You did recognize him, didn't you?"

He had gone too far. Bollhardt pulled himself erect. "I don't think so." He looked at the little attorney with the contempt of the soldier for a civilian, and a Jew at that. The sharpness of his tone indicated that he had either been poorly paid or that Bernstein had overstepped the limits of their agreement. He probably felt that Eulenburg—a prince and a friend of the All Highest—might, if angered, take revenge on him, a common man.

Bernstein refused to give up. "Are you positive that you never saw Prince Eulenburg at the Lynar parties?"

"I've told you so, haven't I?"

"You're testifying under oath."

The attorney's persistence flustered Bollhardt. "Well, I might have, then again I might not. It's hard for a person to tell after all these years."

"Only ten," Bernstein argued.

"It's hard even on the morning after. No lights, only candles, and everyone drunk."

Bernstein conceded defeat. "No more questions."

His adversary having failed to extricate any incriminating statement from the witness against either Moltke or Eulenburg, Counselor von Gordon abstained from cross-examining him.

Bollhardt was followed by five enlisted men of the Gardes du Corps. Three were still in active service but transferred to other regiments. All under thirty, they were rather ordinary-looking sons of the Prussian proletariat or peasantry, none of them the kind of girlishly handsome youths most people might think of as homosexuals.

In response to Bernstein's rapid-fire questions, they readily admitted having taken part in homosexual orgies recently hosted by Count Wilhelm von Hohenau, general à la suite to the emperor. They became tonguetied only when pressed for details.

Watching them squirm on the witness stand, Nicholas wondered about the ways and means by which Harden had succeeded in picking them from the ranks of a whole regiment, how he had managed to focus on the five who *had* participated in orgies. He must have received help, even sanction, from someone very high up.

Suddenly a familiar name dropped by the last of the five, Corporal Johann Sommer, hit Nicholas's ear. For a long moment he sat petrified. Telling of a party held at the Hohenau residence during the month of May, Sommer testified to having had sexual intercourse with, among others, Major Hans Günther von Godenhausen. Once again Counselor von Gordon objected to the testimony on the grounds of irrelevancy, but Bernstein shouted him down.

"My learned colleague is wrong, Your Honor," he protested. "Major von Godenhausen's moral conduct is of great importance to the case. So is the conduct of General von Moltke's other close friends. We all know the old proverb: Birds of a feather flock together. My duty to my client is to prove the homosexual tendencies of the plaintiff. One way to prove them is by showing the prevalence of pederasty in the circle of his intimates."

The judge threw an "objection denied" in Gordon's direction.

His face turning ashen, Gordon sat down. By trying to protect Godenhausen, he had achieved the opposite. Instead of letting the major's name drop unnoticed, he had held it up for special attention.

Of all the soldier witnesses, Corporal Sommer seemed to bear the deepest grudge against his superior officers, who had used alcohol, money and their rank to prostitute him, a naive farmboy who had never experienced abnormal desires before falling into their clutches.

There had been rumors circulating in the barracks, he said, about the orgies at the Hohenau residence. Nevertheless when his turn came to be selected for special duty, he reported proudly and unsuspectingly as a well-disciplined cavalryman should. Only later, when told to join the officers in the salon, did he begin to feel uneasy. The rest of the evening was a blur. It was either the amount of liquor he drank or some mysterious substance mixed in the wine that caused him to lose consciousness. When he awakened he was naked and in bed with a man. Much too sick and drowsy to protest, he had no choice but to submit. Next morning, going through his pockets, he found a twenty-mark gold piece in one.

To Counselor Bernstein's probing questions he admitted having gone on subsequent occasions to his commandant's quarters for more parties and more gold pieces.

After Bernstein finished questioning the witness, Counselor von Gordon had his turn in cross-examining Sommer. Despite the young man's evident willingness to be helpful to the defense, he lost his assurance when told to identify General von Moltke as one of the participants at the orgies.

He had been shown photographs of the general by Herr Harden, he replied, and thought he recognized him as one of the guests, but now, confronted with the general in person, he was no longer sure.

When the court adjourned, Nicholas went to the nearest winehouse and ordered a double brandy. He wondered what effect Corporal Sommer's testimony was to have on the Godenhausens' marriage. That it would put an end to the major's military career was without doubt. He should have felt a malignant satisfaction over the misfortune of the man who was his mistress's husband, but all he could feel at the moment was fatigue and disgust.

6

Alexa stared at the newspaper in utter disbelief. Her husband's name was printed in thick black letters on the front page. Of the soldier witnesses, she personally knew only one: Corporal Sommer, who the year before had been on duty at the Reitbahn, where she frequently rode. He once escorted her and a group of regimental ladies on their horseback excursion to Borstedterfeld to watch the cavalry exercises. She remembered him as a slim young man with surprisingly smooth manners for a noncommissioned officer. She took a liking to him and often wished she could disregard the class barrier and talk to him about matters more personal than the temperament of her mount and the probability of sunshine in the afternoon.

Now the same polite young man was implicating her husband in certain hideous depravities, the nature of which she still failed completely to understand. In April, when the Harden piece in *Zukunft* exploded like a bomb and was followed by General von Moltke's and Prince Eulenburg's falling from grace, as well as the Lynar and the Hohenau indictments for transgressions against Paragraph 175 of the State Penal Code, she had asked Hans Günther to explain what the whole uproar was about. He brushed her off, saying that well-bred women weren't interested in such smut. She looked for the word "homosexual" in her dictionary but failed to find it. For months, except for an occasional reference to the upcoming libel suit, the name of Count Kuno von Moltke seldom appeared in print. Hans Günther subscribed to a local paper in which she usually skipped politics and news and read only the society column and the court circular.

Nevertheless for some murky reason the date when the Moltke-Harden libel trial was to open remained etched in the back of her mind. Then on the morning after the first day of the trial the paper was missing. She looked for it on the small table where Hans Günther used to leave it before reporting to the barracks, but it was not there. At first she paid no attention to its disappearance, but when there had been no paper for three consecutive days she sent Thadeus to buy the midday edition at a nearby kiosk. Later she recalled the strange reluctance with which he tried to disregard the order. She had to repeat it three times before he ran out of excuses and trotted off to fetch the paper.

Alexa read and reread the report, searching in vain for a word that would redeem Hans Günther. It contained references to the ex-Countess von Moltke's testimony of days before. Whatever the woman had said might hold a clue to the mystery of Hans Günther's involvement, Alexa thought. This time she didn't send Thadeus but slipped a coat on over her housedress and went to the kiosk herself. She asked for a week's back issues, but the blind vendor told her that he had none left. He had sold out all publications that carried the reports. He would become rich if papers always sold as fast as they had during the Moltke trial, he added with a chuckle. He advised her to try the stand at the Teltower railroad station. This she did and with success.

She managed to reach home a few minutes before Hans Günther. Without reading the papers, she quickly hid them under her bed.

While waiting for the midday dinner to be served, Hans Günther immersed himself in a French novel. He kept reading throughout the meal, which was not his habit. His manners had always been impeccable—almost always. He had his strange moods, though they were never quite as mean as his uncle's, the general's. There had to be a neurotic streak running in the family, Alexa thought as she gazed at his perfect face seemingly untouched by the inner turmoil that must have been seething in him since the morning headlines.

He put the book down to help himself to the meat course, then immediately picked it up again, holding it, she noticed, upside down. She could no longer keep silent.

"That book must be fascinating," she said more shrilly than she had intended to.

Startled, he looked up: "How was that?"

Her throat constricted and she almost choked on the words. "I said your book must be fascinating, or you couldn't read it upside down."

His face reddened and he dropped the book. "I wasn't reading it upside down."

"You were too." She was unable to control her bitterness. Her eyes brimmed over. "You were hiding behind that damned book so you wouldn't have to talk to me. You don't have to, you know. I've learned to read the signals. I can tell when the DON'T DISTURB sign is out on your door, when I am supposed to be seen but not heard."

"You are heard now." His tone was icy and hostile. "Heard louder than necessary." Suddenly he flared. "Can't a man have peace in his own house? Where the hell can I go to have peace?"

She almost said, *To the Hohenau residence,* but the expression of unconcealed pain on his now sickly pale face kept her quiet. They had reached the threshold that, instinct told her, would be disastrous to cross. It would mean the end of a relationship that had probably never existed except in her mind. Still she had to cling to its illusions, for she was not yet ready to exist without them. Hans Günther was her husband, her family, her first and only love. She had been unfaithful to him, which now that she had broken off the affair strengthened rather than weakened her marriage. She had found out that the man she slept with was making love not to her but her dead sister. It was a sobering discovery and it sent her back repentant and humiliated to the man who had married *her* because it was *she* whom he wanted and nobody else. True, he was cool and distant at times, but evidently that was his nature. At least she had no reason to suspect another woman in his life. But suddenly now even a woman would have been better than Corporal Sommer.

They finished the meal in silence. Later Hans Günther, without a word to her, left for regimental headquarters or wherever he was supposed to do duty that day. The front door had hardly closed behind him when she dug up the back copies of the *Täglicher Rundschau* from under her bed. With trembling fingers she opened the October 23 issue to the case dealing with the Moltke-Harden trial.

Reading Countess von Moltke's testimony, she felt herself turning into a chunk of ice. The countess's words stirred up reminiscences in her that supported Corporal Sommer's accusations. Although Hans Günther had never called marriage an abomination, he did make facetious quips that now in retrospect were equally disturbing. She had heard him referring to women—not to her, others—as bitches in heat or brood mares whose brains were between their legs and who on certain days of the month emitted the odor of decomposing bodies. True, she had never seen him kiss a friend's handkerchief, nevertheless he *had* manifested rather ardent affection for some of his fellow officers. The difference between him and Moltke was that the object of his devotion changed frequently. Hans Günther's friendships were short-lived, and he could be interested in more than one man at the same time. Alexa often wondered what caused him to become rather intimate with a new acquaintance, then drop him after a few weeks' time. Young subalterns, who were greeted like long lost brothers on two consecutive at-home Fridays, often failed to reappear on a third.

There was a nucleus of social contacts that remained unchanged during the four years of their marriage: members of the General Staff, aides-de-camp to the emperor and to royal princes and regimental commandants. Hans Günther considered them to be the right people to further his career, yet he found their company à tiring and boring obligation. With Alexa he attended their stiffly formal tea parties and soirees, patiently listened to the men's long-winded anecdotes and dutifully whirled their wives and daughters around on the dance floors. It happened more than once that later he vented his spleen on her, as though she had been to blame for his rotten evening. She endured his moods because she knew that in a way he was right. She was no help to him, fell short of what a Prussian officer's lady was supposed to be. A sloppy housewife, with a wit much too flippant and disrespectful, she often drew criticism from regimental and General Staff wives. She had been presented at court, attended galas and receptions, yet failed to make friends with any member of the empress's entourage. She used to attribute the cooling of their marriage to his disappointment in her, the imperfect partner. Now, reading the Moltke-Harden trial report, she knew better.

She still failed to understand what "indulging in unnatural acts" meant. Men in love with men and men making love to men were concepts beyond her grasp. They kissed and embraced, lifted each other's handkerchiefs to their lips, wrote saccharine letters to friends, but what else? Hans Günther had never done any of these grotesque things. On the contrary, he seemed even more masculine among males than he was with women. He would act with a touch of youthful exuberance, become noisy and waggish like a schoolboy on vacation. Still there had to be more to it than quips, badinage, playful slaps on backs. The paper mentioned "abominations" for which men were sent to prison. It had to be something simply horrendous. Whatever it was, it left no mark on a man's body; at least she never noticed any on Hans Günther's.

She had to talk to someone, have her numbing confusion cleared up once and for all. She had no woman friend to turn to, and from her aunt she could expect no enlightenment, only outraged reprimand. With sudden alarm she realized that in the first real crisis of her life she had not a soul to help her. In the past whenever she had a problem she took it to Hans Günther. At times she had to wait for the right moment, but in the end they had their talk and, whether to her liking or not, the question became resolved. But now how could she ask *him* what abominations he had committed ten years before at the Adler Villa and more recently at the orgies at Count Hohenau's house? She visualized the angry scowl that would spread over his face, turning it into a savage mask.

She thought of Nicholas and realized that his name had been at the back of her mind ever since she had read the headlines. He was the only one she could turn to. The desire to see him came over her with an irresistible force. Without bothering to dress, she slipped a coat on over her negligee and covered her hair with a wide-brimmed hat.

It was early afternoon, so she assumed Nicholas was still at the Embassy. In the Berlin train the thought that she might have acted too hastily slowly dawned on her. She ought to have phoned him from Potsdam before buying a round-trip ticket. The fare and the cab rides would certainly cost her fifteen marks, all wasted if she failed to find him. She would have to ask Hans Günther for an advance on her November household allowance and give him an opportunity for a lecture. But wasn't squandering fifteen marks a small vice compared to the "abominations" he had been charged with in the Moabit courtroom?

After getting off the train in Berlin, she went to the Austro-Hungarian Embassy. To the receptionist in the lobby she gave her name as Fräulein Rethy. The brisk traffic of staff, visa applicants, petitioners and visitors surprised and disturbed her.

She was afraid of being recognized and regretted that she had come. She realized only now that the hem of her challis negligee peeked out from under her black fur coat and that she had forgotten to pin up her hair.

Then she saw Nicholas coming down the stairway and, as if by miracle, all the pressure lifted off her chest and she was able to breathe. She rose from the bench and crossed to meet him halfway.

"Alexa, what happened?" He saw she was trembling and took her in his arms, although he knew people were watching them.

"I must talk to you," she said through chattering teeth.

"All right, let's go." They started for the exit and were already in the street when he realized that he was without side arm, coat or shako.

"You'll catch your death," she said to him as a cold gust of wind hit them in the face. It was a woman's simple reaction to see a man without a warm coat in near freezing weather, but to him it sounded like an avowal of solicitude, even love. He felt neither the wind nor the cold, only rapturous, light-headed happiness.

"And fourteen days' house arrest on top," she added with a wry little smile.

"Never mind. It would be worth it," he said. He signaled to a cab parked a few meters away. They climbed in and he gave the driver his address. "You're with me and that's all that matters. It's been too long."

"We should've talked at the Embassy. Because that's what I came for. To talk. Nothing else but that."

He felt the euphoria leave him. "We'll talk and nothing else. Just as you wish."

She threw a worried glance at him. "Did I say the wrong thing?"

"You always do, but that's all right. I am used to it." She had bumped her head against the car door when they entered the cab and her hat dropped down over her eyes. He reached out, lifted it off and gently stroked her mussed hair. "What's bothering you?"

She pressed her face to his shoulder. "Oh, Nicky, I am so confused."

He knew that she was thinking of the trial. "Who wouldn't be."

They rode the rest of the way in silence. In the past she had always crossed the threshold of Burg Strasse 62 torn between desire and self-hatred, then traveled in the gilded cage of the elevator with fingers poised over the HALT button, ready to push it before reaching the second floor. Now Burg Strasse 62 was an asylum, a sanctuary where she hoped to find deliverance from a nightmare. She wanted to be told that Corporal Sommer's testimony had been a vicious lie and that Hans Günther never committed "abominations." She knew that Nicholas would tell her the truth; she had complete confidence in him, had always had without being aware of it. Up to now she had harbored a touch of hostility against him which prevented her from appreciating his tact, his patience, his worldly wisdom. It had eased her guilt to blame him for her cheating on Hans Günther. In the past she had considered him a menace to her marriage; what she sought from him now was its very preservation.

Despite her warm coat she was shivering. After they entered the flat and he had helped her to shed the coat, an amused smile flashed across Nicholas's face.

"I might be wrong, but this thing you're wearing looks like a nightgown to me."

She was on the brink of tears. "Not nightgown. Negligee. I was too upset to change."

He cradled her in his arms and she snuggled close to him, resting her head on his shoulder. The shivers left her and she felt warm and protected. The dimly lit drawing room with its large tile stove radiating mellow heat was like a safe port to the shipwrecked. The problem that had brought her here lost its pressing immediacy. She wished it could be kept stored away for a while, leaving the blissful silence undisturbed.

He released her and she reclined on the sofa. The touch of its silk upholstery fabric recalled to her mind the first afternoon of their affair. Now it seemed as if that interlude had happened ages ago and to someone else.

"What did you want to talk to me about?" he asked.

"You can guess, can't you?"

"The Moltke case?"

She nodded. "Corporal Sommer's testimony. It was in this morning's paper. That's how I found out about it." They had been talking Hungarian, now she switched to German. "What *is* a pederast?"

The question took him by surprise. He had slept with her without ever really knowing whether her sensuality indicated a lack or an abundance of previous experience. "Don't you know?"

"Would I ask if I did? Would I have come here if I did?"

She sounded convincing, yet it was hard to believe that a woman in her position could be so innocent. After all, it was the year 1907.

"It is a male who sexually desires males. According to our laws, intercourse between members of the same sex is considered a crime, but there are many societies in Africa and Asia where pederasty—homosexuality—is openly practiced. So it was in ancient Greece and Rome and—"

"But how— What—what do they do?"

He felt the blood surge to his face. Her naiveté embarrassed him. "My dear girl," he said, somewhat peeved, "the human body, male as well as female, has quite a few orifices." Realizing her incomprehension, he raised his voice. "For God's sake, use your imagination!"

She contemplated for a long moment. "I see." She nodded and made a wry face. "But why? I mean what makes them do such a thing? It's . . . it's ugly, filthy. Why?"

He was supposed to explain to the blind how the color red differed from the color blue. "It's instinct—preference. Some are born with the inclination; for others it's an acquired taste."

She was deep in thought. "Is that what Hans Günther did at the Hohenau parties? Doing it to another man?" she asked in a hollow tone.

"I don't know what he did. There are many facets—call them embellishments—to lovemaking between men and women. The same goes for two men. I can't tell you who did what to whom."

"My God," she muttered. She seemed to be smiling, which he didn't like. It was a strange, eerie grin. God, don't let her break down, he prayed. "Now look here." He tried to calm her. "You can't take every word that was said in the courtroom for gospel truth. You must understand the background of that case. It's not a simple libel suit, it's much more. Probably the future of Germany depends on the outcome of that trial. Forces more powerful than a general in disrepute and a cocky little journalist are fighting it out in that courtroom. Harden is only a straw man."

"But why did Sommer involve Hans Günther? Count Hohenau, Lynar, Moltke and Eulenburg I understand. The *Täglicher Rundschau* editorials say it was politics. But Hans Günther is no politician. Not even a general or an aide-de-camp to the emperor. Just an average officer. Not all that important."

Nicholas wished she would stop asking questions. She had come to him for the truth, but that was what he could not tell her. It would have been incompatible for the lover to tell on the husband.

"I don't know, Alexa."

"Nicky, you do get around. Tell me frankly, have you ever heard rumors that Hans Günther was ... whatever Corporal Sommer called him?" She had switched back to Hungarian. It was their own private language. For her it had the same intimacy a secret cave has for children playing hide and seek.

Nervously he rose, crossed to the stove, opened its lower door and stirred up the smoldering coals on the grate with a poker. "You are putting me in a very difficult position, Alexa. This city is full of rumors. Before, it used to be *So-and-so is sleeping with his best friend's wife*. Now, since the *Zukunft* attack and the scandal around Prince Friedrich Heinrich, it is *So-and-so is sleeping with his best friend*. No one is spared, not even Chancellor Bülow. He was forced to sue a yellow journalist named Brand who accused him of having an affair with his bureau chief, Councillor Scheefer. The case was tried a couple of weeks ago. Brand was found guilty and given a prison sentence. It was in all the papers. Haven't you read it?"

"I wasn't asking you about Bülow, Nicky."

He groaned. "Alexa, you must know how I feel about you. If I told you that, yes, I've heard some gossip, I'd be a heel. If I said no, one day you might reproach me for having misled you."

"So you have heard."

"About the entire Gardes du Corps. I'm telling you, it's a craze. A witch-hunt. Lynar and Hohenau were forced to resign from the army, and anyone who's ever shared a glass of wine with them is in disrepute."

"But I've met this Sommer. He seemed such a decent, polite young man. Had manners like an officer."

"Too bad he isn't an officer. Then he could be challenged to a duel, wounded or killed, and your husband's reputation could be restored. Counselor Bernstein knew why he produced witnesses solely from the ranks. Your husband could still shoot Sommer, but that would be common murder and, as such, against the law."

She looked at him, startled. "You're being cynical, Nicky."

"Sorry. At times, I can't help questioning the sanity of our world. If a poor soldier strikes an officer, that's ten years' hard labor. If I kill the same officer in a duel, that's two months' house arrest. In the worst case, barracks arrest. Justice. For instance, you'd have to have the faith of a St. Anthony of Padua in the basic goodness of men to believe that justice will be done in Moabit."

"You'd want Moltke acquitted?"

"What difference does it make whether he is or is not? I've told you, *he* isn't on trial. Neither is Lynar, Hohenau or your husband. They'll probably be ruined for life, but not because they are guilty."

Suddenly she looked daggers at him. "I wish you weren't so damned gallant. You won't give me a straight answer, because Hans Günther is my husband and it wouldn't be cricket if you told me he is a—" She jumped up and angrily paced the floor. "I can't say the bloody word! It's such a horrible—" She halted, glaring at him. "Isn't there anyone in this rotten world I can ask for an answer?"

Her furor failed to disturb him. He'd become used to her sudden fits of anger. "Yes, there is," he said calmly. "Hans Günther. He is the one to ask."

She suppressed an expletive and threw herself into an armchair. Her anger gone, she looked confused and scared, like a newly orphaned child. He was tempted to tell her the truth, which would keep her from returning to her husband. She was bewildered and lost enough to stay with him now, but later, when the fog cleared, she would probably accuse him of taking advantage of her moment of despondency. Besides, he wasn't completely sure of himself either. Seeing her broken and vulnerable, he was inclined to forget that her character had too many facets and all its facets weren't completely smooth. He wanted her more than any other woman in his life, which, he was afraid, included Beata. Her unpredictability attracted and at the same time repelled him, and he was still not certain which force was stronger.

"I must go," she said, but didn't move. He remained silent. After a while she rose. "I shouldn't have come. I hoped you would tell me what to do, but . . . ." She gave him a petulant look. "I always thought you were my friend."

He felt angry at her. "I am your friend and that's why I can't tell you what to do. It must be your decision. What I can tell you is this. You are young, you have your whole life before you. If your marriage is not happy, end it. *If,* I said. If. There is always a solution. There is—" He stopped. He wanted to say, *I love you and am ready to marry you,* but the words stuck in his throat. "Be sure and talk to your husband," he said instead. "You won't have your peace of mind unless you openly discuss it with him."

She put on her hat and tightened the belt of her negligee, hitching up its skirt so it wouldn't peek out from under her coat.

"Remember one thing," he told her. "Whatever you decide, you can always count on me."

He offered to drive her to Potsdam, but she only accepted a ride to the station. "Lately I've had such a strange feeling. I think I am being watched," she told him as they drove down Wilhelm Strasse. "Potsdam is a small nest, and everyone knows everyone else. There's a retired colonel who lives in the next block. He sits behind his closed windows and keeps his field glasses trained on the street. And the army wives! They're all over the place. You can't enter a shop without bumping into them. They're so friendly, although I know they don't regard me as one of their own."

"You're different."

"I don't want to be. It's so strange. Nicky, if I come to think of it, all my life I've been a round peg in a square hole. I never really belonged. Not since Sarkany. But of course there I was always mistaken for Beata. And when I told people I was Alexa, they were disappointed." She paused and remained silent for a while. "Now I am married, yet . . ." They were at the station, and she left the sentence unfinished.

"Don't get out," she told him. "At this hour the train is full of regimental wives on their way home after shopping in Berlin. I'm afraid that since Corporal Sommer's testimony I'm even more closely watched than before."

"When do I see you?"

The question startled her. "I don't know. Before this . . . this awful thing I honestly wanted to stay away from you. But now it's different. You are my friend, the only friend I have." She reached for his hand and gave it a gentle squeeze. "You've been most considerate today."

"I didn't rape you. Is that what you mean? Let me assure you, you may come to me any time. I won't touch you unless you want me to. And even then I must be pretty sure that you really do."

"I'll phone you."

She leaned over, lightly pecked him on the cheek, then opened the car door and slid out. He watched her scurry up the steps to the station building, more of her slim ankle showing under the fur coat than was considered proper. She was probably right when she felt herself resented by the regimental wives in Potsdam. Provincial Prussia preferred conformity, especially in women. He wondered how Vienna would react to her, the city that had never quite taken to her sister. It had misinterpreted Beata's shyness as lack of wit; and one year had been too short a time for her to cause the city to change its mind.

He realized that he was speculating on the reception Alexa would be accorded in Vienna. It had been years since he had indulged in daydreams, but now he conjured up the image of Alexa arriving at the station, riding through the Ring, receiving her first dinner guests in the high-ceilinged salon of the Karady palace.

Do I really wish to marry her? he asked himself. His motive for a *yes* was very simple: she was like Beata. For a *no* equally simple: she was not like Beata. Enclosed in Beata's body there was Alexa's restless, capricious spirit. His common sense warned him against her, the male animal in him yearned for her. It was a relief to know that the decision was not up to him but rested with Hans Günther von Godenhausen.

She had forgotten to take the front door key with her and had to enter through the kitchen, which opened off the back staircase.

"The major has been asking for you," Anna told her with a touch of reprimand. Although Hans Günther treated the servants with the aloofness of an Oriental despot, both Anna and Lotte were clearly infatuated with him. Arrogant and disrespectful to her, they cringed before him and fawned upon him. They reacted to his virile handsomeness like elephant cows to the top bull in the herd.

"Has the major been home long?" Alexa asked.

"At least two hours. He wondered where you'd gone, but we told him we didn't even know that you'd left the house."

The bedroom, with no separate access, had to be reached through the Herrenzimmer, a combination library, study and morning room with Hans Günther's hunting trophies decorating its walls. She found him seated there in a chair, stiff-backed, like a patient waiting to have his tooth pulled at the dentist's.

"Where the hell have you been?" he asked the moment she entered.

Surprised by the harsh tone, she froze. "Out."

"Out where?"

She didn't want him to notice that she was wearing a negligee. "I'll tell you. Just let me take my coat off." She started for the bedroom.

He rose and barred her way. "Will you answer me?"

She felt hot anger rise from the pit of her stomach. A surge of vomit tasting of coffee and bile filled her throat. She swallowed hard to keep herself from spewing it into his face. Feeling ill and faint, she tried to walk past him, but he reached out and grabbed her by the shoulder.

"I asked you a question."

His expression of righteous indignation infuriated her. She lost her self-control, and the question slipped out before she had time to weigh the consequences. "Are you a pederast?" Her tone had the irrevocability of a falling guillotine blade.

For a second he stared at her, his eyes unblinking. He seemed neither hurt nor angry. She had committed a tactical

143

error when she confronted him without a plan, without deciding what she wanted from him: a denial, an apology, a promise to reform or her freedom.

He opened his mouth as if wanting to answer, then turned away. "You'd better start packing," he said after a long pause. "I'm supposed to report to my new post by Monday."

"What new post?" she asked, confused.

"The First Army Corps in East Prussia. As a matter of fact, it's not so new. That's where I was stationed before Potsdam. Only at that time it was Königsberg, now it'll be Allenstein." When Alexa remained silent, he raised his voice. "Don't you understand? I've been transferred."

There had to be a connection between the transfer and the Sommer testimony, she decided. "I'm not going with you," she said.

He seemed taken aback. "You are not?" He stepped nearer to her. "Oh yes you are!"

"You can't force me!"

"I won't have to, because you'll come to your senses and do as you're told." His face flushed, he suddenly turned on her, shouting at the top of his voice. "You're my wife! You come with me no matter where I go. You damned well better!"

She stared at him, wondering what had prompted his outburst: male vanity, jealousy or anger over her rebellion. "What do you need me for? You don't love me!" Her eyes were filling with tears. His announcement of the transfer had taken her by surprise. It caused her to lose her equilibrium, the little self-command she'd had when she entered the room.

Exasperated, he threw up his hands. "Jesus Christ! Love! That's all you women jabber about. In case you don't know, there are things more important than love."

"Name one."

"Duty. Your duty to me and mine to you."

"Did you ever love me, Hans?"

"I married you, didn't I?"

"So you did. But why?"

"That's a damned fool question. If you haven't found out in four years you never will."

His voice sounded suddenly dull and emotionless. Only now did she notice the deep rings of fatigue under his eyes. Once again he was moving away from her to hide behind the invisible wall that rose between them whenever she attempted to have a husband-to-wife talk with him. She was determined to prevent him from escaping her.

"Hans, I've felt for quite some time that our marriage wasn't what it should have been. There's been something wrong. I'm begging you, tell me the truth. Are you . . . are you a — Whatever Corporal Sommer called you? Are you a— Oh, I can't say it."

He looked at her with the lifeless blind eyes of a statue. "You'll find out."

"When? How?"

"When my case comes before the Court of Honor."

"Why the Court of Honor?"

"You didn't think I'd have to answer the charges of a blackmailer in a civilian court, did you? In case you have forgotten, I'm a Prussian officer."

"Is Sommer a blackmailer? He was testifying under oath. In a courtroom. That can't be blackmail."

"Not exactly. It was vengeance. He wanted one thousand marks from me and I refused him. I hope that answers your question."

"It doesn't. What gave him the idea to ask money from you? He must've had some special reason."

"He likes money. Isn't that reason enough?"

"But why from you?"

"Because there is a conspiracy. Certain people are determined to undermine the reputation of the Gardes du Corps, His Majesty's own regiment. I refused to pay Corporal Sommer for keeping his mouth shut, so he found someone who paid him for not keeping his mouth shut."

"Not keeping his mouth shut about what? Was there something he learned about you—found out? Was there, Hans? Was there?"

He contemplated for a second, then crossed to the wall and pulled the bell cord.

"What do you want?" Alexa asked, surprised.

"I've had a hard day. I'm tired. I want to eat early and go to bed."

Lotte entered and the promptness of her appearance caused Alexa to wonder how near she had been to the door when the bell rang.

"Tell Anna we want to eat early tonight," Hans Günther said.

"How early, sir?"

"Now."

"I'm afraid Anna will need a little time. If the major had told her when he came home—"

He turned on her ferociously. "I said now! Must I hand in a petition to get fed in this bloody house? If supper isn't on the table in five minutes, you get the hell out. That goes for both of you."

Withering under the glare of his eyes, the blue of which glistened like tinted glass, Lotte bobbed an awkward curtsy. "Yes, sir, Major. Yes." She scurried from the room.

With her heavy coat still buttoned over her dress, Alexa felt rivulets of perspiration running down her back. Her chemise clung damp and hot to her body and the sour odor of her own sweat made her feel queasy.

She tried once more to elicit a satisfactory answer to her questions from Hans Günther. "You never told me you'd been to parties at Count Hohenau's house. Or to Lynar's."

He gave her a look of cold anger. "My wife siding with the blackmailers! Now get this through your head. I'll kill you before I let you go. I'll strangle you with my bare hands. And as to Corporal Sommer, the subject is closed. Don't you bring it up again, because—"

146

Seeing Lotte enter the adjacent dining room with a trayful of dishes, he halted.

"Don't set a place for me," Alexa told the maid. "I won't be eating supper."

Lotte made a face. "I wish you'd told me that before. I wouldn't have lugged in all this stuff." She threw a side glance at the major to see his reaction to her insolence. When he seemed to ignore it, she rambled on: "Honestly, a person doesn't know what's what in this house."

Too exhausted to reprimand her, Alexa dragged herself to the bedroom. It was a relief to throw off her clothes and rub her body dry with a towel. She dropped her perspiration-soaked underthings into the laundry hamper and sprayed herself from head to foot with eau de cologne. Stark naked, she pulled off the bedspread and slid under the eiderdown quilt. The crisp linen of the bedding felt cool and soothing against her skin. She shivered a little, more with unhappiness than with cold. What to do next? she wondered.

Lotte came in to turn down the beds. Ignoring the maid's grumble about the bedspread dropped on the floor, Alexa pretended to be asleep.

Lying in complete darkness, she could not tell how much time elapsed until she heard Hans Günther enter. He switched on his bedside lamp, then began to undress. Keeping her eyes closed, she followed every phase of the slow, methodical procedure: pockets emptied of their contents to the dressertop, tunic hung on the back of the straight chair, breeches clamped into their hanger, drawers and socks neatly folded on the chair, boot trees slipped into boots and boots placed outside the door for Thadeus to polish in the morning.

Next on the agenda should have been the narcissistic reverence in front of the mirror, but tonight it was being skipped. Her heart stopped as she heard him approach her bed. The thought that he might strangle her flashed through her mind. She was not alarmed. On the contrary, she felt

147

strangely elated. Anything was better than his dispassionate indifference. If she could rouse him to violence, it would prove that she still mattered to him.

She lay motionless, her face buried in the pillow. He lifted her comforter and slid under it. A quiver ran through her as she felt his naked body pressing to hers. His arms encircled her; his lips, hot and dry, traveled from her face down her neck and breasts; his legs gripped hers like a vise. At first she was too surprised to realize that it was not anger but desire that had brought him to her bed. It had been a long time since they'd made love, and even then he had been drinking and performed the act with the detachment of a person playing solitaire. Now he seemed to be on fire.

"You won't leave me, will you?" he whispered to her. "Promise you won't. Say it. I want to hear you say it."

There was an urgency to his tone, a humility he had never before displayed. His caresses became bolder and more insistent, as if this time he wanted to make certain that she was not merely acquiescent but deeply aroused. He was making love to her the way she had always hoped he would. Still she was much too surprised and confused to react to his eagerness. She lay shivering in his arms with the Sommer testimony buzzing in her head.

"Swear that you won't leave me!" he urged her. "Swear on the memory of your mother. On your immortal soul. Swear that you won't ever sleep with another man, that you'll never belong to anyone but me. Alexa, I want you. I need you. I can't live without you. Don't ever leave me, Alexa. I'll kill myself if you do."

Slowly his wild, insane babble melted the ice that encrusted her senses. She succumbed to the frantic note of desperation in his voice. There was a hint of terror in his passion, and he was clinging to her like a shipwreck victim clinging to a lifebelt. The realization that he was capable of such tempestuous emotions astounded her. In the back of her mind there lingered the suspicion that suddenly he would withdraw from her and tell her in his clipped, sarcastic way that the fireworks had been a game to prove how easily she could be fooled.

Despite her mental reservations she was much too hungry for tenderness not to respond to him. Besides, she loved him. The only man she ever had. What was happening to her now was the fulfillment of a wish she had made at sixteen, probably even before that, when she had first glimpsed his photograph in the family album. No longer holding back, she gave in to the wave of mad joy that suddenly surged through her whole body. For the first time in years he was able fully to satisfy her.

Later she tried to remember what she had answered to his pleading. She must have said what he wanted to hear, for it was with a new contentment that he kissed her goodnight and returned to his bed.

During the rest of the week they were busy with preparations for their move to Allenstein. Hans Günther behaved as though the question of her leaving him had never come up between them. Neither did he talk of Sommer and the rest. He remained considerate and affectionate and did his best to take the burden of packing off her shoulders. At times, when things would bog down, he would still display bursts of impatience and annoyance, but never against her. They had long talks and he admitted that he had often failed in his duties as a husband. Allenstein was a demotion, but he was not unhappy about the transfer, because both he and Alexa needed a change. The proximity of the court had added excitement and color to their life in Potsdam, but it also kept them from seeing things in their proper perspective. The time had come for them to have children. To wait longer would serve no purpose. He was against large families; in his view two boys would be ideal. Of course, one had no choice. A boy and a girl, even two girls would be fine, provided they would inherit their mother's beauty.

She agreed to all his preferences, whether they concerned the number and sex of their future children or the pieces of furniture to be discarded or shipped to Allenstein. He no longer hid the morning paper from her, and she was able to follow the Moltke-Harden case up to the verdict. As neither Corporal Sommer nor the other soldier witnesses were recalled to the stand, the Godenhausen name was not mentioned again. Anyway, Alexa decided to accept Hans Günther's explanation of the Sommer testimony and ascribe it to an unsuccessful blackmail attempt.

Hans Günther insisted that she leave most of the arrangements for the dissolution of the household to her aunt Rose and—instead of joining him later—accompany him to Allenstein. They were to stay in a hotel until they found a suitable flat or house for rent. In a way, she was flattered by his decision. He seemed to be clinging to her as if her physical presence meant shelter and security to him.

They paid the obligatory farewell visits to his regimental superiors. Most were new men, freshly promoted to take the places of officers discredited by the Lynar-Hohenau scandal. Whenever it was possible, Hans Günther timed their calls so that those they visited would not be home, and they could drop their card without having to endure ten awkward minutes of forced pleasantries. A transfer from Potsdam's most prestigious regiment to East Prussia was almost as bad as a dishonorable discharge, and Alexa knew that the days prior to their departure were sheer torture for Hans Günther.

He made it clear to friends that he wanted no hearty sendoffs, no crowd of well-wishers on the platform, no handkerchiefs waved after his train. After their luggage was dispatched ahead of time, he and Alexa took a taxi to the station and, carrying a small suitcase each, slipped away with as little fuss as if they were escaping the law.

Up to the last minute, she hoped for some privacy, so she could mail a farewell note to Nicholas, but time ran out and she left without writing him. Unable to rid herself of a nagging guilt feeling, she kept thinking of him throughout the long journey and later too during the weeks of finding her place in the new and alien environment.

As the days dragged on in Allenstein, it seemed increasingly difficult for her to find words that could serve as explanation and apology; and she finally gave up composing letters she knew she would never mail.

Up to the fourth day of the trial, the testimony of his ex-wife was the only incriminating statement against General von Moltke, but even this could be dismissed as a "wronged woman's" vengeance. The turn in Moltke's disfavor occurred when his attorney called Dr. Magnus Hirschfeld, world-famous authority on sexology, to the witness stand. An ardent crusader against laws that made homosexuality a criminal offense, he was supposed to support the plaintiff's case. Instead he dealt a shattering blow to it by delivering a long statement in which he characterized Moltke as a man of undeniable homosexual leanings, unable to satisfy a healthy and normal woman. After this disastrous pronouncement it helped little that he carefully explained the difference between latent and practicing homosexuals. To the best of his knowledge, Moltke belonged to the former group, he stated.

Counselor von Gordon attempted to correct the damage by having a second expert, a certain Dr. Merzbach, testify for the general; but Bernstein succeeded in forcing the judge to disallow the witness's cross-examination.

By the end of the morning session a large crowd had assembled in front of the courthouse. When Harden stepped from the building, eager hands reached out to embrace him, and for a moment he seemed in danger of being lifted off his feet and carried in a triumphant march to the Weinstube around the corner where he usually took his midday meal. It was with some difficulty that he managed to free himself and remain ambulatory.

At the opening of the afternoon session, Gordon appealed

to the judge to have some female witnesses called who were to attest to the affection ladies of the highest society had for Moltke. On grounds of irrelevancy, the judge rejected Gordon's plea and instructed both attorneys to deliver their summations.

Gordon spoke first. He pointed out that Harden had based his slanderous allegations on guilt by association, which, however, no law could accept for evidence. What his friends had done in the intimacy of their bedrooms had been as much of a secret to the general as it had been to the emperor, who up until their fall from grace had honored both Hohenau and Lynar with his personal friendship.

The mention of the emperor had an electrifying effect on the courtroom. The rustle of fans, shuffle of feet and purr of hushed voices continued in defiance of the judge's gavel long after Counselor von Gordon had resumed his seat.

His weasel face flushed with righteous indignation, Counselor Bernstein rose to address the court in behalf of the defendant.

He talked a full hour. Calling Prince Eulenburg the emperor's eminence grise, he warned the nation against being led into perdition by a clique of homosexuals. Their cabal had to be exposed and crushed. The depravity of the prince's circle had been no secret to the world, otherwise pederasty would not be called "le vice Allemand" by foreigners, he said.

Throughout the tirade the plaintiff sat in frozen silence, an expression of helpless bewilderment on his face. After each one of Bernstein's vocal exclamation marks his glance wandered to the three seemingly deaf and dumb individuals who composed the tribunal. He searched for a sign of protest or disapproval on their faces; finding none, he closed his eyes, as though trying to hide from the horrors of reality behind the screen of his lowered lids. Counselor von Gordon made a few unsuccessful attempts to stem the flow of slop from Bernstein's mouth. His objections overruled, he slumped down as if his bones had turned to rubber. To all appearances, he had conceded defeat.

Visibly exhausted by his physical as well as mental calisthenics, Bernstein resumed his seat beside the beaming Harden. In complete silence the plaintiff and his attorney collected their papers and made their slow, listless exit. The realization that he was a ruined man was written all over Moltke's face.

The court recessed. On the following morning, to no one's surprise, and that included the broken Moltke, Harden was acquitted. The verdict drew loud cheers from most spectators, a few angry noes and stony silence from the rest.

His face deathly pale, his eyes glassy, General von Moltke sat like a figure in a wax museum. From the street came the noise of a loud and triumphant demonstration for the hero Harden, who single-handedly had saved the country from the rule of an unholy camarilla.

Except for a few cheaply sensational publications, the German press refused to share the mob's high glee. All respectable newspapers called the Moltke-Harden trial a travesty of justice.

Combing the daily press, Nicholas was impressed with the sober tone of the editorials. They shared a deep indignation over the tribunal's obvious intent to have Moltke discredited by allowing testimonies that had no bearing upon the case. The fact that orgies had taken place with the participation of men belonging to the emperor's entourage was shocking, but so was the judge's permissiveness when he tolerated intrusions upon innocent people's personal privacy.

Through the Embassy grapevine, Nicholas learned about a coded telegram Chancellor Bülow had sent to the emperor the day before the verdict was announced. He thought that the airing of the Gardes du Corps scandals in an open court would be a serious mistake. To placate public opinion, he advised the military authorities to make an example of every man involved, no matter how remotely, in the case.

Reverberations of the verdict were felt in cafes, ministries, stock exchanges and embassies all over Europe. The Austro-Hungarian Embassy on Alsen Strasse was no exception. The entire building was pervaded by a Mardi Gras gaiety over the humiliating blow suffered by the Kaiser's own regiment. "Schadenfreude" was the proper word for it, practically untranslatable. Although other races, among them the Anglo-Saxons, experienced the emotion also, they were too hypocritically proper to coin a word for such an ungentlemanly feeling as gloating over a fellow man's disgrace.

It was pure unadulterated Schadenfreude that induced Second Secretary Schiessler to send an Embassy footman for a magnum of champagne and to invite Nicholas and a few others to his office for an impromptu celebration. The Prussians had made no secret of their belief that they considered themselves militarily superior to the Austrians. Now the tables were turned.

"Hell, if someone had told me a year ago that the commandant of the Gardes buggered privates, I would've laughed into his face. Officers maybe, but not men from the ranks," Schiessler crowed.

Count Victor Novakov, a young Czech on the military attaché's staff, came to the defense of Prussia. "Class distinction stops at the bedroom door, my friend. Remember our Archduke Ludwig Victor. He carried on with an attendant at the public baths. A civilian. Even worse."

"Have you seen the London *Times?*" Schiessler asked. "It gave a whole column to the Harden verdict. A fine prelude to the Kaiser's state visit next month."

"It might be off. At least that's the rumor," Novakov said. His sister, married to one of the crown prince's house marshals, was a constant source of information on the imperial family's private life. As with all intelligence, her reports were promptly forwarded in locked diplomatic pouches to the Monarchy's Foreign Office in Vienna.

"I wouldn't be surprised if the visit were canceled," Schiessler said. "Old Willy kept shooting off his mouth about King Edward's affair with Mrs. Keppler. A woman. Now *his* name is linked with a pederast's. Damned embarrassing."

Schiessler's remark annoyed Nicholas. "I wouldn't call Philipp Eulenburg that."

Schiessler grinned. "Nicky, where there is smoke there is fire. Incidentally, have you heard that your friend Godenhausen was sent to Siberia?"

The name caught Nicholas off his guard. "What do you mean, to Siberia?" He hoped no one had noticed the nervous tremor in his voice.

"East Prussia. A nest called Allenstein. Just as bad as Siberia. Poor bastard. Another victim of the October twenty-ninth carnage. There will be more victims. The entire First Cavalry of the Gardes is suspect. Including the horses. There's been a deluge of transfers. Regardless of background, connection, service record. No such housecleaning since Hercules swept out the Augean stables."

Ever since Alexa had come to him that afternoon to ask about the trial, Nicholas had lived in a state of suspended animation, waiting to hear from her. She had asked him for advice and he gave her none.

Nicholas glanced at the clock on Schiessler's desk. It showed ten to five. The thought that Alexa might be at his flat flashed through his mind. If Godenhausen was really transferred to East Prussia, she might not want to go with her husband. Not after the Sommer testimony.

He rose. "I'm afraid I'll have to run. Thank you for the wine, Hannes."

Out of the room, he heaved a sigh of relief. The name Eulenburg was beginning to grate on his nerves. He also found his countrymen's gloating over the disgrace of the Gardes in bad taste. The Germans were their sole allies—one never counted the mercurial Italians—and if it came to war, he and Schiessler and the rest would fight and die on the same battlefields with them.

Alexa was not at his flat, nor was there any message from her. He knew that once she had left she would be lost to him for months, years, probably forever. The thought benumbed him. The realization that at the age of thirty-six he was in love—romantically, carnally, boyishly, hare-brainedly in love —with a woman who didn't care a damned bit about him elicited a bitter chuckle from him. He cranked up the phone and had Central connect him with Hans Günther's regimental command post in Potsdam.

"May I speak to Major von Godenhausen?" he asked the man at the other end of the wire.

"I'm afraid the major cannot be reached at the post" was the switchboard operator's terse reply. He refused to tell whether the major was still in town and suggested that Nicholas call again in the morning.

If Godenhausen had received the transfer order days earlier, he might already have left for his new post, with or without Alexa. The army could be merciless when meting out punishment. On occasions a family would be given a twenty-four-hour notice to pull up stakes, regardless of what accommodations, if any, were available at the new post.

What choices did he have, Nicholas wondered, if Alexa *had* gone to East Prussia with her husband? Follow her to Allenstein? Then what? His sole chance was to catch her if she was still in Potsdam. He had to talk to her, at least find out where she was.

In Prussian military circles visiting hours were as strictly defined as in prisons and hospitals. Even if he started immediately for Potsdam, he would not reach the city before seven, too late for a social call, even from an ex-brother-in-law. He had no choice but to wait until the morning.

A chance meeting on Wilhelm Strasse with an officer of

Hans Günther's unit saved him the unnecessary drive to Potsdam. The captain, one of the few spared in the great housecleaning, was the Godenhausens' neighbor and had seen them leave for the station the day before. He also knew that the supervision of the packing and moving had been left to Frau von Sedlitz, Alexa's aunt.

It was from Rose that Nicholas received the final, crushing word. When he telephoned her, Rose first said that her niece and Hans Günther had taken a short vacation in the mountains, then, pressed by Nicholas, admitted that her nephew had indeed been transferred to Allenstein. Quite naturally Alexa was with him.

"They're not gone for good, though," she said. "Sooner or later Hans Günther will be exonerated. I could strangle that Jew Bernstein with my bare hands—and Harden. I wouldn't be surprised if it turned out that Harden is a spy, hired by France or England to discredit the Prussian army. Believe me, Count Karady, what this country needs is a Siberia for troublemakers like Harden. The Czar is smart; he knows how to handle revolutionaries. Not like our Kaiser. He's much too kind, too tolerant. He pays too much attention to the Reichstag, an assembly of cutthroats. There is—"

Nicholas unceremoniously cut her short and hung up. What he felt was no pain, only emptiness. The same vacuity that had benumbed him in the library of the Sarkany castle after he had descended from Beata's gutted room to share a glass of Törköly with old Rethy.

The realization that he was responding with the same despondency to the loss of a live woman as he had to Beata's death dismayed him. There had to be more to a man's life than chasing a ghost. His love for Alexa had taken on the aspects of drug addiction. To be with her was a shot of morphine. It was only during the short hours they spent together that he felt alive; the rest of the time he was dead.

Were it morphine and not a woman, he would be man enough to submit himself to a withdrawal cure. Was addiction to a woman a more lethal habit than dependency upon a drug? Wasn't there a cure for it too?

First a change of scenery. Physically, Alexa was five hundred kilometers or a ten-hour train ride away, yet in spirit she was still very much present. The repercussions of the Moltke trial still intrigued people, and the Godenhausen name kept popping up in conversations. He had to get out of Berlin, go someplace where the name was not a household word.

With sudden decision, he rose and crossed to the military attaché's office. Luckily he caught the general between appointments and was immediately received. He asked for and was granted a four-week leave of absence. On the same day he wrote his mother that he was coming home on a visit.

PART TWO

7

The journey from Berlin by way of Thorn, where they changed trains, took ten hours, including the wait for their connection. They traveled through a landscape that even in July would have seemed bleak. Now, with its denuded trees, mud, ice and stagnant waters, it looked as foreign and forbidding as the face of the moon.

Hans Günther dozed almost throughout the journey. Dead tired, but seemingly at peace with himself, he acted like someone who had been through an excruciating experience and was glad to have survived it, no matter in what condition. He treated Alexa with a new tenderness, as if she were a child entrusted to his guardianship.

She tried to discuss the future with him. Would they rent a house or a flat in Allenstein; was the First Army Corps an important enough post to satisfy him, or would he try for a transfer back to Brandenburg? His answers were lame and evasive. Seven years before, while stationed in Königsberg, he had been to most of the small towns of the region, among them Allenstein, but he did not remember them clearly. As to the duration of his new tour, in the army anything was possible.

Allenstein was not quite as bad as she had feared. It was

situated on the River Alle. Its medieval castle, once a bishop's seat, and its narrow winding streets straight out of a Grimm fairy tale gave it an ingratiating charm. The houses around the castle looked as though they were made of gingerbread. One could hardly dislike a town that appeared to be edible.

They stopped at the Reichshof, an inn masquerading as a hotel. Their first meal was atrocious—tough meat, thick soup, mushy vegetables, glutinous pudding. Their room had the same quaint charm as the whole city. Waxed oak floor, hand-loomed curtains, wardrobes, chests, four-poster bed, all looked as immovable and indestructible as the Castle of the Teutonic Knights. Unfortunately the same was true of the mattress. It slanted toward the middle, and the moment they fell asleep they invariably rolled into the deep valley running through its center. There they lay, pressed against each other by the force of gravity.

Their first days were taken up by house hunting and obligatory calls on fellow officers at Hans Günther's command post. The memory of similar visits they had paid as newly-weds in Potsdam was still very vivid in Alexa's mind, and she detected a discouraging difference between the receptions they had been awarded then and were given now. From the regimental commandant down to subalterns, the men displayed uneasiness, suspicion, a wait-and-see attitude, treating Hans Günther the way a concierge treats a hotel guest registering without luggage. Their reactions to her seemed even more disconcerting, a mixture of doubt and surprise. One of the dim-witted wives let it slip out that the garrison had expected her to be plain and past her bloom.

Hans Günther weathered his first difficult weeks with an equanimity that amazed Alexa. He revealed so little concern over the coolness of their reception that Alexa sometimes wondered whether he had noticed it at all. Her heart ached for him, because she knew he would always remain a misfit in Allenstein, even without the cloud of scandal hovering over him. His easy manners, his sophistication, assets in Potsdam, were liabilities here.

Later she was to recall these first weeks in East Prussia as probably the pleasantest period of their marriage. Hans Günther spent every moment of his off-duty time with her. In the afternoons, after leaving the barracks, he would meet her at the Confiserie Colbert for coffee and cake; and on Sundays, weather permitting, he would take long horseback rides over the countryside with her. They went to plays presented by touring companies and to concerts in the auditorium of the Konversationshaus. He seemed to be clinging to her with the insistence of a medieval knight clinging to his shield in combat. People noticed his devotion and commented on it. Frau Notze, the owner of the Reichshof, spread the word that the Godenhausens were the most loving couple ever to stop in her hotel.

Acceptance by the military community was not immediate. For a while they were left to themselves, then slowly, very slowly, they began to receive invitations—to a tea, occasionally to a dinner, and finally to an at-home afternoon at the regimental commandant's. The frost, as though warmed by an unseasonal heat wave, was melting around them. That they were the best-looking and best-mannered couple in town might have had something to do with it. Their appearance invariably caused a flutter at parties and in restaurants. Prim regimental wives tingled with ill-concealed excitement when their hands were kissed by Hans Günther, and Alexa's presence seemed to rejuvenate the men.

By the first week of December they had found a house. Situated on Parade Platz, a wide square with a fountain in the center and planted with now bare trees and shrubbery, it was two-storied and glumly impressive. What caused Hans Günther to choose it was its old-fashioned grandeur and low rent. A high stone wall enclosed its two acres of grounds, and it had a coach house and stable in back of the main building.

Alexa disliked it from the very first. She found it too big and was afraid that heating it would be a problem. Later she was proved right, because not once during their tenancy, not even in June, could she feel pleasantly warm within its fortress-like walls.

"It feels positively haunted," Alexa said. She was making her first thorough inspection of the house. "And the smell. We won't ever air it out."

"What smell?"

"The smell of death. It's coming out of the walls."

"Don't be absurd. We won't find anything better."

"A flat would have done for us."

"Not for me."

"It's too pretentious. It would be too grand even for Potsdam, but this is Allenstein."

"Because it *is* Allenstein. We'll spend more time at home than in Potsdam. I hate to be cramped. Small rooms give me claustrophobia. I need space. Existing in one miserable room at the Reichshof has been driving me mad."

She looked at him, hurt. "I've found it very cozy."

"There are people who could find a prison cell cozy. I can't."

Tears surged to her eyes and she quickly walked away to hide them from him. The more she saw of the house the more it depressed her.

It had an entrance hall spacious enough for a hotel lobby. A ballroom, which they agreed to close off and leave unfurnished, opened to the right, the future salon to the left. Three somewhat smaller rooms—one was to be Hans Günther's study—opened off a hallway leading to the service wing of the building, which contained kitchen, larders, laundry and servants' quarters and had an exit to the back yard. The upper floor had only one large room, a bathroom, lavatory and storage space. The rest was attic.

"I'll feel lost in this house," she sighed.

164

"You won't once we get settled. We'll make it very elegant. Impress the peasants. I'm planning to entertain more than we did in Potsdam. In six months' time I want to have the entire First Army Corps command flocking to our parties. Including General von Hammann. Nothing but the best. That's how you play this game. Have the right friends."

"Like General von Moltke and Prince Eulenburg?" Alexa asked, then immediately regretted she had.

Hans Günther turned red in the face and nervously fingered his collar. "That was uncalled for, Alexa."

The business of getting settled in a strange city kept her busy and left her no time for brooding. Neither Anna nor Lotte had been willing to accompany them to a dreary East Prussia teeming with Poles and Jews. The prospect of hiring a new staff terrified Alexa. Luckily, Frau Notze of the Reichshof found her a German housekeeper, a Fräulein Anni Busse, daughter of a retired infantry captain, and two Polish maids, Bona and Svetlana, who had worked for army families before. The stableboy, Jerzy, took care of the garden and the two saddle horses Hans Günther had bought in Königsberg. His orderly, Dragoon Jan Dmowski, completed the household.

It was quite an establishment and Alexa let Anni Busse, a spinster of uncertain age who looked like the image of Germania as reproduced on drinking mugs and patriotic posters, run it. She had flaxen-blond hair, except at the roots, where it grew out telltale brown, and she treated ethnics such as Poles, Russians, Jews and—Alexa was afraid—Hungarians with the hauteur of a Valkyrie. She could work maids and laundresses to exhaustion and squeeze formidable deals out of the Jewish tradesmen who supplied the house with coal, firewood, imported liquor, real and fake antiques. She was supposed to have driven a certain Lebowitz, the house Jew of her former employer, into emigrating to the United States. Alexa suspected that she accepted bribes from tradesmen but decided to shut her eyes to it, as she did to the vanishing bottles of wine, padded grocery bills and the nightly visits of a cavalry sergeant to Anni's bedroom.

Their furniture arrived on the tenth of December, and they were more or less settled by Christmas. Through the agency of a red-bearded young man named Finkelstein, who had out-maneuvered his coreligionists in Anni Busse's good graces, Hans Günther bought paintings, Persian rugs, tables and settees to supplement their own furniture. Hans Günther had impeccable taste, and whatever he chose fitted in beautifully; nevertheless, to Alexa's eyes, 14 Parade Platz continued to look like the House of Usher. In Potsdam she had felt rather like a permanent guest, never like the mistress of the house. Here she was a transient, mentally prepared to move on at a moment's notice.

Despite her unsettling moods, she enjoyed Christmas of 1907 more than any past holiday during her marriage. Hans Günther was in exceptionally high spirits. The foggy gray that had dulled the blue of his eyes since the Sommer testimony seemed to have lifted, and he more than ever resembled the photo of the young cadet in the Sedlitzes' family album she had fallen in love with. His spell of lightheartedness coincided with the court decision in Berlin that exonerated General von Moltke.

As a result of unanimously condemnatory press notices and the changed attitude of the public, General von Moltke's appeal against the verdict of the Moabit tribunal had been shifted from the civil to the criminal court, where the crown's case was pleaded by the attorney general.

The trial opened on December 16, 1907. This time Moltke had the eminent Counselor Sello representing him instead of the easily demoralized Gordon. Sello proved to be Bernstein's equal. To begin with, he succeeded in persuading the bench to exclude the public, then he had Prince Eulenburg take the witness stand in behalf of the general. Testifying under oath,

166

Eulenburg denied ever having had any sentiment other than friendship for Moltke. Illness and pain had etched his face with deep lines, yet his voice was clear and firm when he declared that he never had committed such abominations as were attributed to him by Maximilian Harden.

In the entire courtroom Counselor Bernstein alone seemed unimpressed with the dignity and sincerity of the witness.

"I fully believe Your Excellency's statement," he addressed the prince. "However, Paragraph 175 of the State Penal Code refers only to a very limited field of homosexual activities. We all know that a variety of intimacies can be indulged by deviates—"

Outraged, the prince cut him short. "I never engaged in any such filth!" he shouted.

On January 3, 1908, the court honored Attorney General Isenbiel's recommendation, found Maximilian Harden guilty of libel and sentenced him to four months in prison.

Allenstein reacted as though Hans Günther and not Moltke had been the winner of the libel suit. Regimental couples who had been the coolest before were now the most anxious to let him know how happy they were about the turn. Alexa learned —not from Hans Günther but from Anni Busse, who seemed to be the depository of all local news—that the Military Court of Honor proceedings against her husband had been quashed by imperial order.

Only now that the danger had passed did she find out how serious the charges had been. She felt relieved and at the same time hurt. Why did he hide his distress from her? Didn't he know that she would stand by him if he confided in her?

During the past months the possibility of his guilt had kept flashing through her mind. As time went by, the thought of a man making love to another man had lost its sickening, execrable connotations to her. Since Nicholas had told her that such practices were common in many parts of the world, she looked up references to them in books and newspapers. Some of her reading material treated them not as depravities but as weaknesses of the flesh. Had Hans Günther confessed to her, she would have found excuses for him. Bad company, drunkenness, curiosity. After reading a book on life in nineteenth-century Egypt, she suddenly recalled the whisperings concerning Hans Günther's mysterious uncle who had become rich in the service of a Mohammedan potentate who ruled a pashalik.

At the time, she had often wondered why the Sedlitzes reacted to any mention of the man's name as if he had been a criminal, or at least a source of great embarrassment to the family. Hans Günther seemed to share their attitude by keeping silent about the year he had spent under the uncle's roof and their subsequent travels together. There must have been a close tie between them, though, as proven by the generous trust fund the uncle settled on him. Once or twice Alexa ventured to ask Hans Günther about the places they had visited, but he parried the questioning by saying that he had been too young to remember, and quickly changed the subject. Now she wondered if it had been the uncle and his circle who had initiated him into the fraternity, in which case he had really been the helpless victim of an evil man's lust and not a deviate by inclination.

She was willing, in truth rather anxious, to blame the defects of his character on this youthful experience. Capricious, restless and driven by ambition, he was also burdened with a self-destructive urge, a sign of mental instability.

From what little she knew of his past, she gathered that whenever he had taken a long step forward he soon took a step back. Now once again he was forging ahead. The future looked rosy. Good God, she prayed silently, make him learn from his errors, keep him out of trouble, lead him not into temptation, whatever kind it might be.

The costume ball given by Divisional Commandant General von Hammann was held on the twentieth of January, seven-

teen days after the Moltke verdict. As a final sign of acceptance, the Godenhausens received an invitation.

Königsberg was not Potsdam and the divisional commandant's ball was a very modest affair compared to the galas at
the New Palace, but for the officers of the First Army Corps
and their ladies it was the high point of the year. For Alexa
and Hans Günther, it meant a meeting with their destiny in
the person of First Lieutenant Otto von Ranke, an artillery-
man stationed in Allenstein.

Lieutenant von Ranke was twenty-seven, single, a dreamer,
a daredevil, an intellectual, a mama's boy or a fool, depending
on whose word one believed. He had few close friends among
the younger set, or any set for that matter. A passionate horseman, he spent his off-duty hours taking long lonely rides over
the countryside. He drank with moderation and—aside from
an occasional visit to a luxury-class bordello in Königsberg,
where he was always serviced by the same flat-chested blonde
—showed little interest in women. He belonged to that legion
of faceless shadows who aroused people's curiosity only if
they committed a crime, became the victims of a crime or
won a million in the state lottery. It so happened that he *had*
committed a crime, a mortal sin in the Biblical sense of the
word, though more an act of bravery in the eyes of his judges,
the Military Court of Honor. In 1904, when stationed in
Bernstadt, a small garrison in Silesia, he had killed a fellow
officer in a duel.

Alexa danced with him twice that night. She danced with
at least twenty other men, and several days later when she
received a bouquet of roses from him she was unable to recall
the face to go with the accompanying card.

Long-stemmed and exquisite, the roses were the kind seldom available even in Berlin during the winter. Alexa was
delighted with them, mainly because they proved to Hans
Günther that men still found her attractive.

"Do you have any idea what this Lieutenant von Ranke

looks like?" she asked him. "I found his name on my carnet de bal, so I must have danced with him. I still don't know why the roses."

Hans Günther threw a taunting look at her. "He seems in a hurry to stake out his claim. First come, first served, you know."

"What do you mean?" She wasn't sure she had heard right.

"I'd look him over if I were you. He might qualify as a successor to our friend Karady. At least he isn't Jewish."

She stared at him, stricken. "You don't— How can you?" Her throat constricted and she was unable to continue. Their eyes met, his spelling malice, hers brimming over.

"For Christ's sake, be discreet. This is a small town, so beware! Besides, Ranke is supposed to be a bit peculiar—a man who shot his best friend dead. Of course, it happened in a duel . . ."

For a second she lost all sense of reality. It wasn't Hans Günther she was facing but a stranger. Perhaps not a complete stranger, because she had had a few encounters with this side of him in the past. In Baden-Baden, when he wrenched that silly hat off her head, and time and again in Potsdam too, when his eyes threw darts of pique at her for no conceivable reason.

She regained her voice. "Be discreet? Beware? About what? Hans, I don't know what you mean."

His lips twisted into a wry grin. "Nothing. I was joking. It's just that a man with Ranke's reputation has a kind of a morbid attraction for some women."

"I am not 'some woman.' I love you, Hans. I never loved anyone but you."

"I was joking." He patted her lightly on the shoulder.

"What made you bring up Karady?"

"No reason."

"Now you've clammed up again. You do it all the time— keep moving away from me." She closed her eyes to escape his amused glance.

170

"I haven't moved."

"Yet you can't be reached. It gives me such a terrible feeling of loneliness. Please don't do it to me. I need you so. I need to know what you think, that you still love me, still care." She halted because she heard him turn. She opened her eyes and saw him crossing to the door. "Hans!" she called after him, but he ignored her and walked out.

For days afterward there was a tension between them that she could not explain. Since their moving into the house they no longer met at the Confiserie Colbert for coffee in the afternoon. As she slept late and he breakfasted at six in the morning before leaving for the barracks, she saw him only at midday and in the evening. He began to bring work home from headquarters. It was a treatise on the advantages of light cavalry over bicycle units in reconnoitering enemy terrain. He told her that he undertook the task in the hope that it might secure him an appointment to the General Staff. It was a chance to leave field service and give a new impetus to his flagging career.

Arriving home, he would invariably lock himself in the study, emerging only for meals, which they took in the company of Anni Busse. In the evenings they spent at home he would work after supper too. By the time he went upstairs, Alexa had often tired of waiting for him and had fallen asleep. She began to suspect that he was intentionally avoiding being alone with her.

About a week later at the dinner table he unexpectedly brought up the subject of the bouquet. "Have you thanked Lieutenant von Ranke for the roses?"

Caught unprepared by the question, she let the fork slip from her fingers. It fell to the floor. "No. Should I have?"

He gave her a reprimanding look. "Most certainly." Svetlana had crawled under the table to retrieve the fork. "It's there, behind the chair leg," he said to her. She found the fork and handed it to Alexa.

"Don't!" Fräulein Busse shrieked at her. "Fetch a clean fork from the kitchen." She heaved an exasperated sigh. "Dumb Poles. They'll never learn."

Alexa was grateful for the interlude with the fork. It gave her time to collect herself. "Thank him how? I told you I can't remember what he looks like."

"Write him a note. Manners, my dear, manners."

All ears, Anni Busse pretended to concentrate on her meat.

"I don't have his address," Alexa said.

"I'll give it to you." He turned to the housekeeper. "Fräulein Anni, remind my wife to write that note."

This was a new routine. As though trying to isolate himself even more, reprimands, instructions and suggestions were no longer given directly to Alexa, but conveyed through Anni. It was from her that Alexa learned that they were going to give a supper party for General von Hammann and his wife. When she was handed the guest list she found Lieutenant von Ranke's name on it. She was offered no chance to strike it out, as the invitations had already been mailed.

Ranke dropped his card at the house the day before the party but made no attempt to be received by her. Later, meeting him face to face, she recognized him as one of the young men she had danced with at the Hammanns' ball. Now she even recalled his costume—turban, embroidered vest over a white shirt, voluminous Bosnian pants. He had been a Janizary, though to her he had looked more like a eunuch. Certainly not like a man who had killed his best friend in a duel.

Now in his artillery lieutenant's dress uniform he looked virile and ordinary. What set him apart from his fellow officers was the unconcealed dreamy admiration lighting up his eyes each time he looked at her. Her beauty, youth and elegance had not gone unnoticed by the men of the command post, even the enlisted men, but none appeared so completely mesmerized as Otto von Ranke. As hostess, she had to observe protocol and ignore the eagerness with which he tried to capture her

172

attention. He went as far as cutting in on the general when he danced with her.

"I can't help it. I adore you," he whispered when she reprimanded him.

Men had fallen in love with her, but never this heedlessly. She wondered if he was drunk or drugged. "You don't even know me," she told him. "Please don't hold me so tight. People are looking."

"I don't care."

"I do. I happen to be married. Very much married."

"That's beside the point."

She gave him a long hard look. He had regular features, straight nose, a somewhat weak chin, full soft lips under a well-trimmed mustache. Only the eyes were a discordant note in the dependable plainness of the face. They were deep-set, had long silky lashes and a strangely fixed stare. The eyes of a killer, she thought.

"There is something I want to make clear, Lieutenant," she told him. "I liked your roses, they were beautiful. I like you too, but if you act like a moonstruck adolescent I'll never speak to you again."

"I love you so," he muttered. She was startled to see tears in his eyes. He failed to notice that the musicians had stopped playing, and he continued whirling her about to the strains of a tune heard only by him. She forced him to halt and disengaged herself.

"Remember what I told you. No sottise." She allowed him to escort her to the group of ranking ladies, then kept away from him for the rest of the night. Next day when he paid the obligatory courtesy call, she had Anni Busse tell him that she was not receiving.

Evidently he took her warning to heart, because during their ensuing meetings his conduct was impeccable. He managed to be invited to most of the parties she and Hans Günther attended, which was surprising, as cavalrymen formed a close clique and rarely mixed with the other branches. It seemed he had a special gift of endearing himself to the elderly women of the garrison. Alexa learned through the grapevine that the only photograph on his desk was that of his mother, and that he had spent his last two vacations hiking with her in the Riesengebirge. Such filial devotion was unusual among the younger set and accounted for his popularity with the ranking wives, especially with those who had marriageable daughters.

Existence in a small garrison town under the wintry sky of East Prussia had some aspects of life in a psychopathic ward. Day after day the same gray walls, the same faces, the same inescapable routines, the same isolation from the outside world.

After the incident with Ranke's roses, Alexa tried desperately to re-establish the relationship that had existed between her and Hans Günther during their first weeks in Allenstein. Whenever she approached him, though, it was like crashing into a wall of ice. After a while she felt as if her inner self had become covered with ugly black bruises. His attitude toward her had taken on a cruel edge. It was not just moody, but deliberately malevolent. He acted the considerate husband when others were around, then turned deaf and dumb when left alone with her. She could understand that after Potsdam he considered Allenstein a penal colony. His punishing of her, who voluntarily shared his exile, she could not.

She had been lonely in Potsdam too, but there she lived in the now. In Allenstein people lived in the yesterday. It was as though she were on a time machine flying back to a generation that had died long before she was born. She had nothing in common with it. She even found nature to be completely alien: the unrelieved flatness of plateaus, lakes frozen over to resemble blind mirrors, acres of moor, sand and bog inhabited by lynx and wolf packs. It was like living on a barren island, or worse, on an iceberg slowly drifting into the inexplorable nowhere.

There was little to occupy her in the house. Even when

disagreeing with Anni's modus operandi, she kept quiet. The thought of losing her and having to cope with the problems of a household in which the servants treated her with the polite indifference usually accorded to poor relations frightened her. At times she felt too listless to get up in the morning and stayed in bed reading, dozing or just staring at the ceiling. She seldom dressed until it was time to go downstairs for the midday meal.

The nights were even harder to bear than the days. Darkness had a strange effect on her; instead of lulling her to sleep, it kept her awake. Wide awake, yet dreaming, which puzzled her. Or were the images projected onto the black screen of her closed lids not dreams but fantasies? Most of the time they centered on Nicholas. From letters of mutual friends she had learned that while vacationing in Vienna he had become engaged to a certain Countess Francesca Winterfeld, a young woman of plain good looks and immaculate reputation. According to gossip, she had been Countess Melanie's choice. Instead of a glamorous daughter-in-law, Melanie settled for one who would be willing to overlook her Nicholas's occasional trespasses, be a loyal wife to him and a loving mother to at least half a dozen little Karadys. Francesca of the poor, devout and very prolific Winterfeld family ideally fitted all these requirements.

There had been an elegant engagement party at the palace in Herrengasse, and the wedding was scheduled for not later than the autumn of 1908, when Nicholas would have completed his tour of duty in Berlin. The fact that he seemed to be in no special hurry to wed consoled Alexa. Not that she hoped for the breakup of the engagement. She had left Nicholas without a word of goodbye, which must have hurt him badly. She wished him happiness with a good woman, yet deep down she also wished he weren't so completely out of reach.

Lately she lived in a constant state of discontent. The slightest annoyance put her out of countenance. For reasons she could not explain, a definite resentment was building up in her against Jan Dmowski, Hans Günther's orderly. He had been a disturbing presence from the day he had first reported for duty, probably because he was so very different from big bearish Thadeus, whom she had grown very fond of in Potsdam.

Of middle height, with the slim wiry body of a circus acrobat, Dmowski looked like one of Murillo's street urchins grown into manhood. His smooth ivory skin, chestnut hair, straight narrow nose, girlish lips and knowing eyes did not fit the name Dmowski. Anxious to please without being obsequious, he had a ready grin that illuminated his face as if hit by sudden sunlight. There was a touch of smugness to his grin, though, which seemed to escape everyone except Alexa.

He sensed her dislike, but he refused to keep out of her way. He used excuses to enter a room where she was and to perform a maid's or a stableboy's tasks. He would unexpectedly materialize in front of a store where she had shopped and relieve her of her parcels. In the mornings, after Hans Günther had left the house, she would not so much see him as sense his presence in the dark upstairs hallway that ran between the bath and the bedroom. When she told Anni that she wanted Dmowski to remain downstairs in the mornings, the housekeeper protested. She had a hard time keeping the huge house immaculate, she said, and neither Bona nor Svetlana could be trusted with the polishing of the brass lamps on the upper floor and the waxing of the balustrade. Dmowski was a wizard cleaner. Had Alexa noticed the improved condition of the warped floor in the upstairs hallway? She would have if she had paid attention to such prosaic matters. The sole concession Anni was willing to make was to keep the orderly on the ground floor while Alexa was still asleep.

For a while there was peace, then Dmowski began to disregard the ban. Alexa would wake to the sound of his rolling up the carpet, waxing the floor or wiping the outside of her door. At times he whistled while he worked, as if wanting to dispel any doubt in her mind that it was he moving about in the hallway.

One morning she could no longer control her temper. She jumped from bed and without bothering to slip on a negligee threw open the door.

"Get away from here! This very minute! Weren't you told to stay downstairs?" she shouted at him.

He let the long-handled brush with which he had been cleaning cobwebs from the ceiling drop to the floor.

"You're beautiful when you're mad," he said, grinning impudently. His Polish-accented German was in odd contrast to his Mediterranean looks.

"You heard me!" She raised her arm and pointed at the stairs. "Down!"

He refused to budge. "Down! That's what you tell a dog, lady. I am no dog." He took a step forward and touched her face, then his hand slid to her breast which was covered by only the thin lace-trimmed linen of her nightgown. For a moment she stood petrified, then she let out a screech and ferociously slapped his face. Immediately there was a thin trickle of blood from his nostril. He was still grinning.

"That was not very nice, Baroness," he said, pulling out a handkerchief to wipe off the blood. Later she remembered that the handkerchief was of fine linen, hemstitched and immaculately clean. The expression of mocking amusement seemed irremovably plastered on his face. "What if I'd hit you back?"

She retreated into the room and slammed the door shut. She threw herself on the bed. Dmowski had to go. Not a day longer would she tolerate him in the house. She should've objected to his presence long ago, but she couldn't dismiss him just because she noticed a lewd expression on his face.

She was dressed and downstairs seated in an armchair in the study when Hans Günther arrived home for the midday dinner.

177

As usual he dismounted in front of the carriage entrance, leaving his horse in the care of Jerzy, the stableboy. She heard Dmowski open the front door for him. She couldn't tell whether they exchanged words or not. During the winter, doors between rooms and hallways were kept closed.

Hans Günther entered and was surprised to find her in the study. She had violated an unwritten house rule when she intruded upon his domain. He noticed the nervous quiver around her lips.

"Anything wrong?" he asked.

"Yes. Dmowski must go."

He stood with arms folded, eyes narrowing to slits. "Go where?"

She rose and moved close to him. "He's . . . he's been— He did something outrageous today and I won't have him in this house." She sensed an inexplicable hostility in him which bewildered her.

"What the devil did he do?"

"He— To begin with, he had no business to be upstairs. I gave orders. I told Anni she mustn't let him work upstairs —not in the morning."

"So he was upstairs. What's so outrageous about that?"

"I told him to go down and he refused and I hit him."

"*You* hit *him?* Were you out of your mind?"

"I'm telling you, he did something outrageous. When I ordered him to go he made a gesture as if—"

"What gesture?"

"He touched me."

"Is that why you hit him? Because he touched you? Most likely by accident."

She raised her voice. "It was no accident. He sort of—he put his hand on my breast."

There was a pause. "Where were you? In bed?"

"Of course not. In the hallway."

He contemplated for a moment. "All right. I'll talk to him. Alone. Tell Busse to send him in."

She resented his calm and the abrasive edge to his tone. "Tell her yourself," she snapped. "Anyway, there is nothing to talk to him about. It's very simple. Send him back to his unit and get somebody else. We never had any trouble with Thadeus."

Without deigning to answer, he crossed to the bell cord and pulled it twice. Two rings were for Anni, but it was Dmowski who entered. He had been waiting outside the door, anticipating the summons, Alexa figured.

"Fräulein Anni is preparing a soufflé. She can't leave now or it won't rise." He stood at stiff attention, his gaze fixed on Hans Günther. He gave no indication that he noticed Alexa. "The major wishes?"

Alexa thought she detected a nervous flicker on Hans Günther's face. He crossed to the window and halted there with his back turned to both of them. "It's you I wanted to talk to, Jan," he said. Then after a pause: "Alexa, will you leave us alone please."

She rose. On her way out she had to brush past the orderly, who was barring the doorway. She felt red hot anger searing her insides. "Let me pass, will you?"

With a cutting look at her, he goose-stepped out of the way. She rushed from the room feeling beaten and humiliated. She sensed a bond between the two against which she felt powerless. Not wanting to know how long their talk lasted and how it ended, she went to the bedroom and came down only when dinner was announced.

During the meal, in the presence of Anni, Hans Günther was his usual proper self. The latest national news was discussed. Wilhelm II was spending his spring vacation on the island of Corfu, at the Achilleion, the palace built by the late Empress Elisabeth of Austria, which he had bought recently. There were rumors of a new controversy between the Kaiser and King Edward because of a private letter the nephew wrote to his uncle's First Lord of the Admiralty.

Seething with impatience, Alexa listened in frozen silence

to the two Prussian patriots sneer at perfidious Albion. When they agreed that nothing short of a war could bring England to her senses, she almost added that she too welcomed a war, provided all men were killed in it.

After the dessert she waited for Anni to leave the room, then confronted Hans Günther. "Are you getting rid of the man?"

He gazed at her fixedly. "If you mean Jan, the answer is no."

Strangely, she was not surprised. "I told you I don't want him in the house. Isn't that clear? He is impertinent and disrespectful. I am afraid of him. I don't feel safe when he is around. He is liable to—"

"Do what? Rape you? Is that what you are trying to say?" He rose and stepped to her.

For a moment she thought he was going to hit her, but she stood her ground. "Yes."

"Now listen to me. I had a talk with him about that . . . that incident this morning. You're a damned tease, that's what you are. Running around half naked. I wish he had raped you. It would've served you right."

She gasped for air. "You are insane."

"You're not afraid of him; he is afraid of you. From now on you're not to leave your room unless fully dressed. And I don't mean a flimsy negligee with your tits showing. You are my wife and this is a repectable house, not a brothel."

Jan Dmowski was a shameless liar, but that was beside the point. She no longer felt angry at him. The intensity of her indignation against Hans Günther exhausted all her strength and left no room for other emotions. She knew that the orderly would remain, if for no other reason than to spite her.

One late March night she had her eyes opened, simply and cruelly.

A northeasterly had been blowing all day, its savage force uprooting trees and tearing clumps of thatch from the roofs of the poor. There was a howling sound from the chimneys, gusts of icy draft chilled the rooms, defying the kapok-filled bolsters placed between the double windows and the quilts hung over the sills.

It was close to midnight. Anni Busse had retired early to her room with the latest installment of the serial in the *Täglicher Rundschau*. The maids had finished cleaning the kitchen and were probably sound asleep in their cubicle behind the laundry room. Neither Jerzy nor Dmowski slept in the house; the stableboy stayed in the stable and the orderly in the coach house.

Suddenly there was the sound of a shutter slapping back and forth. It came from the unused ballroom. It woke Alexa and kept her from dozing off again. She turned on the light and saw that Hans Günther's bed was empty. He was still downstairs, probably working on his treatise, she thought.

Access to the ballroom was through a wide door set in a nook of the entrance hall. She descended the stairs and, not wanting to disturb Hans Günther, went straight to the ballroom. As she went in, she was hit by the icy chill of a place left unheated throughout the winter. Remembering that there was a naked bulb hanging from the ceiling, she groped for the switch on the wall. A sudden violent squall whipped through the garden and the flip-flop of the loose shutter grew louder and faster. Unable to find the switch, she was reluctant to go into the dark room and she decided to ask Hans Günther to help her hook up the shutter.

She saw light escaping from under the closed door of the study, so she knew he had to be in there. Later she could not recall whether she had knocked or simply walked in. She probably didn't think of knocking. After all, she was in her own house and the man behind the door was her husband.

The room was dimly lit by a single candle burning on the desk. At first sight the two shapes on the sofa, casting huge and grotesquely entwined shadows on the white wall behind them, appeared to be engaged in a wrestling match. The skin of their bare buttocks had taken on a reddish hue, at least so it seemed against the paleness of the wall. There was something clownishly comical about their heaves and bumps and their complete absorption in the burlesque act.

She stood in the doorway unable to move. She felt sick with shame as if she had been the one caught committing an outrage.

It was Dmowski who became aware of her. He hooked his gaze to hers, hypnotizing her into extended immobility. The timeworn spring of the antique sofa stopped squeaking and there was a moment of deadly silence in the room. Hans Günther propped himself up on one arm and glared at her. In the flickering flame of the candle, his pale face with deep shadows under the eyes looked like a death mask.

"What do you want?" he asked in a voice that seemed to come from the cellar.

She stared at him open-mouthed, then heard herself say, "The shutter in the ballroom. It's—" She choked. The absurdity of the scene caused her to emit a demented giggle. She wheeled about and ran.

She negotiated the stairs without turning on the lights. Later she tried to reason out why she had thought that darkness would be a refuge. She groped her way into the bedroom and crawled under the covers. She could not tell how long a time had passed when she heard Hans Günther enter. He switched on his bedside lamp and began to undress, neatly, slowly and methodically as always. Tunic hung on the back of a chair, breeches clamped into their hanger, shirt, drawers and socks laid on the bench, boot trees slipped into boots. There was the rustle of the nightshirt, then the groan of the mattress under the weight of his body.

For the first time the routine was incomplete. He had skipped the good-night kiss, the light peck on her forehead that over the years had become the symbolic reaffirmation of the marriage vow. He had steadfastly adhered to the ritual of the kiss, even on nights when, coming to bed, he found her asleep. In the morning she would have a vague recollection of his bending over her, exhaling a whiff of toothpaste and brandy. If she was awake, she would occasionally respond to his kiss by throwing her arms about him, trying to pull him down to her, giving up when she felt his resistance. Repeated disappointments had taught her that the kiss was no more than a parishioner's coin dropped into the collection plate— a gesture, a duty, an observance of a long-established custom. In an oblique way it also signaled Hans Günther's decision not to make love. The day was done, the hour ripe for the energy-restoring repose. That and nothing more.

Now he tossed and turned for a while, then his even breathing told her that he had fallen asleep. His sangfroid astounded her. It was more than sangfroid; it was cruelty, in-human callousness, a complete disregard for the pain he had caused her.

She wondered if she had ever really known him or had merely dreamed up a specter to fit his perfect face. He had married her knowing that he could never return the love she had felt for him. To him she was—as Natalie had been to Moltke—a human latrine, foul, malodorous, distasteful.

Suddenly she was overcome by a wild, murderous fury. Five years, five irreplaceable years of her life, had been wasted. As a child she had fallen in love with a photograph and been tricked into marrying not a man but an image. The image was kept intact by a brazen lie, then abruptly it was torn to shreds. The photo in the family album was re-placed by an obscene picture showing two half-naked men locked in a sick embrace.

She marveled at her own naiveté, which let her ignore signs—even after the Sommer testimony—that must have been obvious to everyone else. Had she been hoping for a miracle? Was it the challenge that intrigued her? Was she a freak who could love only if rejected?

She turned on her night lamp, propped herself up on her elbow and looked at him across the space that separated the two beds. His mouth softened by a half-smile, a curl falling over one eye, he lay on his side, breathing calmly and evenly. In the past the sight of his tanned face, boyish and innocent in sleep, filled her with almost maternal tenderness. That was all over now. The daydream of his changing into a tender and passionate lover had yielded to reality. There was not going to be a miracle. For no matter how firm her breasts, how slim her waist, how welcoming her thighs, it was the hirsute burliness of a Sergeant Bollhardt, the puppy-dog charm of a Corporal Sommer and the gypsy animalism of a Jan Dmowski that Hans Günther lusted for.

Her fury evaporated. She felt no hatred, only leaden weariness. Her arm began to hurt, but she was too tired to shift position. Later, much later, the lamplight shining in her eyes woke her and she realized that she had fallen asleep.

It was already morning, gray and wintry, when she awakened for a second time. She glanced at Hans Günther's bed. It was empty. He was gone. He had got up as quietly as on any ordinary day, dressed and left for the barracks.

8

It was a Wednesday morning like any other. When she finally forced herself to rise and cross the corridor to the bathroom, the noises rising from the ground floor told her that the household was awake and functioning.

On the first Wednesday of every month, provided it was not raining, the Persian rugs of the salon were picked up and taken outdoors to have the dust beaten out of them. It was the orderly's job, and the dull thuds coming from the service yard indicated that Dmowski was at work as usual.

She rang for her breakfast and it was brought up by Svetlana. She was the older of the two maids and the one with the gentler disposition. In the beginning Alexa had tried to strike up a conversation with her, but received mostly monosyllabic answers, some completely non sequitur. She came to the conclusion that Svetlana failed to understand her, although she had no difficulty understanding Anni Busse's German; but then, the housekeeper always used the local dialect when talking to "dumb Poles."

This morning the silence of her room was unbearable. She had to hear the sound of a human voice, even if it was only her own.

"What's new in town, Svetlana?"

The question had the effect of a sudden gunshot on the girl. She wheeled about and stared at Alexa, frowning.

"New in town . . . in town . . ." She repeated the words as if she had never heard them before and was memorizing them.

"Anything interesting?" There was silence again. Alexa felt like screaming but kept her voice low. "For God's sake, something must be happening. Even in Allenstein. Or are only zombies living here? People who walk and talk as if they were alive but are really dead?"

The girl looked terrified. "No . . . No zombies. Only Poles and Jews and Germans too."

"Never mind." She dismissed the girl with a tired wave of her hand. Relieved, Svetlana scurried from the room. Alexa's call caught her as she was about to pull the door shut. "Tell Fräulein Busse I'm not feeling well and won't be down for lunch."

She knew she could not stand eating at the same table with Hans Günther. She had to think, make plans. This time she had to be strong and resist his ruses. Back in Potsdam when she confronted him with Corporal Sommer's testimony, she allowed him to fool her, probably because deep down she wanted to be fooled, because she wanted to hold on to him no matter what. It suddenly dawned on her that throughout their relationship their man-woman roles had been reversed. She had played the part of the seducer and he the seduced—rather, the unseduceable. She had loved him long before the thought of bedding her first occurred to him.

She went back to bed. After a long while—she must have dozed off—she heard him riding through the gate and up to the front entrance. A few minutes later someone was climbing the stairway. She knew it was not Hans Günther, because she would have recognized his steps. It was Anni Busse.

"Svetlana said you were not feeling well. Do you want your lunch brought up?"

"Just some soup."

"We have potato soup. Will that do?"

"Only a small plate. I'm not very hungry."

Anni left the room without asking what ailed Alexa. Her deliberately indifferent tone was meant to convey to her employer that sympathy was not included in the services she had been hired to render. When indisposed, ladies could stay in bed, housekeepers could not. That was the message written all over her face.

Wavering between expectation and apprehension, Alexa waited in vain for the sound of Hans Günther's steps accompanied by the soft jingle of spurs scaling the stairs. When her soup was brought up by Svetlana, she heard the clatter of dishes from the dining room, indicating that the midday meal was being served as usual. Afterward, all was quiet for a while, then the front door opened and closed and a horse trotted down the driveway, its hoofbeats becoming lost in the soft sand of the bridle path on Parade Platz.

All afternoon she remained in bed staring at the ceiling. She knew she had to put an end to her marriage or lose her sanity. Two solutions were open to her, suicide and divorce, of which the first seemed more feasible. It was within easy reach, while the other meant insurmountable obstacles.

She was not totally unarmed though. Her charges against Hans Günther could be a devastating weapon if told to a judge. Getting that far was the problem. At the age of twenty-four, she did not have enough money to live on her own for a week. Her education enabled her to make intelligent conversation, tell the difference between real and fake art, between trash and literature, and to dress with taste; but she had learned no trade, could not compose a business letter, take dictation in shorthand, work a sewing machine or cook a meal. Her freedom depended entirely on Hans Günther's whim; she was not only his consort but also his partner, his chattel.

If she were in Berlin, she would at least have one friend, Nicholas. The irreparable stupidity of her leaving him without a word of explanation filled her with disgust. She had treated him disgracefully, had driven him into the arms of another woman and now could no longer turn to him for help.

She dozed off and was awakened by Anni asking if she cared to go downstairs for supper. It took her quite some time to collect herself. Unthinking, she threw back the comforter and was about to get up when it suddenly dawned upon her that she would have to face Hans Günther across the dinner table. The thought caused her to drop back on the pillows.

"No," she said. "I'll have some cold ham and a cup of tea up here."

"Do you want some rice pudding left from dinner?"

"No, thank you, only tea and ham."

The woman nodded and turned to leave. Later Alexa tried to explain to herself how the sudden decision had come to her. She spoke without taking time to reconsider. "Something else. Tell Svetlana to collect the major's bedding and carry it down to the study."

Anni wheeled about, ennui changing to open-mouthed astonishment on her face. "To the study? What for?"

"To make up his bed on the couch."

"You want the major to sleep in the study?" Anni asked, shocked.

"Exactly."

"Just tonight?"

"Tonight and every night."

There was a long pause. "He didn't tell me anything about that."

Alexa derived a perverse pleasure from the woman's surprise. She was sending a declaration of war to the enemy. And as it was also done between nations, sending it by an intermediary. "*I* am telling you."

"I'd better ask him."

"If you wish."

Anni was still rooted to the threshold. Her big blue eyes, fixed on Alexa's face, appeared to be as sightless as those of a dead fish. She was torn between confronting the major with the message and refusing to deliver it. Like every successful tyrant, Hans Günther kept an even balance between being a charmer and a menace. That was how he ruled his entourage. Including his wife, Alexa thought ruefully.

"I'll tell him, if that's what you want," Anni muttered at last and shuffled from the room. She was hardly gone when Alexa heard the jingle of spurs coming up the stairway. Suddenly she wished she had not said a word to Anni. It was too late for regrets, because Hans Günther was already in the room.

"What is this you told Busse? To make my bed downstairs?"

Alexa pressed her hands together to keep them from shaking. Her lips felt painfully dry, her tongue stuck to the roof of her mouth.

"Yes, I don't want to sleep in the same room with you. I don't want to breathe the same air as you." She raised her voice. "I want a divorce."

He stepped closer. "Are you out of your mind? Do you want people to talk? I don't give a damn about your feelings for me, but I won't have the servants spread the news that things aren't well in this house."

Nervously she jumped from bed and slipped on her robe. If this was to be a fight, she had better be on her feet. "You heard me. I want a divorce. And I don't have to tell you why."

"And *I* won't give you a divorce. Certainly not right now. Maybe later, but not now."

"But why? You don't love me, don't care about me. We've become strangers. We don't even talk anymore. And after what I saw last night—"

With a lighted cigarette in hand he crossed to her. "You'd better forget what you saw last night."

She shrank back, because for a moment she had the strange feeling that he was going to burn her with the cigarette. "I am not an animal. I am a human being. You can't

189

keep me against my will. If you don't set me free, I'll set my-self free. I'll find a way. I am not alone in this world. I still have—"

"You still have Karady? Is that what you were going to say?"

The name caught her unprepared and she felt the ground slipping from under her feet.

"I am amazed at you! Sleeping with a Jew. Couldn't you find anyone better?"

His tone told her that he was not guessing, that he knew. Nevertheless she protested. "You're mad. I never slept with him or anyone else. I—"

He was staring fixedly at her. "You carried on with him throughout last spring and summer."

"That's not true. Whoever told you—"

He cut her short. "You kept seeing him in his flat on Burg Strasse. Later you would meet in Potsdam and drive away in his car."

"He took me for rides—"

"I don't give a damn where he took you. I assume he treated you to a good fuck, otherwise you wouldn't have spent whole afternoons with him. You saw him once again in his flat shortly before we left Potsdam."

He knew. He had probably known it ever since she'd first been to Burg Strasse 62, but kept quiet about it, holding on to the truth as though it were a deadly weapon to be used only as a last resort. His reason for confronting her with the charge of adultery was to scare her into obedience, yet it had the opposite effect on her. It was fuel to her defiance.

"All right, I did have an affair with Karady. But if you knew it all along, why did you want me to come to Allenstein? Why didn't you kick me out? Kill me? Kill him?"

He smiled mirthlessly. "Frankly, the thought did occur to me. To kill him. Jealous husband taking revenge. Would've looked good in the papers. And to the Court of Honor."

Suddenly realization dawned. The Court of Honor. On that

evening in October he had said that his case was to be tried by the Court of Honor. "Oh, now I understand!"

"Understand what?"

"Why you insisted that I come with you to Allenstein. To prove to the world that Bollhardt and Sommer had lied, that you were a model husband! That you were normal! Dear old Frau Notze told everyone in town that she'd never seen a more loving husband than you. If she had only known!"

"Don't twist things around. Be grateful I was willing to forgive and forget."

"I have nothing to be grateful for. Yes, I had a lover and he was a complete man. He loved me, but I was a fool. I left him and came to this damned place with you. I didn't realize I was being used to save your bloody career. But that's over now. I no longer care what happens to you or to your career. I'm leaving you."

He listened in grim silence. "No, you won't," he said when she ran out of breath.

"You cannot force me to stay. If I open my mouth, you're finished, disgraced, kaput—kicked out of the army, sent to prison."

"Blackmail, is it?"

"Yes. So you'd better let me go quietly. Tomorrow I'll leave for Berlin. We'll think of some excuse to tell the people here. Illness, visit to relatives, anything."

"And where, may I ask, will you stop in Berlin?"

"Some hotel."

"And what will you use for money?"

She frowned. "You'll give me a certain amount every month—and pay for the legal expenses. That's customary, isn't it?"

"And if I don't?"

"I'll go just the same."

Her reply seemed to strike him funny. He shook his head, laughing. "I wouldn't if I were you. You might be in for a big surprise. Your great lover is getting married, you know." Playfully he chucked her under the chin. "He's become engaged to a Countess Winterfeld in Vienna. The wedding is planned for the fall."

She felt a sharp pang of anguish and hoped it did not show on her face. "I wasn't counting on him," she said, trying to keep her voice even. "Besides, I knew of the engagement. I just want a divorce, that's all there is to it."

"There won't be any divorce." Hans Günther started for the door, then suddenly stopped on the threshold. "Let me warn you once and for all, I won't have any disruption of our regular routine. No stories spread by servants about trouble in the Godenhausens' marriage. I have a very good chance to end this tour soon, become assigned to a more important post. I won't have my career wrecked by you. You don't know me, Alexa. I can be very tough if I have to be."

He left the room. Exhausted, she dropped into a chair. Nicholas's engagement still hurt her more than she had ever believed it would. Not only because she had counted on his support, but also because now that she had lost it she was belatedly aware of what his devotion had meant to her. She had been loved by a strong, bright, passionate man willing to accept her on her own terms. He transferred to her the love he once had for her dead twin, which she, Alexa, should have accepted gratefully. What a fool she had been to resent a fire that warmed her, just because it had been lighted by another woman and she had merely rekindled it. How she needed its warmth. But the fire had been extinguished, not by the Countess Winterfeld—whoever she was—but by her own insouciance.

Hans Günther's bedding was not taken to the study. He came upstairs as usual shortly after the bell of the nearby Catholic church struck ten. While he undressed, Alexa lay, eyes wide open, shivering under the warm comforter. After getting into bed, Hans Günther read for a while, then turned off the lamp on his night table and minutes later was fast asleep.

The realization that night after night she would have to listen to an enemy's steady breathing, interspersed with an occasional snore, filled Alexa with bitter rage. If Hans Günther died, she would be free, she thought. Immediately she felt a pang of remorse.

She slept fitfully and was wide awake when he rose in the morning. She waited for him to leave the house, then slipped out of bed. Anni Busse, the maids and Dmowski were busy with their endless task of removing yesterday's grime from floors, furniture, silver and brass to make room for today's. She dressed and, unnoticed by them, left the house through the rear entrance. She returned the same way half an hour later.

She had gone to the post office to mail an express, registered letter to her aunt in which she announced her inalterable decision to divorce Hans Günther. She asked Rose for support—first of all for a train ticket from Allenstein to Berlin and some cash. In a postscript she warned Rose against refusing her request, for in that case she would be forced to reveal certain facts that would destroy not only Hans Günther's reputation but discredit the entire family as well. It would be wise, she added, if Rose sent her answer poste restante.

She had also written to the wife of an officer still with the Gardes du Corps in Potsdam. Of all her acquaintances, she felt closest to this young woman and had kept up a correspondence with her throughout the past months. She asked her whether she had heard anything new about Nicholas Karady's engagement.

For a whole week she waited in vain for Rose's answer. The letter from Potsdam arrived by return mail. The woman wrote that Count Karady seemed sincerely devoted to his Francesca, although everyone thought that she was a rather surprising choice for a man as sophisticated as dear Nicholas. She was pretty, but far from beautiful; good family, but poor as a church mouse, a very fitting phrase, for her mother was rumored to be a religious fanatic, practically living in churches.

The Sedlitzes arrived without any prior notice. At least Alexa had not been warned, though Hans Günther might have been, and he had subsequently alerted Anni Busse, which explained the sudden flurry of housecleaning the day before.

It was the sound of Rose's voice coming from the ground floor that awakened Alexa that morning. She sat bolt upright, then dropped back and pulled the comforter over her head, trying to escape reality by sinking back into the blissful refuge of sleep. The next thing she knew, Anni entered and was standing beside her bed telling her that her aunt and uncle had arrived and wanted to see her.

She slipped on a robe and rushed to greet them. They acted with the icy stiffness of an investigating committee descending upon a criminal's house. It caused her to suspect that the general knew of her letter to Rose; nevertheless, she cautiously asked what had brought them to Allenstein.

"We'll tell you when Hans Günther is home," Rose answered. "Fräulein Busse will kindly show us where we can clean up and rest a bit. We had a long trip and neither of us slept a wink."

"Aunt Rose, I must speak to you," Alexa said. "To you alone. I must—"

"Not before Hans Günther gets home."

Anni's presence kept Alexa from insisting. Her aunt's forbidding stare told her that she could count on neither her compassion nor her understanding.

What a fool she had been to expect help from Rose or the general. After twelve years she should have realized that they would always side with Hans Günther. Whatever differences the three—nephew, uncle and aunt—ever had had, they had always settled them in private. To the outside world they presented a defiant oneness, a monument carved of the same block of marble, a grotesque Laocoön group clasped together in the unbreakable hold of two sea serpents: the Sedlitz blood and the Lutz money. After Corporal Sommer's testimony, it was the general who prevented Hans Günther's dishonorable discharge from the army and had him transferred to East Prussia instead—a rather mild punishment, considering the crime. And since those days it was he who kept working untiringly on the nephew's recall from exile to a more advantageous post.

Hans Günther returned home an hour earlier than usual, which also proved that he had been notified in advance of their visit. Surprisingly, dinner was ready and could be served immediately. Conversation during the meal was low-keyed and strained, as if someone lay dying in the house. There were only the four of them at the table, because, assuming that they had family matters to discuss, Anni tactfully decided to eat in her room. The gesture was unnecessary, as the debate was postponed until after they moved to the more guarded privacy of the study.

During the meal the general brought his nephew up to date on the latest news from Berlin, including the progress of the Harden vendetta against Prince Eulenburg.

"It looks as if Harden is closing in on his quarry," Sedlitz said with a strange flicker of malice in his eyes. "Have you heard that a publisher in Munich called Staedele has, in his little yellow journal, accused Harden of having accepted a million marks from Eulenburg for keeping his mouth shut?"

"No, I haven't. A million marks? That means Harden has gotten hold of some damaging facts against the prince," Hans Günther said.

"Oh, but the case isn't that simple, my boy," the general cackled. "Would you believe it if I told you that Staedele's article was commissioned by Harden himself?"

"I don't get it."

"Of course not. You're a dumb Prussian and not a crooked

195

but brilliant Jew like Harden or his attorney, Bernstein. Harden *does* have some defamatory information about Eulenburg's little peccadilloes and is ready to make it public."

Alexa listened with grim fascination. The chatty way in which her uncle discussed the Eulenburg tragedy, which, after all, had affected their own lives, disgusted her.

"Why didn't he just print it in *Zukunft?*" Hans Günther asked.

"Because the people he needed to corroborate his charges had refused to cooperate. So in the course of his libel suit against Staedele he had them subpoenaed as witnesses who, testifying under oath, had no choice but to tell all they knew."

"I still don't see the reason for the whole complicated maneuver."

"Don't you remember that last December, during the second Moltke-Harden trial, held in front of the Berlin Court of Corrections—a trial which, as we all know, ended in Harden's defeat—the prince volunteered to testify in Moltke's behalf? Cross-examined by Counselor Bernstein, he declared under oath that he never participated in any unnatural sex acts."

The words "unnatural sex acts" caused Alexa to pale, but no one paid any attention to her discomfort.

"Now, last week," Sedlitz went on, "at the Municipal Court in Munich, two men testified that about twenty years ago they had been the prince's lovers. What is more, they named others who had also been involved."

At last Hans Günther appeared worried. "Jesus Christ, is the whole nightmare going to start again?"

Sedlitz reassuringly patted his hand. "No, no. All this concerns Eulenburg and no one else. That's been the case all along. In a matter of days, or hours, the Royal Prussian Ministry of Justice will order perjury proceedings instituted against Prince Philipp zu Eulenburg und Hartefeld which will irrevocably put an end to his glorious career as His Majesty's eminence grise."

Throughout the meal the Sedlitzes had pointedly ignored Alexa. Not one word was addressed to her, not a glance cast in her direction. Even her husband joined them in the silent treatment. She felt enclosed in a glass case that not even a bullet could have shattered. Prompted by a sudden fit of loathing, she broke out of it.

"Why are you so happy about his disgrace?" she shouted at her uncle. "I remember the time not so long ago when you had nothing but praise and gratitude for the prince. Now all of a sudden you are on Harden's side. Why? Have you forgotten that Hans was one of Harden's victims? That without that man we'd still be in Potsdam and not in this godforsaken hellhole!"

The three stared at her dumbfounded. Hans Günther was the first to regain his composure. "Would you stop screaming, please? You don't want the servants to hear you."

The warning came too late, as Svetlana, bringing in the dessert, had already entered the room. She was followed by Bona, who collected the meat plates and exchanged them for clean ones. After both left, the clatter of forks and spoons was the only noise in the room.

Hans Günther broke the silence. "There must have been someone very powerful behind the whole plan. Eulenburg still has friends, while Harden or Holstein—"

"It is not Harden or Holstein." The general lowered his voice to a whisper. "The prince committed a fatal error. He underestimated Chancellor von Bülow. He maintained, despite Bülow's warning, that His Majesty's building a fleet to compete with England's was a folly that would lead to war. At last Bülow got tired of his meddling in politics. Eulenburg has called himself a man of peace. Now he'll have perfect peace in a prison cell of the Moabit courthouse."

Rose had two helpings of the dessert, the general three. Alexa took a bite of hers, swallowed it with some difficulty, then ate no more. Once again she was excluded from the

197

conversation; no reference was made to her outburst in behalf of Prince Eulenburg. She had been rebuked for raising her voice; to insist on an answer would have been sheer effrontery.

Now they were seated, the general behind the desk, Rose and Hans Günther on the couch and Alexa on a straight-backed chair, facing them, she told herself with a bitter inward grin, as it behooves the defendant.

Without waiting for Alexa to speak, Rose opened the session. In a breathless, plaintive flow of words that didn't permit interruption, she delivered a long tirade damning enough to serve as a public prosecutor's summation in a criminal case. If her intent was to intimidate her niece, she missed her aim, though. Her accusations were much too familiar to make an impression on Alexa. They were the same ones delivered each time they had had an argument in the past: Rose's recapitulation of her sacrifices, complaints of having failed to make a silk purse out of a sow's ear, a Prussian lady out of a Hungarian savage.

"I wasted my time, my money, my love on you," she said. "I gave you a decent, respectable home, an education, a dowry, a trousseau, a gorgeous wedding, a social position. I didn't expect thanks from you, only that you wouldn't disgrace us. But no, even that little was too much to ask. You're shameless, irresponsible and rotten to the core." She ran out of breath and clutched at her heart. Her eyes closed and her face twisted into a mask of tragedy.

"Shall I bring you a glass of water, Aunt Rose?" Hans Günther asked, making no attempt to rise. He had been sitting stiff-backed and marble-faced, the embodiment of wronged innocence.

Alexa felt strangely detached, as if she were present in two identities—a performer and also an uninvolved observer. Four people were acting out a trial: she as the defendant, the general the judge, her aunt the prosecutor and Hans Günther the witness for the crown.

"I'm afraid, you haven't been told the truth, Aunt Rose. It's not I but my husband who wrecked this marriage. I'd rather not tell you in what way. Just take my word for it. And help me. I want a divorce. You'd better accept my decision because I won't change my mind."

Rose pulled a handkerchief from the pocket of her skirt and dabbed at her eyes with it. "Did you hear that, Adalbert?" she asked her husband. "She won't listen to me. Perhaps she will to you. It's your duty as the head of the family to—"

He cut her short. "Don't remind me of my duty."

"I'm sorry, Adalbert. I didn't mean to, nevertheless—"

He raised his hand to silence her, then cleared his throat, signaling that he was going to speak. "My girl," he began, enunciating every word as though Alexa were hard of hearing, "what you've done is despicable. But your husband is willing to let bygones be bygones. That is, if you promise never to break your marriage vow again."

Now at last she understood. Hans Günther had told them about Nicholas, but certainly not about Dmowski. Or had he?

During her six-year stay at the Sedlitzes, she had been summoned to the general's presence for lectures only when Rose felt helpless to cope with her "wickedness." In those cases the general administered justice with the dignity of a supreme court judge, seemingly forgetting their encounters in the dark passage outside his door, his fumbling caresses, his drooling and panting over her and the kicks and slaps she occasionally meted out to him. Now once again he represented the law and she the criminal.

"I have a very valid reason why I want a divorce." She tried to control her anger and keep her voice down. "Please help me. There must be some way to arrange things quietly, without a scandal. I don't want to hurt Hans Günther, or his career. Don't force me to reveal the truth."

199

"Reveal what truth?" Rose flared. "Have you heard that, Adalbert? She is threatening to blackmail Hans Günther. She's handing us an ultimatum."

The general glared at his wife. "Will you let me handle this, woman? You insisted I do, so let me." He turned to Alexa. "You want to desert your husband at a time when he most needs your loyalty. There was a campaign against us, all of us—our class—the elite of our officer corps. If you started divorce proceedings now, it could be interpreted as a corroboration of certain charges against him—unfounded charges, to be sure, but still very vivid in the public's memory. Deserting him would be like joining his enemies, an act as contemptible as defection in wartime—unethical, un-Prussian—"

"I never said I was Prussian."

"You're a Prussian officer's wife."

Rose jumped to her feet. "You're a shameless bitch," she shouted. "Hans Günther is a saint, willing to forgive your whoring—"

"Shut up, Rose," her husband bellowed. "And sit down, damn it. I promised to handle this matter, but only if you keep your bloody mouth shut. Now listen to this"—he turned to Alexa—"you won't leave my nephew. And you won't ask for a divorce."

"I'm sorry, Uncle, my mind is made up."

"No, my girl. *My* mind is made up." He took a deep breath. "I've tried to reason with you. Now I am telling you." He picked up a paper from the desk and unfolded it. "I have here Professor Dr. Popper's medical opinion declaring that you are a manic-depressive. In other words, of unsound mind."

"What!" Alexa cried. She was not sure she understood the general.

"Consequently," he continued, "you have the choice of assenting to our wishes or being committed to the Kortau lunatic asylum for observation and, possibly, prolonged psychiatric treatments."

Alexa covered her mouth and swallowed hard to keep from

200

vomiting. She had to take a few deep breaths before she was able to speak. "You can't have me committed. That Professor Popper, or whatever his name is, has never laid eyes on me. How can he say I am crazy?"

"Wrong, my dear," the general said, throwing a glance at the paper before him. "He last examined you on September fourteenth, a little over six months ago at the Charité in Berlin."

"I had my lungs examined and not my head. I was running a temperature. I was X-rayed and had blood samples and sputum taken. Sort of precautionary measures because of the TB I'd had as a child."

"Professor Popper was one of the doctors."

"I'm telling you, they examined me for TB."

"In addition, I also have the expert opinion of Dr. Brandt who treated you between 1897 and 1903. He found you suffering from a type of psychoneurosis characterized by such symptoms as convulsions, fainting spells, emotional outbreaks."

"No! No! No!" she cried. "He was your family doctor. He was called when I had an upset stomach, a sore throat or things like that. He was no psychiatrist. He also came to see you when you had your gallstone attack and treated Aunt Rose against her hot flashes. If anyone was crazy in that house it was she and not I!"

The general's fist slammed down on the desk. "Enough of that. Not another word! You have your choice."

Alexa rose with a force that sent her chair crashing to the floor. "No! I am through with Hans. Forever. And there is no judge or court or doctor who could make me stay with him. I am not sick! He is!" She confronted her aunt. "I found him on that couch. Right where you are sitting! Making love to his orderly."

Rose emitted a startled *No!* She blinked dazedly, then lumbered to her feet and threw a strangely measuring look at the couch as if searching for proof of Alexa's allegation. Hans Günther also rose. Till now he'd been sitting motionless, his arms folded, his eyes fixed on the glass-fronted bookcase at the far end of the room. Now he nervously fingered the collar of his tunic. His lips trembled as he turned to the general. "She's lying. She wants to squeeze a big alimony out of me and doesn't care how she gets it."

"Don't worry," Sedlitz reassured him. "We won't have another Moltke case."

"Poor Count Moltke," Rose said. "That woman certainly ruined him. Nothing can help him, not even Harden's conviction. He's finished, disgraced—"

"Nothing like that will happen here. Not while I am around," the general said. *"No scandal in this family."*

Alexa made a last try. "There won't be a scandal. I won't say or do anything to hurt Hans Günther. I'll take the blame if necessary. Please, Uncle Adalbert, you must understand. This marriage can't go on. I'll lose my mind if I have to stay in this house. It's like being chained, being in prison—"

"My dear girl, four years ago you entered into a covenant before God. You can't just walk away from it."

Alexa tried to remain calm. "Tell that to Hans Günther. That covenant binds him too. Although he entered into it in bad faith. He knew he could never give me the kind of love a woman has the right to expect from her husband. Don't you understand? He's different. He's not normal. He is sick."

The general rose with the abruptness of a jack-in-the-box. Placing his palms on the desktop, he leaned forward to shout into Alexa's face. *"You* are sick, woman, not he! Sick, sick, sick. A shameless, cheating slut!"

For a moment Alexa stared at him in mute hatred. Then suddenly she heard herself pouring out all the misery and anger that had accumulated in her during the past terrible days. "You call me sick? Immoral? It's you who are sick and immoral. I haven't forgotten those awful moments when you fell upon me in the hallway, grabbing me, pawing me all over, reaching under my skirt. I was your ward, a child entrusted to your care, and I had to fight you tooth and nail to defend myself. Oh, God! You want me committed? It's you who should be. So you wouldn't abuse another helpless child."

Rose had been staring at her in open-mouthed disbelief. Now her eyes shifted to her husband, who was emitting what sounded like the raucous sputters of a car engine being cranked up. Suddenly she lunged at Alexa, hitting her across the mouth. "You filthy whore!" she screamed. "You bitch! Take that back or I'll kill you."

The impact threw Alexa off balance and she fell back, hitting the edge of the cabinet with her head. She landed on the floor, her legs twisted awkwardly, her hands shielding her face against Rose's slaps. She was saved from getting her nose bloodied by Hans Günther's presence of mind. He leaped at Rose, grabbed her around the waist and pulled her off his prostrate wife. There was the creaky sound of a seam parting, mixed with Rose's asthmatic wheeze and the general's inarticulate muttering. Hans Günther managed to push Rose away, so he could gather the dazed Alexa into his arms and lift her to her feet. He touched her head where it had hit the cabinet edge and saw blood on his hand.

"Look what you've done," he said to Rose.

"I should've killed her. Killed her long ago. Strangled her before I took her into our home. I've had nothing but sorrow ever since."

Hans Günther parted his wife's hair to inspect the injury. There was a small gash where the skin had broken open. "Come, let me wash this out."

Alexa pulled away from him. "Never mind. I'll do it myself."

"Let's put a bandage on it."

She was still too dazed to fight him. He led her to the bathroom, dabbed off the blood and painted the cut with iodine. By then it had stopped bleeding and she refused to let him bandage it.

"If the servants see the bandage, they'll think someone took a shot at me. And we don't want that, do we? The town talking about us?"

"The cut might become infected."

She threw a sarcastic look at him. "Wouldn't that be nice? I'd die of blood poisoning and you could marry Dmowski."

"No such luck," he grunted and walked from the room, slamming the door shut with a loud bang.

Their visit was announced to Allenstein as a family reunion, and the Sedlitzes stayed a week. Alexa learned that her uncle had recently been appointed liaison between the General Staff and the Kaiser's Military Cabinet. His position so close to the source of supreme power explained the flurry of excitement his presence created among the military stationed in East Prussia.

It was a memorable week, with visits exchanged and a reception held at the First Army command post in Königsberg, a very proper and elegant affair. The Godenhausens gave a dinner in honor of the divisional commandant and his staff, and the commandant reciprocated with a supper party that stretched into the early morning hours.

The weather had turned mild for the season, the young green of the trees against the cloudless blue of the sky made people forget the long doldrums of the winter, the pea-soup fogs drifting in from the Baltic, the rivers covered with meter-thick ice, the Sisyphean labor of snow shoveling, the rural postmen found frozen after sudden storms, the roofs caved in under the weight of snow, squashing whole families as though a giant foot had stepped on them. General von Sedlitz's visit to Allenstein added an extra festive touch to the pleasures of spring.

With the excuse that she had grippe, Alexa refused to play hostess at the dinner for the divisional commandant. Next day she miraculously recovered and attended the party Hans

Günther's regiment gave for the Sedlitzes. As always, she was closely watched by army wives—her looks, manners and clothes. Their husbands watched her too, mostly from the corners of their eyes; it wasn't her clothes they were interested in. They envied the single men who were free to make fools of themselves over her, especially First Lieutenant Otto von Ranke, whose new nickname became the Shadow, meaning Alexa von Godenhausen's shadow.

Ranke was the ideal companion for a married woman anxious to preserve her unblemished reputation. He was adoring, faithful, dependable and—allegedly—impotent. His infatuation with Alexa was laughed at, mainly because it seemed beyond reason that a woman of her beauty would choose poor little Ranke—even a potent little Ranke—for her lover. Although Allenstein was beginning to doubt the myth of the Godenhausens' perfect marriage, it did not suspect either the husband or the wife of sleeping around. They were much too well matched, much too attractive together, to be involved in extramarital affairs. And perfection was not easily obtainable in Allenstein.

Of course there was still the cloud of homosexuality hovering over Hans Günther, but his five-year marriage to Alexa offered a strong argument against it. People assumed that he might have strayed once or twice but had been straightened out for good by her.

The Sedlitzes' visit was not without benefit for Alexa. Hans Günther yielded to her most emphatic demands short of divorce. He had Dmowski replaced by Johann Blaskowitz, a heavyset dragoon with coarse white-blond hair, huge hands and a flat boxer's nose. At the same time he consented to move out of the common bedroom. His bed, chiffonnier and wardrobe were taken to a downstairs alcove that opened from his study and had been used before as a depository for odds and ends. Now its window was hung with drapes ordered from Berlin and its floor covered with an antique Tabriz. To keep people from jumping to conclusions, Alexa told Anni that the change was only temporary, until her husband completed his work on a treatise.

It was a few days after the Sedlitzes' departure that Alexa went horseback riding with Lieutenant von Ranke. She had been in a depressed mood, at times filled with venomous anger over Hans Günther. She suspected that he had banished Dmowski from the house not to please her but to comply with his uncle's wishes. The general must have realized the dangers of the affair and convinced his nephew to end it.

As usual, Ranke was pouring out his heart to her. She was destroying him, he said. He could no longer sleep, eat or think and spent his evenings alone in his flat drinking himself into a stupor. As a result, he was neglecting his duties and feared he might be relieved of his command.

His laments bored her. He was quite good-looking, slim and athletic, but still he reminded her of a slug. A large pale-skinned slug, wet and cold to the touch and very vulnerable without the protective cover of a shell.

"Stop whining!" she flared. "What can you possibly want from me? My husband will never give me a divorce—he said so many times—so marriage is out of the question. An affair? He is your comrade. It wouldn't be chivalrous to cuckold a comrade, would it? Besides, Allenstein is a small nest. You can't even sneeze without everyone hearing it. So why don't you find yourself a nice girl and—"

"I hate nice girls."

"I was a nice girl once."

"I could die for you," he said. She found the stare of his gray hyaloid eyes strangely disconcerting. It frightened and at the same time excited her. "Could you kill for me?" The question leapt from her mouth before she could weigh its ominous portent.

His reaction was not immediate. For a few seconds he

rode in silence. Suddenly he reined in his horse. "What do you mean, kill?" he asked in a muffled voice.

She laughed. "Nothing. I was joking."

She too had slowed down her horse. They were turning into the road that ran along the Alle. Spring had changed the forbidding bareness of the riverside into a marvelous park. Grass and shrubs were jubilantly green and the white trunks of the birches glistened like snakeskins in the sun. It was too beautiful a world to be unhappy in, Alexa thought.

"Yes," she heard Ranke say. "I think I could kill for you."

The tone of his voice startled her. She looked at him. His face was flushed and his jaw was quivering. A man possessed, she thought, and watched him with the same mixture of curiosity and abhorrence that a lewd act or an execution elicits from a spectator.

"Is it true that you once killed your best friend?" she asked and held her breath.

The jaw stopped quivering, and for a second the face turned into stone. "It was a duel. And he wasn't my *best* friend."

"Nevertheless, a friend."

"That's a rather vague term. There are friends and friends."

They left the Alle and turned into the road leading to Parade Platz. "You asked me if I could kill for you. I've told you I could. Next question please."

"Forget it. It was a bad joke. I'd heard rumors about you and they made me wonder. They didn't fit the image I had of you—gentle and sensitive, a Prussian Roland. I might have been wrong, but that was the way I saw you."

"The way you saw me?" he asked with a touch of rancor to his voice. "I'm surprised and flattered that you *did* see me at all. I used to think that you didn't even know I existed. I still do at times."

"Don't be absurd," she protested, though not too convincingly.

When they reached the house, she asked him in for a cup

of tea. He noticed Hans Günther's horse being walked by Jerzy around the stable yard, which indicated that the major was home.

"Perhaps some other time," he said.

She felt the wicked excitement that had gripped her during their ride get hold of her again. "Don't be silly. Hans Günther will be glad to see you. He loves company." She almost added that he preferred even Ranke's company to an afternoon spent alone with her, but thought better of it.

Leaving their mounts in Jerzy's care, they went inside and found Hans Günther, wearing a brocade smoking jacket and suede slippers, engrossed in a book. If he resented the unexpected visitor, he failed to show it. In his contacts with fellow officers, even artillery subalterns, he was always impeccably cordial and hospitable. Now that the blind spot of love that had dimmed her vision before was no longer there, Alexa could coldly and cynically appraise the eagerness with which he tried to charm and conquer all. He was like a politician running for office, shaking every reachable hand in the hope that it was attached to a voter. She knew how little he thought of Ranke, whom in one of his more fractious moods he would coolly snub; but Ranke didn't know this and was overwhelmed and at the same time disconcerted by the kindness of the comrade whose wife he loved.

With teacups in hand, the men were discussing the rumor that King Edward, claiming indisposition, had canceled his state visit to Berlin, yet felt well enough to pay an informal call on Czar Nicholas in Reval.

"Edward is courting Russia, which means that the ring around Germany is growing tighter and tighter, my dear Otto," the major said. "It won't be long before your howitzers will be firing live shells."

"The sooner the better," Ranke said. "I'm constantly plagued by the fear that war will come when I'm too old for combat service."

"That's the spirit, Otto. There's nothing like a healthy

bloodletting to clear the air. We might have a two-front war, but I'm not worried. England has no army, the morale of the French was crushed for good at Sedan, the Russians are cattle. First we must finish off the enemy within, though. The pacifists, the Socialists, the rabble-rousers. The trouble is, the police have been hitting the demonstrators with the blunt edge of the sword; it's high time they use the sharp edge. Or if the police won't, let the army do it."

"How true." Ranke beamed.

Alexa felt a sudden urge to dispel the ménage-à-trois coziness of the visit. "Apropos bloodletting. Lieutenant Ranke practices what he preaches. Did you know that he once killed a man? Shot him dead."

Ranke squirmed, embarrassed. "It was a duel."

"Does that make any difference?" Alexa asked. "What do you think, Hans?"

Her husband frowned. "Of course it does. What a question!" He turned to Ranke. "Forgive my wife, Otto. She is in one of her épater-le-bourgeois moods again. Why she's brought up the subject is beyond me."

"We discussed it on our way here," Alexa said.

"Did you?"

"I asked the lieutenant if the rumor was true and he said it was."

"That was very tactless of you."

Ranke's face turned crimson. "I didn't mind it. It's really—"

"Some more tea, Lieutenant?" Alexa asked. Not waiting for his answer, she filled his cup. "I apologize. I'll never mention it again. I promise."

"I'm not ashamed of it," Ranke hastened to reassure her. Or was he reassuring the husband? "It was an unfortunate affair, but it happened and—"

"But you wish it hadn't," she said as Hans Günther fumbled with his collar, which, she knew, was a sign that he was angry.

"I wouldn't s-say that," Ranke stuttered. "What I mean is, once you find yourself in a situation like that—"

209

"Let's change the subject, shall we?" Hans Günther cut in.

"Why should we?" She thoroughly enjoyed the discussion —her husband's loss of aplomb and Ranke's cringing. "I find duels most intriguing. You shoot a man, but because there were four seconds looking on you're not a criminal but a hero. Why, Hans?" she asked.

Hans Günther rose and crossed to a framed painting, an autumn landscape done in the manner of Constable, hanging slightly askew on the wall, and straightened it. "Why don't servants ever right a picture after dusting it?" he muttered. "Another mystery."

"Hans, do you think it's no crime to kill a man in a duel?"

"It depends."

"Depends on what?"

"On how you look at it. According to the Bible it *is* a crime, but according to our code of honor it is not. You're not shooting a defenseless person. He is armed with the same weapon as you. He can kill or wound you just as you can kill or wound him—" He stopped suddenly and raised his voice. "Please let's stop this, Alexa! We're embarrassing our guest."

Ranke had risen when Hans Günther had. He giggled nervously. "I really don't mind—"

"It's a subject that has always intrigued me. This is my first chance to talk about it to someone who was personally involved." She turned to Ranke. "Is it the preceding formalities—the challenge, the seconds, the choice of weapons— that exonerate duelers?"

"They're part of it. You're expected to defend your honor as officer and gentleman. If you refuse to fight, you must leave the service," Ranke answered evenly. His attitude seemed to have undergone a change. He was no longer discomfited. He even sounded as if he welcomed the attention.

"Could there be such a thing as a duel without seconds, without witnesses?" Alexa asked.

Hans Günther returned to the table. Emitting a loud grunt,

he dropped into his chair. "For heaven's sake, Alexa, why this sudden preoccupation with bloodshed?"

She ignored him. "What did you feel when you were told your friend was dead?" she asked Ranke.

"I wasn't told, didn't have to be. I could tell he was."

"And what was your reaction?"

"Relief that it was all over."

"Didn't you feel guilty?"

"The matter had been before the Council of Honor, a reconciliation had been attempted, and when that failed we were ordered to go ahead and—"

"And you weren't even sent to prison?"

"No. Only detained at the regimental command post."

"For how long?"

"Four months."

"Is four months proper punishment for taking a man's life?"

She had gone too far. Ranke threw a nervous glance at the small Empire clock on the console table and took a deep breath as though ready to speak, but Alexa intercepted him. "How about the same duel without the sanction of the Council, the presence of the seconds, the doctor and all that stuff?"

"What is this, an inquest?" Hans Günther asked.

"A philosophical discussion. Can't we just once talk about something more interesting than who is going to ride what mount in the next horse show?"

"No," Hans Günther said. "I may not be a deep thinker, but I'd rather talk about horses than crime and punishment. I'll leave that to Dostoevski. So let's declare the debate closed."

Ranke hurriedly rose. "I'm afraid I'll have to be on my way. Baroness . . . Major, it's been a pleasure."

"I'm glad you think so," Hans Günther said with a hollow chuckle. "Though I doubt you do. So please accept my apologies. It was really my fault that you were exposed to my wife's interrogation."

"Oh, but why—"

"I shouldn't have raised objections, then she wouldn't have gone on with it. She loves to spite me. You weren't the target, I was. You're not married, so you're a stranger to the insidious ways of the female mind. Women create conflicts to keep in training. Over any nonsensical object, so they'll be in shape for the real issue. When that comes up, God save the poor husband."

Ranke responded with an uneasy grin. Hans Günther saw him off, then returned to the salon. "You're impossible, Alexa. I'm inclined to agree with the medical opinion that you're a bit unhinged. What the hell are you up to? Whatever you feel about me is your business. I don't give a damn. I merely insist that you keep up appearances, or take the consequences."

"The consequences?" She massaged her temples, trying to rub away a sudden headache. She repeated it without a question mark. "The consequences."

Lieutenant von Ranke had a four-room ground-floor flat on Nikolai Strasse, a narrow street winding its way behind the Castle of the Knights of the Teutonic Order. Not many subalterns could afford the luxury of such quarters. Most were boarders, renting one or, at the most, two rooms in homes of local families. He was considered to be well off, even rich by regimental standards, though no one knew for certain, because despite his cordial manners he had made after two years in Allenstein a flock of acquaintances but no close friends.

It was on an early May afternoon that Alexa first slipped through the dark porte-cochere from which his front door opened. She had been riding with him in the morning, and her spur-of-the-moment promise to see him at his quarters was almost as big a surprise to her as to him. It caught him wholly unprepared. She detected a labored note to his much too effusively expressed delight.

Up to the last moment she hesitated. She was starved for

love, but Ranke was not the man to satisfy her. He was not Hans Günther, with whom she had been enamored, nor was he Nicholas Karady, who had attracted her physically. Ranke bored her. What compelled her to choose him for her lover and not one of the more winsome and eagerly willing young bucks of her circle was the touch of insanity she sensed in him. There was madness in the glassy stare of his eyes, in his passion for her, in his doglike compliance with her whims. She was the prisoner of a marriage that was like a granite wall around her. Nothing less than a charge of nitroglycerin could demolish it. In Ranke she hoped to find the explosive to blow it up.

She arrived half an hour late and found Ranke in a state of suicidal despair. He had bunches of violets—her favorite flowers—in small vases all over the place, champagne chilled in an elegant silver bucket he had rushed out to buy an hour before and candles burning in candelabra and chandeliers. All the drapes were drawn to shut out the daylight.

"I was afraid you forgot," he whispered as he peeled off her coat. There were tears in his eyes. "I love you so."

She let him embrace her and endured his awkward fumbling with the hooks along the back of her dress. He freed her shoulders and showered them with kisses. Then suddenly he pulled away from her. "How stupid of me. I haven't asked you if you would care for a glass of wine or—"

"Wine would be nice." She had to bolster up her courage or, she feared, the escapade would come to an end before it began.

With trembling fingers he uncorked the bottle and poured for both of them. She emptied her glass and held it out to have him refill it. "I don't know what makes me so thirsty. Probably the sauerkraut we had at noon."

"Yes, sauerkraut has that effect." Then, without a pause, "I love you so."

She downed her second glassful. "You're repeating yourself. Can't you think of something more original to say?"

"You're making fun of me. I'm afraid I bore you, but when I am with you my mind becomes a blur. I'm not myself. It's like being drugged. Away from you, I can think of a million things to say, but when with you . . ."

There were fat pear-shaped tears rolling down his cheeks. Laughing, she pulled out her handkerchief and patted his face dry. He pressed the handkerchief to his lips and kissed it, inhaling the fragrance of her perfume. The scene was like one of those romantic postcards so popular with lovesick seamstresses and parlormaids, she thought.

"You puzzle me, Otto. Here we are alone, just the two of us. You told me you'd be the happiest man on earth if I came. Now I'm here and you're in tears."

Suddenly his arms closed around her with a force that caused her to cry out. "You're hurting me!"

"I want you!" He breathed heavily into her ear. "I want you so much that it's driving me out of my mind."

For a moment she wondered if she had delivered herself into the hands of a madman. He lifted her off her feet, carried her into the bedroom and fell upon her with the carnivorous hunger of a wolf. He snorted inarticulate half-words while his fingers struggled clumsily with the snaps and hooks of her clothes. Afraid that he might tear her dress to shreds, she stripped to her chemise.

Suddenly she was thinking of Nicholas. She recalled his gentle touch, his knowing ways that turned lovemaking into a game and a celebration. She felt disgusted with herself for being in bed with a man who left her so completely cold. She braced herself to push him away, when as abruptly as he had attacked he pulled back and collapsed. "I'm sorry," he muttered and was crying again.

Her first reaction was relief. She had to cover her face with her hands to keep from laughing. At him and at herself. What a stupid, irrational idea to choose him to be the instrument of her liberation. She had judged him to be man enough to kill

214

for her; now she discovered that he wasn't even a man. Instead of disappointment, she felt glee. The absurd adventure was over and she could return to normalcy.

He rose to his knees, took hold of her stockinged feet and pressed his lips to them. "I am so ashamed. I was sure with you it would be different."

She was beginning to feel sorry for him. "There's nothing to be ashamed of. It happens to everybody."

"I love you so much."

"Yes, I know."

"Don't leave me. I'll kill myself if you leave me now!"

She stroked his head soothingly, as if he were a frenzied dog. "No, I won't. Anyway, I told my housekeeper I was going to a tea party and wouldn't be home before six." She looked around the room, really seeing it for the first time. "You have lovely things. That chest in the corner is exquisite. Must be an antique."

"It's Mama's. She furnished the place for me, to make it homelike. She knew Allenstein wasn't going to be a happy tour for me."

"Isn't it?"

"No. And now this." He shook his head in despair.

Reassuringly she patted his hand. She was afraid he would burst into tears again. "Is that your mother?" She pointed at the framed photo of a dark-haired woman with the hint of a mustache—or was it just a shadow?—heavy brows and eyes that had Ranke's glassy stare.

He looked lovingly at the picture. "Yes, that's Mama."

"What an interesting face. Tell me about her." She wanted him to talk, fill the oppressive silence around them with sound, any sound.

"Oh, she's really remarkable. The best. We've always been very close. Especially after my father's death. He died in an accident." He paused for a second, his lips twitching nervously, then continued with sudden animation. "We lived in a big house in Grunewald, which was practically country in those days. Had a swing in the garden and a croquet court. We knew no families with children, and I had no playmates except Mama. I didn't miss them, because I had her. We played cards and other games and—" He choked with fits of unmotivated laughter. "She would hoist me up on her back, pretending to be my horse, and would take me on long gallops around the house and garden. I think that's why I like riding so much." He giggled, with a strange glow on his face. "Sometimes when I ride, I imagine I'm still a child." Embarrassed, he fell silent. There were beads of perspiration on his forehead and he was breathing heavily.

She watched him, torn between repulsion and curiosity. "So you liked being carried around by your mama?"

He nodded, ill-at-ease. "Oh, yes, I suppose all children do."

She stayed another hour. They talked, had more wine, kissed and petted some. When she left, she promised to see him again, although she was not certain she would. For the moment she merely wished to get away without having to watch another hysterical outburst.

A few days later, on a sunny warm afternoon, she yielded to his pleas to go riding with him. He was in an unusually lighthearted mood, as frisky and playful as a young animal put out to pasture after a long winter in the barn. They left the cultivated tracts behind and rode out into the country, where wooded spots alternated with sandy hills and small stagnant water holes. After a while he became oddly quiet, his face screwed up in pained concentration, his spine stiffly erect. They were moving through a clearing in a forest when he suddenly reined in his horse, dismounted, then brought hers to a halt. Without a word he lifted her off the saddle. Too surprised to resist, she tumbled down on the moss-covered ground with him.

He made love to her on a thick mat of last year's fallen leaves that smelled, not unpleasantly, of decay. Later the odor of rain-soaked forests always reminded her of their first coupling, performed by him with the breathless speed of a tardy passenger jumping onto an already moving train.

She began to see Ranke regularly, once or twice a week, mostly at his flat. She no longer had to find excuses for staying away from home, for Hans Günther never asked her where she had spent the afternoon. For the sake of appearances, she seldom went riding with Ranke; the less they were seen together the better, she thought. When going to his place, she always wore a hat with a thick veil and over her dress a voluminous duster of the kind that had become fashionable for automobilists. She failed to realize that after a while it was her disguise that caused people to wonder about the identity of Lieutenant von Ranke's lady visitor.

It didn't take her long to tire of Ranke. What had initially attracted her, the touch of the diabolic in him, was nothing more than the emotional instability of a twenty-seven-year-old mama's boy. He was too sentimental and melancholy to be good company, and he made a queer and inconstant lover. His bizarre behavior shocked and amused her for a while, but she was willing to play his games, because at the same time she was playing hers.

The games that would precede his bedding her were the re-enactments of his childhood romps with his mother. At least she suspected they were. They aroused him and helped him to overcome his defects. By turning him into a complete man she performed a miracle and subsequently became the object of his fanatical adoration. His dependence on her bordered on the pathological. She was unable to determine what she found more disturbing—his ecstatic celebrations of his resuscitated manhood or his despondency each time she was late or canceled a date.

They had nothing in common. What bound them together was his desire for her and, on her part, the possibility that he might serve as her revenger and liberator.

Since the late March night when she stumbled upon Hans

Günther and Dmowski in the study, she had been preoccupied with the idea of Hans Günther's death. At first it was a scheme to keep her mind busy during her empty hours, then for a while it became an obsession. She hinted at it to Ranke only after they had become lovers. Afraid to shock him, she made a few cautious allusions.

To her surprise, he reacted with a knowing glint in his opalescent eyes. "Remember how long ago I told you that I would be willing to kill for you?"

For a second she froze. An inside voice told her to retreat; later she wished she had. "I wasn't thinking of *him* at the time."

"But now you are."

She covered her face with her hands to escape his penetrating gaze. "I don't know. Sometimes I feel so wretched that I get the craziest ideas. If he only would give me a divorce, but he won't."

"Would you marry me if he did?"

She kept her hand pressed to her face. It was a childhood habit to hide her eyes when telling a lie. "You know I would."

They were in bed after some rather arduous lovemaking that had invigorated him but had exhausted and depressed her. She had never told him about the real cause of the rift between her and Hans Günther, only that they had become estranged.

He reached out and peeled her hands off her face, forcing her to look at him. "Do you love me?"

"For God's sake, how many times shall I tell you! Would I be here if I didn't?"

"I wonder," he said in a muffled voice. He watched her pensively. "What made you bring up the subject of duels in front of him? To warn him? To threaten him? It was a mistake. He is no fool, and now he suspects that you want to pit us against each other. But he won't let you. He's been avoiding me like the plague. The other day when I ran into him at the officers' club he was more cordial than ever before. I can't just walk up to him and slap his face."

"How did it come to a duel between you and the man you killed? I heard you'd been friends." She had asked him before, but he always evaded the issue. "Did he challenge you or—"

He cut her short. "I challenged him." He turned his back on her, got out of bed and began dressing.

"But why?"

"He'd been drinking and made a quip I didn't like."

"What kind of a quip?" When Ranke ignored the question, she went on. "Weren't you sorry for him? I mean, later?"

"No. He'd asked for it."

She reflected. "What if there hadn't been any Council of Honor or seconds or attempts at reconciliation? In other words, no witnesses, just the two of you? Would you have shot him dead?"

He answered after a long pause. "I suppose so; it was inevitable."

Duel without witnesses. For the following weeks this was the topic they toyed with. She couldn't be sure whether he was serious or merely willing to go along with her fantasies to humor her. Neither was she certain about her own commitment. At times the plot seemed nothing more than food for some conversation to fill his long oppressive silences.

Once or twice Alexa suggested a bona-fide duel, but the idea failed to appeal to Ranke. He said he would wait until the fall and for the right circumstances, when the shooting could be staged to look like a hunting accident. Even though Hans Günther was no passionate sportsman, he was looking forward to the opening of the season. Game was plentiful around Allenstein, and hunting was one of the few pastimes to relieve the monotony of life in a small garrison.

Ranke's plan was to catch him alone in the woods, approach him and challenge him to a duel. Despite Alexa's skepticism, he stuck to the concept of a confrontation between two equally armed men. The thought of shooting down an unsuspecting victim from ambush was against his credo as officer and gentleman, he said. He even composed the phrases with which to address Hans Günther before their taking up positions and aiming their pistols at each other. Alexa clearly saw the fallacy of his version. Ranke was no fool. After having once gotten away by the skin of his teeth, he would not tempt his luck for a second time. Facing a good shot like Hans Günther, he was not going to wait to be gunned down but would fire first and be done with it. The myth of the chivalrous duel was invented for her benefit, to be adhered to even after the act.

Slowly the plan was losing its allure for her. It was the first of June and the hunting season still months away. She and Ranke had discussed the duel without seconds in such detail that it began to seem as if it had already taken place in the past. She saw the absurdity of it. Envisioning Hans Günther's violent death so many times and so vividly caused her to feel, if not compassionate, at least tolerant about his person. She was like a viper whose poison gland had been drained of its venom; she still hissed and coiled herself to attack, but she knew she intended no harm.

Having abandoned the plan, she was determined to break with Ranke.

"I'm afraid I won't see you for a while," she told him after a lackluster afternoon. "I suspect Hans Günther has found out about us. We had a fight the other day and he warned me that he won't stand for being cuckolded. It's his vanity, you know."

"Not see you for a while?" Ranke wrinkled his brow as if he had trouble understanding. "No, that can't be—"

"We've taken awful chances, Otto. Someone must've seen me coming here. I knew that sooner or later it would happen."

"You mean, I won't see you at all?"

"Of course you will. We'll meet as before, when others are around. But not here, it would be too risky."

He wasn't duped. "You're through with me. You don't love me anymore."

"Don't be absurd. For God's sake, I'm a married woman. I'm not free to do as I please."

"You could be free. Tomorrow, today, right now."

"That's nonsense, Otto. Anyway, this whole thing about the hunting accident—it's just not realistic. I've been thinking a lot. It was a crazy idea. Frankly, I never really meant it. Neither did you."

"We both did. But now you want to back out."

"I'm telling you, it's insane. You're not a murderer and I am not Lady Macbeth. It was . . . it was a moment of madness. I was furious with Hans Günther and—"

"And you wanted him dead."

"No, not really. I lost my head. Please try to look at it rationally. Here we are, two sensible adults indulging in a fantasy. You must realize that it can't be done. No one would believe it was an accident. They would look for a suspect and immediately spot you. People would remember having seen you following him into the woods—"

"It doesn't have to be in the woods."

"Where else?"

"Anyplace."

"In Allenstein? Where everyone knows you?"

"Two years ago there was a case here. A house had been broken into on York Strasse. Both the owner—I think he was a saddle maker—and his wife were killed. It was a clear case of murder, and the culprit was never found."

"I've heard of it. Of course if you're lucky you can get away with anything. Not every crime is solved. Nevertheless, let's forget it. At least for the time being. No matter how I look at it, I still think that the idea of the hunting accident is the safest. So let's wait until the fall and see what happens in the meanwhile. Hans Günther might decide to give me a divorce after all."

She saw him nod. She couldn't tell whether it was in agreement or because he'd run out of objections. Anyway, she could hardly wait to be out of the flat. Its closely drawn drapes, burning candles and air heavy with the fragrance of a potted tuberose reminded her of a mortuary. He followed her to the anteroom. He unlocked the door for her with a key that he'd had in his pocket all the time. She realized that she had virtually been his prisoner.

"When do I see you?" he asked, holding on to her arm.

"Next Monday we'll ride out to the Wartenberg Inn with the Seifferts. Join us."

"I meant here."

"I told you I won't be coming here. Please don't let's fight over that again."

Without a word he stepped back and allowed her to leave. She rushed out without looking back, although she knew he was standing in the open door staring after her. For the first time in more than two months she was glad to go home. She felt like a person who had been in a serious accident and survived it unharmed. She vowed never to cross Otto von Ranke's threshold again.

9

July second began like any other summer day in Allenstein, probably a little cooler than average because an unexpected cold current wafted in from the sea. The sun had risen behind a threadbare layer of clouds, and a thin haze lingered on, softening the green of the vegetation and the red of the roofs to the muted hues of a Claude Monet landscape. By six the clouds had drifted away and the sun became bright enough to sting eyes used to the veiled skies of a spring that had been reluctant to observe the calendar and yield to summer.

At five-thirty sharp, Dragoon Blaskowitz had Hans Günther's horse saddled and led up to the house. In the kitchen Fräulein Busse had filled the silver coffeepot and the milk pitcher, buttered two rolls delivered a few minutes earlier from the Krumm bakery, and spooned strawberry jam into a glass-lined silver jar, placing everything on a tray to be taken to the dining room as soon as the major rang for his breakfast. She waited for the familiar footsteps from the study, but there was silence.

She was used to hearing the bell at five-fifteen, and when the big clock on the kitchen wall showed five-twenty-five she began to wonder whether to reheat the milk. The major liked

223

his café au lait piping hot. She could not remember when during her six-month tenure in the house he had been late on duty mornings. As far as she knew, he had stayed home the night before and gone to his study right after supper while she and the girls were still doing the dishes in the kitchen. He had looked well, ate moderately and drank no more than one glass of Rhine wine. Her premonition of something being wrong grew more and more pronounced as the minutes ticked away. The possibility that he was off duty and had decided to sleep late seemed unlikely, because even on such days he was up before six.

A fear of his unpredictable reaction kept her from knocking on his door. After more minutes passed, she decided to have Blaskowitz wake him. She found the orderly out front walking the horse. Johann Blaskowitz had not been with the major long enough to think his tardiness unusual or alarming. When Anni Busse told him to leave the horse tethered to a tree, he insisted on leading it back to the safety of its stall and looking in on the major afterward. For cavalrymen, horses had precedence over humans, even humans in officers' uniforms. Johann considered Fräulein Busse a pain in the ass. He suffered her in silence because he considered her to be the price he had to pay for the comparative luxury of being an officer's orderly.

"What the hell am I to tell the major?" he asked the woman. "He might be furious if I wake him. A cousin of mine lost an eye when his captain threw a boot tree at him because he'd entered the room without knocking and found the captain in bed with the parlormaid."

"So knock first. I promise you won't find Major Godenhausen in bed with the parlormaid." She realized much too late what she had said and slapped herself on the mouth. Luckily Blaskowitz was too simple-minded to catch the innuendo.

He trotted off to the study. Holding her breath, Anni followed him, then halted a few meters' distance from the door. What happened from then on had the eerie quality of a dream. Later, when she tried to recall the sequence of events, she saw scenes as diffused and nebulous as if they had taken place under water. There was Blaskowitz's loud animal cry, then, for what seemed an interminably long time, silence. Finally, his face ashen, his mouth wide open, he staggered from the room, holding high his right hand like a crucifix carried in a procession. The hand shook violently and was smeared with blood.

The sight of blood elicited an ear-splitting cry from Anni. Later she denied that she had screamed, but Bona and Svetlana, who had been in the laundry lighting the fire under the big caldron, insisted that it had been her scream that brought them running to the study. Johann's stance as he leaned for support against the doorpost—his bloody right hand still in the air and the expression of pain, or was it terror, on his face—caused them to think that it had been he who had met with an accident. Fräulein Busse, no longer shrieking, was emitting low moans.

"Jesus Maria, what happened to you?" Svetlana asked Johann.

"It's the major . . . the major. He's dead . . . dead."

Anni stopped gurgling. "Dead? How do you know he's dead?"

"I don't know. Maybe not. I felt him . . . he seemed warm . . . but he's dead."

Anni started for the door. Scared of what lay behind it, she halted in her tracks. "I knew it when he didn't ring for his breakfast."

Bona's eyes traveled from the orderly to the woman. There was an expression of contempt on her face. "Call a doctor!"

Anni stared at the girl. "A doctor?"

"Don't just stand there like a sick mule!" Bona shouted at her. "Didn't you hear what Johann said? He might be alive."

Anni suddenly remembered who she was. Officer's daughter and lady. "Yes, we must call a doctor." Once again in command, she threw back her shoulders and pulled herself erect.

"There is a Dr. Brück. I've seen his shield . . . corner of Schiller Strasse. But hurry, will you?"

Bona was already storming out through the front door, unmindful of the house rule that servants were supposed to use the delivery entrance.

Svetlana squeezed past Johann and, crossing herself, entered the study. Its drapes were still drawn. Before her eyes could penetrate the gloom and see the nightshirted form stretched out in front of the bedroom door, she was ordered back by the housekeeper.

"Come back, Svetlana. No one's supposed to touch anything in there." She raised her voice. "Out! Right this minute!" When Svetlana emerged, Anni turned to Johann. "I hope you had sense enough not to move anything." No longer shaken, she was herself again.

"No, I didn't. I mean, I didn't move anything. Tried to lift him, but—"

"You shouldn't have. There will be an investigation and—" Suddenly she halted. "Good God, the baroness. We must wake her. Svetlana go and—"

The girl backed away. "Not me! No! No! I won't. *You* wake her!"

"Svetlana, that's an order!"

The girl laughed hysterically. "Order! You sound like Captain Kleinmeister. That's the one I worked for before coming here. He was crazy too."

"Stop laughing, you idiot! Don't you have respect for the dead. Dumb Pole." Anni emitted a loud unhappy sigh. "I'll wake the poor woman. Someone's got to." Slowly, reluctantly, she started for the stairway.

Johann intercepted her. "You must report the major's death to Colonel Seiffert. That's regulations, you know."

Anni frowned. She resented being reminded of a duty. She was always ready to give advice but not to receive it. Especially not from a private. "Go and report it then. What are you waiting for?"

226

"I've got to wash my hands," he mumbled. He stared at his blood-smeared hand.

"Then wash them. But hurry."

He started for the kitchen while she climbed the stairway. Barely five minutes had passed since Johann had found the major's body, but they seemed like an eternity to her. The thought that she should have taken some action, gone into the study herself and from there into the major's bedroom, flashed through her mind. If he was murdered, the murderer might still be in the house. In that case it had been insane of her to send Johann away. Now the murderer might come out of hiding and kill them all.

She reached Alexa's door. It could have been suicide, she reasoned. It most likely was. She had to wake the woman. No sound came from the room, so she assumed that her mistress was still asleep. She could easily be, despite the commotion downstairs. The walls were thick and the study was in the opposite wing of the house.

Anni Busse wasn't heartless, only frustrated and, at times, uncharitable. Of good country stock and an Obere Töchterschule graduate, but still unmarried at forty-five, she had to work for a living, be ordered about by women who, she felt, weren't half as well bred as she was. Deep down she hated all her employers, and Alexa was no exception. Nevertheless, now that she had to confront her with the shattering news of her young husband's sudden death, her heart went out to her. Gently she knocked on the door and waited for an answer. When none came, she entered and tiptoed to the bed.

Alexa lay on her side, her disheveled hair spread out over the pillows. Breathing quietly, she seemed to be fast asleep. When Anni touched her shoulder, she stirred, turned on her back and opened her eyes. Catching sight of Anni, she blinked, then sat up frowning. "What time is it?" she asked drowsily.

"Baroness," Anni whispered to her, "I'm sorry to wake you, but—" Her eyes filled with tears. "It's terrible, I don't know how to tell you." She dropped to her knees beside the bed and

227

with a sisterly gesture, so alien to her nature, gathered Alexa into her arms. "The major— Something terrible happened to the major."

Alexa looked down at the blond head resting on her shoulder and wondered how she could push it away without appearing rude. There was a spot on its top where the hair was thinning that she had never noticed before. "To the major?" She repeated the words like a parrot. Awakening had always been a slow process for her. Now too she was reluctant to emerge from the blessed state of semiconsciousness. She pulled away to escape the rancid oily odor of Anni's hair.

"He had— He was— I sent for Dr. Brück, but I'm afraid it's too late," Anni cried. Her heavy body was shaken by a fit of sobbing and the whole bed shook with her.

Slowly Anni's babbling began to make sense to Alexa. It concerned Hans Günther. A doctor had been sent for, although her husband was beyond help. Her eyes shifted to the clock on the dresser. It showed twelve minutes to six, approximately the time of his usual leaving for duty, so whatever happened to him had taken place in the house. Or while he was on his way out. She shuddered, because the horrible inference she drew from Anni's words chilled her. She managed to take hold of herself seconds before the name Ranke could slip through her lips. Breaking the stranglehold of Anni's sympathy that threatened to choke her, she threw her legs over the side of the bed and stood up.

"Is he dead?" she asked. Then without waiting for the answer, "Where is he?"

"In the study. He must have stepped from the bedroom and collapsed. But please don't go down. Not before the doctor comes."

Alexa slipped on her negligee, recalling with bitter irony that once she had been told not to leave her room unless properly dressed, and descended the stairway. Crossing the entrance hall, the stone floor felt icy cold to the soles of her bare feet. She heard Anni's heavy breathing following close

228

behind. Svetlana was still in the hallway. Catching sight of her mistress, she covered her face with her apron and began to sob softly.

Alexa entered the study and was halfway across the room when the sight of Hans Günther's body stretched out in front of the bedroom door brought her to a sudden halt.

Wearing a long nightshirt of Irish linen, a sock on his left foot, the right one bare, he lay on his stomach, his head turned to the side as though taking a look at something over his shoulder. His hair, in need of the cut he had planned to get that week, fell tousled over his forehead. His mouth was open and so was the eye that showed in the pale profile outlined against the dark carpet on the floor. A few centimeters to the right of his spine there was a dark spot the size of a man's palm on the white linen.

She stood petrified, soundlessly staring at the form before her. The realization that she was responsible for the bloodstain on the back, the sightless eye, the irrevocable finality of death hit her with the force of an iron fist. She had played a game to fill hours of boredom: freedom at any price, hunting accident, duel without witnesses—empty words uttered carelessly. She had not once contemplated their possible consequences.

What she felt was no grief but the painful recognition of her inability to make a happening unhappen again. In the game she had played, Hans Günther's death marked the end of a tale. Now she knew it was only the beginning. It was all terribly confusing, and the most confusing part of it was her own reaction to the denouement she herself had plotted. Or had she? Had she really believed that Otto von Ranke could kill in cold blood? Even now, as she was looking at his victim, the assumption seemed incredible.

She heard the front door open and the sound of footsteps and voices. A tall, slightly bent man with a short dark beard, his white shirt tieless and unbuttoned under a black suit, appeared in the doorway. She had not met him before, yet knew he was Dr. Max Brück, the physician who lived in the next block. She had frequently seen him drive by in his buggy. He had a fine reputation and, although a Jew, had many officers' families for patients.

"I'm afraid you're late, Doctor," she told him. There was no need for introductions.

Dr. Brück stepped to the body. "May I have some light?"

She signaled to Bona, who had returned with the doctor. "Will you pull the drapes open?"

The girl looked at her, terrified. "No." She huddled with Svetlana and Anni on the threshold. None of them moved. To reach the windows and the drape cords meant passing the dead man. Alexa gritted her teeth and crossed first to one window, then to the other. As the heavy drapes parted, the room became flooded with the brightness of the July morning. A shaft of light fell across Hans Günther's face. With the mouth open, it had stiffened into a rigid mask, the pink of his suntanned complexion giving way to a sickly yellow.

What had been ghastly in semidarkness, became sheer horror when bathed in light. Dr. Brück knelt down beside the body, examining it for life signs. Slowly he rose and crossed to Alexa.

"I'm terribly sorry, Baroness, there is nothing I can do for the major. I won't even move him from his present position, not before the arrival of the military authorities."

"He was shot, wasn't he?" Alexa asked and immediately wished she had not. People might wonder how she knew.

"Yes, madam, he was shot."

"But why? How?"

"That's for the inquest to find out." He gave her a long concerned look, then turned to Anni. "Would you please bring a glass of water for the baroness?"

"Bona, a glass of water, quickly." Anni relayed the request to the girl. Even murder in the family was no reason for letting people mistake Fräulein Anni Busse for a servant.

The doctor handed a pill to Alexa. "Take this, Baroness. With a lot of water. I think you need it."

"What for?"

"To calm you."

Alexa smiled feebly. "Thank you, Doctor, but I am calm."

He sorted out more pills. "One every four hours. And these two when you go to bed." He handed them to her. "I'll come by in the afternoon, or if you need me at any time, just send for me."

When Bona appeared with the water, she obediently swallowed the pill. A moment later she was glad she had, because she heard the sound of a carriage rolling up the driveway to the entrance. Whatever the pill contained, she hoped it would help her live through the next hours.

"I think the gentlemen from the regiment are here," she told Anni. "Will you let them in?" She turned to the maids. "Go to your room. And don't leave the house, because you might be needed."

They scurried off like two frightened rabbits. Anni left to answer the door and was now ushering in two captains and a colonel. Alexa had met Colonel Seiffert, Hans Günther's commandant, and Captain Draeseke, but not the third man, who was introduced to her as Judge Advocate Captain Yves. Of the three, the colonel alone appeared personally affected by the tragedy. The captains expressed their sympathies, but their stiff carriage, clipped tones and searching glances warned Alexa that for the moment they reserved their judgment regarding her role in her husband's sudden and violent death.

Captain Yves suggested that she leave the room while the doctor examined the body for the cause of death. "But I must ask you to remain available, Baroness. That goes for the members of your household. I'm afraid we'll have a few questions of them—and you."

"It doesn't have to be right now, Baroness," the colonel said. He seemed to be anxious to take the edge off the captain's gruffness. "We're fully aware of the impact this terrible tragedy must have on you. I myself am benumbed, crushed."

It was only now that Alexa realized that she was barefoot,

with a flimsy negligee covering her nightgown and her hair falling loose and uncombed over her shoulders. "You'll excuse me while I put on some clothes," she said. "Then I'll be at your disposal. It's— I can't believe it's true. Last night I said good night to him and now this—" Her voice broke, then quickly she regained control of herself. "I'm sorry. I'll be all right."

"Oh, but you are. I admire your composure, Baroness," the judge advocate said. She detected a touch of irony in his tone, or was it only her bad conscience playing a trick on her? "An exemplary officer's lady," he added.

She thanked him with a forced smile. Assisted by Captain Draeseke, Dr. Brück was lifting Hans Günther from the floor to the couch. As she left the room and the door closed behind her, she heard the word "revolver" uttered in a loud surprised voice by one of the men, probably Captain Yves. She halted to listen, but the sight of Anni waiting for her at the foot of the stairway prompted her to continue.

"There is a big crowd outside the gate," Anni whispered excitedly, "but the colonel posted guards to keep the people out. And he gave orders that no one is supposed to leave the house. A soldier caught Jerzy as he was trying to sneak out. Now he's locked up in the tool shed. Wouldn't it be awful if it turned out he did it?"

"Did what?" Alexa asked shrilly.

"Killed the major."

"You idiot! You goose!" Alexa screamed at her. Suddenly she was no longer in control of the excitement churning in her. "How can you say such a thing? Don't you know what harm you can do that boy?"

"He was trying to run away, wasn't he?"

"He was scared. Aren't we all?"

The outburst, although it failed to relieve the dreadful pressure on her, had one beneficial result—it kept Anni subdued for the rest of the day. Upstairs, Alexa splashed cold water on her face, pinned up her hair and changed. Her winter wardrobe had been put away in moth balls, so she had no dress at hand that fitted the occasion. She chose a gray wool with a white jabot. She would have to order some black summer outfits for her year of mourning, she thought. One would have to be ready in a day so she could wear it to the funeral.

"Hans Günther's funeral." She enunciated the words slowly, tasting every syllable separately. Hans Günther was to be placed in a coffin, lowered into a grave, covered with a six-foot layer of earth. All that because there had been some frivolous talk about a duel without witnesses. At the moment there were four men in Hans Günther's study dealing with the consequences of her bizarre playacting. They needed no extrasensory perception to discover the truth. She felt an irresistible urge to rush to them and tell them to halt their probing; it was a waste of time for them and the prolongation of an unbearable suspense for her.

Although barely fifteen minutes had passed since Dr. Brück had handed her the first pill, she swallowed a second one, then went down to the salon to wait for whatever was in store for her. The door to the study was still closed; she heard the men talking but was unable to catch more than a jumble of words.

It was a few minutes later that the doorbell rang. After a pause it rang again. Alexa wondered if she should answer it, when she heard Johann's footsteps coming from the kitchen, then the squeak of the front door being opened. The visitor asked to see her. Shocked and incredulous, she recognized Otto von Ranke's voice.

The orderly knocked on the salon door. "Lieutenant von Ranke is here," he said. She noticed astonishment written all over his usually blank face. "I told him I was not sure the baroness would see him, but he said he won't go away."

Her first impulse was to say no, then she reconsidered. It was most reckless of Ranke to come to the house. Was he out of his mind? she wondered. She had to talk to him, if for no

233

other reason than to prevent him from committing another folly. Now she could see him alone, which would not be possible later.

"It's all right, Johann. Ask him in."

"I've just heard the dreadful news!" Ranke cried as he was ushered in. The orderly remained on the threshold, his eyes darting back and forth between the visitor and the hostess. "I'm crushed," Ranke went on. "I came to ask you if there is anything I can do. It's unbelievable. Someone from the cavalry command post telephoned us. First I thought it was a joke. Of course, who would joke about a tragedy?" Alexa thought he was overacting. Deathly pale, his eyes red-rimmed, and despite the coolness of the morning his forehead glistening with perspiration, Ranke looked definitely deranged. "My deepest sympathy," he muttered as he lifted her hand to his lips. The feel of his damp mustache reminded her of a dead squirrel she had found in the garden the day before.

The orderly kept lingering in the doorway.

"Johann," she told him, "bring in a bottle of Steinhäger with"—she counted—"one, two, three—six glasses." She turned to Ranke. "Colonel Seiffert is here with two gentlemen from Division and Dr. Brück." She waited for the orderly to move out of earshot. "Have you lost your mind?" she whispered to Ranke. "To come here? Now? The colonel brought along a judge advocate. They've been in the study at least twenty minutes. God only knows what's taking them so long."

"I had to see you."

"You're insane. You shouldn't have come. Anyway, how could you get in? I understand there are guards posted around the house. They've been ordered to keep everyone out."

"I told them the order didn't apply to me. I was a friend of the major's."

"Some friend!" Angrily she jerked her hand from Ranke's clasp. "You said you'd wait until the fall, make it seem like a hunting accident. But to do it now and right here in the house! We never talked about the house!"

234

He stared at her, not comprehending. Her rage, like an unexpected blow, stunned him for a second. "I was going mad," he mumbled. "Do you realize that it's been a week since I last saw you—and I couldn't even talk to you, because there were people around—and a month since you'd been to my place. It suddenly came over me—now or never—I wasn't going to wait another day. I came here and when I found the window of the hallway open . . ." More composed, he added, "We *did* talk about the house, Alexa."

"That I don't remember."

"Oh yes you do. I said I could make it look like it was done by a burglar. And you didn't object. You said if one was lucky one could get away with it."

"I didn't believe you would really do it," she protested lamely.

He gave her one of his one-way-mirror looks. She used to tease him about his strange stare, call him the man with two glass eyes. "I told you I'd do anything for you. Steal, rob, kill. You wanted me to kill. I did."

She wondered how to make him understand the change in her, something she herself was unable to explain. Perhaps what had happened to her happened to all sinners. After the crime, repentance. Or was it merely fear? Fear of punishment, retribution.

"You had better leave now."

"I want to be with you."

"For God's sake, don't you understand?" she said to him angrily. "You'll have to stay away from me for a while. Maybe it's already too late. We've been seen together so much, you'll be the first they'll suspect. You shouldn't have come here, but as long as you have—" She stopped because she heard the study door open. The men were leaving the study and crossing the entrance hall. There was a knock on the salon door.

When she called to them to enter, there was a bit of polite jostling in the doorway, with the colonel insisting that the doctor, a sexagenarian, enter first. The matter of precedence

235

was settled in the colonel's favor and the four trooped in. Ranke jumped to his feet and stood at attention in the crossfire of surprised and, Alexa thought, condemning glances.

"Why, Lieutenant von Ranke! When did *you* get here?" the colonel asked. Alexa noticed the two captains exchanging covert glances and felt her heartbeat accelerate. It was as though she had one of those cheap but dependable alarm clocks, the ticking of which could be heard rooms away, planted inside her rib cage.

"A few minutes ago, sir," Ranke said. "I came to offer my condolences— I mean, to ask Baroness von Godenhausen if there was anything I could do for her."

"How did you know condolences were in order, Lieutenant?" the judge advocate asked. "Incidentally, I haven't had the pleasure." He offered his hand. "Captain Yves."

"Otto von Ranke." Bowing stiffly, heels clicking, the lieutenant shook the hand. "Someone telephoned the tragedy to my command post."

"Someone. Could you be more specific?"

"I assume a dragoon from Major von Godenhausen's regiment."

"Who received the call?"

"I did. I happened to be in Major Brausch's office when the phone rang. He's my commandant."

"I know, I know. Was he present when the call came?"

"No, sir. He'd just stepped out."

With his eyes fastened on the lieutenant's face, the colonel listened attentively. Now he turned to the judge advocate. "Let's not digress, Captain. You wanted to talk to the baroness, didn't you? I'm sure the lieutenant will be at your disposal any time should you need him. But now, may we have a word with you alone, Baroness?"

She felt grateful for the colonel's tact, that he refrained from ordering Ranke to leave and allowed her, the lady of the house, to send him on his way.

"Thank you for your concern, Lieutenant." Not having been

236

told otherwise, he was still standing at rigid attention. "I appreciate it." She offered him her hand, then quickly pulled it back, barely letting his lips touch it. "Goodbye, Lieutenant." She made the dismissal sound cool and final. He reacted with an unhappy twitch of his facial muscles, nevertheless obediently bowed and marched from the room. In the doorway he almost collided with Anni, who was bringing the bottle of Steinhäger and glasses on a tray. She had changed, was now dressed in black from head to foot and wore an expression to go with the clothes. Her eyes were red-rimmed.

Alexa dismissed her with a gesture, then filled four glasses with schnapps. The officers thanked her and downed their drinks. Only the doctor declined.

"I'm afraid I'll have to leave now." He addressed the colonel. "Unless you, gentlemen, or the baroness need me."

"Not for the moment," Seiffert said.

After the doctor left, there was a long strained pause. Alexa sat down and so did the men, she on the sofa and the three facing her. Her heart was still beating madly, but she felt a creeping numbness slowly reaching her brain. If she could only break down sobbing, it would relieve the pressure on her lungs that made breathing difficult, but it was as though her lachrymal ducts had become clogged. Not a single tear filtered through them.

"Was he really shot? Any idea why and how?" she asked.

The colonel motioned to the judge advocate. "I'd rather you answered that. You have the advantage of being a neutral party. I was very fond of Major von Godenhausen. A first-rate officer, one of the best in the regiment, if not *the* best. I'm shattered by this senseless loss."

With an inward smile of irony, Alexa recalled the cool welcome extended by the colonel to Hans Günther after their arrival in Allenstein. Death, the great writer-off of debts, had restored Hans Günther's halo.

Captain Yves rose. Crossing his arms, he planted his legs wide apart as he faced Alexa. It was the stance he was accustomed to take when addressing a court-martial, she thought.

"As far as we could establish, death occurred in the early morning hours. The major was shot twice, one bullet, still lodged in the body, entered under the left breast nipple, the second below the left shoulder and exited through the back. Dr. Brück expressed the opinion that the first shot was the fatal one and I, as a layman, agree with him, although we'll have to wait for the autopsy to confirm it."

Alexa wished the captain would lower his voice. He spoke in a loud authoritative tone, each word hitting her eardrums like a dart.

"Shot twice?" she asked. "I didn't hear any shots."

"I'm sure you didn't. But they were fired and with the obvious intent to kill. When we lifted the major, we found this under his body." He pulled a small Browning automatic pistol from his pocket and showed it to Alexa. "Have you seen this pistol before?"

Alexa knew she had, but for a moment wondered if she should admit it.

"I think . . ." she began.

"Have you?" he pressed on.

She opted for the truth. "I think I have. It looks like one of the guns my husband kept in a case in his bedroom. Was this the gun that—" She could not bring herself to say, *that killed my husband.*

"No. At first we thought it was. Which caused us to think of suicide. Incidentally, has the thought occurred to you?"

She nodded. "For a moment."

"A close look proved us wrong," the captain continued. "The position of the body made it unlikely. Then we found the bullet that had exited through the back. It was imbedded in the upholstery of the desk chair. It is of a larger caliber than the cartridges of the major's gun, which, incidentally, was not fired at all. Our theory is that the major became aware of the intruder while still in the bedroom, grabbed the gun, crossed into the study, but before he could fire was shot from a range of about two meters."

To escape the stare of the men, Alexa buried her face in her hands. "But who? He had no enemies."

"At this stage we have no clues. By all appearances, the murderer entered through the window in the hallway. We found the window still open and the flower bed under it trampled upon. Nothing seems to have been touched or disturbed, either in the study or the bedroom, so robbery wasn't the motive, unless the intruder panicked after the shooting and fled. Incidentally, it would be a great help if you gave both the study and the bedroom a thorough going over— cupboards, drawers, shelves—to make sure nothing is missing."

"If it wouldn't be too much of an imposition," the colonel gallantly intervened.

"Certainly not. Right now if you wish."

"We'll come to that in a minute," Yves went on. "First I'd like to have a talk with the people who were in the house at the time of the murder."

Alexa pulled the bell cord, and when Anni entered she told her that all members of the household, including Jerzy, the stableboy, were wanted in the salon. A minute later they all trooped in looking awed and troubled. Their master had been murdered. Having been in the house when the fatal shots had been fired made them all suspect. They imagined seeing a big question mark in the eyes of the judge advocate as he asked them one by one where and how they had spent the night.

There was little they could tell him to help the investigation: they had gone to sleep as usual and had the first inkling of something having gone wrong when the major failed to ring for breakfast. Of the five, Anni alone gave a long and voluble account of her time between ten at night and five in the morning and of her apprehensions. The others answered in mumbled monosyllables. Captain Yves had a hard time drawing even these out of them.

"With your permission, Baroness." He turned to Alexa. "We'd like to have a tour of the house. Frankly it seems incredible that two shots were fired and not one person out of five on the premises heard them."

"Not one out of six," Alexa corrected him. "I too was on the premises."

The captain ignored the remark, but when he addressed the servants his tone took on a sharpened edge. "You all wait here. No one leave! I might have more questions."

Alexa felt a growing animosity toward Yves, or was it fear? She was the newly bereaved widow of a fellow officer, yet he failed to show the slightest consideration for her. True, she did not scream, sob or tear her hair; still he had to assume, unless he was deliberately cruel, that she was on the brink of a breakdown. Even if he suspected her of involvement in the murder, which he probably did, he did not have the right to treat her with the same haughty disregard as he did the servants. What's more, he didn't have the right to treat them that way either. Her growing indignation gave her a stamina which enabled her to keep Yves at bay.

"If it's all right with you, I'll show you through the ground floor first." She pointedly addressed herself to the colonel.

Before reaching the door, they were intercepted by Anni. "Could I please give the house a quick cleanup before the gentlemen go through it? I'm afraid everything is upside down —beds unmade, dirty dishes in the kitchen—"

Yves gave her a withering look. "You were told to wait here. Isn't that clear?" he barked at her.

The housekeeper dissolved in tears. Alexa was afraid she would slump down in a heap like a rag doll. "Yes, Captain," Anni whispered, "it is."

Alexa patted her on the shoulder. "Don't worry about the

condition of the house, Fräulein Anni. The gentlemen know this is an extraordinary day for us. At least I hope they do."

"Wouldn't you rather have one of your staff show us through the house?" the colonel asked, suddenly concerned. "You've been very brave, but there is a limit. I would also suggest that you let my wife stay with you. Even better, that you come to our house. My wife will be happy to—"

Alexa cut him short. "Thank you very much, Colonel. You're most kind, but I'd rather stay home. And as to the domiciliary visit"—she deliberately called it that—"I know it is necessary. So we might as well go on with it."

She led the three men from room to room, through the kitchen, the larders, the pantries, the servants' quarters and finally upstairs to her bedroom and the attic. With the patience of a real estate agent taking prospective buyers on a guided tour of a house for sale, she watched them examining the thickness of the walls and testing the acoustics by calling to one another from behind closed doors and down the well of the stairway. They even lifted the Persian rugs to see if the floorboards weren't eaten thin and porous by dryrot.

They returned to the salon. Captain Yves submitted the servants to another interrogation, asking them the same questions they had answered before and obtaining no new information from them. He dismissed them with the warning to remain in the house, to speak to no one, not even the guards who were posted in the garden. He and the colonel left to make arrangement for the transfer of Major von Godenhausen's body to the garrison hospital, where the autopsy would be conducted. Captain Draeseke stayed behind, later to be joined by Lieutenants Stoklaska and Heinrich, both of the First Army Corps Judiciary. They were to undertake a thorough search of house and grounds for the missing murder weapon and look over the dead man's papers and correspondence.

The search lasted until the early hours of the afternoon.

Alexa ordered a quick midday meal prepared for the officers. Their acceptance reassured her that she was not yet considered a suspect. Nevertheless, she decided against eating with them and had a tray brought upstairs with tea and cold meats.

At five in the afternoon, after the futile search had been concluded, the body removed and quiet returned to the house, she fell into a restless sleep plagued by nightmares in which she dreamed that Nicholas was dead.

An hour later she was awakened by someone shaking her by the shoulder. She opened her eyes and saw Anni's discreetly rouged face bending over her.

"I'm sorry, Baroness. Captain Yves is here. He wants to see you."

Alexa sat up quickly as a bolt shot into a slot. "Who wants to see me?"

"The judge advocate who was here earlier today. I'm so terribly sorry to have awakened you. When I came in you were talking in your sleep."

Alexa paled. "What was I saying?"

Anni's eyes brimmed over. One big tear dropped on Alexa's hand. "Oh, you sounded so happy. You said, 'Thank God, he is alive!' That's what you said. You were dreaming about the major, that he was alive. Poor, poor Madame. How I hated to wake you." She broke down, sobbing.

No doubt repentance played a part in Anni's wild outburst of sympathy. Ever since the morning, she had been watching Alexa from the corner of her eye, waiting for signs that would betray, if not her complicity in the murder, then her lack of true sorrow. But now the muttered words she overheard convinced her that Alexa was grief-stricken. They transformed her suspicion into pity.

"What does Captain Yves want?"

"I don't know. I told him that you were resting—God knows you need it—but he insisted that I call you." There was a long pause, then, embarrassed and repentant, she added, "He's been here for some time."

"Doing what?"

"Asking questions. Of the girls, Johann"—a pause—"me."

Alexa tried to reassure herself that the captain's return was no cause for alarm, but deep down she knew it was. Her hands were shaking so uncontrollably that she had to ask Anni to button her shoes. By the time she had her hair pinned up and slipped on a dress, she was able to control her panic and descend the stairway with fairly stable steps.

The captain greeted her and apologized for the intrusion. In a high nasal voice that sounded like the squeak of an unoiled cartwheel, he told her of General von Hammann's wish to wind up the investigation before the civilian press could turn the case into a slanderous campaign against the military.

"I don't see how they could," Alexa said, puzzled. "My husband surprised a burglar who had broken into the house and—"

"That's it. Someone broke into the house, but it wasn't a burglar. Burglars are seldom armed with expensive foreign-made pistols. In fact they're rarely armed at all. The murderer came to settle certain personal differences with your husband, so we have to look for someone in the circle of his friends, acquaintances, contacts—a man or woman familiar with the layout of the house." He waited for Alexa's reaction, and when none came he continued. "I understand it was only recently that your husband changed his sleeping habits."

"What do you mean?"

"He used to sleep in the same room with you. Upstairs. Then he moved into the room adjacent to his study. Why?"

It was a question Alexa had been prepared for since the beginning of the inquest. "It was a temporary arrangement. Lately I've been plagued with a touch of insomnia. Could not fall asleep before dawn. The lack of sleep made me tired and nervous, so he suggested that we try separate bedrooms for a while."

"He did? Wasn't it a rather elaborate operation for a temporary arrangement? New drapes, carpets, the walls painted."

"We thought we might use the room later as a guest room."

"With access only through your husband's study? Anyway, didn't you have a fight shortly before he moved?"

"Not a fight, not really."

Yves sounded like one of the master detectives in the penny dreadfuls she had read. She had better watch out, she thought, because it was always the master detective who had won in the books.

"I've told you I wasn't well. At times I made a nuisance of myself. Nagged him or—"

"So it was you and not he who suggested the move?"

She tried to hide her alarm under the pretense of annoyance. "What are you driving at, Captain? Are you implying that I deliberately set him up to be a target? That I—"

"Just a second," he interrupted her. "After the move, did you continue to have marital relations with your husband?"

She gasped. "How dare you?"

Unflinching, he continued. "You two had an argument in the presence of General von Sedlitz and his wife. A rather noisy argument. What was it about?"

"Why don't you ask the servants? Ask them and they'll tell you all you want to know. You must have found them very cooperative up to now, so why ask me?"

Captain Yves clipped the monocle into his eye and gave her a look that seemed to go through her like an X ray. "Baroness, I am trying to find Major von Godenhausen's murderer. At this stage everyone is suspect. The men of his squadron, the servants, his friends, you, Lieutenant von Ranke."

Her breath stopped. Forgetting to exhale, her lungs became filled to bursting. When she finally did exhale, it was like rolling a stone off her chest. "Why Lieutenant von Ranke?"

"He's been your constant companion lately. Supposed to be very much taken with you. A sentimental, emotionally unstable young man who—"

Although it was warm in the room, shivers ran through her

body. "Perhaps unstable," she cried, "but no murderer! My God, I used to ride with him because my husband didn't want me to ride alone. I'm not a very good horsewoman, had a few bad falls in Potsdam and—"

"I didn't say he was the murderer, only a likely suspect. For instance he couldn't come up with a foolproof alibi for the crucial hours. He was at home asleep. Anyone can say that."

So Ranke had already been interrogated. How long would he be able to hold out? she wondered. "For your information, Captain, I went riding with others as well. Danced, even flirted with others. Why don't you investigate them all? Every man who's ever crossed our threshold. Why not begin with General von Hammann?"

Her defiance seemed to make no impression on him. With arms crossed, eyes squinting, he confronted her as if she were already in the prisoner's dock. Suddenly it came to her with painful clarity that for the first time in her life she was completely alone, with no one standing beside her, no parent, aunt, uncle or husband. She was one small vulnerable figure against a hostile world, her own advocate with no one lending her advice or support. No matter how dismally Hans Günther had failed her in many respects, as protector he never had. There could have been no situation in which she—right or wrong—would have been as defenseless as she was now. He would be her shield, her fortress. If he were still alive, no Captain Yves could subject her to a nerve-racking cat-and-mouse torture. Of course, if Hans Günther were alive, there would be no Captain Yves to contend with, she realized with a pang of remorse.

"Baroness." The nasal voice stirred her from her musing. "You don't seem to understand. One of our officers was killed in cold blood. By all appearances the murderer was personally motivated, an inside affair. Each time an officer is involved in a scandal, it discredits the entire army, so—"

She cut him short. "A scandal? What is so scandalous about being killed?"

The captain ignored the interruption. "We have to solve the case before the press sinks its teeth into it."

"Keep it in the family?"

"Exactly."

"You seem to forget, Captain, that I too am of the family, yet you've been treating me as if I were a street girl rounded up in a police raid. And on the very day when my—" Suddenly the tears that had failed to flow all day flooded her eyes. "Couldn't you wait?" she sobbed. "Don't you see I am at the end of my wits? Haven't I had enough for one day?"

Surprised by the outburst, he blinked nervously. The monocle dropped from his eye to dangle for a moment on its black ribbon. He was used to dealing exclusively with men in the army, and as long as she had behaved like one—defiant, self-possessed and unemotional—he could handle her. Now her tears confused him. Perhaps he had gone too far and too fast. Nevertheless he refused openly to concede defeat.

"I'm only doing my duty, Baroness." He kept his tone deliberately firm. "To your knowledge, was there anyone with a grudge against your late husband?"

"I can't think of anyone." She rose. "Captain, must we go on? I'm terribly tired." Again the tears were flowing.

At last he felt he could beat a retreat with some dignity intact. "Forgive me if I made a nuisance of myself. It was all in the line of duty. Please do contact us should you recall any detail or incident that might help the investigation."

She promised she would and he left. Shortly afterward Colonel Seiffert's wife accompanied by Frau Draeseke called on her to ask if they could be of any help. Frau Seiffert had already sent for her dressmaker to come to the house and take Alexa's measurements for two black dresses, and Bona was dispatched to Moishe Lebowitz, owner of Allenstein's biggest dry-goods store, with the request that he open his already closed shop for the dressmaker to select the necessary fabrics.

The division was waiting for word from the Sedlitzes, who had been notified of the tragedy by telegram, before making arrangements for the funeral. It was assumed that after the services in Allenstein, Hans Günther would be taken to Schivelbein in Pomerania and laid to rest in his family's crypt there.

Frau Seiffert repeated her husband's offer of hospitality, but Alexa insisted on staying home. If for no other reason, she said, but to be an example to her servants, who seemed afraid of spending the night in the house. As the guards posted on the grounds were still on duty, she did not fear the murderer's return.

Secretly she was grateful to the guards for keeping Ranke away from her. He was the last person she wanted to see. She had moments when she almost wished he would be found out, regardless of what harm it would do to her. Then she would be free of him forever.

Hans Günther was dead less than twenty-four hours, and she already knew that her widowhood would be an ordeal. There would be another interrogation by Captain Yves—if she survived it without breaking down—and then the arrival of the Sedlitzes. She expected no benevolence from her aunt, only suspicion, meddling, reproaches. Then the burial. People staring. Eulogies. Long, ponderous Lutheran funeral orations. Sententious references to her grief. Endless outpourings of condolences. And after that, what?

Hans Günther had never considered it necessary to tell her about his finances. Whether he was rich or merely better off than most of his fellow officers she did not know. Was there a will, she wondered, and if so, with what provisions for her? What was she supposed to do about the lease on the house, the servants, the horses? Should she stay in Allenstein or return to Berlin? The knowledge that the death of a husband was not the last paragraph of a book but a series of puzzles became disturbingly clear to her.

She slept restlessly. Every creak of a floorboard or of a beam, every rustle of a tree branch against the house wall, awakened her. Twice she thought she heard footsteps on the

247

stairway and broke out in cold sweat. It was not the dead man she feared, but the live one, not Hans Günther, but Ranke. She no longer doubted that Ranke was unbalanced and capable of committing any lunacy regardless of the consequences. He could outwit the guards and sneak into the house the way he had the night before. But she hoped against hope that his being interrogated by Captain Yves had been a warning to him and would keep him from taking chances.

The morning passed without any disturbing developments. The modiste brought the dresses to be fitted; officers from the division, among them General von Hammann, called to offer their condolences. Before noon Lieutenant Stoklaska came to ask Alexa in the judge advocate's name whether she had found any valuables missing from the house. She told him that, although she had not been through every nook and cranny, she felt pretty certain that nothing was missing.

Shortly after supper a carriage rolled through the gate, and up to the front entrance. She had just seen off the dressmaker who had delivered one of the finished outfits, promising the second one for the morning.

The ring of the doorbell, like every single ring throughout the day, took her breath away. Unable to endure the tension, she didn't wait for the servants but answered the door herself.

As she had feared, Captain Yves, this time accompanied by Lieutenant Stoklaska, was the visitor.

"Isn't eight-thirty a little late for a social call, Captain?" she asked with deliberate sharpness. Her virulent resentment of the man overshadowed her alarm.

"It certainly is. But I hoped that this time I'd be forgiven." He smiled with disconcerting heartiness. "May we come in?"

His cordiality disturbed her more than his arrogance had. She suspected a trick, a trap, a bolt from the blue. Ranke had confessed, and the grin on the captain's face indicated victory. The fear of such a turn had been in the back of her mind all day, and now she wondered how to react to a charge of complicity without knowing how much Ranke had divulged.

248

"Well, certainly, come in." She tried to sound calm. "Or do I have the right to say no?"

The captain kept smiling. "We have good news. That is, if one can use the word 'good' in connection with yesterday's tragic events."

Bona made a belated appearance to answer the door. Alexa told her to return with a bottle of schnapps and glasses, then led the way into the salon.

"What is your good news, Captain?" she asked after they settled down.

"We have the man!"

"What man?"

"Your husband's murderer!"

Alexa felt as if a hand were pressing down on her windpipe. She took a deep breath, but the sensation persisted. The captain's voice seemed to be coming from the bottom of a deep pit.

"It happens to be a person you know. That is why we took the liberty of calling on you at this late hour. There are some muddles you alone can clarify."

Come to the point, you bastard, said a voice inside her. Aloud she asked, "Who is he?"

The captain clamped the monocle on his left eye. "Dragoon Jan Dmowski," he announced, stressing every syllable.

She stared at him, dumbfounded. "No!" was all she could utter.

"He is the one!"

Instead of feeling relieved, she suspected a trap. With all the perquisites of his office, how could a judge advocate err so blatantly? she wondered. "You can't be serious."

"I am. I have not the slightest doubt, Baroness. Tuesday, the night before last, he was seen by one of the sentries posted at the Castle of the Teutonic Knights. He was headed in the direction of Parade Platz. Then, at one-fifty in the morning, the two privates who were to relieve the sentries at the castle—the guards are changed at two sharp—saw him leaving your grounds through the small gate leading to the alley."

"Were they sure it was Dmowski? How could they tell? It was a dark night."

"One of the sentries at the castle knew him well; he and Dmowski are from the same village. The two privates hadn't known him before but recognized him at the confrontation as the man they'd seen in the alley."

Yes, it *was* Dmowski they had seen, she thought. Evidently he had paid a secret visit to Hans Günther and was on his way back to the barracks. It probably wasn't the first time he had sneaked into the house for a tryst. When Hans Günther had suddenly agreed to separate bedrooms, she had wondered what made him change his mind. Now she understood.

"The fellow might have more on his conscience than one murder," the captain continued. "He's been in the habit of slipping from the barracks after taps and staying away all night. Prowling the streets, I'd say. We found a bundle of cash and some valuable jewelry—a watch, a ring, a gold chain— hidden in his mattress. My theory is he broke into your house to commit burglary and was caught by your husband. When recognized by the major, Dmowski drew a pistol and fired. Simple as all that."

The resentment she had felt against Dmowski flared up once more in Alexa. She recalled the mocking glint in his eye, his lewd grin when she had slapped his face. Then suddenly her indignation gave way to the sobering thought that Dmowski was being accused of a crime he hadn't committed.

"I'm afraid you're holding the wrong man." She tried to defend him. "He's loud-mouthed, impertinent, disrespectful— but no murderer."

Yves glared at her. "Dmowski told us it was you who insisted that he be relieved of his duties as the major's orderly. That you didn't want him in the house."

Alexa pretended surprise. "Did he say that?"

Stoklaska came to the captain's aid. "He said no matter how hard he tried to please you, you would always find fault

with him. Wanted him chucked out. I'm quoting him ver-
batim."

"I wasn't satisfied with his work. Besides, he wouldn't take
orders from me. That was all."

Yves seemed annoyed over Alexa's refusal to support his
case against Dmowski. He paced the floor with the impatience
of a caged lion. "Baroness, he also stated that he was dismissed because he failed to respond to—how shall I put it—
to your allure. That you'd taken a liking to him and when he
resisted your approaches—"

Outraged, Alexa cut him short. "That's a lie!"

"Also that you were afraid he'd tell on you to the major."

"Tell what?"

She had the feeling that the captain was willfully distorting
Dmowski's account of his dismissal to wring incriminating
statements from her against the young man. He grinned tri-
umphantly.

"Are you still convinced he is innocent?"

"Innocent of lying? No. But innocent of murder? Yes."

Yves shook his head. "You amaze me, Baroness."

She felt cornered. If she continued protesting Dmowski's
guilt, she would in the end lead the captain to re-examine his
theory regarding the crime and look for another suspect, inevitably for Ranke. She ignored the remark.

"We have sufficient evidence to have the man convicted,"
the captain said. "Two witnesses saw him leave the site of the
murder. Then the jewelry and the money. You told Stoklaska there wasn't a thing missing in the house. Nevertheless,
if you'd be kind enough to look at the pieces, you might recognize them as having belonged to your husband."

She wished she could tell him that they had indeed, except
that they were not stolen by Dmowski but given to him. She
wondered why Dmowski had not said so to clear himself of
the robbery charge. And why it did not occur to Judge Advocate Yves to examine the nature of the relationship between
the major and his orderly. No doubt he had heard of Corporal

Sommer's and Sergeant Bollhardt's testimonies in the first Moltke trial. Was it an oversight or was it deliberate? Were all military investigators as biased and inflexible as Yves? If they were, then the statue of Justice was correctly depicted as wearing a blindfold.

"I'll look at the jewelry if you think it necessary." Assuming that the visit was over, she rose and offered her hand to Yves. He bowed smartly and lifted it to his lips.

"One more favor. At the same time we'd like to stage a confrontation between you and Dmowski."

She stiffened. "What for?" Immediately she wished she had been able to control the sharpness of her reaction.

"We'd like to learn more about Dmowski's feelings regarding the dismissal. To be an officer's orderly is an easy job compared to field service. Perhaps his motive wasn't robbery, but revenge."

"Oh, Captain, that's too farfetched."

"Madame, we cannot present a case to a court-martial unless we cover every angle."

She had to give in, if for no other reason than to be rid of the visitors. Anyway, she had been skating on thin ice. She felt she mustn't tempt her luck by being uncooperative, and she agreed to present herself at the judge advocate's office on the following morning.

After they left, she took a walk in the garden. It reassured her to find soldiers posted at both the front and rear gates. Ranke had made no attempt to contact her since the day before, which indicated that he had come to his senses and become more cautious. She wondered if he knew that Dmowski was now the main suspect in the case. She hoped he did not and would not be told for at least a few days, until she could decide about her plans for the immediate future.

She ordered a hack for eight in the morning, a closed hack to shelter her from the stares of the curious. The divisional command post was a good twenty minutes' ride away along the Alle, past the Bishop's Castle, the Botanic Gardens, the cavalry barracks and the parade grounds. A fresh breeze was blowing from the east, chasing fat white clouds looking like beaten egg white across a brilliantly blue sky. A bridle path followed the opposite bank of the Alle, and a group of riders, the women in dark habits and the men slim and glossy like tin soldiers, were cantering in the direction of Osterode. She thought of Hans Günther and felt a sudden, stabbing pain. The descent from the peak moment of his first kiss in Norderney to the present depths of her despondency had been much too fast and ugly. Their love had had the beauty of a myth. He was Eros and she Psyche, but in defiance of his warning she held her lamp over his bed and the oil dripping from it killed him. If she could only go back to Norderney and start anew. Remain duped. There would be no Ranke in her life and no Captain Yves and she would be one of the carefree riders on the opposite shore of the Alle.

She found Lieutenant Stoklaska waiting for her in front of the command post. He escorted her through the inner courtyard to the judge advocate's office. On their way they passed a group of officers, among them men she knew. They must have heard of her coming to the post, hence their urgent need for a breath of fresh air. They threw discreetly guarded glances at her that felt like the burns of branding irons on her skin.

Yves thanked her profusely for her cooperation, then took a small box from his desk drawer. It contained a gold watch with a heavy chain, a signet ring, a tie pin and a bundle of bank notes. Alexa assumed they were the things found in Dmowski's mattress.

"Do you recognize any of these objects?" the captain asked.

She recognized the ring and the pin, but not the watch. The ring was of heavy gold and had been in the possession of the Godenhausen family for at least a century. The signet on it was of unknown origin. According to Hans Günther it had been used by his great-grandfather to seal letters written to his wife from the battlefields of the Napoleonic wars.

She reflected for a moment before answering: "No, I don't." No doubt Hans Günther had given the ring to Dmowski, as he had the rest of the things in the box, including the money. Her "yes" would have meant tightening the noose around the dragoon's neck, the proof Yves was so eagerly waiting for in order to prefer the charge of murder against the young man. "I don't remember ever having seen them," she added to avoid any misunderstanding.

The captain acted surprised. "That's very strange, madame, because we succeeded in tracing the watch and chain to the Herbert Jewelry store in Königsberg. Jeweler Herbert not only remembers having sold them to your husband on the tenth of March of this year, but has the copy of the bill to prove it. Are you certain you haven't seen them before?"

This time she did not have to resort to a lie. "I am positive."

There was an exchange of amazed glances between the judge advocate and his aide. It seemed that Stoklaska's assignment was mainly to mimic his captain's facial expressions.

"Didn't you know he'd bought them?" When she shook her head, he went on: "Was your husband in the habit of making expensive purchases without informing you?"

"He evidently made this one. However, you can't call it a habit." Fleetingly, Hans Günther's generosity to Dmowski engendered a touch of bitterness in her. She received presents from him only for Christmases and birthdays. He had forgotten her last one.

"Have Dmowski brought over," the captain told Stoklaska, who relayed the order to the sergeant in the anteroom.

He must have been kept somewhere in the building and not in the regimental guardhouse, because minutes later he was escorted in by the sergeant. Wearing a fatigue uniform, he was bareheaded. When he spotted Alexa, his face flushed and his dark eyes glared murder at her.

254

"Well, Dmowski, did you have a good sleep?" Yves asked, sounding cloyingly cordial. There was no answer. "I hope you've given a thought to the mess you're in."

Dmowski shifted his dark gaze to the captain's face but remained mum.

"Do you have anything to tell us?"

"What about?"

"Sir," Stoklaska rebuked him.

With a contemptuous twitch of his lips, Dmowski echoed the "sir."

"While you slept, we succeeded in ferreting out some interesting facts. Regarding that watch, for instance. It belonged to Major von Godenhausen."

The dragoon threw a side glance at Alexa. "If she told you that, she was lying."

"No. Not the baroness. The jeweler did who sold it to the major."

"He might have sold him one like it."

Yves shook his head with avuncular exasperation. "Dmowski, Dmowski, that won't do. This *is* the watch. Expensive watches have serial numbers and other marks of identification. All that's on the jeweler's bill. There is no way out for you, my friend. You took this watch Wednesday morning after you shot the major dead."

Gritting his teeth in anger, Dmowski threw back his head. He reminded Alexa of a frenzied horse champing at the bit. "All right." The words erupted like fragments of exploding shrapnel from his mouth. "I took it, but not Wednesday morning. Long before that, while I was still living in the major's house. I sort of found it. He left his dresser drawer unlocked. I noticed it and took the watch. I don't think he ever noticed it was missing." Suddenly he became animated. "I can prove that I had it long before Wednesday. I have a witness, the owner of the Rahaus Weinstube, Herr Rahaus. I showed it to him one evening. It must have been shortly before Easter."

Alexa listened dumbfounded. Why did the boy refuse to tell the truth that the watch, the ring, the chain, the money were given to him, that they were gifts. Even if he cleared himself of the murder charge, he would still be accused of stealing them. He had not sold the pieces, so he was not protecting a fence. Whom was he protecting? A dead man who no longer needed protection?

"Now where did the ring come from?" Yves continued the questioning.

"The same drawer."

"It did not. The baroness testified that it had not belonged to the major."

Dmowski threw a surprised look at Alexa. "Did she say that?" Their eyes met for a brief moment. His expression mellowed, and he blinked a signal that she interpreted as *Stick with it*. He shrugged. "All right. I must have gotten it someplace else. I don't remember."

"So you admit having broken into other houses?"

"I do not."

"On the night of January twentieth did you break into Number Twenty-three Hohenzollern Strasse and did you steal a silver dinner set for twelve?"

"Of course not. What would I do with a dinner set for twelve? For the slop one's fed in this army a spoon is all one needs."

Captain Yves rattled off the list of other unsolved robberies in Allenstein, to which Dmowski responded with bored noes. After the last one he exploded. "What are you trying to do to me, sir? Make me out a one-man crime wave? Just because Allenstein has a bunch of imbeciles for a police force? Am I to be responsible for all their damned mistakes? First I was a murderer, now I am a cat burglar."

"Apropos murderer"—Yves clamped the monocle on his eye to examine the papers on his desk—"we want to hear the details of your dismissal by Major von Godenhausen. You told us that it was at the baroness's insistence that you were returned to your squadron—when you failed to respond to her advances. Madame denies that."

"Wouldn't you if you were in her shoes?" Dmowski asked with a grin, then added, "Sir."

The captain jumped up and advanced threateningly on him. "I'll put you in irons for that, you bastard." Quickly he turned to Alexa. "Pardon my language, Baroness. One needs the patience of a saint in dealing with his kind." He glared at Dmowski. "Now, will you face the baroness and repeat what you told us regarding your dismissal? Madame, would you please rise?"

What an ordeal, Alexa thought. Yves believed he had caught his man; his harping upon the dismissal was prurient curiosity.

She rose and turned to face Dmowski. When their eyes met, she felt the blood rush to her face. Gritting her teeth, she willed herself to play the game according to the rules set by the captain.

"She wanted me kicked out," Dmowski said. "So I was kicked out."

"What was her reason?"

"Why ask me, sir? Ask her."

She looked him in the eye. "You're a liar, Dmowski. Whatever you told the captain was not true."

Appearing even more ill at ease than she, the young man shrugged. "You were running around half naked," he muttered.

"I was not."

"Yes, you were. And you slapped my face."

"I slapped your face because you were impertinent." She was furious. Her indignation was not directed against Dmowski, but against Yves for staging this inane travesty of a confrontation.

"The major told you to put more clothes on when people were around. That's why you had me chucked out."

"I wanted you out, but for other reasons. And you know the reasons."

With an abruptness that caused her to recoil, he stepped closer.

"What reasons?" His eyes hooked into hers; he was not asking, he was warning her. She tried to escape his stare by turning her head, but it held her fast. An order was being beamed at her as clearly as though it had been written in big black letters on a poster. She was to keep silent about the relationship between him and her husband, although the disclosure of the truth could save him from the firing squad. Why was he willing to take the risk? she wondered. Was it to protect the honor of his dead lover?

"You were impertinent," she repeated lamely.

Later, when she recalled the scene, she concluded that Dmowski had hypnotized her. It wasn't such a farfetched idea, after all. Hadn't she heard that his mother was a gypsy? It was not his looks that set him apart from other Poles but also his fearless arrogance. He was uneducated, but far too smart for an ordinary private, perhaps even smarter than his officers. He had cast a strange spell on everyone who had come in contact with him. Alexa suspected that both Bona and Svetlana had a secret yen for him. He had tamed the untamable Anni Busse, and as to Hans Günther . . .

"In what way was he impertinent?" Yves asked.

Alexa felt that she could not endure another minute of the man's wretched probing. "For God's sake, Captain"—she raised her voice—"if you don't know what impertinent means, look it up in the dictionary. Do you expect me to remember every single time he got fresh with me, was caught smoking in the house or ignored an order?" She hated to find herself allied with Dmowski. On the other hand, Captain Yves's method of interrogation troubled her. It lacked a system, logic. He was liable to be confronting her with a question that, because of its irrelevancy, would cause her to let her guard down. "I would like to leave now, Captain," she told him.

"You must realize that I've been through a lot these past days. You asked me to come. I came, but I don't see any point in rehashing every detail you've already covered more than once."

"I'm afraid that's up to me to decide."

"All right. What do you want to know next?"

It took him a while to answer. "For the moment nothing that couldn't wait. I realize that the inquest has been a harassment for you, but that couldn't be helped. We do value your cooperation and won't trouble you again, unless it becomes absolutely necessary. You will forgive me if I have the lieutenant see you to your carriage. I'm not quite finished with Dragoon Dmowski. Maybe he'll be more talkative when left alone with me."

He bowed stiffly and kissed her hand, letting his lips linger for a long time. Leaving the room, she had to pass Dmowski. He leaned against the wall as bored and unconcerned as a man waiting for a tram. What she felt for him was no longer hatred but admiration mixed with remorse and concern. She was almost at the door, held open for her by the lieutenant, when she turned back to throw a parting look at Dmowski.

"Goodbye, Dmowski, and good luck," she said.

He responded with a knowing look. There was a touch of the old irritating impudence in it.

"Thank you, madame. Same to you."

During the first days of her stay, Alexa was sincerely grateful for the hospitality her aunt and the general had offered her. The ordeal, beginning with Hans Günther's death and ending with his funeral, left her completely drained of her strength, moral as well as physical. She could not have carried through the removal from the Allenstein house or settled in Berlin on her own. Stopping at hotels, even entering restaurants unescorted, terrified her. She was twenty-four, widowed after a marriage of five years, and had never traveled, handled money or run a household alone. She knew

259

that taking shelter in the Kronen Strasse apartment was a temporary arrangement and that sooner or later she would have to look for a flat and make decisions on her own regarding her future, but not this early after the smash-up of her life, not while her wounds were still open and bleeding.

She was given the same cheerless room she had occupied as a girl. She tried to convince herself that Allenstein never existed. What helped her for a short while was a milieu untouched by the passing of time. The people were the same, the place was the same, decorated with the same ugly monstrosities of imitation Gothic, thick velvet drapes, Oriental rugs, and paintings in heavy gilded frames, all grown a trifle shabbier and drabber, as had the people who lived among them. Katie, the old cook, was as loud, disrespectful, jolly and quarrelsome as ever, only now she walked with a slight limp because of her rheumatism. The general had the same stony silences, only now they grew more impenetrable. Rose engaged in the same silly discussions with Fräulein Elsa about the imperial family's activities, only now they were closer to soliloquies, as Elsa was turning incurably deaf.

Dmowski's arrest had had a deep effect on the Sedlitzes. It made them realize that Alexa could throw light on the Dmowski–Hans Günther relationship, and by doing so posthumously dishonor the memory of their nephew. They treated her with great caution, as if she were a time bomb to be defused gradually. The general warned Rose to avoid antagonizing her and to order the servants to cater to whatever whim she had.

Alexa spent the entire first week in bed, getting up only for the midday meal. There was a constant stream of people offering their sympathies. Rose received them without ever insisting that her niece accept their condolences in person, as it behooved a dutiful army wife. On the whole, the Sedlitzes tried their best to keep their grief private, as if they wanted the world to forget all about Hans Günther and his violent death.

Alexa's meals were brought to her room on a tray by old Katie. While the young woman ate, she would sit at the foot of the bed entertaining her with comments on the events of the day. Despite Rose's warning to avoid the subject of Alexa's recent widowhood, she repeatedly hinted that she held the Sedlitzes responsible for Alexa's tragedy. She was convinced that Rose and the general had maneuvered Hans Günther into a marriage that they knew he was not prepared for. Their aim was to keep him from getting involved in the same kind of scandals that had almost wrecked his career in Munich by making shrewd use of Alexa's naive infatuation with him. They gave no thought to the harm they were causing her. Their main concern was appearances; a beautiful and loving wife shielding her husband from scurrilous suspicions.

Alexa also gathered from old Katie's chatter that, despite the army's best efforts to squash speculations, the public refused to accept simple robbery as the motive behind Hans Günther's murder. The yellow press dwelled repeatedly upon Corporal Sommer's testimony given during the first Moltke-Harden trial, and reporters were dispatched to Allenstein to search for new clues in the case. They could unearth no scandalous facts, only oddities, which, neverthless, could be blown up into colorful stories on army life in East Prussia. Hardly a day passed when men claiming to be journalists would not ring the Sedlitzes' doorbell. Some had to be bodily removed by the general's orderly.

After a week or so spent in Berlin in a state of blessed apathy, Alexa received a short letter from Ranke inquiring about her health. It unleashed all the demons she thought she had left behind in Allenstein. What disturbed her most was the realization that she had completely forgotten about him, shut him out of her mind. Now he was back, her abominable centaur-lover—half man, half horse—claiming his due.

That night she didn't sleep a wink. In the morning she got up and dressed, hoping that moving about would calm her. She was mistaken; having to make small talk with Rose and the general merely added to her nervousness. They noticed her discomfort but failed to comment on it. She knew she could never turn to them for protection against Ranke. Even uttering his name would be taking risks. No doubt they had heard the gossip linking them in Allenstein, so her mentioning him would merely add fuel to their suspicions.

The only living soul who could have helped her was Nicholas, yet she could never tell the full truth even to him. It had been nine months since she had last seen him, during which time he became engaged to a girl in Vienna. He would be a saint or a fool if he still cared for her, Alexa told herself with a sad inward grin.

What added to her wretchedness was the realization that she missed him. At first it was only a faint sense of loss, which slowly grew into a longing for his affection and, more painfully, his embraces. She had been mad to stay with an on-and-off husband when the love of a normal, healthy, passionate man was hers for the asking. To escape the humiliating memories of Hans Günther's vapid and Ranke's perverted lovemaking, she spent hours fantasizing about her afternoons spent with Nicholas.

She decided to leave Ranke's letter unanswered, hoping that her silence would keep him away from her, at least for a while. Her restlessness grew more and more unbearable. She went for long walks, but no matter how thoroughly she exhausted herself she had trouble falling asleep at night. Her short naps ended in nightmares, from which she woke trembling and soaked in cold perspiration. The erotic dreams she had were no less disturbing. She caught herself looking at strange men in the street, disrobing them with her eyes. She longed for Nicholas, yet she feared that sooner or later she would yield to the first able-bodied male who approached her.

Ranke wrote again. His letter had been tampered with—opened and clumsily resealed—which led to a clash between her and Rose. Anger mixed with fear caused her smoldering resentment to burst into flame. Ranke was growing careless. He intimated that he would come to Berlin as soon as he was granted a leave of absence from his commandant.

Rose denied having opened the letter, but at the same time she reproached Alexa for encouraging a former beau so soon after her husband's death. They fought as fiercely as in the old days, with Rose the victor this time. She held the trump card: she could decide how long she would be willing to grant asylum to Alexa.

Hans Günther had left no money to her, only heavy debts. He had lived beyond his means, even borrowed a small fortune from the Sedlitzes. Of course, Alexa was entitled to a pension, but it would take quite some time for the army to begin paying it. Until then what would she use for money?

Much too weary to answer impossible questions, Alexa again withdrew to the relative safety of her bed.

Rose had sense enough to stay away from her. It was no peace, merely an armistice, but it gave Alexa a breathing spell.

"You can't hide out forever, child," old Katie scolded her. "It won't solve anything. You're not sick, you're lazy. You'd better get on your feet and start living."

"I can't, Katie, not yet. I need help—and I have no one to help me."

Katie gave her a stern look. "Oh yes you have. You have somebody: yourself. You mustn't forget that you *are* a somebody, the only somebody to count on."

Her words kept reverberating in Alexa's mind long after Katie left the room. The old woman would have been right in other people's cases, but not in hers, she thought. She no longer had herself, not since the morning she had found Hans Günther dead. At that moment she had become an empty cocoon left behind by the live creature it had once encased. A bit of refuse to be crushed underfoot or swept away by the wind.

"Help!" she murmured. "Help! Please help me! Somebody help me, please!"

There was no answer. There could be none. She was alone in the room.

PART THREE

PART THREE

10

Nicholas spent most of June 1908 away from Berlin. He accompanied the military attaché on an inspection tour to training areas where minor war games were taking place. He happened to be present at Döberitz when, addressing the troops, the Kaiser first expressed his concern over Germany's encirclement by hostile neighbors. Though it was one of his favorite topics, he had never before given voice to his fears in public. The statement created great consternation all over the world, and its importance was blown up out of proportion by the international press.

As a rule, Nicholas seldom read the Socialist papers, but on this July morning he bought the latest edition of the *Vorwärts* to find out its reaction to the imperial pronouncement. Thumbing through its pages, he caught sight of an article with the title "Violent Death at Army Post in Allenstein." It dealt with with the shooting murder of a major by a dragoon of his own squadron. The First Army Corps had refused to disclose the details of the case, yet the reporter managed to learn that the victim had been one of the officers involved in the Gardes du Corps scandals stirred up by the first Moltke-Harden libel suit.

For a long moment Nicholas stared benumbed at the page. All hints contained in the report fitted Godenhausen's person.

Since his engagement to Francesca, Nicholas had considered Alexa to be a chapter in a book he had long ago thrown away. He had reached a comfortable plane of tranquility which was now being threatened by the report. In self-defense, he clung to the slim hope that the story was empty speculation and the alleged murder victim in Allenstein was not Alexa's husband.

When he reached the Embassy, he phoned a captain assigned to the staff of General Hülsen-Haeseler, chief of the Emperor's Military Cabinet. The captain was one of the few Prussian officers he had been friendly with. After making him promise to keep the information confidential, the captain confirmed his premonition that the article *had* referred to Godenhausen.

"It's a ghastly affair," the captain added. "I personally suspect that there were some unsavory undertones, although the motive was supposed to be robbery. Yes, the poor fellow was shot by one of his own dragoons, a man named Dmowski."

"Shot dead?" It was a senseless question, betraying utter confoundment.

"Very dead. He was buried last week. The dragoon was arrested and is now held in the military prison in Königsberg. He's denied having committed the murder, yet there is strong circumstantial evidence against him, so his case is being prepared for court-martial."

"What about Baroness von Godenhausen? Is she still in Allenstein?" Nicholas asked, hoping that the tremor of his voice would go unnoticed.

"All I know is that she attended her husband's funeral in Pomerania. She might be staying with the Sedlitzes in Berlin. I am merely guessing, as they are her only close relations in Germany."

After he hung up, Nicholas stared for a long time at the silent telephone. Whatever happened in Allenstein must not affect *his* life, he told himself. Nevertheless, a few days later he called at the Sedlitz home on Kronen Strasse to express his condolences. By then Major von Godenhausen's sudden death, attributed to heart failure, had been reported by the daily papers, so he considered his visit to be an act of courtesy expected from an ex-in-law.

Frau von Sedlitz's parlormaid took his card and, after what seemed an interminably long wait in the dank entrance hall smelling of mothballs and warmed-over sauerkraut, she returned with the message that neither Frau von Sedlitz nor Baroness von Godenhausen was receiving, or would be in the foreseeable future.

The meaning was clear. In a way he was relieved. It would have been irrational for him to see Alexa again. He had loved her because she was the double of Beata, but a double as incorporeal and unpossessable as a reflection in a mirror. In her case, a cracked mirror.

Of all human emotions, love is the most incomprehensible. He tried to put together the fragmented episodes of their relationship: her random materializations, her unmotivated disappearances, her ardors, her gelidities. She was a ghost. Beata's ghost. She never visited, she haunted him.

He tried to convince himself that the impulse that had driven him to her was plain sexual desire, yet even now, after their separation of many months, he sometimes remembered her with a kind of chaste yearning. He adored and hated her. He would visualize her as a cruel child playfully tearing the wings off a butterfly; then the next moment as the butterfly torn to pieces by a cruel child.

She had told him over and over that she loved only Hans Günther. It had to be more than love, otherwise it wouldn't have survived his perversion, infidelity, indifference. But now Hans Günther was dead, and Nicholas wondered if her infatuation would survive his death as well—the way his love for Beata had survived her death. There was one fundamental difference though. Hans Günther left no identical twin behind.

Nicholas was dining at Baron von Stoka's house. As always at the baron's stag parties, dinner was sheer perfection and champagne flowed as freely as if Stoka owned a cellar at Haut-Villiers. The wine loosened tongues, and despite the presence of Councillor von Thören of the German Foreign Office, someone uttered the name of Philipp Eulenburg.

"I understand there won't be a trial," Stoka said to Thören.

The councillor shook his head vigorously. "No trial? Of course there will be a trial. The prince has been under arrest since the eighth of May."

If there was anything written about Eulenburg in the press recently, it had escaped Nicholas's attention. His last information had come from Vienna. Prominent Austrians, among them the Princess Metternich and Baron Albert Rothschild, had been subjected to interrogations concerning Eulenburg's sex life during his tenure in Vienna. This Prussian gaucherie called for a protest from the Monarchy's Ministry of Foreign Affairs. The case caused a far louder uproar than any recent international incident. The Viennese knew that the prince had been in poor health, suffering from blood poisoning and a dangerous phlebitic condition in his left leg. They remembered him as one of the most cultured and tactful diplomats Germany had ever sent to Franz Josef's court and were puzzled by the persecution he had to endure in his own country.

"How could they arrest a sick man?" Nicholas asked Thören. "Couldn't the Kaiser protect him? They were friends for twenty years."

The councillor smiled icily. "It was His Majesty's expressed wish that the case be brought to a conclusion. And rightly so."

"I don't understand. What did the prince do that was so disgraceful?"

Thören threw up his hands in astonishment. "Oh, you

Viennese! You're much too permissive. Just because a man has a title, has written a few songs, and at one time had entree into His Majesty's private circle doesn't give him immunity from the law. This isn't Austria, you know. This is Prussia."

Nicholas was ready with a cutting answer when Stoka's admonishing glance restrained him.

"After the prince's indictment for perjury," Thören continued, "an investigating judge, accompanied by two witnesses for the prosecution, was sent to Liebenberg. At a confrontation staged in the prince's bedroom, the witnesses—both ex-employees of the prince and deeply devoted to him—admitted having engaged in certain intimacies with their master. After this the judge had no choice but to issue a warrant for Eulenburg's arrest."

Stoka had been pensively puffing on his cigar, now he abruptly squashed it out in the nearest ashtray. Nicholas knew him well enough to recognize the significance of the gesture. It was anger. "Wasn't there a medical opinion," Stoka asked Thören, "confirming that the prince was in no condition to travel? Why couldn't he be kept under house arrest in his own home? Especially after the family had offered bail of five hundred thousand marks."

"Unfortunately, bail was unacceptable. By leaving the prince in Liebenberg, the crown prosecutor would have risked jeopardizing the course of justice."

"You mean he was afraid the man would flee the country? Good God, he couldn't even go to the toilet on his own!"

Nicholas marveled at the change of sentiment in favor of Eulenburg at the Embassy. Of course a critically sick man could no longer harm the Monarchy's foreign policy by preaching peace and tolerance to the emperor.

Thören sensed his host's disapproval. "Everything was done to make the prince's trip from Liebenberg to Berlin easy and comfortable—ambulances, a special compartment on the train, attending physicians, nurses—and as an unprecedented favor, instead of a cell in the house of detention at Moabit he was put up in a sickroom of the Royal Charité, the most reputable university hospital of the country."

"With an armed guard posted in front of his door," Stoka muttered.

"But with his windows overlooking the hospital garden," Thören retorted. "A few days ago I happened to visit a friend at the Charité and passed the wing where the prince is being held. There is a flower bed with the most gorgeous peonies and a patch of lawn in front of it. His valet, Emanuel Bartsch, is with him; and his wife, Augusta, has visiting privileges. For the time being only once every week, but that too will change. Be fair, gentlemen. You cannot call detention under such conditions barbaric or endangering a man's health."

Nicholas could no longer hold his tongue. "For heaven's sake, Herr von Thören, why the whole stupid detention? What for, when the crown prosecutor's own medical staff has declared the man too ill to stand trial?"

"Now. But his health might improve. Besides, when His Majesty heard of the medical report, he wired Chancellor von Bülow and instructed him to keep the prince under arrest until he is fit to be tried. His Majesty insists on a verdict, so that all this cochonnerie can be forgotten at last."

"Herr von Thören," Nicholas exploded. "More than twenty years ago the prince had a fling with two young men. Ask any boarding school pupil about the things that go on in their dormitories."

"In England!"

"In Prussia. Even in your military academies."

The councillor bristled. "How do you know? Have you ever been to any of our military academies?"

Nicholas grinned. "Of course not. I wouldn't have been admitted. You see, I am half Jewish."

Thören pretended to be surprised. "That's interesting. Well"—he beamed an avuncular smile at Nicholas—"I admit we used to have prejudices against Slavs, Catholics and Jews, but not anymore. Now an Albert Ballin can be His Majesty's

272

confidant, attend the Rominten hunts and, what's more, be privileged to shoot! Last year he bagged a royal stag."

Being offered such undebatable proof of Prussia's racial and religious tolerance, Nicholas conceded defeat. A few minutes later the Prussian rose to say good night, which broke up the party, not one of Baron Stoka's most successful suppers despite the excellent food and champagne he had served.

Although it was past midnight, Nicholas found his entrance hall brightly lighted and his housekeeper, fully dressed and visibly indignant, seated on a fragile chair that accommodated no more than one third of her ample derriere.

"What's the matter, Frau Gerhardt?" he asked. She had risen and was staring at him reproachfully. "How come you are still up?"

"Well, the lady said it would be all right if I just let her wait in the salon, but I'd never seen her before, and with all that silver and expensive china around . . ."

Perhaps it was Baron von Stoka's champagne that had blurred his mind, but he failed to understand her. "What lady?"

"I couldn't leave her alone. She might have walked off with some of the silver, and you'd have made me responsible, so—"

Suddenly the fog lifted. "You mean there is a lady waiting for me?"

"That's what I keep telling you, don't I?"

He didn't have to ask who the lady was. He handed his shako and sword to the surprised Frau Gerhardt and made a dash for the salon.

It shocked him how drawn with grief—or was it defeat— her face looked. She sat leaning against the upholstered back of a chair, apparently very tired, nevertheless refusing to give in to fatigue: a traveler waiting for her connection to continue a long and exhausting journey.

"Forgive me, Nicholas. I should have telephoned you, but"

—she forced a smile—"I'm being inconsiderate, as usual."

Slamming the door in the face of Frau Gerhardt, who had tried to follow him into the room, he embraced Alexa, lifting her off her feet. For a second he himself felt as if he were losing contact with the ground, drifting away from all reality toward a disembodied state of Elysian joy. He was filled with pure unadulterated happiness, the kind one can experience only for brief moments and only a few times in a lifetime.

"Oh, my dearest" was all he could say.

She disentangled herself and pulled away. "Nicky, I came because I had no one to turn to, no place to go."

"You're here, that's all that matters."

"I was staying at Aunt Rose's. I mean, since . . . since the funeral. But I won't go back to her—ever. I'd rather die. I just couldn't stand another moment in that place. I left a letter telling her that I won't go back—"

"Of course you won't. You'll stay here."

She threw him a confused look. "But you're engaged to a girl in Vienna. All I'm asking you is to help me until I have my affairs straightened out, receive my widow's pension and . . ."

Oh yes, he was engaged. The image of Francesca surfaced in his consciousness the way a dolphin breaks through the mirror of calm ocean water for a breath of air, but only to dive out of sight again.

"True, I am . . . I am engaged. But that is something we'll sort out later. Now, forget it."

"I won't. Because I'm afraid I'm doing the same thing I've done before. Making a mess of your life. I've been beastly to you. I let you down, hurt you."

Her face no longer reminded him of Beata's. Feature by feature it was the same, but torment, restlessness, despair and fright had changed it. Nevertheless, he loved her more than he had ever loved Beata.

"You did, yet it makes no difference."

As if he were a blurred script she was trying to decipher,

she gazed at him intently. "I had a dream about you," she said. "A very odd dream. You were killed, shot by men I didn't know. Then suddenly you came to life and I felt immensely relieved. I was fantastically happy that you were alive." She reached out for his hand. "The strangest part of it was that I had this dream on the day of Hans Günther's death." She paused for a second. "You know he was killed, don't you?"

"Yes, I do."

"It was Wednesday three weeks ago. His orderly found him dead in the morning. Shot dead. It was a horrible morning. I don't know how I lived through it, but I did. Then I went to my room and fell asleep and had this dream about you. Can you explain it?"

"Explain what?"

"That I wanted you to be alive and not him."

He almost said, *Because you'd wanted him dead for a long time,* but he thought better of it. "You were in shock, that's all."

"Nicky, I did love him."

"I know that." He felt a slight pang of bitterness. "You told me so more than once."

"That was last summer. But later too. This is what I've been trying to sort out in my mind. The truth. I loved him even after I'd seen him with a man. I told myself that I hated him, despised him, but it wasn't true. Now I know it wasn't true."

"Is that why you didn't leave him?"

"Oh, but I desperately tried to get away. Living with him was so terribly degrading."

He suspected that she was telling only half the truth. The rest she suppressed, probably even from herself.

"Last October, when you left with him for East Prussia, I must admit I was badly hurt. Now I understand."

"Hans Günther swore that Corporal Sommer had been lying. That he tried to blackmail him, and when Hans Günther

275

refused to give him money he became vindictive. I believed the story because—"

He ended the sentence for her: "—because you wanted to."

"For a while I didn't regret having gone to Allenstein. Hans Günther seemed like a changed person. In the beginning, that is. Later I found out why. He needed me. He had this scandalous charge hanging over his head." She wasn't really talking to him but to herself, recapitulating the strange ups and downs of her emotional life between November and July. "The second Harden-Moltke trial with the verdict against Harden sort of exonerated him. Things changed between us. He no longer felt his career endangered. Perhaps it was because of Dmowski, his orderly. From the day he came to the house—"

"Isn't that the man who shot him?"

She seemed strangely disturbed. "Yes, they think it was he, but—"

"—but you don't agree."

She evaded his eyes. "He denies it." She shrugged nervously. "So I really don't know."

"I read in the papers that there was strong enough circumstantial evidence to charge him."

Her lips twitched nervously. "All that legal talk. Circumstantial evidence! They rely too much on law books and forget that they're dealing with people, not with paragraphs." She shook her head with sudden vehemence. "No, that man didn't do it."

"Why are you so sure?"

She was chewing on the nail of her index finger. He had never seen her biting her nails before. "It's just a feeling. He was part of the household for—let me see—almost six months. Long enough time to get to know a person."

"I see. You liked him."

Although it was warm in the room, she shivered. "No, I hated him. I insisted that Hans Günther get rid of him. That was after I'd seen them together."

276

She fell silent. Her face buried in her hands, she sat hunched, hardly breathing. It was long past midnight. He wondered if she had fallen asleep. Suddenly she looked up, her eyes wide with pleading and, it seemed, with terror. "Please, Nicky, help me get away. I don't want to upset your life, but I have no one else to turn to. I've told you, there is a pension coming to me, but I can't wait for that."

"Get away? Where to?"

"It makes no difference as long as it's not Germany. Africa, Asia, the South Seas. I've read about that French painter who went to Tahiti. Gauguin, that was his name. He painted wild pictures with fantastic colors, lived like a native. Have you ever heard of him?"

"I certainly have. What about him?"

"That's what I'd like to do. Just go. Leave this rotten world behind. Never speak another word of German, never have anything to do with a Prussian—military or civilian."

There were tears rolling down her cheeks and she was shaking, either with cold or fear. To quiet her he pulled her into his arms. "Calm down. You've been through hell, but that's all over and done with. Now leave everything to me."

"I want to get away."

"I'll take you away."

"You can't. You'd have to ask for a leave of absence, and the army might refuse you. And that girl in Vienna. What about her?"

"I don't know." He felt wretched. He cradled her chin in his palms and lifted her head to look into her eyes. Their lips almost touched. "I don't know," he repeated. "I am very fond of her. I was ready to settle down with her, have a family, then . . ." He wanted to say, *Then I walked into this room and saw you sitting in that chair and that changed everything.* But he kept silent.

"You thought I was living happily ever after in Allenstein." She emitted a short bitter laugh. "This will surprise you. Hans Günther knew about us. He'd known it all along and

277

told me only after I'd found him with Dmowski. I wanted a divorce and he refused. He even had the Sedlitzes come to Allenstein, and the three banded together against me. You were engaged to the girl in Vienna, so I couldn't turn to you." She nervously rubbed her eyes with her fists. "At that time I wasn't quite as desperate as I am now. So I gave up the idea of the divorce and stayed with him."

Once again he had the distinct feeling that she was not telling the full truth. "Were you afraid of him?"

As if he had given her the cue she had been waiting for, she answered with sudden animation. "Yes, I was. He could be warm and charming, but oh, did he have a cruel streak!" She rose. "Let's not talk about him. I want to forget." She paced the floor, then suddenly halted to face him. "What now? Can you take me to a hotel? The trouble is, I don't have any luggage. I left without so much as a toothbrush. I walked all the way from Kronen Strasse to here. I have about fifty marks in my purse and that's all."

"I'm not taking you anywhere. You'll sleep here, and tomorrow when you're rested we'll talk."

She shook her head. "No, I can't stay here. What will people think?"

"What people?"

She laughed nervously. "Your housekeeper, your orderly, the postman, the world."

He screwed up his eyes to see her better. Her unexpected presence had had the effect of a strong drug on him, lifted him above reality. Now he began to wonder.

"You said you were finished with the world, wanted to leave civilization behind. Now you worry what the postman might think. Let's get things straight. You said you came to me because you had no one to turn to. You needed help. I'm willing to give you all the help you want."

"I want out! Out of this town, this country!"

"Alone? With me or with someone else?"

She jumped as if she'd been struck an unexpected blow.

278

"What makes you think there is anyone else? Would I come to you if there was?"

Her frenzied protest disturbed him. He wasn't ready to commit himself to change his entire life for her. At least not on the spur of the moment. He placed his hand soothingly on her shoulder. "Listen to me. If you want to leave Berlin for your desert island or whatever spot you have in mind and live there in splendid isolation, I'll help you. You won't owe me a thing."

She rose to her tiptoes and rubbed her cheek against his. "I love you, Nicky."

He wasn't sure he heard right. "How was that?"

She laughed at his expression of confused incredulity. "I love you. I've probably loved you all along without realizing it. There have been many men—young, old, poor, rich, all kinds—who let me know that they wanted to sleep with me. I chose you. Remember last summer? Our afternoons in Glienicke? If that wasn't love, what was?"

He also remembered that she had left him twice without adieux or explanations. "You loved your husband."

Her smile faded. "Perhaps a woman can love two men at the same time. It's not proper, so she won't admit it. Even to herself." She glanced at the clock on the baroque secretaire. "Heavens, it's one-thirty!"

"You're exhausted. I think it's time I put you to bed," he said.

She frowned. "Wouldn't it be better if I went to a hotel? That housekeeper of yours treated me as if I were a streetwalker. Tomorrow it'll be all over town that you had a whore spend the night with you."

"I'll call her in and have her move my bedding to the sofa here. You'll sleep in my room. Alone. Propriety will be observed." Silently he wondered about her sudden concern. She was a widow, accountable to no one.

"You can't wake her at this time of the night."

"I won't have to. She is still wide awake, sitting in the

279

kitchen with the door open, trying to catch every sound coming from here."

He rang, and a fully dressed Frau Gerhardt appeared in less than a minute's time. Her searching glance flitted across the room, then up and down Alexa and Nicholas: a detective inspecting the scene of the crime.

"Did you ring, Captain?" The questioning tone was to convey to Nicholas that one-thirty in the morning was not the proper time for an employer to call for the services of an employee.

"I knew you were still awake, Frau Gerhardt."

"I was getting undressed."

"I'm glad I caught you in time. Would you please make up a bed for me here on the sofa. My sister-in-law will sleep in the bedroom. She arrived in Berlin unexpectedly. That is, she wrote me, but her letter seems to have gotten lost in the mail."

Frau Gerhardt sighed and her lips curved downward. "That surprises me. The mail service has been very good lately."

Nicholas thought it advisable to refrain from mentioning Alexa's name. After the *Vorwärts* article there had been several reports on the Godenhausen case in the Berlin press. He doubted they had escaped Frau Gerhardt's eyes. Next to sex, murders were her favorite news items, closely followed by court circulars.

After exchanging a chaste good-night kiss, they slept in separate rooms. The feeling that Alexa was more deeply perturbed than she cared to admit remained with him.

In the morning he stayed home and had breakfast with her. She had borrowed a nightgown from Frau Gerhardt and over it wore his Turkish brocade dressing gown bunched up with a belt around her waist so she wouldn't drag it all over the floor. She seemed relaxed and at ease, yet still oddly secretive about her abrupt decision to leave the Sedlitzes. Neither was she willing to talk about Hans Günther and the circumstances of his death. This in a way he understood. From what little he knew of the murder, he gathered that it had been a terrible shock to be awakened one morning with the news that her healthy young husband had been found in a puddle of his own blood, shot dead. He noticed that at odd moments in the middle of a conversation she would freeze and stare fixedly, as if watching a scene visible only to her.

With tacit understanding, they avoided discussing the future. He needed time to reach a final decision regarding Francesca. It was Alexa's strange secretiveness that kept him from breaking off his engagement. At thirty-seven, he no longer cared for an on-and-off affair. He wanted stability, a home, a family, but not without a binding promise, a covenant, a solemn contract from the woman who was to be his wife.

"Alexa, all this has been much too sudden. Your desert island can wait for a while. Let's find out how we really feel about each other, not rush into resolutions that we might regret later. Right now it would be impossible for me to leave Berlin. You have been through hard times. Stay here and give yourself a chance to forget and be yourself again."

They agreed that moving in with him would be awkward for them both. A suitable furnished flat had to be found for her, and until then she would take a room at a hotel. At this point she raised a condition that seemed unreasonable to him. She insisted upon registering under a false name.

"But why?" he asked.

"I don't want to Sedlitzes to find me."

"What if they do? At twenty-four, you're of age, a widow, a citizen. They have no power over you. As relatives, they can contest your husband's will, but that should be of no concern to you. What reason do you have for hiding from them?"

She fell silent. "No reason," she finally said. "I don't want the press to track me down."

"I have a feeling the army has taken care of that. It seems more anxious to keep the press away from the case than you are. It wants its officers to be as unimpeachable as the knights of the Holy Grail. To have a cavalry major shot by one of his own men reflects badly on the Prussian army's special Valhalla. So don't worry about newspapers, reporters or—"

"No!" she protested. "You don't understand. I am in no condition to face people now. Friends, enemies, press—military or stranger. If I can't get into a place where nobody knows me I'll just—"

He had never seen her more distraught. "All right, I'll see what I can do. The concierge of the Kaiserhof is an old friend of mine, that and a nice tip will keep him from asking questions. If must be, I'll tell him you're a Russian student hiding from the Czar's secret police."

She laughed cheerlessly. She still seemed troubled. "The Sedlitzes might even turn to the police, report me missing. How can we prevent that?"

"Very simply. Write them a letter that you're leaving town and give no forwarding address."

"I have all my things at their place."

"We'll send a porter for them."

"And if they refuse to hand them out to the porter?"

"Then you'll have to buy a new wardrobe. If I know the female psyche, that should be no great hardship."

For the first time, she looked relieved, almost happy. "Oh, Nicky, you make everything seem so simple. Three wishes—abracadabra . . ."

She could not have acted more like a fugitive if she had really been hiding from the Russian secret police. Yet, to be in love is a state of irrationality. It causes the future to appear as if seen through astigmatic lenses, some aspects sharply outlined, others distorted into foggy shapelessness; so he attributed her strange attitude to the murder and its aftermath.

He told the concierge of the Kaiserhof that he wanted a room for a lady who was traveling incognito. The Kaiserhof was no hotel garni but a highly reputable establishment;

nevertheless it occasionally made certain allowances for distinguished patrons. At one time a German princess using a pseudonym had shared her suite with a man who later was convicted of forgery, and once the widow of the Austrian heir to the throne had kept secret trysts there with a Hungarian count. Alexa signed the hotel register as Fräulein Elisabeth Meinhardt. The concierge pocketed a generous tip and there were no questions asked.

Alexa wrote a letter to her aunt saying that she had left for the resort town Warmbrunn in the Riesengebirge. She was in need of peace and solitude and would let Rose know in time when she would be ready to return to Berlin. In the meanwhile, Nicholas was searching for a furnished flat where she could settle and be undisturbed.

By sheer coincidence he found the ideal flat. After lunching in one of the garden restaurants called Zelte an der Spree, he took a walk along the riverbank. On Schleswiger Ufer he passed an attractive two-story building set back from the street by a narrow strip of garden, with a FLAT FOR RENT sign hanging on its front gate.

The house belonged to a widow who lived in the basement and rented rooms, preferably to "gentlemen in governmental service." When Nicholas told her that her tenant would be a lady, she was reluctant to deviate from her rule. In exchange for the round sum of two thousand marks—two months' rent paid in advance—she yielded to his reassurances that the lady would have no male visitors other than himself, no wild parties, no music—piano or victrola—before nine in the morning or after ten at night.

Ever since the building of the Teltow Canal, most tugboat traffic on the Spree had been diverted, and the former waterfront hubbub had quieted to a pleasant rumble. Across the river lay a section of Moabit that had lately been transformed from a neighborhood of slums into a desirable borough of new apartment houses, private residences and tree-lined streets. From her balcony overlooking the water, Alexa could

283

see the garden of Villa Borsig and on the left bank Schloss Bellevue. The Tiergarten, with its wide avenues cutting across grasslands, recreation areas and woods, was a mere block away. Alexa told Nicholas how eagerly she was looking forward to long walks on its shady paths, where she could feel safe from meeting acquaintances or reporters.

On the day she moved into the flat, the haunted expression seemed to fade from her face. The law prescribed that a person's change of address be reported to the police. She filled out the registration form handed her by the landlady using her maiden name and giving a nonexistent street and house number in Königsberg as her last domicile. When Nicholas asked why she still found it necessary to hide, she answered with a shrug.

Despite her announced plan to take long walks in the Tiergarten, she seldom left the apartment, and if she did she crossed to the Moabit bank and strolled along the river or on streets lined with small factories or working people's houses. In the mornings Marie, her landlady's daughter, reported to the flat to clean and cook. She left before Nicholas came from the Embassy to have dinner with Alexa. They would eat at home or in restaurants with strictly bourgeois clientele. The fact that she was in mourning explained, though not entirely, her reluctance to frequent chic places or attend shows and concerts.

She wore widow's weeds every time she left the flat, as if the thick black veil were a screen to hide behind. Although Nicholas tried hard to rid himself of his misgivings, her inexplicable secretiveness marred his delight in possessing her so completely.

Later, whenever he recalled the summer of 1908, all its details seemed crystal clear; only his own reasons for having once again become enslaved by her remained unfathomable. No moonstruck juvenile, he had not been sufficiently blinded by his passion for Alexa to forget the disappointments and

284

humiliations she had doled out to him in the past. True, she had changed, but instead of delighting in her new personality he felt disconcerted. Haunted by some mysterious problems, she needed his help, consequently he could interpret her love-making as her way of paying for it. What did not fit the picture was her desperate need for his affection, much too fervent to be insincere. He was unable to identify this new personality with the Alexa he knew in the Burg Strasse flat or in Glienicke; she was a woman he had once met in a dream and had been looking for ever since.

What troubled him most was the undefined, temporary quality of their relationship. It had lost its roots in the past, yet promised no future. They were to stay in Berlin for the duration of his tour, then what? She refused to make plans. "I want to leave Germany and never come back" was her only answer to his questions. Once he sent up a trial balloon by mentioning marriage. She protested with a vehemence that left him speechless. "Not now. Not yet . . . we'll see. Why rush?" Vague evasions, but no explanations. Later he admitted to himself that in a way avoiding decisions had suited his then troubled state of mind. He had no plans beyond the Berlin tour either. At times he felt ready to leave the army, settle in Sarkany, perhaps enter the diplomatic service or embark on a journey around the world. He had never been to Egypt, India or China. There was so much to see, to learn, to experience. It might have been the sultry heat of August— benumbing, tranquilizing, conducive to easy, irresponsible sex —that caused him to accept his rekindled affair with Alexa for a calendarless sabbatical following and preceding reality.

Trying to write Francesca the day after Alexa's re-entry into his life, he had composed several drafts, then tore them up. Alexa's mysterious attitude made him wait. He continued sending Francesca short bland notes dealing mostly with the weather and social events. He hated himself for their hypocrisy but postponed the break. When he thought of her, he saw her as the only shady green patch in a desert landscape.

He spent almost every night with Alexa. Although no one at the Embassy knew of the affair, people were beginning to notice changes in his conduct and they wondered. He accepted invitations only if refusing them would have seemed rude, and he stopped attending the summer productions at the Neues Opern Theater and the concerts at the Zoologischer Garten. If it had not been August, his disappearance from the social scene would have caused even more speculation. As it was summer, his acquaintances assumed that he had joined the usual exodus for the seashore or the mountains.

His two years in Berlin had been eye-openers in many ways. He had a chance to watch the Prussian military animal at close range and what he saw alarmed him. He had become a friend of Philipp Eulenburg's, and the spectacle of the man's demotion from emperor's favorite to moral outcast by a biased judiciary gave him a frightening insight into the mentality of the ally on which his country's future depended.

He had always known that his wealth, pedigree and connections could unlock doors to him that would remain forever closed to others. He had never before contemplated imparting his potential energy to causes, but now he was beginning to feel a sense of responsibility about the world his generation was to leave to the next.

Undecided about his own future, he did not mind that Alexa was equally vague about hers. She seemed to love the flat and the cozy domesticity of their life. On one of Marie's days off, she even prepared dinner for him. It was her first attempt at the art of cooking, and the result was a three-course disaster, which, however, he valiantly ate. Her eagerness to please him reminded him of the many small surprises Beata had invented to amuse him.

It took him a while to realize that he was thinking more and more frequently of Beata. He would be reading a book, then glance up and catch sight of Alexa bending over some embroidery and suddenly see Beata in her. The ghost's intrusion into their lives began to trouble him, until one afternoon he found out that it was not his imagination but Alexa herself playing tricks on him.

He had never paid much attention to women's fashions unless they were in bad taste or unbecoming, so he failed to notice that several of Alexa's new dresses were copies of the ones Beata had worn during their brief marriage. One afternoon he left his office earlier than usual and found Alexa having a suit fitted. It appeared so hauntingly familiar that he asked the seamstress where she had found the design. Before Alexa could interfere, the woman answered that she was copying it from a photograph Madame had given her. She pulled a snapshot from her purse; he recognized it as one taken of Beata during their honeymoon.

"What on earth made you choose that suit?" he asked Alexa when they were left alone.

She shrugged. "I liked it."

He suddenly remembered. "And what about the blue silk you wore the other day? It looked like the one Beata had her picture taken in at Christmas. And your hair? You never wore it like this before."

He was puzzled by her reaction. All color drained from her face and her eyes brimmed over. "Can't you understand me? Must I spell out everything in black and white?"

"You once broke with me because I'd uttered Beata's name in my sleep."

"Yes, there were times when I didn't want to be confused with her. Even when we were children, she was such a good little girl. I won't say that I was bad, just different." She paused. "Then again, when I did something wrong, like letting the calves out of the barn or breaking a window, I pretended to be Beata, so I wouldn't get spanked. It worked sometimes. We were so alike, and nobody ever spanked Beata—not even Grandmama."

She seemed strangely agitated. He put his arms around her. To feel her face against his was bliss. Her slim body fitted into his embrace as an oyster into its shell. "But I love *you*. The past has no reflection on what I feel for you. You are my life, my love."

She shook her head. "No, don't love *me*. The *me* isn't very lovable. I look into the mirror and don't like the sight of the *me*. I want to get away from the *me*. Would set her on fire if I could."

The word "fire" hit him hard. "What is troubling you?" he asked. She tried to disengage herself, but he held her fast. "Something *is* troubling you. Wouldn't it be better if you told me?"

She clung to him as if he were a rock rising above an incoming tide. "I have nothing to tell you except that I am happy. For the first time in my life. I loved Hans Günther, but I was never happy with him. Not for one single moment. Somehow from the very beginning I felt that it was not going to last. Call it premonition, insecurity, sword of Damocles. Only I didn't expect it to end this . . . this terribly."

Since the night of her reappearance she had not uttered Hans Günther's name. Now, before Nicholas could answer her, she quickly changed the subject. "You don't want me to wear that suit, is that it?"

He looked at her, puzzled. "What suit?"

"The one Frau Louise fitted on me."

"That's up to you." He reflected. "On second thought, no. I don't want you to wear it. And I wish you'd stop this whole masquerade. I don't like it. It makes me feel I am Orpheus descending into Hades to retrieve Eurydice. I am much too normal to enjoy such fantasies."

She looked at him, bemused. "Yes, you are very normal." She sounded as if she had just made a pleasing discovery. "From now on I'll try to be like you. Normal and good."

"Just be yourself."

"For that I'd have to find myself. The myself I could like."

288

A shadow fell over her face. "How long do you want me to stay in Berlin?"

The question took him by surprise, although he had known that sooner or later she would ask it. "As long as I am staying."

"How long will that be?"

"The end of my Berlin tour. Around November."

"But that's months away! You mean you want me to stay here that long?"

"I thought you liked it here."

She looked out on the river. A steamer towing a coal barge was churning its way upstream. It was passed by an excursion boat loaded with children dressed in the uniforms of an orphanage. They were singing a folk song, their lusty voices mingling with the equally lusty bark of a little black dog running up and down on the barge. It was one of those perfect summer days when the view seemed to have been copied from a postcard: brilliant sunshine, clear sky, here and there the puff of a cloud looking like a small furry animal floating on a deep blue lake.

"I love it, but it's still Berlin," Alexa said.

When Marie knocked on her bedroom door to tell her that an artillery lieutenant wished to see her, she didn't have to ask the name. She wondered if she shouldn't instruct the girl to send him away, then realized that hiding from him would be hopeless. Now that he had found her, he would probably leave, then come back later at an even more inconvenient time.

"Offer the lieutenant a seat. I'll be out in a minute."

She ran a comb through her hair, fastened her chignon with more pins, not that it needed it, merely to keep busy while collecting herself. She felt as terrified as if Marie had told her that death was waiting for her in the salon. Maybe it *was* death. Whatever, she had to face it. There was no escaping now.

She found Ranke standing at the window gazing out on

the river. Hearing her enter, he executed the swift, precise about-face of a sentry on duty. The fixed stare of his eyes with their pale vitreous irises filled her with anxiety.

"You left Allenstein without a word to me. For six weeks no letters, not even a postcard." He blurted out the words in a voice hoarse with indignation and hurt. "Didn't you know I was going mad?"

"We agreed we would have no contact for a while," she managed to answer, "yet you kept writing me."

"We did *not* agree. Anyway, 'for a while' is not six weeks. Besides, that was before Dmowski's arrest."

"But he didn't do it."

He threw back his head and laughed hollowly. "What is this —a game? Of course he didn't, but what difference does that make? He'll be convicted, that's all that matters." He grabbed her by the shoulders. "You've been hiding from me. Hiding deliberately. It took me almost a week to track you down."

She realized that she had to change her strategy. To reveal that she was scared would strengthen his hand. She decided to attack.

"You're damned right I was hiding from you. For your own sake, because you're a fool. We did definitely agree to have no contact until it was safe, yet on the very morning of the . . . of the act, you came barging into the house. The typical criminal drawn to the scene of the crime. Yes, I've been hiding from you, but only to keep you from wrecking your own life and mine."

There was a triumphant glint in his eye. "That's not true."

"I was scared! I didn't want my head chopped off because of you."

"Because of me? Just a minute! Don't pretend you weren't part of it. I had nothing against the man except that he was your husband. I didn't want him dead. You did. You said he refused to give you a divorce, so killing him was the only way out." Suddenly, without any transition, he broke down sobbing.

"I love you! I did it for you and I'd do it again." He raised his voice. "I'd kill my own mother for you!"

"For God's sake, don't shout!" Terrified, she crossed to the door, opened it and looked out. Reassured that Marie wasn't lingering in the entrance hall, she returned to him. "When did you arrive in Berlin?"

"Last Thursday. I'd applied for a leave of absence to visit my sick mother."

"Is she sick?"

"No. She doesn't even know I'm here. I was given one week and have already spent five days of it looking for you."

Two more days, she thought. Somehow she must keep him appeased, so he wouldn't learn about Nicholas. "How did you find me?" she asked.

"I went to see Frau von Sedlitz. She wouldn't receive me, but when I insisted she told me you'd left for Warmbrunn in the Riesengebirge. She couldn't tell me the name of the hotel, so I took the next train and arrived in Warmbrunn late that evening. Your name was not on the visitors' list, so I hired a hack and drove from hotel to hotel. Next morning I inquired at police headquarters and was told that you weren't registered in Warmbrunn. Back in Berlin, I went to see your aunt again. This time she told me that you'd been seen at the Kaiserhof. I inquired at Reception there, but they didn't seem to know you. I had your photo along, and when I showed it to the bell-boys one recognized you. I contacted a detective agency and gave them the names of your acquaintances in Berlin, among them that of your ex-brother-in-law, Count Karady. A detective followed him when he came to see you this noon. He stayed two hours. After he left, you took a walk along the river front. The picture I'd given the agency was a poor snapshot and you had a thick veil covering your face, nevertheless the detective identified you as the lady I was looking for."

Not only had Ranke found her, he'd also learned of Nicholas. "Congratulations," she said with bitter resentment. "A fascinating story. You're better than Sherlock Holmes. Wouldn't it be perfect if while you were tracking me down the police had followed you? And if the next ring of the doorbell would be the police coming to get us both?"

He was pacing the floor with the odd jerky movements of a puppet on a string. She noticed now how much weight he had lost, how drawn and bony his face had become—desiccated like the shrunken Papua heads she had seen in the ethnographic section of the New Museum. The pale gray of his eyes, sunken deep into their cavities, imbued him with the sightless look of a marble statue.

"Your fear is irrational," he said. "No one is suspecting us. They've got their man."

"The wrong man."

"They don't know and they don't care. He's been sent to the Kortau insane asylum for psychiatric examination and found to be in full command of his faculties. He'll be tried and convicted."

"And beheaded."

"Or pardoned to powder and lead."

"Some pardon!"

"He might even get away with hard labor for life. Unless he confesses."

She felt a burst of hatred. "How the hell could he confess? He is innocent."

"Leave it to Judge Advocate Yves. He knows how to make his cases airtight."

If she'd had a knife handy, she would have plunged it into him. The clock on the console table was marching on. Office hours at the Embassy were until six in the afternoon.

"You cannot stay here, Otto, not a minute longer. It's bad enough that the maid saw you."

"Are you expecting someone?"

"No. Not really. But one never can tell. Friends might drop in."

"Count Karady?"

She tried to sound casual. "Why Karady?"

"He was here at noon, wasn't he?"

"I happened to ask him to déjeuner. Once in a blue moon I do. After all, he is my twin sister's widower. I probably won't see him for another week or two." She was growing nervous. "Please, please, Otto, be sensible and go."

"Not without you." With sudden vehemence that made her gasp, he wrenched her into a tight hug. His arms were like steel hoops around her, squeezing the air from her lungs. His mouth, cold and moist, traveled all over her face. She pressed her lips together, but he forced them open, his teeth clashing against hers with the force of brass knuckles.

"I can't breathe," she wheezed.

He slackened his hold. "I love you. I can't live without you. Ever since you left Allenstein, it's been hell. So now that I've found you again, I won't let you out of my sight. I leave here only if you come with me."

"Where to? You can't possibly want me to return to Allenstein."

"I'm staying in a small hotel near the Stettiner Station, the Baltischer Hof. The kind of place where the concierge looks the other way when a man takes a woman upstairs."

She was thinking. Two days, then he would have to report back to Allenstein. For two days she'd have to keep him restrained. She no longer doubted that he was unbalanced. A madman who had killed once and would kill again. Since July 22, when she had moved to Schleswiger Ufer, of the three ghosts that haunted her dreams two were of the still living: the murderer and the false accused. The ghost of Hans Günther was the easiest to cope with. She had made her peace with him and dreaded only the other two. With the appearance of Ranke, her hope for escape became blighted.

"All right, Otto, I'll go to your hotel. That is, I'll follow you. I just don't want the maid or anyone else to see us leave the house together." She knew the maid was gone, their arrangement being that after washing up the midday dishes and cleaning the kitchen she could quit for the day. "There is a hack stand in front of the Bellevue Station. Choose a closed carriage and wait in it for me. I'll join you in ten minutes."

He pulled out his watch. "Why ten minutes?"

"For God's sake, I'll have to change into street clothes. Make it fifteen."

"Fifteen then, but not a minute longer."

She changed quickly and scribbled a note for Nicholas saying that she had run into an old schoolmate and gone to a konditorei for ice cream and cakes with her, but would be back for supper. No doubt the note would puzzle Nicholas, she thought. After weeks of shunning people, suddenly she was making an exception for a schoolmate.

She felt the impotent rage, mingled with the fright, of a trapped animal. For the first time in her life she had been enjoying a peaceful and orderly existence, and now it was endangered by a madman.

It was a hot day with the threat of a summer storm hanging over the city. A thick mass of clouds was drifting in from the west; flashes of lightning flickered, followed by distant thunder. It was a short walk from her house to the Bellevue Station, nevertheless it exhausted her. She passed the hack stand. The two-horse droshky Ranke had hired was parked at the corner of Brücken Allee.

He alighted to help her into the carriage. "You're five minutes late," he said petulantly. "I was going to count to one hundred and if you hadn't come by then—"

She felt a sharp pain spread over her forehead. "—you would've shot me," she snapped.

"How can you say that? I don't think you love me anymore."

The desperation of his tone was disturbing. She threw a glance at him. In the semidarkness of the closed carriage his face resembled a skull—no skin or flesh, just dead bones and the eyes like colored marbles stuck into their cavities.

"I'm mad at you," she said. "Don't you remember what I

asked you? To be patient and to wait. But no. You followed me to Berlin, hired a detective agency to find me. What explanation did you give them when they questioned your reasons?"

"They never did."

"They will, if they haven't found out already."

"What's wrong with an officer looking for the widow of a comrade?"

"Nothing, except that the officer was the one to make her a widow."

The hotel, much in need of a fresh coat of paint, lay in a narrow street untouched by the spirit of modernization, that trend of "There shall not be left here one stone upon another that shall not be thrown down" that was transforming a shabby-genteel Lutheran town into the nouveau-riche capital of a self-styled world power. As if the ceremonial proclamation in the Versailles Hall of Mirrors had never taken place, the lobby of this hotel smelled the way it had for the past hundred years: of dry rot, spilled beer and urine. The once red carpet covering its stairway had long since lost its nap and become worn to a gray web. The concierge was in shirtsleeves, and for the five marks Ranke slipped him he pretended not to see Alexa. There was no elevator, which meant a climb of four flights to Ranke's room.

"Why on earth did you choose this hovel?" Alexa asked after she had caught her breath.

"Because it's cheap," he said.

"Obviously."

The air felt oppressively hot and stale. The windows could not be opened, because across the street a family of father, mother and fat daughter were seated on their balcony, most likely to keep watchful eyes on the happenings in the hotel. This was probably how they spent their summer afternoons, munching candy and enjoying the free show offered them by those uninhibited hotel guests who fought, undressed and made love without bothering to close their windows.

Even after she stripped, rivulets of perspiration were running down Alexa's back. The caresses of Ranke's clammy hands and his feverish efforts to possess her drove her close to hysteria. She hated having exposed herself to his blackmail. She had thought him to be soft and invertebrate like a slug, yet he had the truculence and indestructibility of a snapping turtle. Gazing at his nude body, she was suddenly struck by its ugliness—shoulders too narrow for wide hips, arms too bony for muscular thighs, frail wrists sprouting thick-fingered worker's hands. He looked as if he had been assembled from discarded limbs found in the waste bin of a medical school's anatomical theater.

His lovemaking had the same grotesque and embarrassing touches as at the beginning of their affair. His fumblings enraged her. He demanded that she engage in weird and asinine calisthenics, and she complied because that was the price she had to pay if she wanted to leave the hot airless room before nightfall.

She promised Ranke to return the following morning and to spend the whole day with him. In thirty-six hours he was to leave for Allenstein to report back for duty. Until then she had to do her utmost to allay his suspicions. After that she would have to leave Germany. She could not feel safe as long as she remained in the same country with him.

Luckily Nicholas had been invited to lunch at Prince Joachim Albrecht's on the following day. It was to be a stag affair, which meant that it would last into the late afternoon. If only for an hour or two, Nicholas would have to make an appearance at the Embassy, and he would come to Schleswiger Ufer no earlier than suppertime.

The day, her farewell gift to Ranke, passed without any jarring unpleasantness. They spent the morning hours in his room, had a midday meal at a new restaurant on August Strasse, then returned for a siesta to his hotel.

The night before, a long overdue storm had broken loose over the city, showering away the accumulated grime from its roofs and walls and scenting the air with the fragrance of distance forests and meadows. The room was not as stiflingly hot as before, and she lived through the day without too much discomfort. They had a fight when he suggested that she have supper with him and stay for the night. Up to then he had been a blithely debonair Danilo straight out of *The Merry Widow;* her refusal turned him into a Hamlet. Earlier he had agreed to let her leave in the afternoon; now he reneged.

She spotted Ranke's pocketknife, with its large blade exposed, lying on the table beside a handful of peaches they had bought at a fruit stand. For an insane moment she thought of plunging the knife into his back. She reached for it, but her hand froze halfway. The torturous headache of the day before hit her again; she had to hold on to the edge of the table to keep from stumbling. Ranke noticed her malaise and rushed to her side to support her, but she tore herself free.

"Now listen here," she shouted at him. "I am going home right now. And don't you follow me and don't you spy on me, because I won't have it." She lowered her voice. "I'd rather report you and myself to the first policeman than let you terrorize me. You want me to believe that I talked you into shooting my husband. That isn't true. I never wanted him killed. Never, never, never."

He stepped back, his eyes fixed on her. "You're a damned liar," he said tonelessly.

"We did talk about things, but most of it was playing games, fantasy."

"Liar."

"You never told me you would *really* do it. Or when. If you had told me that you were going to break into the house and shoot him point-blank, I would've said don't."

He shook his head in utter disbelief. "You suggested a duel without witnesses. You must remember *that.*"

"Sneaking up on an unsuspecting man and shooting him in the back is not a duel."

"I didn't sneak up on him and didn't shoot him in the back.

297

He was armed. I'd awakened him and told him to get his gun because we'd have to have a duel over you. When he heard that, he became convulsed with laughter. He thought it was a big joke. He said as far as he was concerned I could have you any time. That's when I shot him. If he hadn't laughed he'd be alive today."

"A Sir Galahad, that's what you are," she said acidly. Her hair had come loose. She gathered up its stray strands and twisted them into a topknot. Reaching for her hat and hatpins, a story came to her mind in which the mystery of the victim's inexplicable death was solved by the master detective who identified the murder weapon: a hatpin still encrusted with the dead man's dried blood. She picked up the pins and took a good look at them. They seemed too short to kill a man.

"I must be going mad," she muttered.

"What did you say?" Ranke asked.

She shrugged, embarrassed. "Nothing, nothing." She quickly put on her hat and fastened it with the pins. "I'm leaving now," she said, although her intent was obvious. "You may write me. A postcard now and then, but no letters, nothing more than you would send to any casual acquaintance. Then after the Dmowski verdict, when we can feel perfectly safe, we'll meet again."

"Meet where?"

"Let's not decide now. We don't know the future. Things may still go wrong." Suddenly she frowned. "Do you think he'll be condemned to death?"

His lips twisted tauntingly. "Let's hope he will be. Then you won't have any reason to avoid me."

"Except that I'll still be in mourning. There are conventions one must observe, you know." She started for the door. "Goodbye, Otto."

His voice, icy and commanding, stopped her halfway. "You don't love me, do you? You never did."

"Not that again, Otto. We've been over that before. I must leave now. I'm late already."

"I only asked if you loved me. A simple yes or no will do."

She stepped to the door. "Yes. Does that satisfy you?" She pushed down the handle and realized with sudden terror that the door was locked and the key gone from its hole. She could not recall when he had removed it, no doubt with the intent to keep her prisoner. "What is this? A game?" She turned on him. "Let me out or I'll scream."

"Scream," he said without moving.

Suddenly she was scared. He appeared calm, yet she sensed menace in his dull loveless tone. For a second she wondered if he had a gun. If he had, he was not carrying it on his body; she would have noticed it when he undressed. A small overnight case was on a chair within his easy reach. A headline flashed through her mind: BODIES OF ARTILLERY OFFICER AND UNKNOWN WOMAN FOUND IN A HOTEL GARNI NEAR STETTINER STATION.

Quite recently she had read in the papers about the violent death of two lovers. The police suspected murder-suicide. Visualizing the site of the tragedy, her mental picture of it fitted the room where she was right now: imitation Oriental runners on the floor, white-painted iron bedstead, nightstand discreetly hiding a chamber pot, single light bulb with parchment shade hung from the ceiling, washstand with bowl, pitcher and bucket for slops.

"Let me out!" she repeated, her voice trembling this time.

"Not before you understand that I won't give you up. I have reason to believe that you have changed your mind about me."

"I have not." Oh God, she thought, help me get out of here.

"That's good. But even if you had, it would make no difference, because *I* still love you and would rather die than give you up."

He pointed at the dresser. On its top, beside his wallet, cigarette case and other small objects he had removed from his pocket, lay the key. With shaking hand she grabbed it and tried to insert it into its hole, but it slid from her fingers and fell to the floor. Before she could retrieve it, he picked it up and unlocked the door. He caught her on the threshold for one long fierce embrace before letting her go.

The corridor that led to the stairway seemed endless. Hurrying through its tunnel-like darkness, she expected to hear the click of a revolver followed by the explosion of a shot behind her, yet nothing happened. Nevertheless she raced down the steps as if she were running for her life. She jumped into the first free carriage at the stand, gave her address in a muffled voice, then lost consciousness. She came out of her twilight sleep only when the cab passed the Royal Charité. Arriving home, she found Nicholas seated in the salon reading the evening paper.

"You are early," she called to him. She knew he was not but said it merely to keep him from telling her that *she* was late.

He threw a searching glance at her. "Is something wrong?" He stepped to her and touched her cheeks with the backs of his hands. "Aren't you running a temperature?"

She realized that the day with Ranke had left its mark on her. "Why?" she asked, trying to sound unconcerned. "Do I look ill?"

His hand slid to her chest, feeling for her heartbeat. "Your heart is pounding like mad." He picked up the newspaper. "Have you read this? Is this what upset you?"

"Read what?" She did not have the vaguest idea what he was talking about. In answer he showed her an item on the third page of the paper. Printed in the column of "News in Brief" was a report from Allenstein.

A court-martial, presided over by Colonel Paul Seiffert, commandant of the Tenth Dragoon Regiment, found Dragoon Jan Dmowski guilty of murdering his superior officer,

Major Baron Hans Günther von Godenhausen, and condemned him to twenty years of hard labor. The prosecution had failed to obtain a confession from the defendant and based the charges on circumstantial evidence alone, which was the reason Dmowski escaped the death sentence.

Alexa read the lines over and over until her trembling hands could no longer hold the paper. At first reading, a faint cry escaped her lips. Now she was staring wide-eyed at Nicholas, her lips moving soundlessly.

"I'm sorry. I shouldn't have shown it to you," he said. "At least not without any warning." Soothingly he placed his arms about her. "I thought you had seen it and—"

When she finally spoke she did with desperate urgency. "Let's get out of Berlin, Nicholas! I can't stand it here. I'll suffocate."

"Calm down, for heaven's sake. The man wouldn't have been convicted unless there had been strong evidence to support the charge." He mistook her distress for worry about the fate of a man she considered innocent. "Should the verdict be a miscarriage of justice, the truth will come to light. It often does, you know. Let's suppose you're right, Dmowski didn't do it. The real murderer feels free now, becomes reckless, commits a blunder, betrays himself—"

She shuddered. "Oh, my God."

He tried to quiet her, but his words seemed to add fuel to the fire. There had to be more to the fatal shooting of Hans Günther von Godenhausen than what the news reports and the grapevine revealed, he thought. He saw torment and fear in her eyes. He was reluctant to upset her even more and tried an oblique approach.

"If you're convinced the man is innocent, we can find ways to help him. You haven't told me much about the judge advocate who investigated the case, but I've known a few in *our* army I wouldn't trust a dog's fate to. We could have a good criminal attorney start a private investigation and—"

"No! Don't! Don't do a thing!"

Her vehemence convinced him that his suspicions were justified. "I'd like to help you, but I can't unless you tell me what's troubling you. The truth."

Her face red with agitation, she confronted him. "I've told you what's troubling me! Berlin! The whole country. I've had nothing but unhappiness here." Abruptly she turned and started for the door.

"Where are you going?"

"To my room. To get out of these clothes. They're filthy. Ought to be burned. I'm filthy too. I must take a bath. I hope Marie didn't forget to prepare kindling and wood under the water heater. And fill the coal bucket."

He followed her and caught up with her in the entrance hall. "I'll bring some from the cellar if she didn't. And light the fire for you and—"

"It might not be necessary. There might be enough warm water left from the morning."

"Then I'll scrub your back."

She halted abruptly and, feet planted firmly on the floor, gave him a push with both hands. "Leave me alone! I don't feel well!" Seeing his startled reaction, she quickly added, "I might be getting the curse. Lately it's been quite irregular." She seemed to be on the brink of tears. "I'm so horribly tired. I just want to crawl into bed and never get up. At least not till tomorrow morning," she corrected herself with a half-hearted giggle. "You'd better have supper out. I don't think I could eat a bite tonight."

He noticed the lanky young man in the ill-fitting gray suit leaning against the lamppost in the same spot where he had seen him the afternoon before. It had been the suit that first attracted his attention. Its unmistakable newness gave its wearer—as he stood motionless, seemingly indifferent to the street scene about him—the appearance of a wax museum figure. On his way to Schleswiger Ufer, Nicholas had encountered the man strolling or window-shopping in the neigh-

302

borhood at least once a day. With the nearest winehouse blocks away, one seldom saw loiterers in this section of town. Maids and housewives carrying shopping bags would stop to gossip, concierges would talk politics with mailmen, old ladies would walk their dogs and nannies run after their straying charges, but otherwise what pedestrian traffic there was would move at a steady and purposeful flow. The closeness of the river caused Nicholas to wonder if the man weren't a potential suicide trying to summon up enough courage for the fatal jump.

When after three days he was still around, his presence seemed even more mysterious. Because of his failure to melt into the background, he could hardly be a private detective or a plainclothes policeman. For reasons Nicholas could not explain, the man's presence disturbed him. Although he was convinced that they had never met, he had the strange feeling that the man knew who he was. Twice he was on the verge of confronting him, then thought better of it. The man displayed no hostility or curiosity, nor did he ever follow him. Nicholas tried to reassure himself that he noticed the man's presence as one does a freshly posted placard, simply because it hadn't been there before.

Alexa had not left the flat for days. She complained of a cold and spent most of her time in bed, getting up only when Nicholas was due from the Embassy. She called in Marie to fix supper so Nicholas could have decent meals. He had the odd feeling that there was a connection between Alexa's indisposition and the stranger's haunting presence in the neighborhood.

From the corner window of the salon, if one leaned out far enough, one could see a section of the Schleswiger Ufer sidewalk. After hanging up his sword and shako in the hallway, Nicholas looked out the window. The man was still there, in the same position as before, seemingly rooted to the base of the lamppost.

"Come, I want to show you something," Nicholas called to Alexa.

303

She crossed to the window but remained behind its lace curtain. "What is it?"

"A young man. He's been loitering around here for days. I wonder what he's up to. If you lean out you can see him standing under the street lamp."

There was a long silence. He turned back and saw her draw away from the window. "I can't," she said. "Heights make me dizzy. A sickness. There is a name for it. Not claustrophobia —that means fear of closed-in places—but—"

Now he knew that the young man was no stranger to her, what is more, that she had seen him keep vigil around the house, probably even spoken to him. Inflamed, he grabbed hold of her by the shoulders and turned her around, forcing her to face him.

"Who is he?"

She paled. "Who is who?" she faltered. "You mean the man in the street? How would I know? I've never laid eyes on him."

"So do it now. He's still there." He half pushed, half dragged her to the window.

Intimidated by his sudden hostility, she obediently leaned over the windowsill, stretching her neck. At the same moment the man looked up. Nicholas, still holding her in his grip, could tell by the expression on the man's face that he caught sight of her. She shrank back as though his glance had burned her. She retreated to the far end of the room—a fugitive dodging her pursuer's bullet.

"Do you know him?" Nicholas asked.

She took a deep breath. "I think so. He might be a lieutenant I met in Allenstein. Lieutenant von Ranke."

"What do you mean, he might be. Is he or isn't he?"

"I never saw him in mufti. Men look different in uniforms."

"Let's suppose he *is* this Ranke. What reason does he have to follow you or to spy on you?"

She shrugged. "I don't know. In Allenstein he was considered a bit on the strange side. Not unbalanced, just peculiar." Suddenly she grew indignant. "Will you please leave me alone? Stop harassing me. He was one of the people we knew in Allenstein. Socially, I mean. He might have found me attractive; some of the younger men did, and even the older ones too. Now that I am"—she looked for the word—"free— a widow—he might have ideas. Please ignore him. When he realizes that I won't have anything to do with him, he'll go away."

Nicholas knew she was telling a half-truth or, worse, a complete lie. He realized once again that life with her was like moving through a terrain exposed to sniper fire; one could never tell from what side the shots would come. He felt the same impotent resentment that her caprices and moods had aroused in him before. "How in hell do you expect me to ignore him when I know he is after you? Just sit and wait till he breaks in here or attacks you in the street?"

"He won't, ever. I've told you. He's peculiar, but harmless."

He started for the hallway. "I'll find out how harmless he is."

She rushed after him, caught him by the arm and clung to him with all her might. "Please, please don't do anything rash. He might be armed and shoot you."

Nicholas was already in the hallway girding himself with his sword. "You said he was harmless. If he isn't, I can handle him better than you can."

With her hanging on to his arm, he reached the door. "Don't believe anything he tells you," she pleaded. "He's unpredictable, sick, a liar."

"He won't have a chance to tell me anything. I'll do the talking."

Impatiently he extricated himself from her grip and walked out. Descending the steps, he could hear her shouted warnings coming from behind the closed door. Although hardly five minutes had passed since he had glimpsed Ranke looking up at Alexa's window, by the time he reached the street the lieutenant had vanished. He could be seen neither on

305

Schleswiger Ufer nor on the cross street, Flensburg Strasse, that led to the Bellevue Station of the Stadtbahn, a stopping place for both metropolitan and long-distance trains.

Moving at top speed, Nicholas rounded the corner of Brücken Allee and, glancing into the doorways, set out for Bellevue Square. He was flustered and out of breath as he entered the station building and crossed and recrossed the circulation area and the waiting rooms. Then, after a long but futile search, he returned to Schleswiger Ufer. When he opened the door to the flat, he found Alexa waiting pale and distraught.

"What happened?" she asked breathlessly.

"Nothing. The fellow vanished. Which, however, doesn't mean that he won't reappear. You must tell me more about him. The truth. Because I'm going to get hold of him no matter what and put an end to his little game. And yours as well."

Without a word she turned and walked away from him. He followed her into the salon and forced her to sit down facing him. "For the last time, Alexa, I want the truth. When you came to my place, you were running from something or someone. You've been running ever since. Was it from him, this Lieutenant Ranke?" When she remained silent, he pressed on. "What was there between him and you? Did you sleep with him? Or promise to? Promise to marry him if you were free? Was there any connection between him and that man Dmowski?"

The last question shook her from her stubborn aloofness. "No," she cried. "They didn't even know each other."

Her protest sounded sincere, nevertheless it failed to allay his suspicion of a link between Dmowski and the lieutenant. "Damn it, Alexa, don't force me to play twenty questions. Tell me the truth."

Her answer exasperated and annoyed him because he took it for a wild lie with which she tried to bluff her way out of a

306

tight corner. Recalling it later, he realized that it was the beginning of her descent into dark and mysterious depths.

"Stop torturing me, Nicky," was her answer. "What is there
to tell? If I come to think of it, I was wrong. Mistaken. The
truth is that I've never laid eyes on the man before."

He looked at her, perplexed. "But you've just told me—"

Haughtily she interrupted him. "Never mind what I told
you. And don't try to confuse me. I'm absolutely sure that
I have never before met or seen the man."

11

Battery Chief Major Brausch was dependable and level-headed and performed his duties to the best of his abilities, which were less than brilliant and more than adequate. His command was run like a good business office; he was respected by all ranks as well as by his wife and children. Admired he was not, which accounted for the peaceful monotony of his life.

When he learned from his adjutant that Lieutenant von Ranke had failed to report for duty after the expiration of his leave, he reacted to the problem in his usual manner: dispassionately and without haste.

"Let's give him three days," he said. "He might be ill or have missed his train. He never caused trouble before. So let's wait and see. Let's keep the matter from Division."

When the three days passed without Lieutenant von Ranke's reappearance, Major Brausch reported his absence to the divisional command, which in turn wired the Ministry of War and the military command of Berlin to have a search ordered for the missing lieutenant.

About the same time the order was issued to various deputy commands, Otto von Ranke, still in civilian clothes, was waiting for his connection in Thorn. His uniform and cap he carried in a small suitcase and his sword wrapped in several layers of brown paper and tied with a string to resemble fishing gear. On the Berlin–Thorn train he had traveled second class; in Thorn he bought a first-class ticket for Allenstein.

There were few passengers in first class and he was alone in a compartment. When the conductor came to punch his ticket, for an appropriate tip he hung an OCCUPIED sign on the compartment door and Ranke locked himself in. He unpacked his uniform, then took off the civilian suit. He stuffed its shoulders and pant legs with the paper he had had his sword wrapped in so they wouldn't wrinkle. He placed the suit in his case, then slipped on his tunic. He realized with sudden alarm that the bottle of perfume he had bought in Berlin for Alexa's use in the hotel room had leaked and permeated his uniform. He had known all along that his return to Allenstein would be a rather trying experience, but to live through it smelling like a bunch of lilies of the valley was to add a painfully embarrassing touch.

When he arrived in Allenstein, the gaslights were still burning in the streets. A moon on the wane, bright with the courage of the undaunted loser, was lending its silvery support to them. It was one of those rare mornings when the air felt soft and slightly humid, as if Allenstein were located not in East Prussia but in the Ticino.

During the walk from the train down the platform and across the circulating area of the station, he noticed the odd expressions on the faces of the few people he passed as they smelled the perfume. As usual, the station was patrolled by the military, nevertheless he left it without being recognized. He did not know, merely assumed, that orders had been issued for his arrest. In a way he wished to be caught. As he wasn't, the next move was up to him, which merely added to his torment. The decision to return to Allenstein had been the result of a long inner struggle. Once he had reached it, he felt as if he were sighting a safe shore after a struggle against wind and sea in a small rudderless boat. He had weighed all

309

his choices: suicide; shooting Alexa or Karady or both; silent acceptance of the unalterable loss of Alexa; and, finally, the disclosure of the truth. Of all choices, he settled on the last. He had left Berlin almost cheerfully, enjoying a peace of mind he had not experienced since firing his gun at Hans Günther von Godenhausen.

Now, riding through the sleeping town in a one-horse hack with its top down, a breeze as soft as a child's hand caressing his cheeks, he once again was troubled by doubts. The four days of his overstaying a leave of absence called for a reprimand, possibly a house arrest. His confession of murder would bring a life sentence or death. He looked up at the truncated moon, half its profile veiled like a Moslem woman's with a threadbare cloud, and at the stars blinking as if sending out Morse signals, and once again felt his inner turmoil melt into tranquilizing fatigue. The emotional and physical exertions of the past days were taking their toll. All he wanted was the feel of cool crisp sheets wrapping his naked body and the restorative peace of a long dreamless sleep.

He dozed off and was awakened by the driver's touch on his shoulder. He looked up, dazed, and saw that they were in front of the gate. The two guards saluted and snapped to attention. He vaguely remembered that sometime during the ride he had intended to order the driver to change directions and head for his Nikolai Strasse flat. Now it was too late. He paid the cabbie, told him to wait for the soldier he would send for his suitcase, then entered through the gate.

He found the duty officer, a second lieutenant, stretched out on the leather couch in the office. The squeak of the door woke him. Sitting upright and rubbing his eyes, he blinked at Ranke from behind spread fingers. "Where the hell have you been?" he asked raucously.

"In Berlin."

"But why report in the middle of the night? Couldn't you damn well wait for the morning?"

"It *is* morning."

"Not by my watch." He scratched his head. "I'm supposed to arrest you. What the hell. Sit down and consider yourself under arrest."

The sergeant on duty stuck his head in from the anteroom. "What do you want me to do with your luggage, Lieutenant?" he asked Ranke.

"Jesus Christ, luggage too!" the second lieutenant bellowed.

"Keep it for the time being," Ranke told the sergeant. He turned to the officer. "Will you kindly send word to Major Brausch that I am here to surrender to him."

"You've already surrendered to me."

"To him and now!"

The lieutenant screwed up his eyes. "Are you drunk?"

Trembling with irritation, Ranke raised his voice. "Will you do as told or shall I order the sergeant to send for him?"

The lieutenant shook his head, puzzled. "What's your damned hurry? The major will think I'm out of my mind if I get him up at his ungodly hour. Sure as hell he'll be here early enough to give you a dressing down." He halted, sniffing. "Say, where're you coming from? You smell like a bloody perfumery."

Ranke dropped into a chair and buried his head in his grimy hands. "I want to confess to the murder of Major Hans Günther von Godenhausen."

The lieutenant's mouth fell open. "You *are* drunk." He chuckled inanely. "Stinking drunk. Stinking of hyacinths."

"Lilies of the valley," Ranke corrected him.

Suddenly, as if wiped off with a rough cloth, the lieutenant's grin gave way to a pained grimace. "What did you say? Confess what? Whose murder?"

"Godenhausen's," Ranke said with a finality disallowing doubt.

The lieutenant stared at him, awed and dismayed. "You *are*

311

mad. A man has been convicted for that. Why stir up the mess? Jesus Christ, old Brausch won't like this. Neither will Army Command."

"Get him," Ranke said in a voice heavy with hidden hatred. Sensing it, the lieutenant scrambled for the door.

Major Brausch went straight to his office, then ordered Ranke to be brought in.

"What's this nonsense, Ranke? It's five in the morning. Couldn't whatever you have to tell me wait? With no exercises scheduled for today, I wasn't going to come in before eight."

Snapping to stiff attention, Ranke had his eyes fixed on his superior's face. "I respectfully report, sir, that on the morning of July second, 1908, I shot and killed Major Hans Günther von Godenhausen."

The written note that Brausch had received had contained no explanation of why Lieutenant von Ranke insisted upon seeing him. Now instinct told him that no matter how weird and improbable the young man's confession sounded, it was the truth. Ever since the murder he had had a vague notion that the Godenhausen case wasn't quite as simple as Judge Advocate Yves maneuvered to make it appear. A man was seen leaving the scene of the crime, which was sufficient evidence for Yves to prefer murder charges against him and have him convicted.

A rather unsociable person, with hunting his only diversion, Brausch nevertheless had been aware of the rumors that involved Godenhausen in the Moltke, Lynar and Hohenau scandals. Through the grapevine of household servants, he had heard that all wasn't well in the Godenhausens' marriage. Notwithstanding the command decision to keep the case quiet, gossip as untraceable and flimsy as gossamer continued floating in the air.

For a while Brausch remained silent, his big neckless head moving up and down like a mechanized doll's between his hunched shoulders. "So it was you who shot him," he finally said. It was a statement, not a question.

"Yes, sir."

Brausch stopped nodding. "Why?" He seemed more distressed than curious.

Ranke took a deep breath. "I was his wife's lover and—" A stab of pain contorted his face into a grotesque mask. Despite his visible efforts to remain at attention, his legs began to tremble.

"At ease," Brausch commanded; then, after a moment's reflection, "Sit down."

"Thank you, sir." Nevertheless he remained on his feet.

"So you were the wife's lover. Did the major find out about it?"

"I don't think he did, sir."

The answer surprised Brausch. Rather unsophisticated in matters of illicit sex, his initial concept of Ranke's motive had been the husband's threat to break up the affair. "Why in the devil did you have to kill him then?"

"He refused to give her a divorce."

"Did she ask for one?"

"That's what she told me."

"Does she know it was you? Did she before or after the act?" Vexed by Ranke's glassy stare, he raised his voice. "Damn it, Ranke, was the woman in on the bloody thing?"

Like a swimmer before a deep dive, Ranke took a long breath. "She wanted him dead. That's why I shot him." He was swaying to and fro with the tempo of a pendulum.

"Sit down, Ranke, before you fall flat on your face." He waited for the lieutenant to comply, then continued. "Now, my boy, are you fully aware of what you've just told me? That on the second of July you shot and killed a fellow officer?"

"Yes, sir. I am, sir."

"Well then, the next step for me is to arrest you and hand you over to Division. But, as your commandant, I first want a detailed account of the whole damn business from you."

"I killed Major von Godenhausen by twice firing my Webley-Fosbery semiautomatic at him. Point-blank."

The hollow despair in Ranke's tone moved Brausch. Despite his better judgment, his sympathy went to the murderer and not the victim. "I said a detailed account, Ranke."

"It was supposed to be a duel without seconds, sir. That's how we'd planned it. To take place during the hunting season, somewhere in the woods, and—"

"Just a minute," the major interrupted him. "Who planned it? You and who else?"

"Baroness von Godenhausen."

"But it didn't happen that way. Why not?"

"I was afraid to wait, sir. She was losing interest in me. Time and again she would make a date with me, then break it. In the beginning I often wondered why she'd chosen me, when every single man in Allenstein would've been willing. That is, almost every man. So when I noticed a change in her, I began to worry. She had expected me to shoot her husband, but I let her down. I figured she was looking for someone else. The thought of losing her—" His voice cracked and he blinked away tears. "I started drinking, but it didn't help. I couldn't sleep. Evenings I would steel myself to live through another night without losing my mind. Like Christ in the Garden of Gethsemane. I kept praying to God to have the cup pass from me, but he didn't hear me." He paused to collect himself. "On the afternoon of July first, I dropped in at Lieutenant Colonel Schimmert's. It was his wife's at-home day. She—I mean Baroness von Godenhausen—was already there when I arrived, but left soon after. I felt she left because she didn't want to talk to me. That night I had supper at the officers' casino and went home early. I knew I wasn't going to sleep, so I had a large snifter of brandy—"

Brausch's eyes lit up. He pounced upon the lieutenant. "You were drunk! Don't forget to mention this when you're interrogated. It might be considered an extenuating circumstance."

"No, sir. I wasn't drunk. I was cold sober. The brandy gave me a bad headache, that was all. I couldn't fall alseep. I heard the church bell strike midnight, then one o'clock, then two. That was when I decided to put an end to it. The night was very dark—overcast sky, no moon—but even a full moon wouldn't have stopped me. I put on the plus fours and the jacket I'd worn on hiking tours with my mother and pulled heavy socks over my boots. I thought of covering my face with a bandanna, but that would've been too theatrical, so I chose an old yachting cap with a wide visor. And . . . yes . . . I slipped the pistol into my pocket." He halted as if there were no more details to tell.

"Go on."

"I'd read in some detective story that what cat burglars did to muffle the sound of their footsteps was to pull socks over their shoes."

"You said you'd heard the church bells strike two. So what time did you leave your place?"

"Fifteen—twenty minutes later. I didn't go straight to Parade Platz but took a long detour instead to approach the Godenhausen house from the opposite direction in case someone saw me."

"Did anyone see you?"

"Yes, sir. There was a man relieving himself in the alley behind the Reichshof. He cursed me when I passed him. I think he was drunk."

Brausch shook his head, puzzled. "Damned if I understand you. You said the woman had been avoiding you. At that stage what did you hope to gain by killing the husband?"

"That was what she wanted me to do."

The major snorted. "Now let me see. You left your place with the definite intent to kill the major."

"To challenge him to a duel."

"How were you planning to go about it? Ring his doorbell and tell him to shoot it out with you?"

Ranke blinked, embarrassed. "Not exactly, sir. I didn't want to awaken the people in the house. I assumed I'd find a door or a window open and—"

"What if you hadn't? What would you have done?"

Ranke shrugged. "Gone home, probably." He reflected for a moment. "But I didn't have to look long. You see, sir, it's a rather big house. There's the entrance hall; to the left is the salon; beyond that is a ballroom that they kept closed off and unfurnished; and to the right is a hallway, sort of second anteroom, with windows overlooking the garden. The study opened off this. There was no access to his bedroom other than from the study. I entered the grounds through the gate behind the stables. I knew the layout well, since I'd saddled her horse more than once when neither the orderly nor the stableboy was around. I circled the house and found one of the hallway windows wide open. It was set rather high in the wall, but there was a ridge on which I could take a foothold, so I managed to climb it without making too much noise. I groped my way to the study, but when I crossed it I bumped into a chair. Godenhausen had either been awake or the thud woke him, because he lighted a candle—they had electricity in the study but not in his bedroom—and came to the door. I told him I was in love with his wife and challenged him. He stared at me, called me a damn fool and burst out laughing. That was when I shot him."

"Is that what you call a duel?" Brausch shouted. "Shooting an unarmed man?"

"No, no, sir," Ranke protested, agitated. "He was armed. He had a pistol. He had it in his hand."

"A lighted candle. That's what you just said."

"No, sir. At that point he *was* holding a pistol. One of us had turned on the light in the study. I mean, either he or me. I don't remember." Ranke closed his eyes in an effort to black out the present. "Yes, he could've been holding both the candle and the pistol when he confronted me."

"Both?"

Ranke shook his head nervously, as if trying to get rid of an

316

insect crawling through his hair. "I don't know, sir. The more desperately I try to remember how it all happened, the more confused I become. I can't even recall how I left the house. Possibly through the front door. Yes, that's how. I did climb *in* through the window, but not out. I reached home without meeting anyone. I said to myself, What a godforsaken little nest Allenstein is at three in the morning, with not a soul awake except patrols, sentries or policemen. From those I kept my distance. I don't think anyone saw me. At home I noticed that the socks I'd pulled over my boots had worn to shreds. I burned them in the tile stove."

Major Brausch lumbered to his feet. He looked thoroughly shaken. "You're guilty as hell, Ranke. I can't think of one mitigating circumstance that could help you. Premeditated murder—" Suddenly he flared. "Why did you have to wait six weeks to make a clean breast of it? Let a man be tried and convicted? Didn't your conscience bother you?"

A small self-satisfied smile played around Ranke's lips. "No, sir."

"Then why now?" Ranke's eyes followed the flight of a fly around the room. The gray tower of the castle had taken on a crimson hue as dawn started breaking in the east. A dormant world was coming to life. "Does it have to do with the woman? You overstayed your leave of absence by four days. Did you go to Berlin to see her? And did you see her? For Christ's sake, Lieutenant, I want to help you!"

"I'm beyond help, sir."

What little social contact Brausch had had during his tour in Allenstein had been with officers of his own command. At the divisional affairs he had dutifully attended he had seen the Godenhausens yet never rubbed elbows with them. In a milieu of mediocrity, they moved as if illuminated by a hidden spotlight, two stairs adding glamor to a provincial production. Frau Brausch, short and compact, weighed 160 pounds, while Alexa von Godenhausen was probably under 110, yet it was not weight, the color of their hair or the shape of their noses that set them apart. They looked as if they had been born on two different planets. Major Brausch was one of the very few men in Allenstein who didn't find Alexa alluring. In his eyes her sophistication rendered her as sexless as a shopwindow mannequin. He would have turned her down even if she had been offered to him on a silver platter.

"Don't be a damn fool, Ranke. You're in grave trouble. You did see her in Berlin, didn't you? And she told you to go to hell? Answer me, Ranke. That's an order!" he barked at him. His male loyalty would not allow him to find Ranke fully guilty of the crime; he was more inclined to regard him as one of its victims. As a judge, he would have inflicted more severe punishment on the woman than on Ranke.

Slumping down in his seat, Ranke let his head hang. "In essence, yes, sir. She told me to return to Allenstein and keep away from her for appearances' sake. But that was only to get rid of me. The truth is she's been living with a man—a Hungarian, the widower of her twin. She was deliberately hiding from me. I had to engage the services of a detective agency to find her."

"What a bitch!" Brausch said and saw Ranke flinch at the word. The poor bastard is still in love with the rotten little whore, he thought.

Captain Yves reacted to the news of Ranke's confession with silent but venomous indignation. Unlike Major Brausch, he let no curses escape his thin lips, which were pressed together into one single line, straight and pink-edged as a half-healed knife cut. Inside him there was a raging volcano of rancor. That Ranke had murdered a fellow officer was at the moment beside the point. In the judge advocate's eyes Ranke's unforgivable offense was having made a fool of him, Yves. He had prosecuted the wrong man with a vigor and expertise that resulted in a twenty-year prison sentence. There was only one way to lift the blot off his service record: if Ranke were found insane and his confession an act prompted by sick exhibitionism. He wouldn't be the first man to admit to a crime he had not committed.

Lieutenants Stoklaska and Heinrich attended the interrogation, with Heinrich acting as a recorder. As the questioning progressed and they began to understand Yves's intent to have Ranke retract his confession, they exchanged furtive glances but remained silent.

Before handing him over to Yves, Major Brausch had ordered a substantial breakfast for Ranke—a large pitcher of coffee with milk, bread, butter and jam—and saw to it that the lieutenant finished it all. Thus fortified, Ranke comported himself more rationally than he had in Brausch's office. He answered Yves's questions with clear and composed recollections of the crime and of the events leading to it and following it. Every new detail made Ranke's guilt more indisputable and Dmowski's conviction more clearly a case of miscarried justice. The judge advocate's growing discomfort gladdened the hearts of his two aides. Captain Yves happened to be the most generally disliked member of the First Army Corps Judiciary.

With a two-hour interruption for the midday meal, the questioning lasted until seven in the evening. When it was time for Ranke to be escorted to the regimental guardhouse, where he was to be held in a cell reserved for officers, Captain Yves ordered both Stoklaska and Heinrich to step out into the anteroom. Left alone with the prisoner, Yves pretended to ignore his presence and immersed himself in the study of some scribbles with which he had filled a notebook during the day. As the minutes ticked away, the dead silence enveloping them began to gnaw on Ranke's already bruised nerves. Close to total collapse from fatigue, he nevertheless forced himself to sit erect, his spine parallel to the straight chair back, his head held high, his eyes searching the captain's eyes which deliberately evaded his. Instinct told him that the silent treatment was to soften him up for a suggestion, and it also told him what the suggestion was going to be. They were playing a game, and the advantage of anticipating his adversary's next move helped Ranke to overcome his mental and physical weariness.

At last Yves's gaze shifted from the notebook and, after leisurely circling the room, settled on Ranke's waiting eyes.

"I am mortified, Lieutenant," he said. "I see the headlines, the nasty attacks of the liberal press, the leering reactions from abroad. A Prussian officer sneaking into an unsuspecting comrade's house to shoot him down in cold blood."

Unflinching, Ranke returned the judge advocate's gaze. "I told you, sir. It was a duel."

"Who challenged whom? Was the Council of Honor contacted? Who were the seconds?"

"There were no seconds. Nevertheless, it was a duel."

Yves rose abruptly and stepped to Ranke, who jumped to his feet. "It was murder. Premeditated murder. You're a filthy coward, a disgrace to the entire officer corps." He crossed back to the desk and pulled out its top drawer. "I'll leave you alone. By the time I return, in exactly ten minutes, you will have expiated your crime and removed the shadow cast upon the uniform you are wearing."

Ranke circled the desk, stopped behind it and glanced in the open drawer. "Are you suggesting, Captain, sir, that I shoot myself with that gun?"

Yves had been headed for the door; now he whirled about. "I thought I was explicit enough for a Prussian officer to understand what I meant."

"That you were, sir. So I'd better tell you that your explicit suggestion was wasted on me. I am not going to shoot myself."

The captain swallowed hard. His sallow skin turned sickly red over the cheekbones. "I offered you an honorable way out of a dishonorable predicament." He raised his voice. "Damn you, Ranke, don't you understand? There is no hope for you. Once you're stood before a court-martial you're as good as dead. There are no mitigating circumstances in your favor. Why go through the whole bloody ordeal when the outcome will be the same?"

"I won't shoot myself, sir. At least not before I am confronted with the woman. I might afterward."

"You're a bastard, Ranke." The red blotches on the captain's cheekbones widened. His forehead glistened with perspiration. "You have no esprit de corps, no consideration for your fellow officers. What kind of a worm are you?"

"Not the suicidal kind, sir."

Yves nervously paced the floor. "I'll make you pay for this, Ranke, because I'm going to get it in the neck from General von Hammann."

"You mean for Dragoon Dmowski's conviction?"

"Don't provoke me, Ranke."

"I'm sorry for inconveniencing you, sir. There is, however, a way to right things. Why don't *you* shoot me and call it suicide. It could be done, you know, has been done before. There would be no questions asked. You might even be complimented on your discretion and competence."

Yves gazed darkly at the gun. A large horsefly materialized on the window and began buzzing up and down its pane. For a while its loud buzz was the only sound in the room. With sudden decision, Captain Yves bounded for the door and threw it open.

"Stoklaska," he called out, "have the prisoner escorted to the guardhouse. I've had my fill for the day. We'll continue tomorrow at eight sharp."

The following two days were spent checking the details of Ranke's confession. A visit was ordered to his flat, also a search for the murder weapon, a .38-caliber Webley-Fosbery semiautomatic.

Accompanied by Stoklaska and two corporals, Yves pried into every corner in the flat. He found several short notes signed by an A, which later were ascertained to have been written by Alexa von Godenhausen's hand. They were messages setting the time and place of rendezvous. To Yves's disappointment, they contained no references to the murder. However, a draft of a letter from Ranke to her proved to be definitely damaging. It was dated on the day before Ranke's departure for Berlin and in it the lieutenant was reproaching her for going back on the promises she had made at the time they discussed the "duel without seconds." It seemed Ranke had changed his mind about mailing the letter and decided to go to Berlin instead and contact her in person. Under a large Bokhara rug in the bedroom the searchers found 2300 marks in crisp new bank notes, evidently destined to be his escape money. The murder weapon, which Ranke had allegedly thrown into the Alle, was irretrievably lost, despite the efforts of two divers who searched the river bottom at the indicated spot. Finding it wasn't essential to the case, because Ranke produced documents proving his ownership of the gun. Besides, the bullets found in the body were of the type used in the .38-caliber Webley-Fosbery semiautomatic, and matched those still in Lieutenant von Ranke's cartridge pouch.

On the third day of the investigation, Ranke was charged with violation of Paragraph 97 of the Military Penal Code: assault against a superior officer. After his transfer to Königsberg, court-martial proceedings were instituted against him by the judiciary branch of the First Army Corps. At the same time, Attorney General Nitzki empowered Investigating Magistrate of the Allenstein County Court Johannes Koller to issue a warrant for the arrest of the widowed Baroness Alexa von Godenhausen. On the basis of Ranke's confession, she was suspected of being an accessory before the fact in the murder of her husband.

12

The night before her arrest, Nicholas persuaded Alexa to have supper with him at an open-air restaurant on the Spree. For three days there had been no sign of Ranke, and she assumed that he had returned to Allenstein. Ever since his materialization under the lamppost, the relationship between her and Nicholas had remained rather strained. The lie, rather the concealment of the truth, lay between them like a heavy fog over a river that prevents people on one bank from seeing the people within shouting distance on the other bank. She knew that he was disturbed by her evasiveness, yet she feared that a confession would make him leave her.

Before the murder she had thought that Hans Günther's death would, by freeing her of the bondage of an unrequited love, restore her peace of mind. She would find herself and know what she wanted from life. She had had no doubt that she could handle Ranke. He loved her and she didn't love him, which would give her control over him. The problem she had not reckoned with was her inability to control herself: the choking attacks of anxiety that befell her when she was alone. They were worse at night. The moment she turned off the light and dropped her head on the pillow, it was as if a noisy alarm clock would start ticking inside her chest. She could feel the ticking in the arteries of her neck, temples, wrists. If she managed to doze off, she would sleep fitfully for an hour or two and dream of strange places where she invariably lost her way. Sometimes, tired of staring at the ceiling, she would try to read, then give it up when she realized that she was unable to grasp the meaning of the simplest sentence. She had the same trouble with writing. The day after Hans Günther's death she began a letter to her Rethy grandparents. Now, weeks later, the letter—rather the fifth draft of it—still lay unfinished on her escritoire. Correct spelling had always been her forte at school, but now she would stare for moments at a very common word and suddenly find its orthography incomprehensibly weird. Should there be an M or an N, a P or a B? If she consulted a dictionary, she found her original spelling was correct. As long as she relied upon her instinct, she was safe. Thinking led her into mazes in which she became hopelessly lost.

The symptoms of this mental disorientation had first troubled her on the day of Hans Günther's death. At that time she attributed them to shock, then afterward to Judge Advocate Yves's probing. He demonstrated an uncanny clairvoyance, which brought him close to the discovery of the truth. Dmowski's arrest and later his conviction should have—but failed to —put her mind at ease. Notwithstanding the hurt and humiliation he had caused her in the past, his image in shackles and prison garb kept haunting her. Then, of course, there was Ranke. A new Ranke, not the toy soldier modeled in pliable wax, but the overlord demanding fealty from a vassal.

Her first days on Schleswiger Ufer had been paradise. The ticking of the imaginary alarm clock inside her chest was replaced by the actual sounds of the thumping of the riverboats that passed under her window and the splashing of waves against the stony bank. Together the sounds blended into a lullaby in the style of those young composers who wrote atonal music.

For a while Nicholas's presence alone could lift the pressure of fear off her chest. Her need for him was beyond love or sexual dependence; it was the opiate craved by a sick person in pain. She felt sheltered in his arms. Their common language, Hungarian, was like a secret island where she could hide from the powers of darkness. In the beginning of their affair, during the spring and summer of 1907, she at times had deliberately clung to German to keep him from identifying her with Beata, but now she found comfort in communicating with him in a tongue unfamiliar to the people around them.

Her state of grace was of short duration and had ended when she looked down from her window and spotted Ranke leaning against the lamppost. She and Nicholas didn't discuss Ranke during supper; yet whenever their glances met, she read unspoken questions in his eyes. She felt more and more strongly that as long as her involvement in the murder remained untold she could pretend it never happened. At first her recollections of the period preceding Hans Günther's death had been frighteningly vivid, but lately they had begun to dim.

On this August morning she was still in bed when she heard the doorbell ring. That night she had slept alone because Nicholas had gone home around midnight to finish a report on the Bavarian army maneuvers he had attended earlier that summer. As always when left alone, Alexa had a miserable night: spells of troubled sleep, upsetting dreams and long hours of wakefulness.

A pale and distraught Marie burst into her room to tell her that two detectives bearing a warrant issued by the office of Police Commissioner Wannowski were in the anteroom and demanded to see the Baroness von Godenhausen. She had told them that they'd come to the wrong address, but they insisted that Fräulein Rethy and the baroness were one and the same person.

Alexa stared at her dumbfounded. She had heard the words but failed to grasp the meaning, especially of the word "warrant." "What do they want?" she asked.

Her question seemed to upset Marie. "How would *I* know? They won't tell *me*. They're the criminal police."

Alexa dropped back on the pillows. "Tell them to go away."

Marie bounded to the bed and with one swift move tore the comforter off her. "Don't you understand? They have a warrant! You must come out and talk to them. You might even have to go with them."

Hastily Marie took a street dress from the wardrobe, underwear, stockings and shoes, even a hat to have it ready in case it was needed. She had literally to lift Alexa off the bed, stand her on her feet as though she were a dressmaker's dummy, peel off her nightgown and throw clothes on her. Alexa endured Marie's not so gentle ministrations in silence. She no longer had doubts concerning the mission of the detectives. This was the moment she had dreaded ever since Hans Günther's death. However, instead of being terrified, she felt almost relieved, because the undefinable chimerical fear that had haunted her up to now suddenly acquired reality. Once again she was going to be questioned about Hans Günther's death. This time the interrogation would be conducted not by Captain Yves but by a police commissioner, and if she was careful she would outwit him as she had outwitted the captain. Suddenly she was in a hurry to confront the detectives and grew impatient with Marie when it took her too long to brush and pin up her hair. Her friseuse, Fräulein Bertha, was not due until eleven, so Marie's clumsy efforts had to do for the day.

One of the men was short, dark and compact, reminding her of the eggplants in the Italian greengrocer's window on Bellevue Square. The other was tall and prematurely gray and comported himself with the dignity of a supreme court judge. They were polite but curt in informing her that they had orders to escort her to Commissioner Wannowski's office at Royal Police Headquarters on Alexander Platz. When she asked what the charges were against her, the fat one shrugged, leaving the answer to his tall colleague.

"Baroness," the tall man said, "that is a question only the commissioner is authorized to answer."

"And what if I refuse to go with you?" Alexa asked.

The men exchanged worried glances. "Don't," the fat man warned her. He had a clear, jaunty tenor, much too high for his bulk. "We'd have to employ force, you know."

"Regretfully," the tall man added.

Alexa reassured them. "I'll go with you, only let me get my hat."

Marie had been hovering in the dark end of the hallway; now she followed Alexa to the bedroom. "Don't you want me to let the captain know about this?" she whispered while Alexa was pinning on her hat. "I overheard him telling you last night that he would not be coming here until later in the evening."

Alexa responded with a blank stare. She failed to understand the girl's excitement; what's more, she suddenly wondered who Marie was. She nervously shook her head to clear her mind of a fog that seemed to envelop it. She was supposed to leave the flat. Why? she wondered.

"Ranke." She uttered the name, trying to link it to a face, but saw only a blur.

"What did you say?" the girl asked. When there was no answer, she grabbed Alexa by the arms to force her to listen. "The captain—shall I go to the Embassy and tell him?"

Slowly realization dawned. "The captain! Of course, you're right. Go find him." The fog had lifted and she became conscious of the meaning of the warrant and the possible consequences of her impending interrogation by a police commissioner. "Yes, by all means, go to the Embassy and look for him." Her heart began to beat furiously, as if it were trying to force its way out of her chest. "Good God, what are they going to do to me?"

She felt like a person surfacing after a long underwater swim. A moment earlier things were diffused and undulating; now they became frighteningly clear. Some new development must have revived the authorities' interest in the part she had played in Hans Günther's murder. With sudden decision, she

327

started pulling out the pins she had stuck through her hat and into her chignon.

"I am not going with them," she said, taking off the hat.

Startled, Marie placed her arms about her. "Oh, you must! You heard them. They won't leave without you. Might even handcuff you and drag you down the stairway. You don't want the neighbors to know—the whole street. You'd just make it more difficult for yourself."

Alexa pondered for a moment. "You're right." She shrugged and put on the hat again. From her purse she handed ten marks to Marie. "Here, take a cab to the Embassy. Find the captain, wherever he is. Be sure and find him."

"Don't worry, I will." During the past few days Marie had noticed that her mistress was losing her hold on herself, said things that failed to make sense, seemed confused, teeter-tottered from cheerfulness to sudden despair.

Alexa flashed a warm smile at her. "I'm not worried." She started for the door. "In case we don't see each other again, I want you to know that I've grown very fond of you. You're a good soul, Marie."

The girl stared after her, nonplused. By the time she collected herself and could think of an appropriate answer, Alexa was out of her sight.

"Sorry to have kept you waiting," Alexa said to the detectives. "I wish modistes would make more sensible hats. One ought to be able to plump them down on one's head without any pinning and fussing." She pulled herself erect. "We might as well leave now, if you please."

During the carriage ride the tall man sat beside her and the shorter one took the jump seat. She repeatedly attempted to make small talk with them, but received only monosyllabic answers. Nevertheless, behind their stiff reserve she sensed good will, even sympathy, which helped to bolster her courage for the impending session with the commissioner.

To avoid being spotted by the swarm of reporters who kept constant vigil in and around headquarters, the detectives had been instructed to hire an ordinary droshky instead of using a police vehicle. They told the driver to pull up to a side entrance that was kept locked to the public. A narrow staircase led to the third floor, where the commissioner's office was located.

With an enormous nose, the reddish tip of which made it seem even more grotesque, blue-green eyes that twinkled even when he was at his most serious, a rasping voice and a strong Swabian accent, Paul Wannowski looked more like a beerhouse comedian than a high-ranking police functionary. Alexa was ushered into his office by an assistant. Wannowski rose politely, introduced himself, offered her a chair placed in front of his desk, but no handshake.

"I'm sure you know why you're here, Baroness," he said after they settled down—she facing the window, its bright light hitting her eyes, he with his back to it. There was a second man in the room, most likely a secretary, she thought.

"No, Herr Wannowski, I don't. I wish you'd tell me." She tried hard to control the nervous churning of her stomach that sent her breakfast coffee up to her throat.

"Lieutenant Otto von Ranke confessed the murder of your husband and named you accessory before the fact," the commissioner told her in a dull even tone, as if reading aloud a news item that had no bearing on her life.

She wondered why she wasn't alarmed, or at least surprised. She must have expected Ranke to do it or something similarly hurtful. "Accessory before the fact—what does that mean?" she asked and immediately regretted speaking. She should have shown shock at Ranke's confession, convinced Wannowski that she had never suspected the lieutenant of the murder. From now on she would have to weigh every word or remain silent, she told herself.

"Lieutenant von Ranke named you to be the person at whose instigation he shot and killed your husband, Major von Godenhausen."

Again the flat unemotional statement. In vain she searched

329

for an expression on the man's face that would give a hint about his attitude, but he seemed inscrutable.

"That is insane," she replied, stressing every word as if talking to someone with impaired hearing. "My husband was murdered by his orderly—ex-orderly—a man named Jan Dmowski."

Wannowski leaned forward. The stare of his bright eyes felt like lancet pricks on her face. "You know that's not true, don't you?"

"He was murdered by Jan Dmowski," she repeated mechanically.

The commissioner rose and crossed to her. His raised hand caused her to flinch; for a panicky moment she expected him to hit her, but he merely placed his hand on her shoulder.

"Baroness, I'll have Herr Staub read the lieutenant's confession to you. Will you please turn to face Herr Staub and listen carefully."

For the next half hour the young man's guttural Hochdeutsch filled the room with the monotonous rumble of a person saying his beads. Ranke had told it all, in explicit detail, beginning with their first encounter and ending with his days spent loitering around Schleswiger Ufer and learning the identity of her present lover, Count Nicholas Karady.

The confession recorded in Judge Advocate Yves's office contained Ranke's recollection of all the varieties of sex play —some referred to in Greek or Latin medical terms, expressions she had never heard before—in which they had supposedly engaged during their trysts in his flat. For the first time she was given a step-by-step chronicle of the murder. That part of the confession was new to her, and she listened wide-eyed. It seemed to her as though Herr Staub were reading a chapter of a mystery story of which she knew the beginning and the end but not the middle. She had trouble understanding that the person referred to as "the victim" by Herr Staub was her dead husband. The last paragraphs of the script—

assignation in the Baltischer Hof in Berlin—made her drowsy. The strange fog that during the past weeks had repeatedly blurred her thoughts seemed to be descending on her mind again. She had to fight with all her might to remain alert.

At long last Herr Staub reached the last sentence and lowered the pages onto his lap. He took off his glasses and carefully cleaned them with his handkerchief before replacing them on the bridge of his nose.

"Have you listened carefully, Baroness?" The commissioner broke the silence. During the reading he had had his eyes focused on Alexa's face, as if to catch every twitch of a muscle, every quickening of the rhythm of her breath. He seemed disappointed by the lack of reaction on her part. "What's your comment?" he asked.

She felt that the less she said the safer it would be. "No comment."

"You mean you're willing to corroborate the lieutenant's confession?"

"Of course not."

"What part do you disagree with?"

"Every word."

The commissioner shook his head, puzzled. To Alexa it seemed as if his nose were moving twice as fast as his face. "But Baroness, witnesses saw you entering the lieutenant's quarters in Allenstein. The concierge of the Baltischer Hof, when shown your picture, recognized you as the woman Lieutenant von Ranke had repeatedly taken to his room, and—"

"They were lying."

"As you've heard, the lieutenant maintained he had sexual relations with you. You don't deny that?"

"Yes, I do. That is, I haven't had any such relations with the lieutenant."

Eyebrows raised. Wannowski shook his head. "What am I going to do with you? You don't seem to realize that this

331

is no game. Acting like a spoiled child won't do you any good. You're accused of being an accomplice in the murder of your husband. This is no joking matter."

Alexa gave him a cool look. "I'm not joking."

Pensively the commissioner rubbed his long nose. "Without being coerced, threatened or mistreated, Lieutenant von Ranke admitted his guilt in your husband's murder. Details of his confession were examined by the First Army Corps Judiciary and found to be true. Now you're telling me that none of it is. How can you explain that?"

"Have *them* explain it."

"Let's concentrate on the basic issue, the murder itself. In your opinion, who killed your husband?"

"Wasn't it Jan Dmowski?"

"Baroness, I want an answer, not a question."

"Wasn't he convicted?"

Embarrassed, the commissioner scratched his head. "That's beside the point. Yes, he was, but now he will be exonerated. These things happen. Even military judges aren't infallible—they're only human." He resumed his seat behind the desk and thumbed through Ranke's confession, which his assistant had placed before him.

"Let's see, madame," he began. "You wanted to divorce your husband, but he refused you. Subsequently you persuaded Lieutenant von Ranke to kill him so you'd be free."

"No."

"You promised Ranke to marry him if—"

"No."

The commissioner completed the sentence: "—if everything went according to plan." The drumming of his index finger on the desktop betrayed that he was running out of patience. "For the last time, do you, Alexa von Godenhausen, née Rethy, admit that it was upon your instigation and with your previous knowledge that your lover, First Lieutenant Otto von Ranke, murdered your husband by shooting him twice on the morning of July second, 1908?"

332

"No, I don't."

"Very well then." The commissioner got to his feet. "You leave me no choice. As there exists a definite danger of prejudicing the course of justice, I am hereby placing you under arrest. You shall be taken to the Charlottenburg County Jail to be kept there until your transfer to Allenstein."

The word "Allenstein" suddenly stirred Alexa from her apparent indifference. "Why Allenstein?" she asked in a shrill, nervous voice.

"Because the Allenstein County Court happens to be the competent authority in your case. They'll appoint a magistrate to conduct a preliminary investigation. Should the investigation lead to your indictment, that is where you will stand trial."

Arms crossed over her chest, head thrown back in defiance, Alexa remained seated. "No!" she said.

"What do you mean: no?"

"I won't go to Allenstein."

"My good woman, you don't have a choice." For the first time, Wannowski sounded irritated. The Schwarzwälder clock on the wall showed ten past one, which meant that even if he started out without any delay, he would be late for his mid-day dinner. His wife, a stickler for observing tight household schedules, wanted the soup on the table at one sharp and, as always, would consider his tardiness a deliberate offense. "Baroness, we have laws in this country," the commissioner said sternly, "and no wealth or social position will grant a guilty person immunity from prosecution."

She rose and confronted him. Six feet tall, he towered over her. Annoyance caused his fleshy nostrils to flare. Looking up at him, she noticed thick bristlelike hairs sticking out of them. He seemed too droll to be taken seriously.

"I am not going to Allenstein," she said in a loud, firm voice.

Since dining with Alexa on the Zelte terrace the night before, Nicholas had been troubled with inexplicable premonitions.

333

At one o'clock he was to present himself at the private residence of Ambassador Szögyény-Marich to attend a déjeuner in honor of the Italian minister of foreign affairs visiting Berlin. He searched for an excuse that would allow him to beg off and spend the day with Alexa, but found none. On his way to the déjeuner he still wondered if he shouldn't drop by her flat, but that would have caused him to be late, an unpardonable offense.

The affair lasted into the afternoon hours. Instead of going straight to her, he had to show himself, if only for minutes, at the Embassy. He entered the vestibule and caught sight of Marie. As their eyes met, her frightened look told him that the chimeric disaster that he had feared for days had finally struck.

"She is dead." The words slipped out before Marie could speak.

She shook her head. "No, not dead!" She felt relieved that her news was a shade better than what he expected. "Two men from the criminal police came to the house and took her away. They had warrants for her arrest. She didn't want to go, but in the end she went."

The wildest speculations flashed through Nicholas's mind. No doubt Alexa was involved in Hans Günther's murder. She had hired Dmowski to shoot him. Ranke had hired him. Or even worse, she killed him herself.

"Did the men tell you why she was wanted?"

"They didn't say much, except that they were the criminal police."

"You said she didn't want to go with them."

"At first she didn't, but they told her if she refused, they'd have to resort to force."

"Do you know where they took her?"

"I imagine to police headquarters." She saw pain and confusion mirrored on his face. "Captain, please don't worry. It might be nothing. You know the police; they often make mistakes. Maybe they just wanted to question her about something. She is such a fine lady, she couldn't have done anything wrong."

Nicholas forced a smile. "I am sure of that." He patted her arm. "Now go home so you'll be there in case they release her."

Together they started for the exit. They were in the street when she suddenly stopped. "Captain, sir, please accept my apologies."

"What for?"

"I've just found out that you're a count. I thought you were only a captain. An ordinary captain, I mean."

Despite his troubled state of mind he had to chuckle. "But that's what I am, Marie. Just an ordinary captain." Silently he added, *The question is how much longer*.

"And that Fräulein Rethy is a baroness, and that her name isn't Rethy, but Godenhausen, von Godenhausen. I hope my mother won't have trouble on account of harboring a person wanted by the police."

"Of course not, Marie. I'll make sure she won't. Anyway, Rethy is the baroness's maiden name. She used it merely to keep the press away."

At police headquarters no one seemed to know of Alexa. As a last resort Nicholas called a privy councillor he knew at the Ministry of Justice and asked him to have the criminal police reveal to him the whereabouts of his missing sister-in-law. The call had results and he was advised to see Commissioner Wannowski in charge of the civilian aspects of the Godenhausen investigation.

A young man who introduced himself as Detective Staub greeted him on the third-floor landing. "I'm afraid, Captain, you'll have to wait some time. The commissioner is busy at the moment. He'll see you the minute he is finished with the people who are in his office right now."

"I've been told my sister-in-law was brought here. Is she still in the building?"

"I'd prefer to have the commissioner tell you that, sir."

335

They entered the anteroom. Seated on a long bench were five people. When catching sight of Nicholas, they rose in respectful haste. In one of the men, a tall bearlike guardsman, he recognized the orderly who had served drinks at the Godenhausen parties in Potsdam. One woman bobbed a curtsy to him. She looked familiar, and he figured she was another one of Alexa's servants.

Detective Staub offered Nicholas a chair, but he remained standing. The wait seemed interminable. When the door to the inner sanctum finally opened, he saw a tall man, evidently the commissioner, escorting General von Sedlitz and his wife through the anteroom. Rose was the first to recognize Nicholas. She paled and pressed her lips together as if trying to keep from spitting. When she opened them again, the sound that escaped them reminded Nicholas of the hiss of an angered goose.

"So you're here too. I'm not surprised." She threw back her head and sputtered a sibilant warning: "This ought to teach you to stay away from other men's wives."

Nicholas stared at her, baffled. He almost forgot to salute the general. Quickly he pulled himself erect and jerked his hand to his shako.

Rose took one threatening step in his direction, but her husband grabbed her by the arms and unceremoniously wrenched her back. He looked murder at her; then, cool but correct, he recognized Nicholas's salute. "Good afternoon, Karady." Evidently he was determined to keep his wife from calling Alexa's lover to account right there in the commissioner's anteroom. To have a case of murder in the family was degrading enough, public scenes and recriminations would have made it even worse.

He extended his hand to Nicholas. "It's been a long time. If I remember correctly, it was at the autumn maneuvers that we last met." He threw a sternly dictatorial glance at Rose, who obediently held out a limp hand to have it kissed by

Nicholas. Having properly dispensed with the social amenities, the Sedlitzes left. As it behooved their status, they were seen to their waiting carriage by the commissioner himself.

"Please accept my apologies for the long wait, sir." Re-entering after the three-story climb, Wannowski was out of breath. "It was most gracious of the general and his lady to see me. It doesn't happen every day that a military gentleman of his rank makes himself available to civil authorities. But, of course, we are dealing with a most extraordinary case." He ushered Nicholas into his office. "What can I do for you, sir?" He pretended to be unaware of the caller's quest.

Nicholas plunged in medias res. "Why was my sister-in-law, Baroness von Godenhausen, arrested this morning?"

Wannowski's eyebrows formed two sharp V's. "Oh, so the baroness is your sister-in-law? I wondered about the nature of your relationship with her when I learned that you'd put her up in a rented apartment under an assumed name and—"

"Her maiden name," Nicholas corrected.

Wannowski acknowledged the interjection with a nod, then continued, "—visited her daily, frequently staying overnight, provided her with the necessary means of support. So she is your sister-in-law? Of course, that explains it. So your assistance was prompted by a kinsman's concern."

Nicholas suppressed his mounting annoyance. "Commissioner, I came here to ask *you* for information, not the other way around."

Wannowski smiled placatingly. "Count, sir, let me assure you that I wouldn't dream of disregarding your diplomatic immunity. I was merely trying to have your kinship confirmed. The police are not obliged to divulge the whereabouts of a suspect. We might make an exception when dealing with family members."

Of the whole sentence, Nicholas heard only one word: "suspect." "Is she a suspect?" he asked.

The commissioner heaved a deep sigh. "A most unfortunate

337

case. I, personally, hope to be proven wrong, but at the moment I have reason to believe that she acted as accessory before the fact in her husband's murder."

Nicholas had been prepared for the answer, nevertheless it hit him hard. "That's insane," he protested. "What proof do you have?"

"Only the murderer's testimony."

"As far as I know, the murderer was tried and convicted without ever implicating her. Why now, all of a sudden?"

His large nose twitching nervously, Wannowski scratched his head. "It seems the army was in too big a hurry. It's never good to rush things. The man you are thinking of is innocent. An unfortunate miscarriage of justice, no matter how we look at it. He's already been released or will be shortly, I am sure. The major was killed by one of his fellow officers."

The picture of the pale young man leaning against the lamppost came to Nicholas's mind. He almost uttered the name Ranke but caught himself in time. For Alexa's sake he had to proceed with caution.

"A fellow officer? What's his name?"

"I'd rather not tell you. Not before the investigation is completed."

"Why did he implicate the baroness?"

Wannowski's gaze became fixed on Nicholas's face. "Revenge. We're dealing with a psychopath. A man of abnormal sexuality. By catering to his perversions, the baroness gained control over him to the extent that he was willing to kill for her. Then, after the act, when he no longer was of any use to her, she deserted him. That explains his delayed reaction, doesn't it?"

Nicholas felt a bitter rage against Wannowski, Ranke and, above all, Alexa. One of the most sacrilegious obscene curses the German language ever spawned was on the tip of his tongue. He suppressed it with an effort that sent the blood rushing to his face.

338

Somehow he managed to regain his composure, although deep down he was still fuming. The bitch, the lying, scheming, whoring bitch! She had used him to fill her sexual needs, then had another hapless fool kill the husband who had found out about her escapades. Ranke's grim assignment completed, he was no longer of any use to her, so she dropped him off at the wayside, as vacationers do unwanted summer pets before returning to their homes in the city.

Part of Nicholas's anger was directed against himself. He had known all along that she was playing a game with him, but, afraid of losing her, he had stopped asking questions he had never really wanted answered.

"Would it be possible for me to see the baroness?" he asked. Before fully condemning her, he felt he ought to hear her side of the story. Secretly he expected to be refused, and to his relief he was. "Has General von Sedlitz made arrangements for an attorney to represent her?"

"I am afraid the general and his wife decided to disassociate themselves from the case. Considering his high position, the general feels that any attempt at interfering with the course of justice on his part would be unethical."

So they had deserted her. Nicholas was not surprised. The murder victim was the general's nephew, and to feel concerned about Alexa would have called for Christ-like compassion, which was not one of the general's virtues.

Nicholas left police headquarters determined to follow Adalbert von Sedlitz's example. By the time he crossed Alexander Platz, he had changed his mind. He had had a taste of the Prussian judicial system when he had followed Prince Eulenburg's case through phases beginning with the Moltke-Harden trials, then the Staedele libel suit, ending with the prince's arrest and detention in a room at the Royal Charité. Could a Hungarian woman involved in the murder of her Prussian officer husband ask for mercy from the Allenstein County Court? he asked himself. His affection may have died for Alexa, but he had been her lover before and after the murder, which burdened him with a certain share of responsibility.

He went over a list of attorneys and settled on Counselor of Justice Dr. Robert Wengraf, one of Berlin's most successful and expensive lawyers. He had met the man at Embassy parties, liked him and now considered him to be the best choice to represent Alexa.

At first Wengraf was reluctant to undertake her defense. He anticipated that the army judiciary would try everything within its power to make her the chief culprit of the case. Mitigating circumstances had to be found for Ranke, whose guilt cast an ugly shadow on the Prussian officer corps. At the end, Nicholas's touching concern for the woman's fate generated a feeling of male solidarity in the attorney and induced him to undertake Alexa's defense. That and the exorbitantly high retainer.

He assumed that she had been taken to the Charlottenburg County Jail, and his hunch was corroborated by Commissioner Wannowski, who at the same time informed him that no one, and that included her attorney, was to talk to her before her arraignment in Allenstein. Disregarding the refusal, Wengraf had his chauffeur drive him to Charlottenburg. But all he could accomplish there was to have Alexa moved to a large and airy cell where she could be alone. For a box of chocolates with a twenty-mark bill under its wrapping, Matron Kudelka disclosed to him that on the following morning Alexa was to be put on the fast train to Allenstein.

An excruciating hunger pain was all Alexa remembered about the carriage ride from police headquarters to the county jail. At police headquarters no one had thought of offering her lunch or even a piece of bread, and she felt reluctant to ask.

This time, Staub and the chubby detective had ridden with her. Arriving at the jail, they escorted her through endless hallways to a door that was unlocked as if by magic from the inside. Beyond it, she was handed over to a short fat woman in a starched cotton uniform with a bundle of keys hanging from its belt. She had coarse gray hair, thinning on the top of her head, a dour expression and a clubfoot. She ordered Alexa to leave behind her hatpins and the small scissors she carried in her purse and to deposit her jewelry and money in return for a receipt. Her way of spitting out directions to her and the women she encountered when walking down a corridor with cells opening right and left from it reminded Alexa of a dog trainer she had once watched working with two Doberman pinschers in the Tiergarten. On the whole, the entire place brought the picture of a kennel to her mind: peeling whitewashed walls, grimy stone floors, cages smelling of disinfectant and urine. Despite her handicap, the woman moved so fast that Alexa had trouble keeping up with her.

The matron unlocked the door to a large room that had benches alongside its walls. Five females were huddled in one corner. The squeak of the door caused them to scatter like a flock of flushed birds. Their alarm conveyed to Alexa that the woman with the clubfoot had to be a formidable disciplinarian. In surly silence she surveyed the room, then walked out, leaving Alexa behind. To the diminishing sound of her orthopedic shoes hitting the stone floor the girls reacted like the population of a conquered city to the departure of the enemy's occupation force.

They bombarded Alexa with questions which were just as hostile as the fat matron's bark. She was a lady and they were trash, most likely streetwalkers or petty thieves. Having been thrown in with them, she was no longer enjoying the privileges of her status, and they felt free to vent their resentment against her class on her.

Their attack caused her to wonder what she had done to arouse their malevolence. The strange fog that had repeatedly blurred her thoughts was once again growing thicker and more impenetrable. She had been arrested and thrown into some sort of a prison, this much she could reason out; but when

341

one of her tormentors asked what the charge was against her, she became confused. She said she didn't know and they reacted with vicious hilarity. Next, the one with the shrillest voice wanted to know what her dress had cost, then decided to try on her hat. Wrenched from her head, it made the rounds from hand to hand, was clamped down upon oily, unwashed hair, stripped of its flower trim and fought over. It was her favorite hat, yet she failed to care. Overcome by uncontrollable fatigue, she slumped down on a bench.

She must have fallen asleep, because some time later she was shaken awake by Clubfoot. Now there were about a dozen women in the room, although two of the previous five had disappeared. In a tone that seemed to have lost some of its harshness, the matron told her to get up. She was taken to an airy cell furnished with a table, a chair and a cot. Giving out a faint yellow light, a gas lamp hung from the ceiling. To her relief, Alexa realized that she would be alone in the cell.

She felt gnawing hunger, but when minutes—or was it hours?—later a girl in striped prison garb left a plate with cold meat and bread on the table, an attack of nausea kept her from touching it.

She lay awake for hours, at least she thought she did. Somehow she no longer could tell the difference between sleep and consciousness. The gas lamp was turned off. Or did it go off automatically? she wondered.

The darkness felt thick and woollen, as if a black hood had been pulled over her face. It frightened her. She heard faint noises: sighs, whispers, the creak of a cot. Her fright was turning into panic. An unspeakable horror was threatening her, reaching out for her from behind the cover of the night. Frantically she tried to rise, but her legs refused to obey her. They felt cold and stiff to her touch as if suddenly turned into wood. Or were the bones broken? Had she been attacked, beaten, crippled? How was she to get away from *them*, whoever they were? She reached for the nightstand beside her bed but failed to find it. The realization that she was not in the flat scared her out of her wits, and she began to thrash about trying to lift her body off the cot. After a while she managed to roll to the edge of the mattress. She fell but instead of the soft rug she expected to hit she crashed headfirst onto a hard stone floor. Dazed, she lay still for a moment, then emitted a terrified scream. From all sides came shouts and curses ordering her to stop, but the louder they grew the less she could control herself. It seemed as if the only way to relieve the terrible pressure inside her chest was to let it escape through her throat.

The cell door was thrown open by two women, who rushed in and tried to lift her to her feet but failed when her legs folded under her like a rag doll's.

"Have you lost your mind or something?" the one with frizzly red hair shouted at her. "Stand up!"

They pushed her against the iron frame of the cot, but she collapsed again. By then her screams were losing their shrillness and came in hoarse guttural spurts.

"Jesus Maria, something *is* wrong with her!" the second woman said. "You'd better go and fetch Dr. Niedermayer."

"She's faking, can't you tell?" the redhead said.

"She might have swallowed something. Let's not take chances. Remember the fuss over the prostitute who hanged herself. And this one happens to be a baroness. You'd better hurry."

Mumbling profanity, the woman left. After a while, in shirtsleeves and tieless, his thinning hair tousled and his eyes blinking sleepily, a middle-aged man, accompanied by the matron, made his appearance. He was Dr. Niedermayer, the county medical examiner, who happened to be on duty that night.

"Take my word for it, Doctor," Clubfoot said, "the woman is malingering. We're supposed to put her on the first train to Allenstein tomorrow, but she doesn't want to go."

For twenty years Dr. Niedermayer had been working in detention facilities, and he made a rule of never accepting professional advice from guards or matrons. He ordered a stretcher brought in and had Alexa carried to the dispensary.

With a nurse's help, the doctor pinned down her wildly thrashing right arm and plunged a hypodermic needle into it. The injection had a soothing effect, and Alexa offered no resistance when he subjected her to a cursory examination.

"There is not a thing wrong with her, is there?" the matron asked. She had followed them into the dispensary and planted herself with folded arms in front of the door as if determined to thwart any escape attempt by the prisoner.

The doctor ignored the question. He sat down at his desk to write his medical report. "What is your name?" he asked Alexa.

Wide-eyed, she was staring at the ceiling. When she failed to answer, he repeated, "Your name?"

She blinked sleepily. Her lips barely moving, she mumbled, "Be-a-ta Re-thy."

The matron pounced upon her. "That's not your name!"

"It is, it is too. Be-a-ta Re-thy."

Clubfoot turned to the doctor. "Didn't I tell you? She is faking."

The doctor rose and stepped to Alexa, who seemed to have dozed off on the stretcher. "Is that what your name is? Beata Rethy?"

She opened her eyes. "Yes."

"Are you sure?"

The corners of her mouth twitched as if with petulance. "I am sure." Her voice had sounded a decibel louder.

"In that case, who is Alexa von Godenhausen, née Rethy?"

She frowned. "My . . ." There was a pause. "My sister." With some effort, she lifted her head. "My twin sister."

Dr. Niedermayer kept his tone low and quiet. "And where is this Alexa von Godenhausen, née Rethy, now?"

Her head dropped back. The dark shadows under her eyes seemed to grow deeper. "I don't know," she muttered. "She was taken away."

344

"Where to?" the doctor asked. "Try to remember. Try hard," he coaxed her.

Reluctantly she yielded to the persuasion of the gently commanding voice. "To Switzer-land." The sounds S and tz seemed to give her trouble. "That's where she is now," she volunteered, "in Switzer-land."

"Why was she taken to Switzerland?"

The answer came faster this time. "Because she was bad, always caused trouble—always."

"She is faking," the matron muttered.

The doctor cast an annoyed look at her, then turned back to Alexa. "Did you miss her when she went away?"

She responded with a bewildered look. "I don't know . . . I don't remember." She began to whimper softly. When her sobs grew louder, she received a second injection, which calmed her down and a few minutes later lulled her to sleep. The doctor telephoned the Royal Charité Hospital and instructed the receptionist on duty to have a room readied in their psychiatric section for a female prisoner who was to be sent over from the Charlottenburg County Jail.

13

Judge Advocate Yves had repeatedly blundered during his investigation of the Godenhausen murder, but he was proving to be right in one respect. The case was causing a press uproar that was extremely harmful to the prestige of the army. Public indignation, aroused by the hasty verdict that had given a twenty-year prison sentence to an innocent private, emboldened the liberal press to launch a devastating attack on the military judiciary. What would have been a simple crime of passion—lover killing jealous husband—was turned into the murder case of the decade and splashed across the front pages like spilled red paint. With Alexa's arrest, the investigation shifted from Allenstein, where the army could keep the details under cover, to Royal Police Headquarters in Berlin, an establishment readily accessible to reporters.

At first some of the stories were full of erroneous speculations. Articles published on the following morning came closer to the facts, much too close for Nicholas's comfort. By then his connection with Alexa had been revealed by a functionary of the homicide division, perhaps by Commissioner Wannowski himself. The triangle of wife, lover, husband widened into a quadrangle, and the existence of a second lover added extra piquancy to the already bizarre yarn. To dig up more scurrilous details became a challenge to reporters, and they threw themselves with unusual vigor into the task.

The moment he saw his name on the front pages, Nicholas prepared himself for repercussions from the Embassy. He didn't have to wait long. After lunch he found a note on his desk asking—ordering rather—him to see Baron von Stoka in his office.

"You're in a hell of a muddle, fellow," Stoka greeted him. "Are you aware that without your diplomatic immunity, you would by now be under arrest?"

Nicholas had had a sleepless night. He was too numb to be disturbed. "Under arrest? What for?"

"For being accessory after the fact. Your mistress is implicated in the murder of her husband, and—"

"On the basis of one man's testimony. What if he is lying?" It was a question that still kept haunting him despite his better judgment.

Stoka ignored the interruption. "You set her up, first at the Kaiserhof, then in a rented flat under an assumed name. Why?"

"She wanted it that way. Anyway, it was her maiden name."

"Did you ask her why she wanted to conceal her identity?"

"She had been through a lot. I couldn't possibly trouble her with questions that would upset her even more."

"Your explanation may sound convincing to me, but not to the investigating magistrate of the Allenstein County Court."

"I don't think she will be taken to Allenstein. At least, not now. Since this morning she's been at the Royal Charité undergoing a psychiatric examination."

The information was news to Stoka. "How do you know she is at the Charité? Who told you?"

"Her attorney, Counselor of Justice Dr. Wengraf."

Stoka frowned. "So she already has an attorney? The most expensive man in Berlin. How can she afford him? According

347

to my information, she has no money." He rose abruptly. Nicholas followed suit. "Would you, by any chance, be paying Wengraf's retainer?"

"I'm afraid so, Baron."

For a while Stoka paced the floor in grim silence, then plumped down in a chair. "Damn you, Nicholas, where were your brains—in your pants? *You* retained the man. What made you do such a fool thing? All right, I accept that the woman kept the truth from you, but by the time you contacted Wengraf you already knew. Didn't you realize that getting involved might cost you your career? Jesus Christ, you're no hotheaded cadet, you're a staff officer. What made you compromise not only yourself but your embassy as well?"

Stoka was sixty, give or take a few years, still not old enough to lecture him as if he were a delinquent schoolboy, Nicholas thought. Nevertheless, the male solidarity filtering through the baron's indignation dispelled his resentment. He knew that only the truth would do. "I did love her," he said, deliberately using the past tense.

Stoka shook his head. "Oh, you poor bastard." There was a long pause. "I'm afraid you won't like this. We've been informed in no uncertain terms that your presence is not wanted in Prussia. You had better start packing."

Nicholas felt the shirt on his back dampen with cold sweat. "She is all alone. The Sedlitzes have washed their hands of her, and—"

"That's unfortunate, but you have no choice. You'll be recalled. If you're lucky, there won't be any further reprimands from Ballhaus Platz or the General Staff."

"She has no one in the world. An old couple on a farm in Hungary, her grandparents."

"There is nothing I can do for you. You've never really been persona grata with the German Foreign Office. Your friendship with Prince Eulenburg didn't exactly endear you to them. I'm sure they've been waiting for an excuse to get rid of you. Now you've furnished them with it. In Dr. Wengraf you've retained a man of influence and power. If he can't help her, no one can." Then, suddenly, "Say, aren't you engaged to one of the Winterfeld girls?"

Blood rushed to Nicholas's face. "I am," he said dully.

Stoka shook his head. "I thought you were. Well, you've certainly muddled up your life." Pensively he rubbed his forehead. "I'm not yet completely fossilized, so I'll help the woman as much as I can. There is one thing, though. You must break with her. Even in the lucky event that she is found innocent." He noticed Nicholas's intent to cut in, but ignored it. "I am not passing judgment, merely calling your attention to certain aspects you musn't ignore. As far as society is concerned, she's become a leper, an untouchable. As an officer, you can never marry her or associate with her. That would cost you your army commission, your friends, your future. Of course, you're a man of independent means, but would the life of a social outcast satisfy you? Don't answer me now, just think about it."

Nicholas was grateful for the baron's tact. It would have been difficult to tell him that he had already made the decision to break with Alexa. The piercing heartache she had caused him was now dulled to a constant corrosive pain. He felt like the victim of an earthquake whose house has been laid waste, lost with all the mementos that had been dear to him.

The baron's voice roused him from musing. "There is one more thing," Stoka said. "An investigating magistrate of the Allenstein County Court is coming to Berlin. Ambassador Szögyény-Marich has already given his consent to a meeting between you and the magistrate. There will be no formal interrogation, mind you, just questions. You're free to refuse to answer any you judge irrelevant or indiscreet. In consideration of your voluntary cooperation, they'll forget that you deliberately misled the police. Twice you let the woman register under an assumed name, which, according to their laws, is a misdemeanor. Should they change their minds and prosecute you, they would naturally have to go through diplomatic channels. I hope they won't resort to that though. Their Ministry of War wants to minimize your part in the affair, mainly to keep the scandal from growing even more embarrassing to all involved."

A day later Nicholas received word that he was being recalled to Vienna. By then he had had another conference with Counselor Wengraf. For the time being, Alexa was to remain at the Royal Charité to undergo an extensive examination by the hospital's staff physician and a court-appointed psychologist. Wengraf had obtained permission from the attorney general's office to have a highly regarded expert in the field of nervous disorders, Dr. Karl Julius Berg, attend the sessions.

Even at this early stage the doctors found that symptoms like her erratic behavior, crying fits, partial paralysis and mental blackouts were indicative of an unsound mind. They all agreed that while she might have been in full command of her faculties at the time of the crime, she was at present incompetent to stand trial. The suspicion that the symptoms could be feigned was ruled out. What supported the doctors' conclusion was a year-old medical report signed by Professor Dr. Popper, at the time chief of the Royal Charité's psychiatric section, that described Alexa to be a person of manic-depressive tendencies. There existed also an earlier medical opinion signed by a certain Dr. Brandt, who had treated her between the years 1897 and 1903 for fainting spells and convulsions.

"She remains silent and withdrawn for hours," the attorney told Nicholas. "The nurses say she has moments of suicidal despondency. Then again she becomes cheerful and rational, except for her insistence on being Beata Rethy. Yesterday she was visited by General von Sedlitz and his wife. She treated them politely—until Frau von Sedlitz called her Alexa. That provoked a screaming fit, and she had to be given morphine to quiet her down."

"I'll have to leave Berlin the day after tomorrow," Nicholas said. "Could you arrange for me to see her before I go?" Later he wondered why he had asked for the meeting when he no longer loved her.

Wengraf was not in favor of the visit, but he promised to try his best. Although she was his client, he had no sympathy for Alexa. He saw her as a selfish woman, sheltered all her life, who fled into insanity once her shelter had crumbled to pieces. He felt sorry only for Nicholas.

He did arrange for the visit, and on the eve of Nicholas's departure a young intern and a nurse from the psychiatric section met Karady and escorted him through the service entrance to Alexa's room.

It was a small cubicle with a narrow barred window facing the yard. Alexa, in negligee and nightgown, lay stretched out on the bed. When she heard the door opening, she sat up terrified. In the faint light of the gas lamp her gaze moved from the doctor's face to the nurse's and came to rest on Nicholas's. Her expression of brooding watchfulness gave way to ecstatic delight.

"Oh, Nicky," she cried. "Where have you been all this time?"

Unable to resist her outstretched arms, with one long step he reached the bed and lifted her from it. As she clung to him, he was shocked to realize how weightless she felt—no longer an adult, but an emaciated adolescent. Holding her in his embrace, his entire being responded to her joy. For that one second the past was gone—her betrayals, lies, guilt, even the pain she had caused him. She was the woman he loved most in the whole world. The only woman.

Her name, Alexa, was on the tip of his tongue, but he had been cautioned by the doctor not to utter it. To call her Beata would have been like playing a game, besides being an affront to his dead wife's memory. Never before had the difference between the twins been so obvious to him as it was now.

351

Suddenly she released him and sat down on the edge of the bed. "Where are my things?" She appeared bewildered. "My clothes? I can't go with you like this, can I?"

He looked at the doctor for instructions. To him she seemed as normal as ever, only physically weakened. He began to doubt the diagnosis that had labeled her deranged. With a gesture, the doctor indicated that they were running out of time.

"I can't take you with me," Nicholas told her.

She reacted with panic. "Oh, Nicky, don't leave me here! Please, please! This morning I was taken to an office and asked all sorts of questions by men who pretended to be doctors but acted more like police. They treat me here as if I were a criminal or a lunatic. It's true, I cried and screamed a lot, but only because I was scared. I still am. Not mad, just tired and frightened."

He felt wretchedly helpless and confused. Her looking so frail and virginal made it hard for him to identify her with the whoring heroine of the newspaper stories. He wavered between resentment and blind all-forgiving love.

"You must be patient," he said. "You've been ill and your doctors insist that you stay here for a while."

"Why here? I don't like it here. I'm not ill. Don't believe *them,* believe me. I've never lied to you, have I?"

"No, you never have." What else could he tell her?

The intern stepped up to him. "Sorry, you must leave now, Captain. We've been lucky so far. The personnel have strict orders from the public prosecutor's office to keep out visitors. There is usually a guard posted at her door. He is at supper right now, but might be back any minute."

Kneeling on the edge of the bed, Alexa threw her arms about Nicholas. "Don't listen to him, Nicky, don't. Please stay. I have no one but you. You've never let me down. Don't desert me now when I need you most."

The muscular strength of her arms, seemingly so thin and

brittle, disconcerted him. There was a strange glint in her eyes. Was that insanity? he wondered. To break the hold of her embrace and disengage himself called for quite a struggle.

"I'll be back soon, I promise," he told her, knowing too well that this was one promise he was not going to keep. With a sinking feeling he lifted her face to his and kissed her lips, cheeks, eyes. She sensed the desperate finality of their parting and as he was about to move away reached out once more for him.

"I won't ever see you again. Isn't that the truth, Nicky?"

The doctor's hand rested on the door handle. "Let's hurry, Captain."

He followed the doctor from the room. During the long walk to the exit he managed to pull himself together. "She seemed perfectly lucid to me," he remarked. "She did recognize me."

The doctor shrugged. "That's how they are—lucid one moment, alienated the next. We know so little about them. Sometimes I think we know absolutely nothing."

"Will she ever be cured?"

"She might. But in this case, isn't she better off if she isn't?"

Nicholas understood what the doctor meant. The Royal Charité, or whatever mental institution she would be transferred to, was still preferable to years, perhaps life, in prison. In the back of Nicholas's mind lingered the grim possibility, never pronounced, merely hinted at by Counselor Wengraf, that her guilt might be heavy enough to call for the death sentence. The investigation had hardly begun and the full extent of her involvement in the murder had not been established yet.

Leaving the building, he turned to the doctor to express his thanks.

"I'll walk you to the gate," the young man said. "It's such a balmy night, probably the last one we'll have this year. I go on duty at eight o'clock, so I still have a few free minutes left." He chuckled. "We're inmates too, you know, even though we dress in white."

They passed several buildings. The doctor pointed at one. "See that lighted window on the second floor? That's Prince Eulenburg's. He has been here since the middle of July. I can't understand why they don't let the poor man go. They won't ever drag him before a court. He's much too ill for that. Sometimes I suspect that it's been decided to keep him locked up in that little room probably for the rest of his life."

The realization that he was not the only loser in the world, that sorrow was as inescapable a human disease as the common cold, caused Nicholas to halt suddenly. He felt a deep, aching pity for the old man behind the lighted window.

"I've known the prince for a long time," he said. "He's always been very kind to me. As I must leave Berlin, perhaps for good, could you arrange for me to see him? If only for a few moments to say goodbye."

The intern scratched his head. "If you had asked me a few weeks ago, I would've told you, Sorry, no chance. But lately they've been treating him as if he were a non-being. We keep sending medical reports to the Appellate Court, but I don't think they're ever read. Sometimes even the guard posted in front of his door fails to report for duty. No one seems to care how many visitors he receives, as long as he is here. They acknowledge his existence only when the family makes another attempt to offer bail. That, of course, is immediately refused."

They entered the cardiological ward where Eulenburg was held. The intern asked Nicholas to wait while he went to look in on the patient and announce the visitor.

A few minutes later he returned. "I'm afraid the prince isn't up to receiving anyone tonight. That phlebitic leg causes him great pain. He is sending you his regrets. He told me he wished he could go with you. He said he always adored Vienna, a city where troops marched to the strains of Strauss' music and the emperor's shirts had frayed cuffs. An odd remark, don't you think?"

Nicholas sighed. "Oh, but so true."

He reached Vienna late at night and was relieved to learn that his parents were out of town. Ferdinand was in Marienbad taking the waters, and Melanie was in Gmunden visiting a friend who had a villa on the lake. He anticipated a far from cordial reception from his superiors, so he could easily do without parental lectures. In Conrad von Hötzendorf's newly reorganized General Staff, errors were seldom overlooked. Their consequences could be demotion, transfer to field service, even drumming out. During the long journey home there had been time to wonder if his resignation from the army would not be the safest way to avoid a peck of troubles.

All Viennese newspapers had reported the Godenhausen murder case, some in truthful, others in sensationally fictitious, detail. His involvement was mentioned in each; he was either referred to as an ex-brother-in-law concerned for the accused woman's plight or—in carefully veiled terms—as the new lover for whom she had deserted Lieutenant von Ranke.

And when he entered the house, the expression of sympathy mixed with reprimand on major-domo Rosner's face conveyed the Viennese consensus of opinion about him: a fool in the clutches of a scheming woman.

He found mail waiting on his desk. On one envelope he recognized Francesca von Winterfeld's handwriting—straight and even as a string of well-matched pearls—and he immediately guessed the letter's contents:

Dear Nicholas,

For days now I have been hearing some ugly gossip linking you with a lady in Berlin. I am certain you remember the talk we had when I accepted your marriage proposal. I loved you then and still do. However, if the allegations regarding your connection with

355

Baroness Alexa von Godenhausen are based on facts, I do not want to continue our engagement. Neither do I wish ever to see you again. I am appealing to your honesty and charity to respond to this letter only if the rumors are unfounded. In case they are not, please, please offer no explanations or excuses, because they would merely add to the pain and humiliation I have already suffered. Simply disregard this letter; I shall interpret your silence to be your answer to it. I shall have no anger or bitterness in my heart, only pity for you and Alexa von Godenhausen, because your lot will be much harder to bear than mine.

    Yours respectfully,
        Francesca Winterfeld

He stared at the beautiful calligraphy with a sense of loss. Neat, even, every single letter conforming to the standards set by the first-grade primer and written in a steady, well-disciplined hand. It told him what life would have been with her. Peace, contentment, security, even happiness. A slow-burning resentment was building up in him against Alexa. Lieutenant von Ranke accomplished something that he would never have been able to do on his own. He put an irrevocable end to the slavish bondage she had kept him in.

On the following morning he reported for duty and was instructed to see General Hartmann at his office. Prepared for serious reprimands, he was pleasantly surprised to find the older man in a benevolently understanding frame of mind.

"You certainly managed to get yourself tangled up in some nasty business," he said after a handshake that was encouragingly cordial. "What I want to ask you is, When exactly did you find out that the woman was involved in her husband's murder?"

"I never did." Responding to the general's frown, he quickly added, "What I mean is, I haven't had a chance to get an answer from her. As to the charge of her complicity, I first heard about it after she had already been arrested."

"Haven't you talked to her since?"

Nicholas contemplated for a moment. "The truth is, I

356

have, sir. On the eve of my departure from Berlin her attorney arranged to have me sneaked into the hospital room
where she was kept. Strictly against rules."

"So?"

"She is—she seemed—no longer rational. That's why she
is being held in a hospital and not a house of detention. She's
been found temporarily unbalanced and is undergoing a series
of psychiatric examinations."

The general shook his head with an old man's amazement
over the readiness of youth to fall into clearly discernible pit-
falls in matters of the heart. "One more question, which you
may refuse to answer. Was there more between you and the
woman than an in-law relationship?"

Nicholas replied in a low, pained voice, "Yes, sir, there
was."

For a long moment Hartmann kept his heavy-lidded eyes
closed. With his wide lipless mouth over a triangular chin, he
looked like a wise old turtle. "Well, for the time being
you'll remain 'en disposition.' When things have quieted down,
you'll be given a new appointment. Incidentally, Ballhaus
Platz responded to the Germans' request to have you recalled
by declaring a member of their embassy staff here persona
non grata. Tit for tat, you know."

Nicholas spent October in Vienna. The Monarchy's annexation of Bosnia and Herzegovina, two provinces inhabited by
southern Slavs, took Europe by surprise. Despite the outrage
it stirred up in the Entente Cordiale, the storm blew itself
out without too many serious consequences. The excitement
was quieting down when another incident upset the international equilibrium. This time the controversy centered
around the Kaiser himself. An interview of his, given some
time before, published in the London *Daily Telegraph,* was
interpreted by the British, the French, the Russians and even
the Japanese as proof that he was a threat to world peace.
Oddly enough, the most vicious reaction came from the Ger-

man press. The devastating cartoons they published depicted Wilhelm as a windbag and a fool.

Shortly after his arrival in Vienna, Nicholas received a letter from Counselor Dr. Wengraf. It read like a chapter in a penny dreadful. The first part of it dealt with Lieutenant von Ranke. Upon the insistence of his commanding officer, Major Brausch, Judge Advocate Yves had agreed to have Ranke receive a mental examination at the Kortau insane asylum. Although he was found to be a person with psychopathic tendencies, he was declared legally accountable for his crime.

While preparing the case for the court-martial, Captain Yves yielded to the lieutenant's demand for a confrontation with Alexa—this despite her physicians' warning that such a traumatic experience might rob her of the last vestiges of her sanity.

The lieutenant, escorted by the judge advocate, was brought to Berlin under heavy guard, and the confrontation took place at the Royal Charité in the presence of a staff physician, a nurse, the county medical examiner and Dr. Karl Julius Berg, the latter representing the defense.

Alexa's first reaction to Ranke's and Yves's appearance was polite curiosity. She wondered what the two men in uniform could want from her and displayed the first signs of nervousness only when Yves addressed her as baroness.

"I'm afraid, Captain, you're confusing me with someone," she said with the childlike petulance she had adopted more and more frequently. "I don't like grown-up people playing games."

"Then why are you?" Yves retorted.

Before he could continue, Dr. Berg raised a hand to restrain him. "Let's not waste time on irrelevancies, Captain. Please remember what I told you. We mustn't tire or irritate the patient."

Ranke kept looking fixedly at Alexa, trying to catch her eye, but she ignored him. Not Captain Yves, though. It seemed his face stirred up memories in her, and the memories weren't pleasant. Seated in an armchair, she rested her hands in her lap, clenching them as the minutes passed into balled fists with the knuckles turning white.

"Will you step forward, Lieutenant, and address the lady," Yves said. "I want you to repeat the accusations you made against her in the course of the investigation. Madame, will you kindly face the lieutenant?"

She responded with a frown, then shifted her gaze to Ranke. His voice breaking after each sentence, he told of their first meetings, then gave a detailed account of their memorable horseback ride during which she had dropped the hint that she wanted her husband dead. Up to this point she had listened politely, now she paled; her hands crept up to her lips and pressed down on them as if trying to stifle a scream.

Ranke held a long pause and continued only after Yves's repeated prodding. He spoke with increasing bitterness of having been her willing slave and tool. She looked at him in puzzled silence. Her bewilderment turned into anger as he recounted the incidents leading to the murder. Her face became flushed and she glared at him with hatred.

"Go on, Lieutenant," Yves urged him when he halted for a long moment. "You were going to tell us that Madame stopped seeing you because you failed to keep your promise to murder her husband."

With an ear-piercing cry, Alexa jumped to her feet and pounced upon Yves, clawing at him like a rabid cat. It took the combined efforts of the nurse and the doctors to restrain her before she could do more damage than leave a few bloody scratch marks on his face. She kept shouting at him in a language none of those present understood. Later it occurred to them that she must have reverted to her native Hungarian.

Ranke stood by and watched the scene in stunned silence. The staff physician gave her an injection that broke her fighting spirit. Moaning, she collapsed in a heap. The doctors suggested that the session be ended for the time being and

359

continued only if and when she regained some semblance of
sanity, at least to a degree that would enable her to understand
the proceedings.

As days passed it became obvious, even to Captain Yves,
that a second try would be meaningless. Reluctantly he agreed
to depart for Allenstein, taking his prisoner with him.

"The confrontation had a shattering effect on Lieutenant
von Ranke," wrote Counselor Dr. Wengraf. "He must have
realized the hopelessness of his situation, and perhaps the fu-
tility of his involving the baroness in the crime. Two days after his return to the military prison, he somehow secreted
away a rather blunt table knife after his dinner dishes had
been collected and cut his throat with it. By the time a guard
looked in on him, he was beyond all human help."

Despite the legal tone that Counselor Dr. Wengraf adhered
to throughout his letter, he could not restrain himself from
adding a personal remark. Ending the description of the unfortunate lieutenant's death, he wrote, "Needless to tell you,
the army emitted a sigh of relief."

By the time of the confrontation, Alexa had undergone an
extensive psychiatric examination. At its termination, a committee consisting of the county medical examiner, physicians
of the Royal Charité, and private psychiatrist Dr. Karl Julius
Berg reached the conclusion that at the present time she
was in a state of complete dissociation from reality, consequently unfit to stand trial. The committee recommended
that, on the basis of Paragraph 203 of the Penal Code, the
public prosecutor's office temporarily suspend all proceedings against her and permit her to be moved from the Royal
Charité to a private institution for continued psychiatric treatment. The public prosecutor accepted the committee's recommendation and released her on a bail of 100,000 marks to the
custody of Counselor Dr. Wengraf.

Nicholas answered the letter by return mail. He authorized
the attorney to procure the bail and to find a suitable sana-

torium for her, possibly in the country, where the air was clean, the scenery attractive and the medical staff first rate. Alexa would be kept in sanatoria as long as the judicial authorities raised no objection. Forever, if necessary.

Having paid his debts—not to Alexa, because he owed her nothing, but to the troublesomely exacting creditor within himself—he decided to leave the past behind and begin to live in the present.

The sanatorium, a large modern building set in a well-kept park, was in Babelsberg. From Alexa's window a lovely view opened on the Havel. In the beginning she spent days with her forehead pressed to the windowpane, staring at the glistening water down below. Being in the country confused her after her confinement at the Charité. It took her time to understand that she could leave her room at will and take a walk in the garden. She made a habit of covering each path that crisscrossed the grounds at least three times every afternoon. She knew that she was not as closely watched as she had been at the hospital, yet there *was* some supervision, because whenever she ventured near the gate a nurse materialized from nowhere.

She was one of the most docile and sweet-tempered patients of the sanatorium and presented a problem in only one respect, her unwillingness to speak German. The staff had been warned by Dr. Berg that since the unfortunate encounter with Ranke and Yves she had become even more dissociated from her real self, Alexa von Godenhausen, whom she had discarded as willfully as if she had been a dress gone out of style. Oddly enough, she understood the German of the doctors and the nurses, except when they addressed her as Baroness or Alexa. Then she ignored the culprit, punishing him or her with a silent disdain that lasted for days.

She still had periods of restlessness, when she slept badly and was irritated by trifling matters, such as a lukewarm soup or someone coughing in the room next to hers. She would

361

give voice to her annoyance in Hungarian, or in a strange German that puzzled the staff until a nurse born in the Palatinate recognized it as a dialect spoken in her native region. Intrigued by the occurrence, Dr. Berg contacted a professor of linguistics at Göttingen University and learned that the same dialect was spoken by the descendants of German settlers brought by the Hapsburgs to the depopulated parts of Hungary after the expulsion of the Turks. For more than two centuries these people preserved their ethnic identities, never melting into the Hungarian majority. Some of Alexa's childhood playmates had been of this breed, and it was from them that she had learned the quaint German.

Doctors and nurses fell under the spell of Alexa's beauty and charm. From their excursions into town they frequently brought her gifts, such as a box of candy or a bunch of flowers. She thanked them with the unself-conscious delight of a child for whom kindnesses from adults are unsolicited gestures that need not be reciprocated.

One Sunday the nurse from the Palatinate brought her a bouquet of violets. Alexa took the flowers to her room, but as she was putting them in a vase she suddenly broke down sobbing uncontrollably. Only after the violets had been thrown out and she was given a sedative was she able to calm down. She could offer no explanation for her violent reaction to the flowers. They reminded her of something unpleasant, yet she couldn't tell of what. There were other memories too that haunted her. Images flickered through her mind, but by the time she could identify them they were gone.

Late in October the monotony of her existence was broken by the arrival of the same committee upon whose recommendation criminal proceedings had been suspended against her. They brought an elderly woman who spoke Hungarian with them to serve as an interpreter. The men stayed for the entire day, firing questions at her that she had trouble answering, naming people she was supposed to remember but did not, no matter how hard she tried. Her inability to cooperate an-

362

noyed and embarrassed her. Nevertheless, the visitors seemed satisfied with her performance, for as the day progressed their initial severity mellowed to avuncular benevolence.

It was a week later that Counselor Dr. Wengraf, accompanied by the lady interpreter, came to inform her of the public prosecutor's decision to drop all criminal charges against her, provided she was willing to leave Germany.

"What criminal charges?" she asked, bewildered. Then, without waiting for his answer: "You mean I can go home?"

Wengraf misunderstood her. "Not to your aunt. I've just told you, the condition is that you leave the country for good."

She frowned with annoyance. "I meant *home!* To Sarkany! Where else?"

Wengraf promptly informed Nicholas of the Prussian judicial decision and asked for instructions. In turn Nicholas contacted the Rethys and inquired whether or not they were willing and able to take Alexa back. When old Rethy answered in the affirmative, Nicholas authorized the attorney to make the necessary arrangements, legal as well as financial, for her return to Hungary. They agreed that one of Wengraf's female secretaries would accompany Alexa on the journey from Berlin to Sarkany.

On the day Alexa passed through Vienna, Nicholas deliberately left the city to visit an aunt in her castle at Rosenegg in Styria. The weather was unseasonably wet, with a cold rain turning the country roads into morasses. Once he had to have a farmer's ox team pull his automobile out of a mudhole and once he got soaked to the skin while changing a tire, nevertheless he considered the excursion a success, the final proof of his having cut the cord that linked him with Alexa.

14

Early in November Nicholas received an invitation to a house party at the castle of Prince Maximilian Egon von Fürstenberg in Donaueschingen. The prince's letter surprised him, as he had heard the Kaiser would also be a guest. Evidently von Fürstenberg ignored imperial piques when directed against an old friend of his. In a fast-changing world where the luster of the greatest historical names was slowly but inevitably fading, the Fürstenbergs' still radiated magic and independent power.

Before déjeuner the party assembled in a courtyard dominated by an elaborate fountain which enclosed the Donauquelle, a thin trickle of a spring, one of the sources of the mighty river Danube.

To Nicholas's pleasant surprise, Baron von Stoka was among the guests.

"What is new in Berlin?" Nicholas asked him.

"The same three-ring circus. In the center is Wilhelm the fire eater, spewing red-hot insults at Victor Emmanuel, his cousin Nicholas, the Socialists and, above all, his uncle Edward the Seventh. In the left ring is Chief of Staff Helmuth von Moltke with his animated tin soldiers. In the right ring we have trainer Chancellor von Bülow with his wild animal act, cracking the whip at the British lion, the Russian bear and the French puma, mainly to distract their attention from what is going on in the two other rings. Incidentally, Helmuth von Moltke was close to losing his job. He was thrown by his horse during a parade, and the Kaiser vowed that no bad horseman could stay on as his chief of staff. It took the concentrated efforts of Moltke's friends to save his neck."

"Any news about Prince Eulenburg?" Nicholas asked.

"Good news, but keep it confidential. On September twenty-fifth, by orders of the Appellate Court, he was released from arrest on a hundred-thousand-mark bail and permitted to return to Liebenberg. The court decision has been kept a secret from Wilhelm because of his insistence that the case be continued and a verdict be rendered, preferably a conviction."

"How incredibly mean."

"I should say it is. Of course, the condition was that Eulenberg stand trial once his health has improved. Which, if you ask me, will never happen."

"We'll have the pleasure of breaking bread with His Majesty today."

"I know. He is coming from Konopischt, where he saw Franz Ferdinand. From here he'll go to Rominten and Schorfheide to hunt some more, then to England on a state visit. What a nervous, restless man."

"That he is," Nicholas agreed. "And to think that, despite the constitutional claptrap, the fate of an empire depends on his whims, perhaps the fate of Europe."

Wilhelm was expected later in the afternoon. During déjeuner there was a surprisingly unrestrained discussion of the *Daily Telegraph* article and its repercussions. Since his departure from Berlin, this was Nicholas's first encounter with members of the Kaiser's inner circle. The rest were Europe's high aristocracy, all nationalities, with only the French and the English missing, which had never happened before at the Fürstenberg house parties.

The frankness of the quips bordered on lese majesty and

Nicholas wondered if such liberties could have been taken had Wilhelm's prestige not become tarnished lately. The only guest who seemed to resent the jokes was General Hülsen-Haeseler, the chief of the emperor's Military Cabinet. Never on friendly terms with Nicholas, the general now treated him with icy disdain, noticed by all.

The Kaiser arrived in a carefree mood, which was remarkable, considering that the aftershocks of the Bosnia-Herzegovina annexation, as well as the *Daily Telegraph* article, could still be felt all over Europe. The fact that he had just now paid a visit to Franz Ferdinand was taken for a sign that he had fully approved of the Monarchy's move.

As in the case of all private parties he attended, the list of the Fürstenberg guests had been submitted for his approval. Nevertheless, he reacted with an annoyed frown to Nicholas's presence. After that he pointedly ignored him.

The Fürstenberg hunt was a great success, although the daily papers and the new arrivals at the castle reported disquieting developments in Berlin. They left Wilhelm unaffected; his sunny disposition persisted throughout the visit, that is, until an incident that followed the festive banquet on the last night of his stay.

As long as he lived, Nicholas remembered the banquet as the crowning event of an era of taste, carefree gaiety and beauty. The castle was a most resplendent backdrop before which a comedy of manners was presented by personages whose brains, inherited riches and power ruled a continent. The ladies appeared in grande toilettes, the men in gala uniforms, green and black tails with decorations. The ones who had taken part in the day's steeplechase wore scarlet.

The mellow flames of the candles made even the ugly and the old seem attractive. There was no discordant sound or sight to mar the perfection of the scene.

After the meal the guests, led by the Kaiser, moved to the great hall of the castle. The Fürstenberg house orchestra,

366

seated on the curving staircase, was playing the latest popular tunes.

Suddenly the music stopped, and from the archway to the adjoining gallery, in flitted General Hülsen-Haeseler wearing tights, a pink tutu and a blond wig. The orchestra played a movement from Tchaikovsky's *Swan Lake* and, rising sur les points, the chief of the German Emperor's Military Cabinet began to caper, whirl and pirouette with a professional skill that elicited amazed cries from his partly startled and partly amused spectators.

Nicholas kept blinking nervously. He didn't trust his eyes. He had heard rumors that similar performances had taken place at stag parties on board the Kaiser's yacht, but even that was hard to believe. His gaze combed the faces around him. He detected no signs of embarrassment. On some there was an expression of polite boredom; after a rich meal and too much champagne the dancer's legs, though rather shapely for an aging general, failed to titillate. The Kaiser alone seemed impressed; he beamed like a ballet master presenting his favorite pupil to a jury of experts.

The agility and grotesquely feminine grace of the fifty-six-year-old male body amazed Nicholas. He expected the general to slow down, but the longer he continued the more playful vigor he infused into his act. Beads of perspiration appeared on his forehead and his costume showed wet spots under his arms, while his feet kept moving with the tireless-ness of a wound-up mechanical doll. As the sound of the music rose in volume to prelude his exit, he once more leaped upward to perform a perfect entrechat. For a moment he seemed to be suspended in mid-air smartly clicking his heels together, then suddenly his grin turned into a grimace of pain and he flopped to the floor, a motionless heap except for the flutter of his many-layered pink tutu ruffled by an air current from the gallery.

At first the spectators took his stumble for part of the performance, then the startled silence was broken by a cry emanating from a lady standing behind the fallen body. It brought people to their feet. Although the empty stare of the wide-open eyes and the slackness of the mouth indicated that the man was beyond help, he was carried to the gallery, where efforts were made by Dr. Niedner, the Kaiser's personal physician, to resuscitate him; this in order to reassure the horror-stricken Kaiser that everything humanly possible was being tried.

Utter confusion reigned in the great hall. The Kaiser had risen and followed the motionless body to the gallery. The orchestra continued playing, until it occurred to the host to stop the musicians in the middle of a bar. Princess Fürstenberg, seated on the bottom step of the stairway, was sobbing hysterically.

At eleven Dr. Niedner admitted defeat and pronounced the general dead. He had probably died the moment he had hit the floor, because by now rigor mortis was setting in. The doctor and his helpers were unable to peel off his tights and tutu and had to cut them open with scissors so that the body could be dressed in the kind of costume a general was supposed to expire in: his uniform. The fact that the chief of His Majesty's Military Cabinet had died in a ballet skirt was to be kept secret, yet within twenty-four hours it became known all over Europe.

The general was temporarily laid out in the grand salon on the second floor of the castle. In the excitement, the absent Countess Hülsen-Haeseler became forgotten. It was past midnight when someone remembered that she had to be notified.

Stunned into silence during the failed resuscitation efforts, Wilhelm now became feverishly active. He categorically refused to take Dr. Niedner's advice and go to bed. Arrangements for the general's funeral had to be made, and he insisted on being in charge. Underneath the mask of the human dynamo a thoroughly frightened man was hiding. When someone called Hülsen-Haeseler's performance a "Dance of

Death," he paled, and his good right arm clutched his heart in an involuntary imitation of the general's last gesture. He had long lived in fear of bacteria and contagion, and now, with the realization that death could come from within, that his own heart might betray him, God's Favorite, the Kaiser suddenly felt helplessly mortal.

The tragedy was the latest in a series of ominous events that had befallen him within a few months' time. The deterioration of his relationship with his uncle Edward VII, the Bosnian crisis, the *Daily Telegraph* article, and now this. A signal that his luck was changing.

The frantic exodus of the houseguests began shortly after Hülsen-Haeseler had been declared dead, and it continued throughout the night. Wilhelm was among the first to leave. His sudden departure aboard his private train played havoc with the timetables of the lines affected by the imperial journey from Donaueschingen to Rominten, where he was to hunt boar. In his haste to get away he allowed his entourage no time to pack his luggage. He himself left as though fleeing from a burning house, without changing his clothes.

The Viennese contingent of the guests, among them Nicholas, took the early morning train home. Once they were aboard, the initial numbness left by shock wore off. For some it turned into hysterical exhilaration. The younger and more cynical men saw black humor in the bizarre episode and kept mining their memories for additional occasions of grotesquerie. For the next few weeks their accounts of the case were to make them the center of attention at parties in Vienna.

Their hilarity began to grate on Nicholas's nerves, and he withdrew to his reserved compartment. He was still under the impact of last night's events. The picture of the little general clicking his heels in mid-air while the grin of death already distorted his features, the jolly approval on the face of the emperor who had sent his best and oldest friend to prison for the same peculiarity that his new friend was now exhibiting in public, the mixture of refinement and vulgarity, of daring and prudery—all blended into the symbol of what future historians were to call the "Age of Wilhelm II." Its perplexing contradictions left their imprint on all strata of Prussian society—on the proletariat and peasantry in a small degree, and more corruptingly on the ruling classes. Men like Prince Eulenburg, Kuno von Moltke, Godenhausen, even Ranke, were not the villains but the victims of the system in which chauvinism came before the inviolability of life, camaraderie before marital love, imperial caprice before justice. To kill in duel was not murder, to prevent a woman from exercising her free will was not slavery. It was a system that lacked humaneness, common sense and logic. No wonder it turned some men into perverts or killers. And women into shrews and harlots.

Alexa von Godenhausen's guardians had unscrupulously maneuvered her into a marriage with a man whose moral defects had been well known to them. Unconcerned about her happiness, all they wanted was to safeguard and further a nephew's military career. Had she been released from the bondage of her wretched marriage, she would never have turned for help to Ranke, whose sole attraction for her was his expertise in committing murder without penalty.

During their days on Schleswiger Ufer, Alexa had seldom spoken of her life in Allenstein, except when describing the East Prussian weather. Her reminiscences conjured up a picture of loneliness, desolation and hopelessness in Nicholas's mind. She was the prisoner of a system alien to her temperament, and it was her misfortune that the only escape route she could find was Ranke.

Nicholas wondered how Beata would have reacted to Allenstein. It was an absurd speculation because, except for their physical resemblance, no two women could be more different than the twins. Or were they really? Wasn't it her childhood illness, her joyless adolescence and her miserable marriage that had turned Alexa into a capricious, restless creature, and finally into a mental case? Beata had been sheltered and loved all her short life, first by her grandparents, then by him, Nicholas. Would Beata have remained her serene self if transplanted into alien Prussia with guardians as crude and unfeeling as the Sedlitzes and a husband as frustrating as Hans Günther von Godenhausen?

On December first, Nicholas was reassigned to duty at the deployment section of the General Staff, even given the same office he had occupied before his Berlin days. He would have preferred a post abroad, but his involvement in the Godenhausen case had remained a bad mark on his service record.

Later he remembered the winter of 1908-09 as just one long arctic day—dusk flowing into darkness, then into dusk again, with never a glimpse of the sun. Even the political sky was cloudy with storms brewing.

After his return from Donaueschingen, Wilhelm suffered a bout of neurasthenia, and speculations on his imminent abdication were reported by the international press; yet by February he felt well enough to play host to King Edward VII and his queen in Berlin.

It was the king's last visit to Germany, and despite his best intentions it did as little good for German-British rapprochement as his previous ones. The entertainment the Kaiser prepared for his uncle included a state banquet, a gala performance at the opera, but also a military parade with thousands of Prussian bayonets sparkling in the first pre-spring sunlight.

Reading the reports, Nicholas was happy to be out of Germany. His personal life was as drab and cheerless as the political scene. His mother treated him with a petulance previously reserved for his father; her constant nagging that he should marry and settle down was getting on his nerves. He had a brief affair with one of the leading actresses of the Burgtheater, but stopped seeing her when he realized that she remained a tragedian even after removing her makeup. She was a passionate lover, with tastes veering toward the bizarre, demands for constant attention and unpredictable moods. The last straw was a spectacular suicide attempt. She took an overdose of sleeping pills, but only after phoning him, her doctor, her director, even the police, to make sure that she would be saved in time. He left her house despite her threat to do a repeat performance. Of course she never did; she married a mysterious Armenian armament dealer a month later.

The hunting season was the only time of the year Countess Melanie liked to play chatelaine. The summer was too hot for her, the winter too cold, the spring too wet. She loved the balmy multicolored St. Augustine's days in Hungary, also called old women's summer in the local vernacular.

In 1909, as in many autumns before, half the Karadys' Viennese household, including major-domo Rosner, preceded her to Sarkany to prepare the castle for her stay. There were house parties and a hunt ball planned, still she found the thought of being—as she expressed it—stranded in the country with her aging husband a bore, and she insisted that Nicholas accompany them.

He had not been to the castle since the fall of 1907. What had kept him away were his painful memories—and Alexa's presence at the Rethy farm.

On the day of his return to Sarkany he wrote to Kalman Rethy telling him that he was back but for Alexa's sake thought it inadvisable to pay a visit to them. Instead, he asked Rethy to come and see him at the castle.

Secretly he wished Rethy would not come. They were no longer family, only ex-in-laws, so the Rethys were none of his concern. Beata had died in the fire and Alexa the night he had last embraced her in the hospital room of the Royal Charité. What he had done for her since was the same he had done for Beata—give her a perfect farewell, the best money could buy.

When Rethy called on him, he deliberately avoided asking the old man about Alexa or the problems her return cre-

372

ated in the family and the community. Rethy, however, in too dire a need for a sympathetic ear, failed to realize that by unburdening himself he disconcerted his listener.

"It was difficult at first," he recalled. "You know how people are. Tactless and often cruel. She couldn't leave the house, because she was gaped at in the street, followed around, called murderess to her face. But soon the excitement died down. After all, mental illness is no rarity around here; every village has its assortment of idiots, madmen, eccentrics. Quiet, sensible people running suddenly berserk. Common occurrence, just like a forest set on fire by lightning, a farm washed away by a flash flood, cattle dying of disease. What I'd been afraid of was the old woman's reaction. She never really cared for Alexa, not the way she did for Beata. I'd thought that having the child come home sick and tainted by an ugly scandal would cause frictions. I'd tried to keep all the nasty rumors from the old woman, but no luck. Sarkany was buzzing with them; you had to be deaf or a recluse to escape them. I expected my wife to be hard on the girl and refuse to go along with her quirks. I needn't have feared. The truth is, the old woman hasn't been herself since the fire. Not deranged, only confused."

"You never wrote me about that. Why not?" Despite himself, Nicholas felt concerned. The worry-and-age-ravaged face of the old man stirred up disturbing emotions in him.

"I didn't want to trouble you. Besides, Dr. Satory told me that in his opinion she was better off this way. She's erased all the hurts of the past from her memory and made peace with herself and her God." He paused. "That's something I wish I could do. I might in time. I already have moments when I forget the girl is not Beata. I don't call her that, of course. I can't make myself do it. I just call her 'angel.' It fits her. She is no trouble at all. I'm glad she's come home to us. Maybe that's what she always wanted. To be home with her own people."

"Is she aware of her condition?"

"I suspect she is. The other day she appeared unusually pre-occupied, so I asked her what was troubling her. She said she had another dream—her dreams seem to puzzle her—this time about a corridor with many doors. They all had heavy ornate keys. When she tried to open the doors, she could not find them. They disappeared, with nothing left but the keys. She asked what the dream meant. Keys to lost doors." He rose. "I'd better be going. I've taken too much of your time already."

Nicholas asked if there was anything he could do for him.

"Not a thing, Nicky. You have already done more than you should have. The harvest was good and I expect to have around three hundred hectoliter of wine this year, which will keep me afloat for some time."

Nicholas saw him to the gate. On his way back up the path to the castle he spotted Melanie on the second-floor balcony surveying the countryside through a pair of opera glasses. He went up to her.

"What are you looking at?" he asked.

She ignored the question. "I bet he wanted money from you," she said shrilly.

"If you mean Kalman Rethy, he did not. I wish he had, though."

Since their arrival in Sarkany he and Melanie had, with tacit understanding, avoided mentioning the Rethys or Alexa. Nicholas had not been certain whether his mother knew of her return to her grandparents' house, which, of course, was pretty naive of him. When had any news in connection with his women escaped Melanie's attention?

"Haven't they cost you enough already?"

"That's none of your business, Mama." He turned to leave her, but she barred his way.

"I wasn't going to talk to you about them, but now that Rethy has had the nerve to come up here—"

"What do you mean, the nerve? He's welcome here any time. I was married to his granddaughter, remember."

374

"You're not now. Anyway, I don't have to tell you how I feel about them. The whole family. If you ask me, they have a mad streak in them. Take the girls' father. Drifter, swindler, embezzler—and at the end suicide. And now Alexa."

"Will you stop, Mama?"

"They say she's gone completely mad. Thinks she is Beata."

"So did I at times. Did that make me mad?"

From the balcony a wide view opened at the hillside sloping downward to the Rethys' farm, beyond that the narrow ribbon of the road to Komárom, and in the distance the fog-blurred outline of hills, forerunners to the Bakony mountains. The sun was setting and its last rays dotted the landscape with patches of brilliance. It was the moment of the day when colors deepened as if brushed on with a double coat of paint.

He stepped to the balustrade and looked down. Rethy was descending a narrow path between an alfalfa field and a freshly plowed tract, a shortcut from the castle to his house. Nicholas looked farther down the path to the acacia-tree-planted boundary of the Karady acres and below it to the Rethys' vegetable garden. Suddenly he spotted a figure in blue moving between the bean patch and the row of strawberry bushes.

On a late June day six years before he had stumbled upon another girl at that very same spot. It had been his second visit in a week to the Rethys' farm. On his way to the house he had caught sight of her and changed directions. Her hair piled loosely on top of her head, with tiny beads of perspiration glistening on her cheeks, she was as beautiful as she had been a few days before in her grandparents' tightly shuttered parlor. A butterfly landed on a beanstalk, and as she stealthily reached out for it, it flew away, its gorgeous wings sparkling in the sun. Nicholas's eyes had followed the girl with the fascination of one watching a prima ballerina perform. She turned back, noticed Nicholas, and her face brightened with a smile.

The encounter and all its luminous details had remained indelibly etched in his memory. What followed was an interlude of contentment and happiness, the kind he, a blasé man spoiled by life, had never hoped for. Then his luck ran out with the same suddenness it had struck. What he had expected to be an endless summer was over in a flash, and now his days were bleak again.

His mother raised the opera glasses to her eyes. "That is she, isn't it? Who would have believed that she would end like this?" She lowered the glasses. "Come to think of it, you almost wrecked your career for her. There were rumors in Vienna that you'd be cashiered. Besides, you lost your chance for a normal happy marriage with a lovely girl. I hope you realize what a fool you were."

He took the glasses from her and adjusted them to his eyes. Through their lenses the slight figure in the blue dress appeared as quaintly unreal as an illustration in a storybook. He felt his heart stop, literally. Seized by a fit of dizziness, he leaned for support against the balustrade.

Melanie gave him an alarmed look. "What's the matter with you?"

He handed her the opera glasses. "Do you believe in fables?"

She frowned. "Fables like what?" And before he could answer: "No, I don't. Certainly not."

He continued regardless. "The fable of Orpheus descending into Hades to bring Eurydice back to earth?"

She looked at him suspiciously. "Don't talk in riddles. It's not like you." She eyed him with a touch of annoyance. "Anyway, Orpheus left Eurydice behind!"

"Only because he ignored the warning not to look back."

"But he did and he lost her. Earth to earth, ashes to ashes, dust to dust."

"He looked back to see if her stay in Hades had left any mark on her. If she was the same as before. How could she be, after her time in Hades? He was a fool even to assume that she could be the same as before. That's why he lost her."

"So he did. So what? Let's change the subject before you rewrite the story." Her fingers drummed nervously on the balustrade. "Getting back to reality, I'm planning a dinner party for next Thursday. You'll be staying until then, won't you?"

"I'm afraid I won't."

"But Nicky, dear, you told me you would. I counted on you."

"I am sorry to disappoint you, but it can't be helped. Just can't be helped, Mama." He turned from her and started for the stairs.

She stared after him, petrified. She had a mind to grab him and hold him back, but instinct told her it would be useless. A few minutes later, as she leaned over the balustrade, she saw him leaving through the park gate. Held by a strange fascination, she remained glued to the spot. The glasses felt heavy in her hands; she lowered them for a second, then raised them again to her eyes.

Down below, her son was descending the path toward the Rethys' farm. The girl in the blue dress must have seen him coming, for she dropped her basket filled with string beans and started running uphill. For a few moments the acacia trees, turning autumnal yellow along the boundary line, obscured Nicholas from Melanie's view. When he emerged again, he was nearing the Rethys' orchard. He was moving faster now and so was the girl. He called to her and she opened her arms to him.

With a sinking feeling, Melanie put down the opera glasses. The sun was about to slide behind the faraway hills, now sharply outlined against the blue of the sky. A squall of wind caused her to shiver. She wondered whether during her long life she had ever learned what love was.